LIBRARY OF DAEMONIUM

ABDUCTION CYCLES

JOHN ELIJAH CRESSMAN

MAVERICK-GAGE PUBLISHING

ISBN: 978-1-954524-02-6 (Paperback)
ISBN: 978-1-954524-03-3 (Hardcover)
ISBN: 978-1-954524-01-9 (Amazon Kindle)
ISBN: 978-1-954524-04-0 (Audiobook)

Any references to historical events, real people, or real places are used fictitiously. Names, characters, and places are products of the author's twisted imagination.

Front cover image by Christina Myrvold

Editing By Celestial Rince.

Printed by Maverick-Gage Publishing in conjunction with IngramSpark, in the United States of America.

First printing edition 2021.

Maverick-Gage Publishing
Allentown, PA
info@maverick-gage.com
www.maverick-gage.com

John Elijah Cressman
www.johnecressman.com

In Loving Memory of Luna Lovecat
12/2012 - 1/2021

Always Loved, Always Remembered

PROLOGUE

Ethan sat surrounded by rabbits. Normally, it might have been a good thing. After all, they'd been hunting and killing rabbits for food during the journey to Castlehaven. But these weren't eating rabbits. These were demonic rabbits. They were "friendly" demonic rabbits, but they were still demonic rabbits.

After helping defend the village of Hawkshead from a tribe of invaders, his kobold companion, Par'karr, had leveled up. At least, Ethan thought that's what Par'karr had done. The kobold had no HUD like Ethan and his companions but now he was able to summon several demonic rabbits. Based on what Ethan knew, that made the kobold a Summoner. And his summoned animal of choice was rabbits. Because, of course it was.

There were three of them at the moment, the maximum he could summon without falling unconscious. Ethan was curious how Par'karr did it without a HUD and knowing his *Mana* and *Stamina* levels. When he'd asked the kobold how he did it, the kobold had shrugged. "Me just do it."

As he thought about *Mana*, Ethan looked down at the wand in his hand. He was no closer to figuring out the wand than he had been when he first got it. And it wasn't like he hadn't been trying. Every night when they stopped, he had tried to focus magic through the wand. Each time it had failed. Par'karr wanted to help him, but the little kobold understood even less about magic than Ethan.

Magic. It was something new to Ethan. A few weeks ago, he'd been a computer tech for a computer repair chain. Then, one night while he was playing an MMORPG with his buddies, he'd been abducted by aliens.

At least, that's what he believed had happened. The house had lost power, he'd walked outside, and a bright light had levitated him into the sky until he had blacked out. He hadn't actually seen any aliens, but what else could it be?

When he woke up from the abduction, he wasn't in Kansas anymore. He wasn't even on the planet *Earth*. The planet he was on now was completely different. He was pretty sure it wasn't even a planet. It seemed like more of a large moon around a gas giant with multicolored rings, in a solar system with two suns. Two suns and a black hole. Plus, it had at least 2 other moons that he'd seen.

And he'd seen other things. Most remarkably was a HUD, or heads up display, that appeared overlaid on whatever he was looking at. He could even call it up with his eyes shut. It displayed statistics and information about him in a very game-like fashion that reminded him of the MMORPGs he'd played with his friends.

The HUD had allowed him to choose the wizard class, which is when he'd started being able to channel magic. At first, it was all accidental. He'd done it without even really knowing what he was doing. But with a little practice, he was able to recreate some of the spells from his favorite RPGs.

Even stranger was that he had received quests through the HUD. And completing quests and killing enemies allowed him to level up and gain additional abilities. It was all eerily like the MMORPGs he played on *Earth*.

Then there were the people and creatures on this world. They were straight out of a table-top roleplaying game or MMORPG. He'd seen kobolds, dwarves, elves, two-headed wolves and foxgirls so far. Some of them were now his companions. And somehow, they all spoke English. Or rather, he heard them all speak English.

Like him, all of his companions, with the exception of Par'karr, had been abducted around the same time Ethan had. They'd all been dropped off at roughly the same spot and had immediately been forced to band together and fend off enemies.

First, there was Ainslee. She was the quintessential dwarf. She was a stout woman just over four feet tall, with deep ebony skin and white hair. She was a knight. Or rather, that was the class she'd chosen to be using her own HUD. Besides acting as their tank, she was also an accomplished smith back on her home world.

Next was Nia, the foxgirl who was an amazing fighter but who was forbidden from taking the lives of enemies by her Pack rules. Despite the fact that the foxgirl was probably hundreds or thousands of light-years from whatever planet she called home, she refused to abandon her Pack's edicts. She also had a HUD and had chosen the acrobat class.

Third was Yuliana, the green-haired elf. The short and willowy woman had an otherworldly beauty and looked like a short runway model. On her own world, she had tended a grove of trees - something she hadn't really elaborated on. It seemed natural that the nature-loving woman would pick the druid class.

Finally, there was Par'karr. He had spared the little kobold when the remnants of his tribe had attacked Ethan and the women. With the rest of his tribe dead and no place to go, Par'karr had joined up with them and had become surprisingly useful.

The kobold was also the only one of them who was a native to this world. Ethan had found out from Par'karr that kobolds had relatively small lifespans - 10 years if they were lucky. To make up for this, their women birthed a litter of three to four kobolds. From what the kobold had learned, his people had been on this planet for at least a dozen generations.

Together Ethan and his companions had managed to fight off an invading army of kobolds who had tried to destroy the village of Hawkshead.

Hawkshead was a village that Ethan had somehow become mayor of after killing some bandits who had been harassing the small town.

It was partially in his capacity as mayor that Ethan and his friends were on their journey. He was given a quest to re-open a trade route with the much larger city of Castlehaven. At least, that was one of the reasons. There was another reason he had wanted to go to the city.

When Ethan had chosen wizard as his class, he'd inadvertently chosen a class that was being systematically killed. And not just killed. Someone or something was murdering wizards and then sucking their brains out.

No one in Hawkshead knew anything more than rumors about what was happening to wizards. But they had all been afraid that whatever was hunting wizards would come to the village, possibly killing some of them in the process.

And despite the fact that Ethan and his companions had saved the town from being burned down by kobolds, not to mention that he was mayor, the villagers had wanted him to leave the village.

They'd been nice about it, mostly. But in the end, the message was clear: please go on a quest that takes you far away from the village so that if you get your brain sucked out, it doesn't happen to us too.

Now, he and his companions were a week into their two-week journey to Castlehaven. It had been an uneventful and uncomfortable journey so far. Uneventful that is, except for an owl-headed bear that had attacked them last night. It had been a tough fight, and the bear meat had been tough and greasy - but no worse than the rabbits they'd been eating.

"You want me try again?" The kobold yawned quietly.

They had both started taking first watch so that they could work on figuring out the wand together. It had seemed like a good idea, but neither of them had managed to channel so much as a single point of *Mana* through the wand. It was frustrating.

Ethan looked up at the moons. When he'd first arrived, telling time had been impossible. Without knowing the positions of the moons or even how long a day or night was, he'd been confused. Now, he was finally starting to be able to gauge the time.

"No," Ethan replied, looking at the moons. His shift was over. It was time to wake up Yuliana to take the second watch. "Go ahead and get some sleep and I'll wake up Yuliana."

"You sure?" the kobold whispered and cast a glance at the

sleeping elf. She was curled up under her blanket with Luna, her mountain lion animal companion next to her.

"I..." Ethan started but was cut off by a loud snore from Ainslee. They both stifled a chuckle. The dwarf snored incredibly loudly but insisted that she didn't snore at all. It had actually kept Ethan up at first, until he'd gotten used to it. He frowned and looked around at his companions and then up at the twin moons. He sighed. It was amazing what a person could get used to.

Ethan walked over to Yuliana, intending to shake her awake. Luna's head shot up and growled before the big cat seemed to recognize him. He held out his hand and let the mountain lion sniff him before gently shaking the elf.

Yuliana slowly opened her eyes and groaned. She blinked several times before she focused on him. The elf yawned. "My turn?"

"Your turn." He nodded.

Pushing herself up to her elbows, she absently moved her hand to Luna's head and scratched the mountain lion between the ears. In response, the big cat purred loudly. She looked at the wand in his hand and started to speak. She yawned instead.

The elf looked embarrassed "Sorry. Any luck?"

He looked down at the wand and frowned. "No. Nothing I did worked."

"You will figure it out." She smiled and sat up fully. "You are very smart."

He grinned but didn't share her optimism. Ethan had tried so many things over the last week and nothing had worked. There had to be some trick to it, but he just didn't understand what it was.

"Get some sleep," she told him and made a shooing motion.

He gave her another tired smile and crawled over to his own bedroll, slipping into the layers of blankets. Ethan had intended to spend some time thinking about the wand and coming up with new strategies to test it. Instead, as soon as he closed his eyes, he fell fast asleep.

1
______

Ethan woke with a start on the eighth day of their journey to Castlehaven. It was barely light out and normally he would have slept later but once again he'd had the same dream. Or rather, a similar dream.

For some time, he'd been dreaming of something chasing him, maybe even hunting him. But over the last few days, the dreams had changed. He no longer felt like something was drawing closer, hunting him down. Now, he felt something in his dreams watching him, or maybe searching for him.

The dreams had started shortly after he'd learned about something killing wizards, so he assumed that his imagination was running away with him. It wouldn't be the first time. He was prone to nightmares after watching certain horror movies and had given up on the genre. An overactive imagination, that's what his friends had called it. The curse of a dungeon master.

He smiled as he thought of his friends and their tabletop RPG sessions. He'd almost always been the dungeon master, the person who created the adventures for the other players to enjoy. Ethan enjoyed doing it. The creative aspect of building fantasy worlds and adventures was the polar opposite of the logical troubleshooting he did for his day job.

"Bad dream?" Nia asked in a quiet voice. The fox girl was looking over at him from across the waning fire. Her expression turned mischievous. "Or still sore from last night?"

Awake now and knowing he wouldn't be able to sleep any more, he sat up. He was still sore from their weapons training, but it was a good sore - mostly. He'd asked the fox girl to train with weapons, especially the quarterstaff, given how useless he was in a fight without his magic.

Training others wasn't forbidden by whatever code she followed, so Nia had agreed. Par'karr had even sat in on some of their sessions, though neither Ainslee nor Yuliana had seemed interested.

The morning air was chilly, even close to the fire and he kept the blanket wrapped around him while he sat up. "Bad dream. The same one."

"You were thrashing in your sleep," she replied, taking another piece of wood and putting it on the fire. "Though not as much as other nights."

"I really thrash in my sleep?" he asked. He didn't remember thrashing in his sleep previously. Certainly, he didn't remember thrashing in bed back on *Earth*. But then again, considering how many times he'd actually had a woman sleeping next to him in bed to tell him, how would he have known.

"From time to time." The fox girl shrugged. A loud snore broke through the silence and they both looked at the dwarf. Nia smiled. "But it could be worse."

He chuckled quietly and moved closer to the fire, trying

to ward off the chill that had settled on him.

"Since you are up, I will hunt for breakfast," Nia said. The fox girl stood up, grabbed her bow and walked into the woods before he could say anything. Luckily, the code preventing her from killing enemies didn't prevent her from hunting food, or prey, as she called it.

Ethan chuckled again and shook his head as he watched the foxgirl walk away, her bushy tail swaying back and forth. Realizing he was staring at more than just her bushy tail, he turned his attention to the fire.

Prodding the fire to try and coax more heat from it, he stifled a yawn and brought out the wand he'd taken from the kobold medicine man. Once more he examined it in his HUD, reading over the description for what seemed like the hundredth time.

```
Crude Wizard's Wand
   Type: Wand
   Range: Special
   Damage: Special
   Durability: 6 of 10
   Special: A wizard's wand allows the
wizard to focus his Mana through the
Chymera crystal at the tip to cast
spells.
```

It was the vague description he'd read multiple times a day since getting the wand. It seemed like it should be so simple, yet none of his attempts had been successful. Instead, whenever he'd tried focusing his magic through the wand, either nothing happened, or the spell used up his *Stamina*.

The situation was driving him crazy. The computer technician in him saw this as a problem to solve and he wasn't used to giving up. After all, people didn't pay for attempts to fix their problems, they paid for solutions to their problems.

He held the wand up. It was simple and crude, a foot-long stick with a clear crystal at the top, held in place by twine. Although the crystal was clear now, like a piece of clear quartz, he'd seen it glow blue when the medicine man had used it. But how? How had the kobold wizard done it?

Experimentally, he waved the wand around. Nothing happened of course. The magic in this world, at least the magic he could do, wasn't like magic from the MMORPGs or tabletop RPGs he'd played on *Earth*. It wasn't a spell that he memorized and then cast. Instead, the magic was something that he "willed" into existence. It was as if the magic responded to his thoughts, even subconscious thoughts sometimes.

To prove his point, he summoned a small ball of fire. He'd used it many times before as a light source and he found that he could manipulate its color and even intensity. It used up only a point of *Stamina*, though he found if he forced it to grow larger, the drain on his *Stamina* went up as well.

He thought about his abilities. Unlike the other magic he could do, the abilities he'd earned, like *Summon Minor Elemental*, did seem to operate more like traditional spells. When he mentally activated the ability, it did the same thing each time, regardless of his will. He'd tested it out by trying to summon a fire elemental in the shape of a bird, but each time, he got the fire weasel.

It seemed his only real choice he had with the ability was the type of elemental. And it was the same with the

Elemental Armor ability. Ethan could choose the element, but nothing else about the ability. What did that mean? Did it mean anything at all? There was just so much he didn't understand. He needed a manual or a FAQ!

He let out an exasperated breath and dismissed the ball of light. He looked down at the wand. Somehow, he was supposed to focus *Mana* through the wand to work his spell. But how?! He had been trying for days but nothing had worked! It was maddening!

He tossed the wand behind him on his bedroll. At least, that's what he had meant to do. Out of frustration, he'd thrown it a little too hard and it hit a large rock just on the other side of his bedroll. When it did, the stick part of the wand bounced one way and the crystal bounced the other way.

"No! No! No!" he cried as he scrambled for the pieces. Ethan swore as he grabbed the wooden part of the wand. It was missing the crystal at the top.

Desperately, his eyes searched the ground for the crystal, and he found it several feet away. He cursed. He'd broken the wand! He reached down and picked up the crystal. Unconsciously, he examined the crystal.

```
Small Chymera Crystal
   Type: Magical Focus
   Range: Special
   Damage: Special
   Durability: 4 of 10
   Special: A Chymera Crystal allows a
wizard to focus Mana to power his
magic.
```

Skill increase: Appraise +1%.

Ethan frowned. The description for the crystal was almost the same as the description for the wand. He examined the wooden part of the wand.

Stick
  Type: One-handed crushing weapon
  Range: 1 ft.
  Damage: 1 points crushing damage
  Durability: 5 of 8

He looked at the descriptions for both again. By itself, the stick was just a stick. It didn't seem to have any magic or special properties at all, other than possibly inflicting a point of damage on something.

The crystal, on the other hand, seemed to have nearly the same description as the wand had before. Was the crystal the part that actually channeled his *Mana*? Ethan had been trying to focus his magic THROUGH the wand and into the crystal the entire time. Had that been his mistake?

Gingerly, he willed some of his *Mana* into the crystal itself. He shuddered as he felt "something" flowing out of him and into the crystal. Immediately, the crystal began glowing a pale-blue color.

Excited, Ethan pulled up the HUD and checked out his stats.

Stamina: **39**
 Mana: **49**

He knitted his brows. Ethan's *Stamina* was just under

two-thirds. That wasn't unusual. Even with the bedrolls, his *Stamina* never regenerated past two-thirds. He'd accepted that it wouldn't get to full until he spent a good night's rest in an actual bed. Since he'd spent a point of it on the ball of light, it was right where it should be at 39.

On the other hand, his *Mana* was at maximum every morning. And now it was down a point! He'd done it! He'd channeled *Mana* into the crystal! But now what?

He focused on the crystal and, just like he did with his *Stamina*, willed it to do his bidding. He focused his will into creating a fireball and shooting it straight up into the air to explode above them. But this time, he focused not on himself, but on the crystal.

In response, the crystal glowed bright blue and then a tiny ball of fire shot from his hand. It was much smaller than his normal ball of fire and it only went about ten feet before exploding into a small fireball that was barely a foot in diameter. Luna opened her eyes and looked up but, seeing nothing interesting, laid her head back down on Yuliana and closed her eyes.

The fireball was completely lackluster, but he didn't care. He'd done it. Ethan had actually channeled *Mana* into a spell! And he'd done it by focusing on the crystal and not the wand! He shook his head at all the time he'd wasted trying to focus the magic through the wand and specifically, the stick part of the wand.

Now that he knew the crystal was the actual channel for the *Mana*, he could begin actually experimenting. If he could channel different amounts of *Mana* into the crystal and then release it, he should be able to replicate the same things he could do with his *Stamina*. Theoretically.

Nia suddenly burst from the underbrush, bow ready and

arrow notched. The motion and noise caused the mountain lion to spring up and the thing growled before recognizing the fox girl. That in turn caused Yuliana to spring up out of her bedroll, eyes wide. "What?!"

Par'karr also shot up from his bedroll, little spear in his hand. His head darted from person to person. "We attacked?!"

The fox girl looked around, eyes narrowed and then turned to Ethan. "What is wrong?! Where is the enemy?!"

"Wrong?" he asked. He was momentarily confused until he remembered the fireball he'd shot into the air. He gave them both an apologetic look. "I just figured out how to channel my mana into the wand... well... crystal. And I may have... accidentally... shot up a fireball as a test."

The fox girl glared at him and lowered her bow. "There is no enemy?"

"No, sorry," he apologized again. Obviously, his finding out how to channel *Mana* wasn't as exciting to her.

"If we have nothing for breakfast, it will be your fault!" Nia chastised him and then spun and stalked off into the forest.

"That's good." Yuliana yawned as she lay back down. Ethan smiled and started to explain what he had done but the elf had already turned away and pulled the covers over her head.

Ethan turned to Par'karr to tell him his exciting discovery, but the little kobold was already curled back up in his bedroll, eyes closed.

"I guess no one wants to hear about my big breakthrough," he muttered to himself.

The only response was a loud snore from the dwarf.

2

Nia did manage to kill a wild turkey for breakfast. At least, it would be a wild turkey if turkeys had bat-like wings, serpentine tails and scales on their underbelly. But despite its strange appearance, it did taste like turkey, or chicken, or some sort of bird-like creature he'd eaten.

As usually, Ainslee ate the lion's share of the kill, though there was so much meat, they each ate until they were full. Yuliana ate well that morning too. The clearing they had picked was surrounded by wild blackberry bushes and she still had half a pouch full of Shagbark hickory nuts they'd gathered from a grove of trees that they'd passed a few days earlier.

Ethan had never heard of Shagbark hickory nuts and wasn't sure if they were from *Earth*, but his Herbalism skill had said they were edible. After Yuliana had reported that they tasted sweet, he'd tried them. To him, they had a pecan taste. He had never really cared for pecans before, but on this world, you had to eat whatever you could.

During breakfast, he'd shown his companions how he'd learned to focus *Mana* into the crystal. The women gave him polite smiles but only Par'karr showed any real enthusiasm for his discovery. The little kobold asked him to demonstrate it several times and he was happy to oblige.

All too soon, they were done eating and then back on trail. While the first few days of hiking had been painful, he'd gradually gotten used to it. He was still tired and sore every night when they stopped, but it was no longer agonizing.

He'd noticed the same change in Ainslee and Yuliana. Like Ethan, neither of the women had done the type of hiking they were doing now. Like him, they'd struggled the first few days but now they walked without complaint. Well, Ainslee seemed to complain about everything but did less complaining about the walking.

As he walked, Ethan continued to channel *Mana* into the crystal and then conjure balls of fire. He did this constantly until his *Mana* got low. Once it did, he'd take a break and let it recharge. When it was back up to maximum, he would pick up where he left off.

He did this so many times that he reached Rank 2 in *Fire* Magic before lunch, which granted him another point of *Intellect*. Once that happened, his skill ups slowed down dramatically for the ball of fire spell.

Instead, he began working on Air Magic. Channeling *Mana* into the crystal, he would pick up a rock and toss it with air. He actually enjoyed the Air Magic more as it made him feel like he was a superhero or mutant with telekinesis. Or even a knight of the old republic. He just needed a laser sword!

So intent was he on practicing, Ethan hadn't even

noticed the air growing salty. Nor had he noticed the strange birds that seem to be this world's equivalent of seagulls. At least, that's how he thought of them. They were smaller than seagulls and had blue feathers on top and white under-bellies.

"That's not something you see every day," Ainslee gasped, causing Ethan to look up from his crystal.

The group had just crested a hill and sprawling before them was the ocean. But it was unlike any open he'd ever seen. The water was a deep purple, instead of the blue or blue green he was used to seeing on *Earth*.

But that wasn't the most striking thing about it. Hundreds of waterspouts appeared and disappeared up and down the shore with even more of them further out into the water. They rose from the water to the height of several hundred feet before slowly spinning back down in the water. All across the surface of the ocean, the strange watery dance repeated. It was both amazing and terrifying to see.

Ethan was no expert on waterspouts or weather, but he thought waterspouts were caused by storms, like tornadoes. Everything he'd heard on the news or read had basically led him to believe that they were really just tornadoes over water. And yet, there were no storm clouds in sight. In fact, and he wished he had some wood to knock on, it hadn't rained all week. So then why and how were the waterspouts appearing?

Looking at the huge shape of the ringed planet that was always visible, he wondered if it had something to do with gravity. Was the gravitational pull from the planet causing the water to act in such a way? Or was it some sort of magic? Or just a unique, naturally occurring phenomenon.

"I have never seen so much water," Nia gasped. "It is... beautiful."

Par'karr didn't say a word but nodded. The little kobold's eyes were large as he took in the ocean.

"What is it?" Yuliana asked, her own voice full of wonder.

"Do you not have oceans on your worlds?" he asked. Considering their levels of technology, if they hadn't lived within ten or fifteen miles of an ocean, chances were they'd never seen one. It wasn't like any of them had TV, streaming video or even photographs to go by.

"We have oceans." The dwarf shrugged. "But not like this. They are underground. The surface is too hot."

"I have never even heard of oceans," Yuliana said, still mesmerized by the shifting, bending patterns of the ocean.

"I have... heard rumors," the foxgirl muttered. "But I thought they were just fanciful stories. And this... this is something else."

"What is causing the water to shoot up like that?" Ainslee asked.

"I don't think this is normal for oceans," Ethan said. "I think it might be because we're so close to the planet."

Nia looked back at him, her brows knit. "The planet?"

Ethan wondered how he could explain the concept of gravity and gravitational forces to someone with a much more primitive culture. Did he even understand it enough himself to try explaining it to someone else? No, he didn't.

"It might have some sort of magic." He shrugged.

The women made sounds of agreement and looked back out over the water. They just stood there watching it as the minutes passed until finally Ethan cleared his throat. He pointed to a larger road down the hill that stretched north and south along the coastline.

The intersecting road was wider and more worn than the trail they'd been following and appeared to be the Dragoon Highway the villagers mentioned in passing when giving him directions to the city. Ethan wouldn't even have realized the name except for a faded sign they'd passed.

From here, they would turn north and follow it right to Castlehaven. "That looks like the road."

When the women continued to stare at the tumultuous waterscape, he cleared his throat again. "Ahem. We should probably get going."

When no one moved after several minutes, he let out a frustrated breath and began walking down the hill towards the road. After a few moments, he heard the sounds of Par'karr and the women following him.

Thirty minutes later, they had reached the coastal road and once again they paused and stared up at the towering torrents of water that rose up out of the ocean, only to sink back down a few minutes later. From their lower vantage point, the waterspouts looked even more awe-inspiring.

They gawked for a bit but eventually, they moved on. The group trekked north along the road for the rest of the day without passing a single person coming or going. While they walked, they all kept an eye on the columns of water and their almost-hypnotic pattern.

Yuliana was the first to point out the large reptilian birds that looked strikingly like the Pteranodons from *Earth*'s history. They were large reptiles with enormous bat-like wings that seemed to glide on the winds. The creatures darted in and out of the spouts.

"What are they doing?" Nia asked.

"Fishing," Ethan replied. At least, that's what he suspected. In that way they were like seagulls or pelicans, only hunting through vertical water instead of horizontal water.

"Let's hope they don't come fishing over here," Ainslee muttered, meaty hands going to her swords. They all nodded in agreement and continued walking.

The more of the spouts and the ocean he saw, the less Ethan imagined that there was any sort of ocean travel. The waterspouts seemed to be completely random and could easily pick up or capsize even a large vessel. That must mean all travel was land travel.

The group continued their own land travel until evening. Once evening arrived, they hiked almost a mile into the eastern forest before setting up camp. None of them wanted to risk a campfire in the open with the flying creatures so close.

It was hard to judge exactly how big the creatures were, given the distance, but given how far away they were and how large they looked, none of them wanted one of the creatures deciding to investigate a fire in the middle of the night.

Once they decided on a campsite, Ethan and Nia did their nightly practice while Ainslee and Yuliana watched. He was getting better. At least, that's what the foxgirl told him. But she showed him no mercy when he did something wrong or missed a block. He had the black and blue bruises to prove it.

He'd learned how to hold the staff and how to do several different types of strikes but was still a long way from being anywhere near as good as Nia. For knife training, they used sticks. It was a good thing because given how pitiful his skills were, the foxgirl would have given him dozens of scars.

After weapons training, Ethan spent the time before and after their dinner of another reptilian turkey, practicing with

Air Magic and the crystal. He was getting quicker at channeling his *Mana* and then using it to shape his spell. He was also getting more creative with what he could do with air.

During his watch, he practiced levitating himself several feet into the air and then setting himself back down. It was surprisingly more difficult to raise himself in the air than it was to lift another object. But after his latest attempt, he finally gained a rank in Air magic and earned another point in *Intellect*.

He grinned, as he slowly lowered himself from a height of about ten feet. "Yeah, I can fly."

3

———

Elated by his recent experiments in levitation, and his rank in Air Magic, he continued practicing. Ethan was just about to wake Yuliana for her shift when he noticed that the forest sounds had suddenly gone quiet.

Reaching out for his staff, he searched the darkness beyond the flames. Unfortunately, since his eyes were used to the light, he couldn't see more than a few feet in front of him. He looked into the air too. Ethan doubted any of the flying creatures could get through the forest canopy, but he wasn't about to take any chances.

Then he heard a snap of twigs to his right and his head snapped around. There was definitely something out there. Something that caused the insects and other animals to go quiet.

Luna, who was curled up next to Yuliana, suddenly raised her head and looked in the same direction as him. The mountain lion's ears went back, and she growled. Obviously, she knew something was out there too. That did it for Ethan. He needed to wake people!

Reaching out with his Air Magic, he nudged the others awake. They had just started to sit up when several shapes emerged from the darkness on the right. Immediately, he called out the alarm. "Attack! Attack!"

The things that emerged from the darkness were the stuff of nightmares. There were three of them and they looked like a cross between a snake and a squid. The bodies were long and slithered like a snake, but the head was a mass of octopus-type tentacles, complete with a snapping beak in the center.

Bringing up his HUD instinctively, he Analyzed them.

Beaked Slitherer
    Level 4

The beaked slitherers moved quickly and closed in on his companions. Still sleepy, their reactions were slowed. One of the slitherers went for Yuliana, who screamed. Luckily, Luna swatted the thing with a large paw, rocking it back.

A second one reached Ainslee as the dwarf was rubbing her eyes and trying to figure out what was going on. The slithering creature reared back to strike her. Ethan was forced to reach out and grab her with air, pulling her just out of reach of the grasping tentacles.

The attempt used up some of his *Mana*, which was depleted from his practice. Ethan hadn't saved much since he thought he'd be lying down to go to sleep right about now. He quickly brought up his HUD and checked on his stats.

Mana: 11

Ethan had only 11 *Mana* left! He cursed himself for using so much for practicing. He should have saved more.

He saw one of the slitherers coming for him. He quickly used Summon Minor Elemental and felt the drain of *Mana* and *Stamina*. The fiery weasel appeared in front of him and the beaked slitherer halted, seemingly unsure what to make of the flaming creature.

Ethan checked his stats.

Stamina: 22
  Mana: 6

He was almost completely out of *Mana* and he didn't have much *Stamina*. He would need to be careful.

The weasel squared off with the slitherer. The serpentine creature struck out several times, but the weasel nimbly dodged out of the way. As the slitherer overextended itself on a lunge, the weasel leaped on its back and buried its flaming teeth just behind the tentacles.

Minor elemental (fire) critically burns Beaked Slitherer for 13 fire damage.

Skill increase: *Fire* magic +1%.

The thing hissed and whipped its head back and forth, trying to dislodge the elemental but the fiery weasel held on tight.

A bellow of pain drew Ethan's attention away from his

fight. Looking over, he could see that one of the slitherers had its tentacles wrapped around Ainslee's left arm. It had pulled her arm into biting distance of the snapping beak and was taking large gashes out of the dwarf's forearm.

Ainslee's face was a mask of pain and rage as she desperately tried to strike at the tentacles with the short sword. Unfortunately, her blows didn't seem to dissuade the creature from its task. If anything, the sword blows seemed to bounce off the rubbery hide.

Minor elemental (Fire) critically burns Beaked Slitherer for 11 fire damage.

Skill increase: Fire magic +1%.

His own slitherer was still twisting and writhing on the ground, trying to stop the burning creature on its back. His elemental was not letting go. It continued its fiery attacks against the creature, which seemed to have more effect than the dwarf's blows.

Turning back to Ainslee, Ethan ran over to her and began raining blows on the "head" of the slitherer, just behind where the tentacles joined the body.

You crush Beaked Slitherer for 0 damage.
Slitherer skin absorbs 5 points of crushing damage.
You crush Beaked Slitherer for 0 damage.

Slitherer skin absorbs 4 points of crushing damage.

"Get it off me!" the dwarf hissed through clenched teeth. The thing continued to bite her with its beak and blood covered her entire arm. "I don't have much health left..."

Ethan swore. His weapon was useless, and it was killing Ainslee. He needed to do something fast or she was going to die.

He looked over to Nia, Yuliana and Par'karr. Nia was nimbly dodging the attacks, but she bled from several wounds. Luna was trying to bite and scratch the creature, but the marks she left were minor.

Par'karr was trying to help with his summoned demon rabbits. The three rabbits were hopping around the creature and biting at it, but their fangs, like Luna's, only seemed to inflict minor wounds.

In game terms, these beaked slitherers must have some sort of damage reduction. From what he observed, it reduced physical damage but not elemental damage - like fire damage. If that were the case, then only massive damage or elemental damage would bypass it.

Knowing he wouldn't get any help from the others; Ethan knew he needed to help Ainslee himself. He double checked his stats again.

Stamina: **20**
Mana: **6**

It wasn't much to work with. He quickly ran through his options in his head. He could create a fireball, but that would drain most, if not all, of his *Stamina*. He could also create a few beams of fire, but would they be enough to kill it before he ran out?

Checking his character sheet, he saw he had just enough *Mana* for *Elemental Armor*. Ethen dropped his staff and activated the ability. Immediately, he felt the fatigue of having his *Mana* and *Stamina* drained and he staggered a step. Blue flames sprung up around him like a second skin. As before, the flames didn't affect him or his belongings.

Gritting his teeth, he launched himself at the body of the slitherer. He tackled the thing around its main body and it immediately began to twist and writhe as its rubbery flesh sizzled.

```
Elemental  Armor  (fire)  burns  Beaked
Slitherer for 5 fire damage.


Skill increase: Fire magic +1%.
```

As he had hoped, the creature released Ainslee and the dwarf fell back, clutching her bloody arm. The slitherer tried lashing out at him with its tentacles but immediately regretted it.

```
Beaked Slitherer slashes at you for 4
points of damage.
   Elemental Armor (fire) burns Beaked
Slitherer for 3 fire damage.


Skill increase: Fire magic +1%.


Beaked Slitherer slashes at you for 3
points of damage.
```

Elemental Armor (fire) burns Beaked Slitherer for 4 fire damage.

Skill increase: Fire magic +1%.

The beak opened and the creature emitted a screech of pain. It tried to rear its head back from him and continued to buck beneath him, desperately trying to get away from the flames.

Elemental Armor (fire) burns Beaked Slitherer for 5 fire damage.

Skill increase: Fire magic +1%.

Unlike the fire elemental, Ethan had no claws to dig in. As the creature squirmed and twisted, he lost his grip and was thrown off the creature. As he rolled to his feet, he received a message.

Beaked Slitherer dies.
  You gain 40 experience. Experience to next level 1255.

Looking over, he saw the fiery weasel hop off the unmoving form of the slitherer it had been attacking. Good. One down, two more to go. He pointed at the one that Nia and the rest were fighting. "Kill!"

The weasel bounded towards the slitherer they were fighting, and Ethan turned his attention to the injured one that was still writhing on the ground. It still twisted and snapped, and he wondered if it realized he was not on it.

Gritting his teeth, he leaped on the twisting mass of tail and tentacles. This time, he wrapped his arms and legs around the body and pressed himself close.

Elemental Armor (fire) burns Beaked Slitherer for 5 fire damage.

Skill increase: Fire magic +1%.

Once again, the tentacles snapped at him. Apparently, they were slow learners - or it didn't realize he was the same person as before. The barbed tentacles raked across his arms and his back briefly before retracting from the flames.

Beaked Slitherer slashes at you for 3 points of damage.
Elemental Armor (fire) burns Beaked Slitherer for 5 fire damage.

Skill increase: Fire magic +1%.

Beaked Slitherer slashes at you for 2 points of damage.
Elemental Armor (fire) burns Beaked Slitherer for 4 fire damage.

Skill increase: Fire magic +1%.

The creature once again went into a frenzy as it sought to get away from the flames of his *Elemental Armor*. It thrashed about but didn't attack him with its tentacles again. He continued to bear hug the creature until it stopped moving.

Beaked Slitherer dies.
   You gain 20 experience. Experience to next level 1235.

Ethan pushed himself off the charred body of the slitherer. He stood up just in time to see the final slitherer go down with his elemental latched to its neck - or at least, what he thought was the neck.

Beaked Slitherer dies.
   You gain 20 experience. Experience to next level 1215.

"Yuliana!" he shouted. "Help Ainslee! She's really hurt!"

The elf rushed over to Ainslee and the green glow of healing magic surrounded her. While Yuliana healed her, the others walked over to Ethan. The elemental was nowhere to be seen and he guessed its duration had expired.

"What were those things?" Nia asked. The foxgirl had gashes all across her limbs and torso from where the creature's barbed tentacles had slashed at her. It was the worst he'd ever seen her. "Are they from your world?"

"Not from mine," he said, looking down at the charred remains of one. "I've never seen nor heard of them. I take it these things aren't from your world either?"

Nia shook her head. "Thankfully not."

"They sure as Loki's toes ain't from my world," Ainslee grunted as the elf cast more healing magic on her. The dwarf's arm was a mess and Ethan wondered if there was a limit to what the magic could mend. Hopefully, the dwarf wouldn't have any permanent damage.

"They beaked slitherers," Par'karr chimed in. "They hard to kill."

Ethan nodded to the little kobold. Par'karr had just stated the obvious but he was trying to be helpful.

"They are not from my world either," the elf gasped in between healing. Her face was covered in sweat and he guessed she had used up all of her Piety and was dipping into her own *Stamina*.

"Maybe we should do double watches for the rest of the night," he muttered as the flames of his *Elemental Armor* faded away.

"I was about to suggest that very thing," Nia said. "You, Yuliana and Ainslee can get sleep first. Par'karr and I will stay up for the first shift."

Par'karr gave the foxgirl a toothy grin. "Par'karr good at watch!"

They dragged the bodies of the slitherers a hundred yards away before fixing up their camp. When he finally lay down, Ethan was out the moment his head hit the bundle of cloth he now called a pillow.

4

They marched another day on the Dragoon Highway. They were all exhausted from the night before. None of them had slept well after the attack.

Around midday, the tired group came across some outlying farms.

Trying to stifle a yawn, he checked out the farms as his companions walked by. They seemed much like the farms near Hawkshead. Perhaps a bit poorer looking.

After passing farms for several miles, the group eventually came to a small village called Birchwood. The village was similar in size to Hawkshead, no more than half a dozen buildings and some outlying farms. Unlike Hawkshead, this village actually looked busy, with people bustling around and kids running through the street.

Most of the activity stopped when he and his companions came through and the group received hard stares. Par'karr got the brunt of their hostile expressions but Nia received a fair number as well.

"Friendly lot," Ainslee muttered as the group walked through the town.

"They do not seem to like me," Nia said quietly, her tail puffy and her ears back.

Par'karr looked at the glares from the villagers. "Not like me too."

When Ethan had originally seen the village from afar, he had thought maybe they could stay the night if it had an inn. Now, he thought it was best if they camped far away from this village.

The companions walked through the village and kept going. They passed more farms on the north side of the village before it reverted back to the dense forest they were used to.

"Did you notice that there was no dock," Ethan said, when they'd finally passed the last farm.

"What do you mean?" Yuliana asked from behind him.

"I mean, this is the coast," he replied. "You'd think this would be mostly a fishing town. Or that there would be boats of some kind."

"Fish?! In that?!" chuckled the dwarf, motioning to the waterspouts to the east. "They'd have to be daft!"

Ethan nodded. "I agree. It just seems weird to see villages along the ocean that aren't fishing villages."

"Is that how it is on your world?" Yuliana asked.

"Yes." He nodded. "The ocean is one of our greatest resources. I'm not sure how we'd be able to survive without it."

"How many people are there where you come from?" the elf asked, her tone light but curious.

He shrugged. "In the whole world? Like 7 or 8 billion, I think."

"Billion?" Yuliana asked, her tone confused. "What is billion?"

"Uh..." Ethan struggled to remember how many that was in millions. "A billion is a thousand million... I think."

"Million?" the elf asked, her struggle with the word making it obvious she wasn't familiar with it either.

"A million is a thousand thousand," he said.

"A thousand thousand?!" Nia and Yuliana said at nearly the same time.

"I'm pretty sure," he said. "You don't have a million people on your worlds?"

The two women seemed unable to speak as their minds mulled over the numbers. He belatedly realized that with their level of technology, they would have no way of knowing how many people were on their entire planet. He doubted they even had an accurate count of whatever countries they lived in - assuming their culture had countries.

"I think you burned out their minds," the dwarf chuckled but then her face turned sour as she probably remembered the events of the previous night. "You must have a huge world. I doubt there are more than a million dwarves on our entire planet. Though in all honesty, I don't think anyone's explored all of it. I don't even think all of it's accessible."

"You two are jesting?" Nia asked with furrowed brows.

"About the numbers?" the dwarf replied. "No. We do a census each year. That's how the king determines taxes. And that's just our king. I know the other nine kingdoms are about the same as ours, so that's almost a million."

"But thousand thousand?" Nia said, her eyes wide. "How can you all fit?"

"Some places are crowded," Ethan replied. "But some places are as sparsely populated as this area."

"So many people," Nia marveled. "Thousand million."

The group lapsed into silence after that and Ethan pulled out his crystal. He'd found that he didn't actually need to hold the crystal to channel *Mana* into it. Having used it nearly constantly for two days, he could sense the crystal now. As long as it was on his person, he'd been able to use it.

He had begun practicing with his *Earth* magic, but that proved more difficult that he'd originally thought. In the MMORPGs and RPGs he'd played, he'd never really been any sort of earth mage. He had found he could cause the ground to cover a person's feet or even their whole body if they stayed still enough.

The biggest surprise had been learning that he could also form things from earth and rock, as well as metal - sort of. Last night, he'd used his practice time to hone the crude flint spearhead on Par'karr's spear to a razor-sharp point.

Once he'd successfully manipulated the flint, he'd shaped several pieces of stone into varying shapes, making stone copies of some of his RPG miniatures. Despite Ethan having no real artistic skill, as long as he focused on the shape in his mind, he could recreate it with stone.

Then he'd tried it on his knife. And he'd almost killed himself and possibly everyone around him as the knife exploded. One moment, he could feel the metal bending to his will and the next, the thing was exploding into shards of metal.

He'd gotten the brunt of the exploding metal shards, dropping his *Health* down to 11 points, but everyone in the camp had been hurt. He looked down at his ripped armor. Had he not been wearing the jerkin, he might have killed himself.

"Are you daft?!" the dwarf had shouted after she had

stopped swearing and he'd explained what happened. "You can't work metal while it's cold! Even with magic! You have to heat it!"

She had berated him for nearly an hour before finally going back to bed. The others hadn't been happy but after Yuliana had healed them, most of them just wanted to go back to bed. Not Ainslee. If the other women wouldn't have shouted for her to go to bed so they could sleep, the dwarf might still be yelling at him.

Ethan looked over and caught Ainslee glaring at him as he handled the crystal. She made a face and shook her fist at him.

"I'm not going to do anything with metal!" he assured the dwarf and she turned away.

He'd learned his lesson. It seemed he could manipulate natural stone with no problems, just not worked metal. Ethan was curious to whether or not he could manipulate metal that had been heated. If they got the blacksmith's tools for Ainslee, so she could restart Hawkshead's forge, maybe he could talk her into letting him try.

An hour before dark, Nia suddenly held up a hand, her ears twitching.

"I hear it too," Yuliana said and pointed east towards the ocean. "Look!"

A flock of twenty or thirty of the large Pteranodons were flying their way. They were flying fast and heading directly for them.

"Into the trees!" Ethan yelled. The flying dinosaurs were large, and he hoped that the thick trees would prevent the creatures from being able to follow them or get to them.

His group made a mad dash into the nearby forest. Once they were in the trees, Ethan turned and looked back out.

The Pteranodons flew over them without so much as a pause, their large forms blocking out the suns as they flew overhead. The group warily watched them all fly by. Even after they had all gone, they stayed in the trees for several more minutes.

"Are they gone?" Yuliana whispered, her eyes searching the sky through the trees. The elf was crouched down, her arms around a tree. At her side, Luna the mountain lion watched the sky, the cat's ears completely flattened against her head.

"I do not hear them," Nia said, her ears twitching.

"Neither do I." The elf nodded, slowly standing.

"What in Odin's beard was that about?" grumbled the dwarf. "Were they attacking?"

"Big birds eat Par'karr!" the kobold cried.

"I don't think so," Ethan said. He'd been looking for any signs that the creatures were after them but none of them so much as paused or circled the area.

"You don't think so," mocked the dwarf. "Like you didn't think the dagger would explode?!"

Ethan winced, knowing that she was right. He'd made a serious blunder last night because he hadn't really thought things through. But this was different.

"Quiet!" hissed Yuliana, her voice full of fear. She was getting lower to the ground. Next to her, the mountain lion was baring her teeth and looking at the sky.

"Yes! Listen," said the foxgirl, who also crouched lower.

They all shut up then and listened. Ethan realized that he didn't have nearly the hearing of either Nia or Yuliana but even he could hear something odd. It was like squawking. Almost like large bird sounds. Was that the sounds the Pteranodons made?

The loud and terrible roar echoed through the forest and Ethan's blood went cold. Whatever had made that sound was large. Much larger than the Pteranodons. It almost sounded like a Tyrannosaurus Rex from some of the Jurassic movies he'd watched.

Was that possible? Were there other dinosaurs on this world? Considering what he'd seen so far, it wasn't completely out of the realm of possibility.

The roar sounded several more times and then there was quiet. Almost. Ethan strained his ears to hear anything else but there were no more squawks and no more roars. Just a rhythmic beating that was getting closer. Then a huge shadow passed over them.

Looking up at the enormous shape, Ethan swallowed hard. The creature which had flown over them was not a Pteranodon or any sort of dinosaur.

It had a large, horned head on a long, thick serpentine neck. The creature had a large muscular body with four powerful limbs that were curled up close to its body. The entire body of the creature was covered in slick green scales that seemed almost incandescent in the waning sunlight. Large bat-like wings beat rhythmically, and a long serpentine tail snapped back and forth as it flew overhead.

He knew what it was, though it seemed completely impossible. It was not a dinosaur and nothing that was even in *Earth*'s fossil record. It was a dragon. A huge freaking dragon!

5
———

No one in the group moved, they barely breathed, until the dragon had passed them. Then they quietly made their way to the edge of the forest and watched as the enormous creature flew towards the ocean. As it got closer, the remaining Pteranodons scattered. The creatures flew in all directions, trying to get away from the dragon.

The dragon pursued the fleeing creatures. The great beast could not match the Pteranodons' speed and maneuverability, but its long neck snaked out to catch the smaller creatures. They watched for five minutes in silence as the dragon fed on the Pteranodons and eventually chased a large group of them to the south.

"Dragon," Nia breathed finally as the huge mythical creature flew after its prey.

Ethan turned to the foxgirl. "They have dragons on your world?"

The foxgirl's eyes never left the dragon. "No, but there are stories of them. Children's stories to frighten pups."

"So, you've never seen one?" he asked.

Nia turned to him, her expression annoyed. "No, they are just stories. Do you have them on your world?"

"No," he replied, glancing back at the dragon disappearing into the distance. "But we have stories too."

"The dwarves have stories of dragons as well," Ainslee murmured softly. "It's said they were the first creatures on our world, and they created all the other races."

Yuliana glanced at the dwarf and nodded. "In our legends, dragons planted the first groves and left us to tend them. Then they burrowed far underground and slept."

"Interesting," Ethan said, trying to wrap his head around the concept that all four of their worlds shared stories of dragons. "In your stories, did dragons generally look like what we just saw?"

The women looked at one another and then, almost as one, they all nodded.

He turned to Par'karr, whose eyes were wide, and his little tail was between his legs. "Par'karr, how frequent are dragons here?"

Par'karr continued to stare at the huge beast, unmoving and unspeaking.

"Par'karr!" he hissed, finally getting the kobold's attention.

"Me heard of dragons," he replied. "All in tribe know of dragons. Me see one once, flying around mountain. Very far. It much more big when closer!"

Ethan's head spun. What did that mean? How did different worlds, who knew how many millions of light-years from each other, all have dragons in their history. And not just dragons, but the same sort of dragon.

For a moment, he considered that dragons might be the aliens who had brought them all to this world. But the idea of massive ships able to hold just one dragon, let alone dozens of them, seemed completely far-fetched. What was the connection? How had all of their planets heard of dragons?

"We should move north before it comes back," Nia said, breaking Ethan from his theory. "When it passed us the first time, it was on the hunt. If it returns this way, it will not have something to distract it from seeing us."

"And we might be dessert." Ainslee swallowed.

"We should leave," Yuliana agreed.

"Stay in the treeline," Ethan told them.

Nia frowned and glanced at him. "That will be slower."

"Maybe," Ethan replied, remembering the stories and stats of dragons from the various role-playing games. "In my world, the stories say the dragons have extremely sharp vision. If we are out in the open, it might see us from miles away."

"Like birds of prey." Nia nodded.

"I'm fine with the trees," Ainslee said and Yuliana nodded her agreement. Luna made a cat noise that could have been an agreement as well.

"Fine," Nia said and adjusted the straps on her backpack. "Let us move swiftly then."

True to her word, Nia kept a breakneck pace that had Ethan breathing hard after only a few minutes. While Nia and Ainslee barely seemed affected by their speed, both Yuliana and Ethan struggled to keep up. Luckily, all of the walking had at least given them a little more endurance.

They kept up the fast pace until the suns had set and the forest had grown too dark to see. Still, the foxgirl continued their pace, her own eyes able to see in the near-complete darkness.

"Let's stop," Ethan hissed as he bounced off a tree he hadn't seen until it was too late. He rubbed at his injured shoulder.

"Why?" Nia growled without casting a backwards glance at him.

"Because... it's too dark... for the rest... of us to see...," he retorted irritably. Ethan was tired and irritable, his breath coming in ragged gasps.

That had been the third tree in the last ten minutes he'd run into. And he hadn't been the only one. Only a couple of minutes ago, Yuliana had almost face planted into the earth when she tripped over some roots.

"Why don't you create some light, wizard-boy," the dwarf snickered.

"No!" Nia snapped. "No light!"

Coming to a halt, the foxgirl was promptly knocked to the ground when Ainslee barreled into her. The dwarf looked down and chuckled. "I guess he's right. It's too dark."

Muttering to herself, Nia stood and brushed herself off. "No light! No fire! It will be a beacon in the darkness."

"Are you kidding?" Ainslee huffed, hands on hips. "No fire?"

"And no hunting," the foxgirl added. "Unless you want to eat it raw."

"No dinner?!" Ainslee growled and then looking back to the south, lowered her voice. "No dinner?!"

Nia folded her arms across her chest. "Do you want the dragon to see the fire and come to see if we are a snack?"

"Nia's... right," Ethan said, still catching his breath. "If the dragon... is flying around... a fire... is sure to... attract it."

Grumbling, the dwarf collapsed heavily on the ground. "Fine. But it's going to be a cold night with no fire!"

Ethan nodded his agreement in the dark. The night air had already turned cool and the only reason he wasn't feeling it was because he was still hot from running. He shivered as the sweat evaporated and left him feeling even more chilled.

They all sat down, slipping their backpacks from their shoulders. They began to riffle through their packs, gathering up whatever nuts that remained. Unfortunately, there weren't many left. Ethan sighed. If only he could create food using magic.

Ethan scrunched up his face as he thought of magic. He'd been practicing manipulating *Earth* all day. Maybe there was something he could do. Not to make food, but to provide them some sort of shelter.

He took out his crystal and held it tightly in his fist so the glow couldn't be seen. He looked around at the others. "Move in closer."

"What?" Ainslee asked irritably.

"If you want some food," he snapped back, "move in closer."

Apparently, food was the magic word and they all moved close, giving him curious and hopeful glances.

He wasn't a student of architecture by any stretch of the imagination, but he still remembered a good deal of what he had learned in high school and college. Perhaps because of his roleplaying games and creating adventures for his friends, he'd always been fascinated with medieval and early cultures. That included Native American cultures.

He remembered that the Native Americans created dome-shaped, tent-like structures called wigwams. They were usually made from a frame of sticks over which the Native Americans would throw hides. They didn't have sticks or hides, but they did have some magic.

Focusing on what he wanted, he began feeding *Mana* into the crystal. As he did, he reached out with his senses and found the dirt around him. He channeled the magic into it, drawing it close and forming it into walls.

He stopped looking through his eyes, depending more on his sense of the *Earth* than his eyes. Ethan was vaguely aware of a few gasps from the women, but he was intent on what he wanted to do.

He formed the walls in a circle of what he guessed was seven or eight feet in diameter. He forced the dirt not only to form the walls, but also to solidify, becoming dense enough to form the walls.

He continued to build the walls up into the dome shape that he remembered the wigwam had. When he got to the apex of the dome, he left a small hole on the top of the earthen structure to let smoke out. Ethan made sure to reinforce the roof of the structure, forcing it to harden to a point where he knew it would not collapse on them.

Finally, he was done, and his eyes came into focus. He looked around at the newly forced structure around him and then saw that all of his companions were looking at him with shocked expressions.

"What?" he asked tiredly. Using so much magic at once had taken a lot out of him and he felt very drained. Ethan saw messages waiting for him in his HUD.

"You have created a dirt house," Nia muttered. The foxgirl was looking around at the structure and reached out a hand to touch it.

"We can build a fire inside," he told them and pointed up

at the roof. "The smoke will go up and out the top but most of the light will stay inside. If we can cover the top with twigs, the smoke will still go through but there should be very little light leakage. Not enough to penetrate the tree canopy."

Feeling weak, he leaned against the side of the wigwam. Par'karr was grinning, running his hands along the walls, but the women were still gawking at him.

"You really are a wizard," Yuliana breathed.

"That's what it says on my character sheet," Ethan chuckled tiredly, barely able to keep his eyes open. The day's walking and last hour of their fast-paced journey were catching up to him. Combined with using his magic to build the hut, it had completely exhausted him.

"Are you okay, wizard-boy?" Ainslee asked.

"Really... tired," he said. Even to him, his words sounded slurred. Ethan tried to keep his eyes open, but they were so heavy. Every part of him just wanted to sleep. He wondered why he was fighting so hard. It was night. It was time to sleep.

The last thing he saw before the darkness closed in was the women looking at him with concerned locks. Then, sleep claimed him, and he knew no more.

6

Ethan was lying on a cold, hard table. He had to be naked, because he could feel the cool metal across his back, legs, arms and his butt. He tried to open his eyes, but it seemed a herculean task.

Straining to open his eyes again, he tried to think about where he was. Thinking was hard. It was almost as if he were drugged. His brain was slow and fuzzy. It was like thinking through molasses.

He tried to move his hand, but the limb didn't respond. Ethan could feel the arm and the hand, could feel the cool metal of the table, but he couldn't move it. Was he paralyzed? Or maybe just too tired.

Reaching out with his other senses, Ethan heard a buzzing noise. And another noise. Maybe a whirring sound? And a humming. It almost seemed like background noise. It was coming from all around him and he couldn't pinpoint it.

Then there was the smell. Ethan wasn't sure what it was. It seemed familiar. Maybe, cleaning products? Rubbing alcohol? It had a very antiseptic smell to it, like a hospital.

Ethan's heart began beating faster. Was that it? Was he in a hospital room? Maybe an operating table? Had something happened to him? Had he been in an accident at work or maybe in a car accident?

He renewed his efforts to open his eyes and a crack of white-hot pain stabbed into his brain as bright light assaulted his eyes. Ethan blinked back tears at the bright light. The pain the light caused was palpable and he desperately wanted to shut his eyes. And yet, he needed to know. Ethan needed to know what had happened to him and where he was.

Forcing himself to endure the pain and blinking through the brightness as his eyes adjusted, things began to take shape. At first, everything was blurry. Then, gradually, things began to take shape. And he wished they hadn't.

The room was dark, but above him were several intense lights, blasting light down on his body. He couldn't actually move his head, so he couldn't see his body, but he could see the bright lights suspended four or five feet above him. Shapes moved in the darkness, but he couldn't quite make them out.

Then a head thrust itself into his view on his right. A head, but not a human head. It was hairless with light-gray skin and large, black eyes. Its nose consisted of only small slits and its mouth was tiny and toothless. It looked down at him and blinked large eyelids.

"It is awake," the thing said, though its mouth did not move. Was he hearing its voice in his head?

Another head appeared, this one from the left. At the same time, he sensed more movement in the room. The second figure looked almost identical to the first. Maybe it was identical. They were both so featureless, it was impossible to tell.

The second face leaned in. Large black eyes blinked several times. "Interesting. It fights the anesthesia."

"The alterations are not complete," another voice said from the darkness. This voice seemed to originate in his head, rather than something he heard with his ears.

"We must complete the alterations," the first voice said.

"Yes," the second head said, its small mouth unmoving. "I cannot help us without the full alterations. Increase the dosage by 5%."

He felt fire in his veins for only a moment before everything faded into darkness. Ethan swam in the darkness for what seemed like eternity, vaguely aware of shapes and sounds before everything dissolved into absolute black.

Ethan gasped awake. He sat up quickly, nearly hitting his head on the domed wall of the wigwam. Next to him, Yuliana and Par'karr looked at him with concern.

"You awake!" The little kobold grinned happily.

The elf gave him a smile and he looked down to see that she was holding his hand in her own. Her hand was cool to the touch yet comforting. Ethan didn't make any move to take his hand away and noticed she made no move to remove her own hand.

He blinked, looking around at the inside of the wigwam. The scene he'd just been experiencing had been so real he felt disoriented. It was as if he'd been watching a movie really intently and then suddenly changed the channel to a completely different type of movie.

Had that been some sort of bizarre dream? Or had that been a memory of his abduction? If it was a memory, what did it mean? What were these "alterations" they had spoken of. And what did they mean about helping them?

"Are you okay?" Yuliana asked. "You were unconscious for a long time."

Ethan looked up through the hole in the ceiling of the wigwam and saw the light was filtering in. It was daylight. But it had just been night a second ago. At least, it had been to him. "What... what time is it?"

His mouth was dry, and he ran his tongue over his lips to find that they were chapped.

"It is just after midday," the elf replied. She took her other hand and placed it on his forehead. It was cool to the touch. "You still have a fever."

He frowned. "A fever?"

"Yes," she replied, her tone scolding. "You created this shelter and then collapsed. We could not wake you and you thrashed and murmured all night, burning up with a fever. None of my healing made you better."

"I think I'm okay now," he said and looked around. "Where are Ainslee and Nia?"

"Nia is hunting and Ainslee went to get more firewood," she said.

"Ainslee not happy," Par'karr added.

"Why?" he asked.

"Dragon," the kobold replied and flapped his arms like wings.

Ethan remembered the dragon. A creature from the very legends and myths of his own planet and other planets. It was to hide them from the dragon that he'd created the wigwam. He'd used his *Earth* magic to do it. And just as the shelter had been created, he'd blacked out.

Trying to make sense of what had happened, Ethan brought up his HUD. He had intended to check his stats, but found a ton of messages he hadn't seen while he was creating the shelter.

```
Skill increase: Earth Magic +1%.
   Skill increase: Earth Magic +1%.
   Skill increase: Earth Magic +1%.
   Skill increase: Earth Magic +1%.
   Skill increase: Earth Magic +1%.
   Skill increase: Earth Magic +1%.
   Skill increase: Earth Magic +1%.
   Skill increase: Earth Magic +1%.
   Skill increase: Earth Magic +1%.
```

There were many more *Earth* magic increases, and he scrolled through them until he saw that he'd reached rank 2.

```
You    have    reached    Rank    2    in    Earth
Magic.
   +1 Intellect.
```

There were some additional *Earth* magic increases, but then a red message caught his eye. The text of the HUD had always been white. But the new message was bright red.

```
Warning:  Mana  at  0.  Channeling  more
Mana  than  you  have  available  can  cause
temporary  or  permanent  injury.
```

He swore silently. He'd been so intent on creating the wigwam that he hadn't bothered looking at his HUD. Ethan had assumed he'd simply be unable to channel *Mana* once he reached 0.

```
You have unlocked a new ability.

Overchannel
   Type: Wizard
   Cost: Special
   Range: Self
   Duration: Special
   Description: The caster channels his
physical and mental fortitude into raw
magical Mana.
   Warning: May cause permanent loss of
ability scores.
```

```
You have temporarily lost a point of
Intellect.
   You have temporarily lost a point of
Intellect.
   You have temporarily lost a point of
Intellect.
   You have temporarily lost a point of
Intellect.
   You have temporarily lost a point of
Intellect.
   You have temporarily lost a point of
Intellect.
```

Ethan read and re-read the new messages several times. Instead of stopping at 0 *Mana*, he had unwittingly consumed some of his *Intellect* points to fuel his magic. He brought up his stats.


```
Intellect: 17


Health: 30
  Stamina: 30
  Mana: 31
```


His *Intellect* was at 17. According to his calculations, it should be at 23 given his recent level up in *Earth* magic and the point he'd gained. His lower *Intellect* score had the effect of also lowering his maximum *Mana* pool.

He cursed as he realized he should have been paying attention to his HUD. Ethan always kept a close eye on his stats when he was playing an MMORPG with his friends. And that was a game. This was his life now. He had been stupid. "Stupid! Stupid! Stupid!"

"What's wrong?" Yuliana asked as she withdrew her hand from his head.

"I did something very stupid," he admitted. "I channeled too much magic and I could have died."

Par'karr and Yuliana exchanged looks. Both looked worried but not necessarily surprised. It was the kobold who spoke up. "Me told them story. Medicine man from my tribe. He try to do big magic. Big magic like you. Him fall over dead."

"We were afraid something similar had befallen you," the elf said. "After all, you did build an entire house."

"It's a wigwam," he muttered and rubbed his forehead. Obviously, this place had rules, just like a game. The problem was, there was no Player's Handbook, wikipage or even a tutorial.

He had flashbacks of his dream with the little gray aliens looking down on him. Was that just a dream? Or was it a memory? It had all seemed eerily real, too real to be a normal dream. He shivered as he remembered the aliens peering down at him.

Ethan wasn't sure what to think. He did have a fever, or so Yuliana had said. Had that just been some sort of fever-induced dream? Or had he somehow unlocked a suppressed memory. Was there any way to know?

Nia ducked her head into the wigwam and looked over at him. "He is awake now. That is good. We should leave this area."

"The dragon?" he asked.

"No, we have not seen the dragon today." The foxgirl shook her head. "But there is something else. We have seen signs of it, marking its territory on the trees."

"What is it?" he asked. His body was aching, but he forced himself up.

"I do not know," Nia replied. "I do not recognize the markings and my tracking skill cannot identify the tracks."

He swore. If skills worked similar to the skills from MMORPGs, that probably meant whatever was marking its territory was much higher level than them.

"He should rest more," the elf protested.

"No." He smiled. "I can move. And she's right. If there's something out there she can't identify, we probably don't want to meet it."

Par'karr looked at the inside of the wigwam. "What about magic house?"

Ethan was about to reply when Ainslee thrust her large

head into the wigwam. "You're awake! Stop your yappin' and let's move it. This area is giving me the willies!"

Yuliana glared at Nia and Ainslee but Ethan nodded. He forced himself up and grabbed his backpack. "They're right. We've lost enough time because of me. Let's get out of here."

The group was packed up and on the road in only a few minutes. Ethan's entire body ached from the fever, but he forced himself to gather his stuff and walk down the hill to the road.

They never saw the creature who had marked up the trees. Whatever it was did not bother them once they made their way down to the road. They spotted the occasional tree with huge claws marks and missing branches, but those became less frequent as they continued their walk north.

While they never saw the creature, Ethan did have the feeling that something was up there in the forest - watching them. He could never actually catch a glimpse of it but the hair on the back of his neck stood up for almost half an hour. Judging by the nervous looks of the others, they felt it too.

Whatever it was, it was content to watch them go and not attack. That was a good thing. Judging by the size and height of the claw marks on the trees, the thing was large. Given Ethan's current condition, he was more than happy to live and let live.

7

Ethan's fever broke later that day, but he continued to feel weak and drained. Yuliana insisted they stop at every brook they passed and allow him to drink, as well as refill their waterskins. Ainslee would grumble each time, but he noticed the dwarf drank almost as much water as he did.

By the time they stopped for the night, Ethan was exhausted and could barely keep his eyes open. He did notice that he had some new messages in his HUD. Bringing it up, he saw a message saying that a point of his *Intellect* had been restored. Checking his stats, he saw that it was true. His *Intellect* was now up to 18.

`Intellect:  18`

He was still down five points but luckily, by the time they reached Castlehaven, he should be completely back to normal. Not that he was expecting trouble in the city, but if they did run into something there, he would feel better knowing he was at 100%.

Nia managed to kill a small wild boar for dinner. Ethan had been expecting something similar to pork, but it tasted and looked nothing like the pork he'd eaten on *Earth*. First, it wasn't a white meat, it was a dark-red meat. Second, instead of a pork taste, the meat had a nutty, yet rich taste.

Unsurprisingly, Ainslee ended up eating seconds. Once everyone else had eaten their fill, the dwarf had finished off the remainder of the boar before finally leaning back against her pack contentedly.

Despite his fever breaking, the group told him not to take watch. Everyone, even Ainslee, insisted that he sleep. Par'karr insisted that he take the first watch by himself and Ethan was too tired to argue. As soon as his head hit his pack, he fell asleep and didn't wake until the next morning.

THEY PASSED many farms and several small villages over the next few days. Like the first village the group encountered, these villages did not seem very friendly. Nia and Par'karr received the most hostile stares. They walked through each village without so much as a word to or from the villagers and kept traveling.

On the evening of the fourteenth day since they'd left Hawkshead, they reached the walls of Castlehaven. The town was set atop a large hill and was easily seen from miles away. But it wasn't what any of them had expected.

It was much smaller than he had thought it would be. Subconsciously, Ethan had been expecting some great city like the ones from the fantasy books and movies. Instead,

Castlehaven looked more like a large castle than a city. He guessed there couldn't be more than a few thousand people in the city. Much more than Hawkshead, but much fewer than the fantasy city he'd imagined.

"So that's it, huh?" Ainslee muttered, as if reading his mind. "I expected it to be... you know... bigger."

Ethan almost said "that's what she said" but stopped at the last second as he realized none of his companions would understand modern *Earth* humor. But he was glad he wasn't the only one who had been anticipating something more grand.

"It is bigger than any city we have," Nia said, her eyes soaking in the large walls. "And those walls make it formidable."

"We have no cities such as these on my world either," Yuliana added.

Par'karr looked around and shrugged. "Kobolds not build cities. We make villages. Move village when nothing left to eat."

"We do something similar." The foxgirl nodded. "The pack moves through the Great Forest, going where there is prey. When we return to a place, the prey has returned."

"At least we can find an inn and sleep in a bed tonight." The dwarf grinned.

"Not so fast," Ethan replied, earning a glare from Ainslee. Ignoring her, he continued. "I think we should wait until morning."

"Why in Odin's beard do we need to wait until morning?" the dwarf demanded. "We're here. We can be at the gates in an hour. We could sleep in real beds."

"And drink real mead?" he asked with a raised eyebrow.

The dwarf flushed slightly but just shrugged and gave

him a defiant look. "Well, if they have mead, I certainly wouldn't turn it down."

"Why do you wish to delay?" Nia asked, casting her eyes from Ethan to the city and then back.

"One, most medieval... I mean, most walled cities close their gates at night. So we may not even be able to get in," he replied. "Also, remember all the looks you and Par'karr got from the villagers? I'm wondering if we need to find out more about what potential reactions to you two we can expect."

"That's the dumbest..." Ainslee started but Nia cut her off with a hiss.

"Why do you say this? Do you expect trouble?" Nia asked.

"I don't know," he said. "But for all we know, there are more of your people and Castlehaven is at war with them. The last thing we need is to walk in and get arrested and thrown in the dungeon."

Ainslee frowned and looked from Nia to Par'karr. "You don't think they'd really arrest us because of these two, do you? They've done nothing."

"So far, the only races I've seen here are humans, dwarves and kobolds," he said, pointing to each of them. "And kobolds do not seem to be held in very high regard."

"Dat true." Par'karr nodded.

"Since we don't know what their reaction might be to a foxling, an elf or a kobold who tries to get into their city, I think we should wait until tomorrow and then Ainslee and I go down into the town and ask around," he offered. "If everything's fine, then we come back and get you. If not, then we'll need to figure something else out."

"We are good fighters, why must we cower," Nia demanded, her hand tightening on her staff.

"They've probably got militia," Ainslee replied, her gaze going to the walled city. "Right?"

Ethan nodded. "That's what I was thinking. A city with walls like that probably has a fairly large militia to defend those walls. Given the size of the town, there's probably at least a hundred guardsmen or soldiers. And they'll be armored and have decent weapons. They could even have knights and cavalry."

The foxgirl's lips were curled back in a snarl and he thought she would argue but then her face relaxed and she nodded. "I will trust your word."

"Yeah," the dwarf sighed. "One more night out here won't hurt, I guess. Better than a dungeon cell."

He looked at Par'karr and Yuliana. Par'karr nodded. He always seemed to agree with Ethan. The elf nodded too, but her expression was more grim.

"Are you okay?" he asked Yuliana.

"Do you truly think there are others of my kind on this world?" she asked. Her tone was sober but she looked at him with an expression of hope.

"I don't see why not," he replied honestly. "There are humans and dwarves, I don't see why they would bring unique... Ah, specimens here."

"Specimens?" Ainslee asked. Her brow furrowed and she frowned. "You make it sound like we're some sort of experiment."

"We could be. None of us really know why we're here," he said. "But it's clear from the humans and dwarves that were already here that we're certainly not the first people who have been abducted. They've been doing this for a long time considering we've seen families with kids."

Ainslee looked thoughtful. "That's a good point. When I

talked to the dwarves in the village, they all said they'd been born here. And Hamish is over two hundred years old."

Ethan nodded. "That's what I mean. They've been 'collecting' people for a long time. Nothing says they had to place them all in one place. There could be elves in another city, another country or even another continent."

The group lapsed into silence. After several minutes, Nia took off her pack and pulled out her bow. "I will go hunt. Find a spot to set up camp."

The rest of the group retreated back to a small copse of trees that offered a little shelter. There they found an area that appeared to be an old campfire.

"Others already camp here," Par'karr squeaked, pointing at the campfire remnants. The rest of them grunted their acknowledgements as they dropped their packs to the ground and slumped to the ground.

An hour later, the foxgirl returned empty handed. She growled as she walked into the camp. "There is nothing!"

"Nothing?!" Ainslee asked, her face horrified. "No dinner?!"

"There are too many farms in this area." She scowled. "They have scared the game away."

"All the game?!" the dwarf asked, voice pleading.

"Unless I wanted to kill the animals on the farms," Nia retorted. "After Ethan's earlier conversation, I did not feel that was wise."

Ethan nodded to the foxgirl. "Good call. The last thing we need is for someone reporting a foxling killing their livestock a day before we enter the city."

"So, no dinner?" Ainslee whined.

Nia shook her head. "There is nothing."

The dwarf looked panicked, her head swiveling from

Ethan to Nia. "No dinner at all? What about nuts? Are there any nuts left?"

Yuliana looked down, her face blushing. "I am sorry. I finished the last of the nuts."

"No food at all?" the dwarf screeched.

"Par'karr can find bugs," offered the kobold helpfully.

The dwarf seemed to consider the kobold's offer before frowning. "No, thanks."

"It looks like we go to bed hungry," he said, looking around at his companions. Other than Yuliana, who looked embarrassed, the others returned his stares with grim nods and began to settle down.

"Okay if me eats bugs?" the kobold asked quietly.

Ethan chuckled softly and glanced over at the pouting dwarf. "Yes, you can go eat some bugs. Just don't eat them in front of Ainslee, she might take them from you."

The kobold cast a furtive glance at the dwarf before nodding and slinking off to find his own dinner.

8

Unsurprisingly, they all woke hungry the next morning. As usual, Ainslee was the most vocal about it and insisted they head into the city right away. His own stomach grumbling, Ethan agreed. After reminding the others to stay hidden until they returned, Ethan and Ainslee began the trek to the gates of Castlehaven.

It was early but they still passed a variety of people on the road. They were a mix of humans and dwarves, with an occasional smaller race which Ethan recognized as similar to the dead halfling they'd discovered the first day they had arrived on this world. A quick check with his HUD confirmed that they were called halflings.

Most of them were farmers headed into the town with small carts full of food. Others appeared to be manual laborers carrying the tools of their trade. All were dressed in simple, and oftentimes extremely worn, clothes.

Of the carts they passed, some of the carts were hitched to a donkey, mule or horse. Others were hitched to some sort of six-legged lizard creature neither he nor Ainslee had ever seen. The creatures seemed docile enough and no one else paid them any heed.

Ethan didn't waste the opportunity to practice his Analyze skill and used it on every person and animal he passed. Doing so gained him another rank by the time they reached the gates but also revealed the name of the reptilian creatures.

Monitor Lizard (Domesticated)
Level 3

His HUD didn't reveal any additional information about the creatures, and he wondered if Nia or Yuliana would know anything about them.

"Look!" Ainslee pointed excitedly at one of the carts. "Bread!"

It was true. One of the carts was loaded down with bread of all shapes. The cart was hitched to a pitiful-looking donkey and a sandy-haired man with a tanned and worn face walked alongside the cart. A girl, maybe 12 or 13, sat atop the cart, keeping the bread from falling out as the cart hit bumps in the road.

He was about to tell the dwarf that they should wait until they were inside the city when a loud rumbling from his own stomach betrayed him. Ainslee gave him a knowing look and gestured again to the cart. "Come on! Let's get some!"

"Fine," he said and walked closer to the sandy-haired man. He brought up the man and his daughter in his HUD.

Jonas

```
Human
Farmer
Level 3
```

```
Uka
Human
Commoner
Level 1
```

"Jonas," he called the man by name as they walked closer and the man started. Jonas and the young girl eyed him suspiciously. Their gaze settled on the swords on Ainslee's hip. Both looked nervous.

"Do I know you strangers?" the man asked.

"You sell bread in the market, right?" Ethan asked. It was a guess but he wasn't sure how much other people knew about the HUD and the Analyze skill.

Skill increase: Bluff +1%.

"I do." Jonas nodded but continued to eye him suspiciously. The man continued to focus on the dwarf, who was salivating over the contents of the cart.

"How much for some loaves of bread?" he asked. "My companion and I ran out of food and we're a bit hungry."

The man opened his mouth to speak but the young girl beat him to it. "2 copper pennies each. Or 3 loaves for 5 coppers."

Jonas shot her a warning glance but nodded. Ainslee could barely contain herself. The dwarf bobbed her head up and down and started to head to the back of the cart. "We'll take some!"

Ethan shot an arm out and grabbed onto the dwarf. She shot him a glare, but he shook his head. "Give us one moment to check our coins."

He practically dragged the dwarf a few steps away before she shook him loose. "What?!"

"Let's make sure we have the money first!" he hissed as quietly as possible. "We don't even know what the coins are!"

"Sure, we do," she said, rolling her eyes. "The gold ones are crowns. The half silver-half gold are knights. The silver ones are marks. The coppers are pennies."

"Wait?! What?!" he asked. How did she know the currency?

The dwarf let out a frustrated breath and threw her hands up. "Didn't you appraise them?"

Ethan opened his mouth and then closed it. He hadn't used the Appraise skill on the coins. It hadn't even occurred to him.

She rolled her eyes and chuckled. "You were always having us appraise this, appraise that. Analyze this, analyze that. And you didn't even appraise the coins? Hah! We have copper pennies! Can we please get some bread?!"

Feeling somewhat sheepish, Ethan nodded, and they bought a dozen loaves from Jonas and Uka. Once they produced the coins, the man's mood towards them shifted quickly and when they walked away, he was smiling. No doubt it meant he'd spend less time at the market.

Keeping one loaf out for himself and two for Ainslee, they stuffed the other loaves into their packs to share with the others. Would Yuliana even eat bread? He was no cook, but he was pretty sure bread had eggs in it. Did that mean she wouldn't eat it? They'd need to bring back some vegetables, just in case.

They also found a cheese merchant and spent another 2 silver marks for a couple hunks of cheese from a halfling merchant named Heribert. The cheese was hard but tasted like a sharp cheddar. Together with the bread, it made a satisfying meal and he stashed away the remaining cheese to share with the others.

When they finally reached the city gates, Ethan realized just how tall the city walls were. They were impressive. The outer wall was at least twenty feet tall and made of gray stones stacked atop each other. He didn't get a good look, but he thought there might be some sort of mortar in between some of the stones.

There were almost a dozen guards at the large wooden gates. Each of the guards was armed with a spear and a long knife. They lounged around on either side of the large doors, looking bored. They lazily waved people inside, occasionally stopping one of the farmers to peek inside their cart. The guards didn't even give Ethan and Ainslee a second look as they entered.

Once inside the outer walls, Ethan could see that there was about 100 feet between the inner and outer and it was quickly filling up with merchants and farmers hawking their wares. It seemed like it acted as some sort of farmer's market. He made a mental note to stop by on the way out and grab some vegetables for Yuliana.

Most of the farmers were turning off to either side, taking their carts between the walls to set up shop. Only a handful of people continued towards the open gates of the inner walls. Ethan became aware of how alone and conspicuous they looked as they approached the dozen guards at the inner gates.

"Halt," said one of the guards, raising a hand. "Name and purpose."

The guard was young, maybe early twenties but his face was weathered. Like all the guards Ethan had seen, this one was garbed in a chain hauberk over which he wore a stained and faded white tunic with blue trim. On the tunic was an insignia of a white castle tower and black griffon on a shield of blue. It was the same insignia as the banners Ethan saw hanging from the walls - probably the city crest.

Coming to a halt, Ethan quickly scanned the guard in his HUD.

Corporal Rollie
    Human
    Fighter
    Level 3

"My name is Ethan," he replied. "I am the mayor of Hawkshead. I have come to re-establish trade with Castlehaven."

The corporal screwed his face up and turned to the other guards. "Hawkshead? Is that even a real place?"

The other guards, who looked younger than Rollie, shrugged and muttered but didn't seem to have any answer.

Finally, Rollie cut them off with a motion. "Fat bit of help you lot are." The corporal turned to Ethan. "Okay, mister mayor of Hawkshead, you may enter. But stay out of trouble, eh?"

"Yes, corporal," Ethan said and started to walk on when the guard thrust out a hand.

"1 silver mark." Rollie grinned. Ethan went to the purse of

coins on his belt and caught the guard eyeing the bag. Almost immediately he added, "Each."

Ethan guessed this was some sort of shake down, but there was nothing to be done about it. The guards may be corrupt, but they were still the guards. He handed over the coins.

"Can you tell me where the traders are?" Ethan asked the man as he dropped the coins into the corporal's outstretched hand.

"Traders," the man repeated as he made the coins disappear into his own pouch. "Yah. You go straight to the center square, then go right and their place is on the right about three blocks."

"Thanks," Ethan replied and started to walk through before stopping.

"Corporal," he started. "Is there a wizard school or mage's guild in the city?"

"Wizard school? Mage's guild?" the man chuckled mirthlessly. "That's funny. Maybe you mean the Order of the Scroll. That's them sages. Lots of books."

"Yes." Ethan nodded. He had been hoping for some sort of mage's guild, like they had in MMORPGs. He had questions about magic, and he needed some answers. Maybe the sages could give him some answers. "The Order of the Scroll is what I meant."

"Sure," Rollie snickered. "It's up past the main square. Can't miss it. Big place. Scroll on the outside."

"Thank you," Ethan replied and, motioning Ainslee to follow him, walked into the inner city.

"Welcome to Castlehaven," the corporal muttered behind him and the other guards broke into laughter. The guards muttered a few words but the only one Ethan could make out was "yokel."

"What do you think that was all about?" Ainslee asked, casting a glance over her shoulder.

"No idea," Ethan said as he surveyed the tightly packed, multistory buildings and the narrow, winding streets that bustled with people of all sorts. Unlike the walls, which were clean and looked almost regal, the inner city looked dirty and stank of too many people in too small of a space. "But let's do our business and get back to the others."

9

The two of them went north along the bustling street. Humans, dwarves and halflings came and went along the narrow street. And it wasn't just adults. Several women, of all races, and a few men, dragged small kids along with them and some kids ran around alone or in small groups.

Ethan saw Ainslee drinking it all in with her eyes and he wondered if her own cities were as packed as Castlehaven. To him, it was nothing new. He'd been to New York City and Philadelphia enough to be familiar with the bustle of city life.

He'd also spent enough time in the big city to be wary. Having spotted a few rough-looking men eyeing them, Ethan surreptitiously slipped his coin pouch inside his jerkin. If this was anything like a MMORPG or tabletop RPG, there were bound to be thieves and he guessed pickpocket was a skill in this world.

"More crowded than I was expecting," Ainslee muttered as they walked.

"Oh?" He looked down at her and raised an eyebrow. "Not like your dwarven cities?"

The dwarf shook her head, glancing around at all the people. "There's never this many people. Except maybe at festivals. How can people stand it here?"

"You get used to it," he replied. At least, some people got used to it. He knew friends who lived in big cities. They loved it and would never leave. Not Ethan. He was more of a mid to small-town guy. He liked visiting the big cities from time to time, but they just had too many crowds.

They walked on to the center square, which was a large open area filled with tents, booths and blankets spread out with various goods. The pungent aroma of human, and non-human, sweat combined with the smell of pastries, cooking meat, herbs and incense to create a cacophony that assaulted his nose.

"I thought the rest of the city stank," Ainslee complained, wrinkling her nose.

Navigating through the labyrinth of merchants, the two of them went right and continued three blocks to a large three-story building. It looked like nearly every other building. The first floor was stone, but the second and third floors were wooden and reminded Ethan of Tudor style. A faded wooden sign hanging from the building had a picture of a pouch with coins spilling out.

"I think this is the place," he told the dwarf and walked over to the wooden door. He knocked and then tried the door. It was unlocked so he pushed it open.

"Hey!" came a high-pitched woman's voice. "What's this now?"

The door opened into a large square room that was littered with crates, boxes, sacks, chests and bags. The odd assortment of things covered nearly every available bit of floor space. The only exception was a narrow passage that led back to a small wooden desk that was covered in books and parchments. Behind the desk was a female halfling.

The halfling was perhaps three feet tall, with pale skin, hazel eyes and dark hair pulled up into a bun. She was dressed in an expensive-looking, low-cut purple and blue dress with flared arms. The dress had a corset that pushed up the halfling's small breasts and made her already-thin waist look almost unnatural.

One thing he noticed immediately about the halfling that was in sharp contrast with every other female he'd met in this world, was that she wore makeup. He'd gotten used to seeing it every day with women on *Earth* but hadn't consciously thought about it until this point. But the little halfling definitely wore some sort of lipstick and eyeshadow.

He was close enough to examine her in his HUD and quickly used his *Analyze* skill.

```
Athalia Brownlock
   Halfling
   Trader
   Level 7
```

Ethan was surprised to see that she was so high level. He thought back but didn't remember encountering anyone or anything with as high a level. Obviously, she was a good, or at least experienced, trader.

Looking over the information, he found it curious that some of the people he Analyzed seem to have professions, rather than classes. He wasn't sure what that meant. Once again, he lamented not having any sort of handbook or even quickstart guide to help make sense of this world.

"Well? Are you going to answer, or should I call for the guard?" the little halfling said.

"I'm sorry, Athalia," Ethan said, remembering to use her name. It was something all of the customer service training had said - always use the person's name to make it more personable. "I'm Ethan, mayor of Hawkshead, and I've come to talk about reopening a trade route."

The halfling sat back in her chair and eyed him up and down before shifting her attention to Ainslee. Ethan noticed the halfling's gaze lingered on the short swords belted on the dwarf's waist before focusing on him again. "What's she? Your bodyguard?"

Ainslee snorted and opened her mouth to say something but Ethan was faster. "She's my advisor and an expert blacksmith."

From the corner of his eye he saw the dwarf looked surprised but then she crossed her arms over her chest and nodded smugly.

"Advisor? Expert blacksmith, huh?" Athalia muttered and then focused her attention on Ethan. "And you're the mayor? What happened to that other fellow? What was his name? Q-bert? Sherbert?"

"Cuthbert," Ethan replied. "He... ah... passed away."

"I am sorry to hear that," the halfling said in an emotionless tone before switching to a more annoyed tone. "What's this about re-establishing trade?"

"There were some kobold attacks and the trade caravans stopped coming to Hawkshead," Ethan replied. "We've come to ask that you restart them."

"Kobold attacks?" the woman said and looked at books on her desk until she found a particular book. She opened it and started flipping through pages. "Kobold attack... kobold attack... ah... here it is..."

Athalia took a moment to read through the page on the book and then looked up at him. "Ah yes, two caravans were attacked on their way to Hawkshead. The trip detour was barely profitable as it was and with the kobold attacks, it is no longer a profitable venture. I'm sorry, that's the way it is."

"We've put an end to the kobolds," Ainslee told the woman.

"I'm afraid I have nothing but your word on that," the trader said, closing the book. She sat back in her chair and eyed them both again. "And your word is not enough for me to risk any more caravans. According to my ledger, I am in the red from undelivered goods, the loss of three mercenaries and two drivers."

"Our word's not good enough?" Ainslee growled and took a step towards the halfling.

Ethan put out a hand to stop the dwarf and she snapped her head up to him, an unreadable expression on her face. Looking down, he saw that he had inadvertently put his hand on her breast. He snatched his hand back, feeling his face grow hot. He sputtered an apology.

Ainslee rolled her eyes at him and snorted before turning her attention back to the gnome, who now looked at them with a bemused expression. "Why is our word not good enough?!"

The little halfling eyed the dwarf; she seemed to realize she may have gone too far. The trader leaned forward and put a smile on her face. "Please don't take it personally. It's just business. While I put together the caravans, each one is underwritten by investors. Those investors aren't about to sponsor a detour to Hawkshead without some sort of proof."

The dwarf opened her mouth, but Ethan beat her to it. "What sort of proof?"

Athalia rubbed her chin for a long moment before answering. "The only thing I can think of that would satisfy them would be a signed writ from one of the guilds. Most likely the mercenary guild."

"How do we get that?" Ainslee demanded.

"Hire them to investigate the area and report back," she told them. "You'd have to check with them, but probably 500-1000 gold should cover it."

"500-1000 gold?!" Ethan and Ainslee gasped at the same time, mouths hanging open.

"What do you expect?" The halfling smirked. "A company of mercenaries, plus a sergeant - or whatever they call them - for a month or more. Right?" She looked back down at the open pages of the book. "Hawkshead is a fourteen-day march. So that's a month of just traveling."

Ethan opened his mouth to object but Athalia waved off any further comments. "Listen, I'm the trader. I don't make the rules. I'm just telling you what you need to do."

"But..." he tried to speak but once again the little halfling cut him off.

"You'll have to sort out the details with the mercenary guild. If you can get a writ, I can look into resuming trade. If you don't, it's not going to happen," she said with a tone of finality.

Ethan grimaced.

She looked pointedly at each of them. "Now, if you'll excuse me, I do have work that I must get back to."

The halfling gave them a dismissive look and then

promptly closed the book that contained the information about Hawkshead and grabbed another book from the pile and opened it up. Without looking up, she began to read the book.

Knowing they'd been dismissed, Ethan turned and left the trader's shop. Ainslee stomped after him, obviously annoyed. She looked like she was about to say something, but Ethan put a finger to his lips and nodded back to the door. "Let's walk down the road a bit."

The dwarf turned and cast a sour look at the trader's door before nodding. She followed Ethan a few doors down before grabbing him by the hand and spinning him around. "500-1000 gold?! That's robbery!"

"Shh!" he said, gesturing for her to lower her voice but the dwarf just huffed. "Not so loud."

Ainslee planted her hands on her hips and gave him a hard stare. "I know we don't have that much coin. How are we supposed to reopen trade? And if we don't reopen trade, how am I supposed to open up the smithy?"

Ethan leaned back against the nearby building. He wasn't sure of the exact value of their coins, but he knew it couldn't be more than 200-300 gold. He frowned. "I don't know."

"So, what do we do?" the dwarf demanded.

"We still need to find out what the deal is with..." Ethan looked around and lowered his voice. "...kobolds, elves and foxlings. I haven't seen a single one in the city."

Ainslee nodded, looking around. "I actually hadn't been looking but now that you mention it, you're right. I just see humans, dwarves and the halflings."

"Let's go check out that Order of the Scroll," he said,

looking back the way they had come. According to the corporal, it wasn't far from here. "Maybe they'll have some answers."

10

The corporal hadn't been lying when he'd said the Order of the Scroll was a large building. It took up an entire block. Unlike the majority of the other buildings, whose first floor was stone and the upper floors were wooded, the entire structure was worked stone.

"That's impressive," Ainslee said, staring at the building. "I can't even see how the stones are fit together."

Ethan knew. He'd done something similar with the flint arrowheads and spearheads. The building had been made, at least partially, by a Wizard. He looked around to make sure no one else was close enough to hear. "Magic."

"Oh, right," she muttered, keeping her own voice low. "I've seen you do it, but I keep forgetting that's a thing here."

"Yeah." He nodded. "You've mostly seen me do combat stuff. Imagine a few wizards working together to make this. They could probably do it in a few hours."

"Impressive," the dwarf murmured, running her hand along the smooth surface of the stone.

A shiny copper sign [C5]in the shape of a scroll and quill

hung from above a large ironbound door. Walking over to it, Ethan knocked. He waited for several minutes before knocking again.

"You think they're closed?" the dwarf asked, squinting at the door.

Looking around to see if anyone was watching, he reached for the door latch to see if it was unlocked. Before his hand touched it, the door swung open. In the doorway was an older man and Ethan Analyzed him on reflex.

Mertin Graystaff
   Human
   Channeler
   Level 3

Unconsciously, Ethan did a double take at the old man's class: Channeler. Other than his own class of Wizard and Par'karr's Summoner class, Ethan knew nothing about the other magic classes. Back on *Earth*, Warlock and Channeler had otherworldly demonic connections in almost all the games and literature. Was that the case here? Looking at the man, he thought it might.

The channeler was human. Or, at least that's what showed in his HUD. And yet, the older man's sagging skin had a deep crimson tint and his eyes were bright yellow. The man had receding gray hair that made the small black horns protruding from his forehead even more prominent. He was garbed in simple, yet well-made black robes and Ethan couldn't help but notice that a pointed red tail stuck out from underneath the robes.

Mertin's gaze shifted from Ethan to Ainslee and then back to Ethan. His eyes narrowed, obviously noticing that they were both gawking at his unusual appearance. "What do you want?"

Pulling his eyes from the man's horns and looking at Mertin in his yellow eyes, he forced a smile. This man was a magic user too, but Ethan was unwilling to reveal his actual class with a stranger. Especially someone who looked like a geriatric version of Satan. Instead, he tried a different approach. "I'm a sage from Hawkshead. I've heard you have an unparalleled library here and I was hoping that I might see it."

Skill increase: Bluff +1%.

The man's yellow eyes brightened, and he opened the door wider. "A fellow sage. Come in, come in. Hawkshead, you said?"

He and Ainslee stepped into a small antechamber that was decorated with glass cases containing old manuscripts and even some stone tablets with writing. Ethan looked back at the man as he shut the door. "Yes, Hawkshead. It's a couple weeks' journey from here."

"Hmm, Hawkshead," Mertin said as he slid the bolt of the door and turned to face him. "That was an old mining town a while back."

"It was." Ethan nodded. He remembered what Hamish and Fearghas had told him. "Until the silver ran dry."

"You're new to Hawkshead I take it." The man chuckled and motioned them to follow him through a set of double doors and into an enormous room that seemed to encompass all three floors of the rest of the building.

The room was open with the second and third floors being little more than balconies that allowed access to the walls. The walls themselves were bookshelves, packed with books of all shapes and sizes. In the center was a spiral ramp that granted access to the upper levels.

As he looked up and down the floors of books, he could see other people on the second and third floors, standing or sitting in front of bookshelves.

"Wow," Ainslee gasped. "I don't think I've ever seen this many books."

Mertin chuckled. "I should hope not. We have the largest library in Sunderland."

The channeler studied Ethan for a long moment. "What is your field of specialty?"

Since introducing himself as a sage, Ethan had been wracking his brain to answer that exact question. He knew the most about computers but that didn't translate into a pre-industrial age society. Obviously, roleplaying games wasn't an option either. Instead, he went with something that actually interested him in this world. "Extraplanetary species origins."

Skill increase: Bluff +1%.

"Interesting," the man said and eyed Ethan again. "An old school of thought. I can't say I've seen any new research in that field in...well... not in my lifetime. I'd be interested in reading your notes."

A moment of panic seized Ethan and he was afraid the man had seen through him. He tried to think of a quick excuse. Then he got a moment of inspiration. "That's actually one of the reasons I came here. My research was recently destroyed in a kobold raid against the village. I was hoping I could restart it by doing some research in your library."

Skill increase: Bluff +1%.

"Kobolds destroyed your research?!" The channeler looked mortified. "I'm terribly sorry. That must have been devastating."

Putting on a solemn look, Ethan nodded sadly. "It was."

Skill increase: Bluff +1%.

The man shook his head sadly and gave Ethan an apologetic look. "I'm afraid the books are for members of the Order only."

"Can I join the Order?" Ethan asked.

The man bit his lip and once again offered Ethan an apologetic look. "I'm sorry, membership is granted through the contribution of knowledge to the Order. Perhaps if you had your research on extraplanetary species origin, and it was a unique perspective, we could have admitted you. But..."

Mertin trailed off, his meaning clear. No research, no admittance. Ethan's heart sank. He'd been counting on being able to learn more about this world - and more about magic - through these books.

"Mertin," a voice said from behind a nearby bookshelf. The figure who emerged was a normal-looking human woman who might have been in her middle to late forties, with just a touch of gray in her auburn hair. She had piercing blue eyes and wore sky-blue robes, similar to Mertin's. Ethan *Analyzed* her.

Charmine Norton
>**Human**
>**Warlock**
>**Level 5**

"I couldn't help but overhear you talking to a possible new recruit," she said in a honeysweet voice. Immediately, Ethan's guard went up. He'd had some bad dates with honey-voiced women. They'd never ended well.

The woman looked over her shoulder and frowned, her voice lowered to a whisper and she furrowed her eyebrows. "I'm about to ask him, shut up."

Charmine turned back to him, all smiles and honey, the sudden change in her voice and expression almost comical.

"Yes, Charmine. He might have made a good recruit. But his research was destroyed." The channeler shrugged.

Once again, the woman looked over her shoulder and ground her teeth. "I know. I'm getting to it."

"Perhaps there's another way," she said sweetly as she turned back around to them.

Mertin shook his head. "You know the rules. You have to contribute to the collective knowledge of the order to become a member."

"Right," she said, her tone so sickly-sweet Ethan felt his skin crawl. "But the rules don't say it has to be his own research."

Scratching his chin, the channeler looked thoughtful. "That is true. But it does have to be something unique, or a unique perspective on the subject."

"What could be more unique than the Tomes of Ashmedai," she purred and then suddenly glared over her shoulder before turning back, once again all smiles.

The channeler went quiet for a long time, looking between the warlock and Ethan. He bit his lip before finally nodding. "If he were to bring those tomes, I don't see how we could deny him access. But..."

"But nothing," the woman interrupted, her voice still sickly sweet. "I can give him a map to their location, he can retrieve them and then we can induct him in the order."

The man glared at Charmine before nodding. "If he agrees..."

```
You have received a new quest
"Retrieve the Tomes of Ashmedai I"

To join the Order of the Scroll, you
must give the Order a unique
collection of knowledge. Retrieve the
Tomes of Ashmedai and deliver them to
Mertin Graystaff of the Order of the
Scroll in Castlehaven.
    Tomes delivered (0/3).
    Reward: 500 experience, +250
reputation with Order of the Scroll
    Accept quest (yes or no)?
```

"He'll agree," the warlock hissed. She looked over her shoulder. "Won't he? Oh yes, you already know he'll agree."

The woman's behavior was starting to freak Ethan out and he was tempted just to say "No" and get out of this place as soon as possible. He looked down at Ainslee and her face told him she was feeling the same.

And yet, he stayed. Ethan needed answers. This library contained thousands of books. If he was going to learn more about this world, he couldn't think of a better place. All he had to do was retrieve some tomes.

He frowned as his gamer instincts kicked in. He looked at Charmine and Mertin. "What's the catch?"

The woman opened her mouth to answer but the channeler cut her off. "The tomes were lost almost 20 years ago by another member of the Order named Justinian Notley, who borrowed them in search of the ancient library of Daemonium, in ruined city of Patheos. His last letter said he had found the entrance to the library and was going inside. When the messenger returned, there was no sign of him and no camp."

"So, the tomes are inside the library," the woman purred. "You just need to go get them and bring them back."

"Ahem." Mertin cleared his throat and gave the woman a hard look; he looked pointedly at her as he continued. "Except no one who's gone into the library has returned."

"He's different," she said and then snapped her head over to her shoulder. "I just said that. I told him he's different." She snapped her head back towards them, grinning.

Mertin turned to Ethan. "You need all of the facts before you go. At least four teams have gone in search of the tomes. They made it to Patheos but none of them ever returned from inside the library."

Ethan had a bad feeling about this, but he could at least go and check it out. It might be his only way to join the Order and get access to the library. Besides, if he got a bad feeling about it, he could turn around and leave.

"I'll do it," he told them and accepted the quest. "Give me a map there and I'll retrieve them."

Mertin nodded grimly but Charmine grinned manically

and turned over her shoulder. "Yes, yes. You were right. He did accept."

The woman produced a folded parchment from inside her robes and held it in her outstretched hand, a huge grin plastered on her face. As he took the note from her, she brushed her finger against his hand, and he shivered as a wave of wrongness rippled through him.

Snatching his hand back, he stared at the woman, who just stared back at him. For a moment, her eyes changed. Not the eyes themselves but something in her eyes. It wasn't like the woman was looking at him. There was something else looking out through her eyes. Something ancient and evil... and hungry.

Ethan and Ainslee walked quickly back to the entrance room. Neither wanted to spend any more time with the strange and unsettling warlock woman. Just thinking about her made him shiver. That malevolent force that seemed to linger around her was not something he wanted to think about.

Mertin followed them to the door but paused before opening it. He turned to the pair and seemed to be struggling with something internally. Finally, he sighed. "Please be careful. Charmine hasn't been 'right' for some time."

"I think that was obvious," the dwarf snickered. "Woman's a loon."

The channeler's face became somber and he shook his head. "No. Not a loon. She is a warlock. Do you know what that means?"

Ethan thought he did have an idea but like Ainslee, he shook his head. "No."

"Some people are born with magic," he said wistfully.

"They have the internal ability to manipulate the elements - and more. We call them wizards."

From the corner of his eye, Ethan saw the dwarf glance his way but Mertin was wrapped up in relaying his knowledge and didn't seem to notice. "If you are not born with the gift, then no matter how much you study or experiment, you can never do magic on your own."

Mertin paused and Ethan gestured for him to continue. "I hear a BUT coming..."

"You are perceptive." The channeler smiled grimly. "Those without innate magical talent cannot do magic on their own, but they can draw on extra-dimensional beings to give them power that rivals that of a true wizard."

"For a price," Ethan said without thinking. Mertin shot him an annoyed expression but then he shrugged.

"Clearly you've done some studying on magical theory." The channeler smiled. "And yes, you are correct. There is a price."

"What kind of price?" Ainslee asked, brows furrowed warily.

"It depends on the way the person goes about gaining the power," he answered. "But it involves a pact with extra-dimensional beings."

"Demons?!" Ainslee asked, alarmed. Ethan saw her take an involuntary step back from him.

"Demon is an oversimplification," he replied wryly. He rubbed his finger along his horns. "Although I can see why you might think that. No, they are creatures from other dimensions that are very similar, and in certain places, or in certain times, overlap our own dimension."

Ainslee put her hands on her hips. "That sounds like demons."

"Regardless of their name," he continued. "They are beings of great power and they can somehow send that power over the dimension barrier." He looked at Ethan. "For a price."

"What's the price?" Ainslee asked cautiously.

"Well," he said, spreading his hands, "that depends on the way the person gains the power. As you may know, there are summoners, channelers and warlocks."

Mertin stopped and looked at them, waiting for them to acknowledge him. Ethan nodded, once again gesturing for him to go on.

"Summoners are the weakest. They somehow form connections with lesser creatures from the other dimensions and they are able to draw them over to this dimension for short periods of time. The creatures don't actually influence the person. Their goal is for the summoner to get strong enough that he pulls them fully into our world permanently."

Ethan raised an eyebrow. "Why?

"We're not sure." The channeler looked thoughtful. "Though there are several good tomes on the subject."

"What about channelers?" Ethan asked, looking Mertin up and down.

"My appearance," the man said sheepishly. "Yes, well. Channelers gain their power by channeling magic directly from an intelligent creature in another dimension. They are not extremely powerful creatures but the more we channel their power, the more we take on their form and, some say, their mannerisms. It's also speculated that the creatures we channel can see through our eyes and hear what we hear."

"Then why do you do it?" Ainslee asked incredulously.

"The ability to do magic is... well... like nothing else," he replied with a small smile. "And now with the wizards disappearing..."

"So, they allow you to channel power like the wizards?" Ethan asked.

The man shook his head. "Sadly, no. A channeler can only channel the element their patron is attuned to."

"Attuned?" Ainslee questioned. "I thought demons were all fire and brimstone and stuff."

Mertin smiled indulgently. "A common misconception. Actually, each entity has an affinity for a specific element. Ability with that element is what they share with us."

"What's your element?" Ethan asked cautiously.

"Mine is water." The channeler smiled.

Ethan wanted to ask about wizards, but he was curious about the warlocks and how they got their power. He had a bad feeling, but he wanted to hear confirmation. "And warlocks?"

"Ah yes," Mertin nodded, "warlocks. Well, they are the most powerful because they manage to gain the attention of a powerful extra-planar being and make a deal with it. They gain incredible power, but they open a conduit between them and the being. The more they use the power, the more it can influence them."

"Like Charmine." Ainslee nodded.

"Yes," the channeler agreed sadly. "She has used a lot of magic and the being she draws it from gains more and more influence over her."

"Why would you do that?" Ainslee asked.

"Power," Mertin said. "You don't understand the power of the dimensional force."

Ethan almost snickered but managed to keep a straight face as Mertin continued. "And once you have a taste of it.

It is hard to say no." He gestured to himself. "Despite the cost."

"And what's HER element?" Ainslee asked.

"Charmine's element is fire," he replied. "And she is very powerful with it."

The warlock might be powerful with fire, but at what cost? Ethan had seen too many horror movies and read too many books to think that making a deal with a demon was a good idea. He still needed to know about his own class. "And what about wizards?"

"They were the foundation of our society," Mertin replied and gestured to the room. "Wizards founded the Order of the Scroll. But, as I'm sure you are aware, something is killing wizards."

"What's killing them?" Ethan asked.

"No one really knows," the channeler replied. 'A few people have witnessed the attacks, but they are never the same afterwards and never remember exactly what happened."

"But their brains get sucked out." Ainslee made a face.

"Indeed." The channeler nodded. "That is the only consistency in the attacks. Each of the wizards has had their entire brain removed."

They were quiet long enough that the silence became uncomfortable. Rubbing his hands on his robes, Mertin cleared his throat. "I'm sure you want to get started on your journey..."

"One more thing," Ethan interrupted. "What can you tell me about elves, foxlings and kobolds? Are there any in the city?"

"The war slaves?" he asked, one eyebrow raised.

"Slaves?" gasped Ainslee. "You can't be serious?"

The man shrugged. "I don't agree with it personally, but since the Prince changed the law, more and more soldiers and mercenaries are enslaving them rather than killing them outright."

"Killing them outright?" Ethan asked, horrified. "Why?"

"Please don't tell me you don't know Castlehaven is at war with Moonpoint," Mertin said, giving Ethan an appraising look.

"I've been so engulfed in my research," Ethan said, trying to pass himself off as the scatterbrained professor type. "I lose track of what's going on in the outside world."

Skill increase: Bluff +1%.

The channeler smiled and nodded. "Ah! A man after my own heart. Sometimes, when I'm in the middle of research, I go days without even eating!"

Ethan returned his smile and nod. "Lately, I've gone without eating myself."

"Where was I?" Mertin asked himself and then he raised a finger. "Oh yes, the war. Yes, Castlehaven and Moonpoint have been at war for the last three years. Well, on and off."

"Why are they fighting?" Ainslee asked.

"It's not completely clear." Mertin shrugged. "And none of our scholars have undertaken a study of the causes of the war. The prince said it was because they began raiding the northern villages."

Something struck a chord with Ethan. He remembered something else had started around two or three years ago. "Was that about the same time that wizards started dying?"

Mertin pursed his lips and rubbed his chin. "Technically, there were rumors of wizard deaths before that, but yes, now that you mention it, that is around the same time the killings became more widely known."

"You think Moonpoint killed the wizards?" Ainslee asked.

"It seems coincidental that the fighting started at the same time," Ethan replied.

The channeler shook his head. "From what little news we did receive from Moonpoint, their wizards were being slain too."

"Maybe each one assumed it was the other," Ethan offered. "Or one of them started it and the other retaliated and it escalated until it was full blown."

"Possibly," Mertin said but his expression told Ethan he wasn't convinced.

"And Moonpoint is foxlings, elves and kobolds?" Ainslee asked. "And Castlehaven is dwarves, humans and halflings?"

"That's an oversimplification but somewhat accurate," the channeler replied. "At least, it's more accurate now. Most of the elves and foxlings that were in Castlehaven left within a year of the war starting. Things became... difficult for them."

"Persecuted?" Ethan asked. He wasn't a big fan of history, but he remembered the Japanese-Americans who were rounded up in World War II. People had a way of turning on others when the going got rough.

Mertin nodded. "The foxlings and the elves. As for the kobolds, they've never really been welcome in the free cities. Mostly they were tolerated and killed if they started making trouble. It's only recently, since the prince's proclamation of slavery that you see them in the city - as slaves, of course."

"That's terrible," Ainslee said and Ethan agreed.

"As I said," the channeler nodded grimly, "I don't agree with it, but it is the law."

"How come we didn't see any slaves?" Ethan asked. He was going back over their journey into the city and then around the city. He hadn't seen anyone in shackles or who looked like a slave.

Mertin looked down and bit his lip. "Most of them have been bought by the temples."

"The temples?" Ainslee asked. "To free them?"

"No," Mertin said, his eyes still looking down. "As... uh... pleasure slaves, or other things?"

"Other things?" Ethan and Ainslee said at the same time.

"Freya's priestesses buy them to uh... work... in their temple," he replied with a blush. "The temple of Hel has been buying them up as well, but not as pleasure slaves. They go into the temple and aren't seen again."

From his role-playing experience, Ethan knew that Hel was the Norse goddess of the underworld. And she wasn't the only Norse god or goddess he'd heard people reference. "And I assume Hel's priests aren't freeing them?"

"Hel isn't exactly the type of goddess who encourages magnanimity." He bit his lip and made a warding gesture. He looked slightly embarrassed. "She's the patron goddess of warlocks, channelers and summoners." Mertin paused and gave an apologetic shrug. "I don't follow her myself, but others do. That's especially true, now that the wizards are gone. Only a few years ago, Hel worship was all in secret. But now that warlocks and channelers especially are in demand, she has a temple."

"Why does Hel need slaves?" Ainslee asked.

"I want you to know that I don't approve of..." he started.

"What are they doing with the slaves," Ethan demanded through clenched teeth. He thought he already knew but he wanted to hear the man say it.

"Sacrifices."

Ethan and Ainslee exchanged looks. Judging by her expression, Ainslee was thinking the same thing he was. They needed to get back to their friends and warn them before they were discovered and enslaved - or worse.

12
———

After thanking Mertin, Ethan and Ainslee quickly headed south, out of the city. On their way through the market square, one of the small vendor stands caught his eye. A thin, pointy-nosed man advertised slave collars. Putting a hand on the dwarf's shoulder, he motioned to the stand.

"I know," she spat. "Disgusting."

"But perhaps useful," Ethan replied, rubbing his chin.

The dwarf looked from the vendor to Ethan and wrinkled her forehead. Ethan ignored her and walked over to the man.

The merchant had tanned skin and a balding head of dark brown hair. His clothes were simple, but well made. He wore an off-white linen tunic over a pair of dark-gray linen pants. On his feet, he wore well-made leather boots with only the slightest bit of wear. When he saw Ethan approached, he grinned, revealing a missing canine on his upper left.

"Ah." The merchant smiled. "How can Shamar help you, good sir?"

"I need 3 slave collars," he replied, keeping his tone neutral to hide the disgust he felt at the man and his profiteering off of slavery. Plus, Ethan never trusted anyone who referred to themselves in third person.

"Ah." The man grinned. It wasn't a pleasant grin, but rather a predatory one. Like a wolf who had just stumbled onto a lost sheep. "A man who wishes to go get him some slaves! Maybe a tender little elf or a feisty foxling?"

"How much for the harnesses," Ethan growled, suppressing an urge to punch the man.

"2 crowns each," the man replied, his smile still in place. "Everyone will know they are your slaves."

"Ethan!" Ainslee hissed. She grabbed him by the arm and jerked him close. "What are you doing?!"

Fighting back the urge to wince at her vice-like grip, he forced a smile and leaned in close. "Trust me. We may need them if we're going to keep our friends from becoming slaves."

A look of confusion passed over her features before the light of understanding gleamed in her eyes and a small smile crept on her face. She released her grip on him. "Oh, right."

Skill increase: Diplomacy +1%.

Ethan had to force himself not to rub his arm where the dwarf's thick fingers had dug into him. Instead he pulled out his coin pouch and removed 6 gold coins. Looking up, he saw Shamar lick his lips as he stared at Ethan's coin pouch.

Replacing the coin pouch under his jerkin, Ethan glared at the man. "Here."

Shamar took the coins and made them vanish into his own coin purse. "Thank you, good sir. You will not regret your choice. This way, everyone will know the slaves are yours."

The merchant retrieved several leather bundles from the far end of his stand and then turned back to face Ethan. "What name should I put on the collars, good sir?"

"Name?" Ethan asked, confused.

"I will burn your name in the leather," he replied and held up one of the collars. The words "Property of" were already burned into the leather in small, clear letters. "This way, everyone will know they are yours."

"Fine," Ethan said. "Ethan."

"Very good, good sir," the man nodded and setting the collars down, he took several metal squares and put them over some goals. They waited in silence for a few minutes as the man laid out all three collars on a bench behind the stand.

Shamar then took out thick leather gloves and put them on. Taking a pair of metal tongs, he turned to an open iron pot containing coals. That was when Ethan saw the small red-hot squares of metal scattered across the coals.

Using the tongs, he lifted several of the squares until he found the one he wanted. Picking it up, he brought it over to the first collar. The merchant pressed it against the collar for a few seconds. When he removed the square, the letter "E" was burned into the leather. He quickly repeated the process with the other two collars.

He did the same with the other letters in Ethan's name. When the job was complete, each of the collars now had the words "Property of Ethan" burned into them. Grinning, Shamar handed the collars to him. "Shamar has done a good job, yes?"

"Thank you," Ethan said tersely. Without another word, Ethan spun on his heel and strode purposefully away.

Ainslee struggled for a second to catch up with him but she quickly pulled alongside him. "You're going to have the others wear those collars?"

"Hide in plain sight." He nodded. "If they look like slaves who belong to me, hopefully no one will bother them."

"Let's hope," Ainslee replied.

"Yeah," Ethan agreed. "Let's hope."

The two were about to leave the city but Ethan stopped at the space between the inner and outer walls. While it was not as packed as it had been earlier, there were still farmers selling all sorts of food. The sight of them had reminded Ethan he needed to buy some vegetables for Yuliana.

As he went from vendor to vendor, he bought some vegetables but also bought some more bread, cheese and some beef jerky. At least, he hoped it was beef jerky. They needed to retrieve those tomes if he wanted access to the library of the Order of the Scroll. The food he bought would at least give them a little variety - while it lasted.

Ainslee came running over, a huge grin plastered on her face. Under each arm was a crude clay pot that almost looked like a vase. Both were sealed with wax. She gestured to the clay pots, still grinning. "Mead!"

Ethan shook his head and chuckled. Trust the dwarf to find a farmer selling mead.

"Let's hurry up so I can crack these open." Ainslee licked her lips.

He quickly finished buying the additional food and drink they needed. Once he had everything, the two of them left the city and found their way back to their camp. When they arrived, the camp was empty.

Ethan felt his heart begin to race. Had his friends already been captured and enslaved? With his imagination running wild, Ethan was about to call out when his companions came out from behind a group of bushes.

"You have finally returned..." Nia started but then her nose went into the air and she began sniffing. As she did, she came closer and closer to him. She stared at him, her mouth practically salivating. "You brought food?!"

Smiling, Ethan slipped his backpack off his shoulders and opened it up, revealing the variety of food. He sat the pack down as Yuliana and Par'karr quickly joined her. The three of them searched through the backpack to find something they could eat.

Before they could dig in, a pop sounded behind him as the dwarf popped the wax seal on one of her clay jugs and brought it to her mouth. She took a long, hard swig and when she lowered the jug, she was smiling. "That hit the spot."

Yuliana went straight for the vegetables, not bothering with the bread or cheese. Nia took a hunk of cheese and a few strips of the beef jerky. Par'karr took a little bit of everything.

Luna sniffed at the jerky but didn't like the taste when Ethan offered the mountain lion a bite. Instead, the big cat seemed to like the cheese. She didn't bite it, but rather licked it from his hand. He gave her several pieces before the cat padded back over to Yuliana and lay down next to her.

Ainslee did pass around the mead and they all had several sips before it was gone. The dwarf polished off the second jug all by herself while the rest of the group ate. As they did, Ethan related the story of what had happened and showed them all the collars. None of them were happy.

"I do not wish to wear something that proclaims me as your property," the foxling growled, ears back and tail puffy. "I am not yours."

"Of course not," Ethan said, keeping his voice even. Once again, his customer service experience helped him out and he treated Nia like he had just given her the bill for his computer repair services. "I don't own any of you. I just want you to wear them so that no one else tries to take you as slaves."

"If anyone tries," she snarled, showing her canines. "I will kill them."

"I thought you couldn't kill?" he asked.

The foxling bit her lip. Her brow furrowed and her tail twitched as she fought some inner battle. Finally, she snarled. "I can render them unconscious. Very unconscious."

"But if you wore it, we might be able to avoid a fight completely," he suggested.

She gave him a sour, dismissive look.

"Me do it," Par'karr said happily. "Me trust Ethan. Ethan friend."

Skill increase: Diplomacy +1%.

"Thanks, buddy." Ethan smiled at the little kobold and kobold gave him a toothy grin. Ethan looked back at the foxling with a raised eyebrow.

Nia looked at the kobold, who was fastening the collar around his neck. Her eyes darted around like a cornered animal and finally settled on Yuliana.

The elf hadn't spoken since she picked up the collar. She simply stared down at it, lost in thought. As if sensing someone was watching her, the elf looked up. She gave them all a weak smile. "I do not like the idea of wearing something that proclaims me as someone else's property. But I will wear it if it means there will be less fighting." Yuliana looked him in the eye. "I too trust you."

Skill increase: Diplomacy +1%.

Nia's eyes went wide, and she took an involuntary step back, eyes darting around. The foxling stared down at the collar in her hand like she was holding a deadly viper. Her breath came rapidly, and Ethan was beginning to think she wouldn't do it.

Suddenly a loud belch broke the silence. They all turned to Ainslee tossing away the empty mead jug. The dwarf shrugged and put her hands on her hips. "Just put the gosh darn thing on."

"But..." Nia objected.

"But nothing," the dwarf huffed. "If he treats you any different or tries to sell you, just beat him senseless."

Ethan rolled his eyes. "Gee, thanks."

The dwarf shrugged and stared expectantly at the foxling.

Nia waged an internal battle with herself for long minutes. As she did, she glanced from Ethan to Ainslee and then over to Yuliana and Par'karr. Finally, her shoulders slumped, and her ears stood up.

"Fine," the foxling said dejectedly. "I will wear your collar. But I am not yours."

"I know," Ethan said. "It's just pretend, so we can avoid unnecessary questions and fights."

The foxling thrust the collar at him suddenly. She looked

at him through narrowed eyes. "I will not put this on myself. You must put it on me."

Ethan didn't really understand the difference but the foxgirl looked resolute. Taking the collar, he fastened it around her neck. When he was done, Nia lowered her head, spun and walked to the edge of their camp to sit down on a stump.

Skill increase: Diplomacy +1%.

Ethan didn't understand what the big deal was, it was just pretending. It was almost like roleplaying or wearing a costume. It didn't mean anything. He tried to think of something else to say to the foxling to make her feel better but nothing profound came to mind.

Instead, he began packing up the rest of the food in his backpack. "Let's get ready to move out. I want to be as far away from Castlehaven as possible."

13

They took the long way around the walled city to avoid as many people as possible. Despite the fact that they hadn't run into trouble on the way to Castlehaven, Ethan didn't want to take any chances.

As they walked, Ethan studied the map the strange warlock had given him. He had more than a few misgivings about both the warlock and the quest. The woman had given him the creeps. And now that he knew she was communicating with some sort of demon, it made him even more wary.

At the same time, he had no choice if he wanted access to their library. And he desperately wanted access to the library. Knowledge was power. Right now, he had very little knowledge. He needed to know about this world, about magic... about everything.

Ethan needed those books. He needed to study everything he could about this world and about the magic he now controlled. And he needed to learn everything he could about whatever was killing wizards.

The Order of the Scroll had the only library he was aware of. If he didn't get access to it, then he would be at a severe disadvantage. Given that it was literally life or death, he needed to find out as much as he could before whoever or whatever was killing wizards found him.

They slowly worked their way to the edge of a vast forest that stretched out before them. It took hours of cutting through thickets, fields and pastures but they reached the edge of the forest in late afternoon.

"Do we camp here or press on?" he asked the group.

Ainslee glanced around. Behind them, it was open pasture. She shook her head. "I don't like this. We'd be really exposed."

"She is right," Nia said. It was the most the foxling had said since she had put on the collar.

Ethan looked at Par'karr and Yuliana. They both shrugged.

"Fine," he said and pointed to a road a few miles to the north. "Let's get to the road and see how far we make it before the sun goes down."

Without a word, Nia turned and began walking north. The rest of them watched her go. The foxling had been moody since donning the collar and Ethan knew he'd need to talk with her. He just had to figure out what to say.

Nia had been quiet all day and Ethan was worried about her. He had tried starting up some small talk but the foxling answered with short, abrupt responses. He quickly got the hint and stopped trying. But given her dark mood, he knew he'd need to talk with her soon.

Something about the collar was really striking a nerve with the foxling. He'd only come up with the idea to help protect them. The last thing he wanted was for one or all of them to be enslaved, or worse, sacrificed. Maybe once they were in the forest, it would be safe for her to remove it.

The group followed Nia to the road and then followed it east, away from Castlehaven. According to the map, the eastern road led inland, back towards the mountains. He had no idea what the scale was, but it looked like at least a week's journey to a mountain range and then they'd head south.

The road was not straight, nor was the terrain level. Instead, the forest wound through the tree-covered hills, making it a difficult trek. Despite all the walking he'd done lately, Ethan quickly became winded trying to keep up with the foxling.

After a few hours, the forest grew dark. Ethan could still glimpse the sky through holes in the tree canopy, but it was simply too thick to let much light in. That meant there would be almost no starlight or moonlight. The nights were going to be pitch black.

"Let's start looking for a campsite," he said and gestured up at the trees. "It's going to get really dark tonight."

They walked for another half hour before Nia pointed out a small clearing that looked like it was used as a regular campsite. It was near the river that ran alongside the road, so there was convenient water. There was even a fire pit dug, though the ashes were old - mostly washed away by rain.

They all stopped and began to drop their packs when both Nia and Yuliana froze. The foxling began sniffing the air with her ears back. Yuliana tilted and moved her head around, obviously hearing something he couldn't.

The mountain lion tensed as well. Ethan wasn't sure if Luna was sensing something or if it was reacting to Yuliana's nervousness but either way, he became instantly on guard.

"Something is coming," Nia hissed, dropping her pack and bringing out her staff. Using the staff, the foxling pointed into the forest to the right. "It smells fouler than anything I have smelt on this world!"

"Two somethings," the elf said. Beside her, Luna tensed even more, the cat's ears back and her tail snapping back and forth.

The rest of them quickly got out their weapons. There was barely enough light to see by and Ethan contemplated summoning some globes of light. He was about to do it when two huge forms burst from the trees.

The creatures were tall and bipedal. Ethan couldn't be sure exactly how tall they were because they walked hunched over, like apes. Similar to an ape, the things had long arms and shorter legs. Unlike an ape, the creatures were almost completely hairless except for a mop of thick, coarse hair at the top of its head.

Like their bodies, the creatures' faces were thin, almost emaciated. They had large, black eyes, bulbous noses and mouths full of sharp-looking teeth. Their skin was a dark green, except for some sort of brown or black tiger-striped pattern on their back sides.

They both had patches of stringy dark hair around their pubic region but one of them had what appeared to be large, droopy breasts. A female?

His nose wrinkled as he got a whiff of them. They smelled like a combination of a sewer and the worst body odor he could imagine. He scanned them without even giving it a conscious thought.

Wild Forest Troll
    Troll

Barbarian
Level 5

Ethan's heart skipped a beat when he read the type of monster. He'd played many MMORPGs and other role-playing games. In nearly all of them, trolls had an unnatural healing ability. They regenerated from nearly any sort of damage. Would these?

He didn't have any time to think about it. The creatures hesitated for only a moment, their enormous noses sniffing. They looked at the group and the one on the right, the one he thought was the male, grinned.

"Meat!" it bellowed and charged Nia.

The other troll, the female, charged towards a wide-eyed Par'karr. The kobold screamed and tried to backpedal but the troll stopped short as two large, demonic rabbits leapt at the thing's throat, digging their overly large fangs into its neck. The little kobold had summoned his rabbits and they were defending their master.

The troll grimaced but reached with its huge hands and pulled the rabbits off its neck. It looked down at the squirming creatures in its massive grip. It brought one up to its nose, sniffed it and then took a bite of it. Instantly, the rabbit turned to smoke in its hands and dissolved away.

The troll seemed to try and chew for a moment before it realized it had nothing in its mouth any longer. Then it looked down at its now-empty hand. It opened and closed the hand several times, seeming unsure where the big rabbit had gone. Then it shrugged and brought the other rabbit up to its mouth.

Before it could bite the second rabbit, it was knocked over by a charging Ainslee. The dwarf slammed into the creature's short legs, sweeping the troll off its feet. It fell towards Par'karr who leaped out of the way.

Ethan jumped forward and brought his staff down on the troll's head.

You crush Wild Forest Troll for 5 damage.

If the creature noticed the blow, it didn't show it. Instead, it quickly scrambled to its feet and lashed out at both Ethan and Ainslee with its claws. It missed the dwarf as she hopped back but Ethan wasn't as quick.

He suppressed a scream as long, sharp claws ripped through his armor and into his skin and muscle.

```
Wild  Forest  Troll  slashes  you  with
claws for 9 damage.
    Leather  armor  absorbs  3  points  of
slashing damage.
```

Clutching his chest and feeling the warm blood flow through his fingers, Ethan stumbled back. As he did, he saw the green glow of Yuliana's healing magic from the corner of his eye. She was healing Nia. He heard the growls of Luna but couldn't spare the time to look.

The troll seemed to sense that he was injured, or maybe it simply smelled his blood. Either way, it turned towards him and took a step forward. Almost instinctively, he used *Elemental Armor*, covering himself from head to foot in writhing blue flames.

```
Skill increase: Fire magic +1%.
```

The troll stopped immediately and in the azure illumination from the flames, he recognized the look of fear on its face. Unfortunately, he also noticed that the wounds the rabbits had made were completely gone. Ethan cursed. These things could regenerate, just like in the games.

He thought back to the games. Trolls could regenerate from most wounds, but not wounds from fire or acid. Would that be the case here too? The look of fear on the troll's face gave him hope that it was.

Still clutching his chest, he took a step forward. The troll took a step back. Then it was promptly hamstrung by Ainslee's short swords.

The troll howled and once again, fell to the ground. In the blue light of his *Elemental Armor*, Ethan would actually see the creature's flesh and the muscle beneath knitting back together. It was both disgusting and fascinating to watch.

A scream from Nia caused him to look just in time to see the troll's claws rake across the foxling's arm. Unable to hold her staff in her injured hand, the weapon fell to the ground. The troll's other claw came across at head level, but Ethan reached out a hand and blocked it with a bubble of air.

Skill increase: Air magic +1%.

The troll looked down at its hand, confusion etched on its features. It didn't seem to understand what it had run into. Its hesitation gave Nia the time she needed to dance away. Yuliana rushed in and healed her.

Luna leaped on the troll's back, raking her claws across the creature but the troll bellowed and began shaking back and forth until the mountain lion was thrown off. Movement turned his attention back to the troll closest to him as it pushed itself back to its feet. The damage Ainslee had done to its legs was completely healed.

"What's going on with these things?!" bellowed Ainslee. "I just cut the monster's legs and it's back up like nothing happened!"

"They regenerate!" he yelled, loud enough for everyone to hear. "They'll just heal any damage we do with normal weapons."

"How do we fight them?" hissed Nia as she dodged out of her troll's range, barely avoiding its long claws.

Ethan thought quickly. The troll seemed to be afraid of fire, but he didn't know if fire would actually prevent it from regenerating.

Fixing an image of what he wanted to do in his mind, he channeled *Mana* through the crystal and a line of fire shot from his outstretched hand and struck the troll in the chest.

You burn Wild Forest Troll for 17 fire damage.

The troll howled, slapping at its chest with its hand. Ethan saw the opportunity and called out to Ainslee. "Hamstring it again!"

Obediently, the dwarf darted in and slashed her shortswords across the back of the troll's legs. Tendons and muscles sliced, the troll fell forward into the ground.

He wasn't sure if the fire worked yet, but he could see that the normally deadly Nia was doing everything she could just to avoid the troll's long arms. She needed help. And Ethan knew exactly what to do.

Using Summon Minor Elemental, he summoned the fiery weasel and pointed at the troll attacking Nia. "Kill!"

The weasel turned and hopped towards its prey. The

thing launched itself into the air and attacked the troll's neck.

Minor elemental (fire) critically burns Wild Forest Troll for 11 fire damage.

Skill increase: *Fire* **magic +1%.**

Nia's troll howled in pain and tried grabbing the elemental, only to burn its hands. Nia shot him a look of thanks and darted in to retrieve her staff. As the troll struggled with the fire weasel, the foxling began raining blows down on the thing's knees and feet.

Turning back, Ethan saw his troll struggling to its feet. The legs were healed but there was still a large charred circle in the center of its chest. The damage from the fire wasn't healing.

"*Fire!*" he yelled. "Use fire!"

"How in Odin's name are we supposed to do that, wizard-boy?!" Ainslee snarled. "You're the one with the magic."

The troll looked at Ethan with fear and hatred and then started to turn. He guessed it was planning on running away but they couldn't afford to have the things get away and then harry them for days. They needed to finish both trolls off now.

"Yuliana!" he yelled. "Use the roots! Bind its legs! Don't let yours get away!"

Summoning air, he wrapped the female troll's short legs together at the ankles. The thing topped over like a felled tree and hit the ground with a thud. As soon as it did, Ethan bound its arms together but had to keep expending *Mana* to keep the air bonds.

Skill increase: Air magic +1%.
Skill increase: Air magic +1%.

Feeling the *Mana* drain, he didn't think he could use a bolt of flame while maintaining the air bonds. Not without running out of *Mana*. Instead, he got another idea. He couldn't exactly create a flaming sword like so many games used to dispatch trolls, but maybe Ethan could do something similar.

Splitting his focus, he willed heat into one of Ainslee'a short swords. He couldn't quite muster the concentration to do both, so he picked the one in her right hand and chan-neled heat into it.

Skill increase: *Fire* magic +1%.

"My sword's getting hot!" the dwarf said, looking over at him. "What are you doing, wizard-boy?"

Straining, Ethan could barely spare the focus to answer. "Making your sword hot enough that you can do some damage."

Skill increase: *Fire* magic +1%.

The dwarf pulled down her sleeve and used it to hold the hilt of the sword as the blade began to glow red and then orange. While this was happening, Ethan was aware of messages from his fiery weasel as it continued to damage the troll.

```
Minor    elemental    (fire)    critically
burns  Wild  Forest  Troll  for  9  fire
damage.
```

```
Skill increase: Fire magic +1%.
```

```
Minor    elemental    (fire)    critically
burns  Wild  Forest  Troll  for  7  fire
damage.
```

```
Skill increase: Fire magic +1%.
```

```
Minor    elemental    (fire)    critically
burns  Wild  Forest  Troll  for  13  fire
damage.
```

```
Skill increase: Fire magic +1%.
```

"Try now!" he said between clenched teeth. The sword was glowing bright orange and he didn't know how much more he could push into it. He brought up his HUD and checked his *Mana*.

```
Mana: 10
```

Ethan swore. He was down below a quarter and he was having to continually expend mana to keep the troll down as it struggled against the air. Even as he watched, his *Mana* dropped a point.

```
Mana: 9
```

Skill increase: Air magic +1%.

"Kill her!" he yelled to Ainslee. "Kill her!"

Ainslee took her glowing sword and began hacking at the creature's neck. The thing howled and screeched but after a few chops, the thing stopped moving and Ethan released his air bonds.

Wild Forest Troll dies.

Skill increase: Air magic +1%.

You gain 35 experience. Experience to next level 1180.

He took the moment's respite to look at his *Mana* level.

Mana: **4**

He released the fire mana he was feeding into the sword. "I can't keep the sword heated. Use it on the other one before it cools too much!"

Ainslee nodded grimly. They turned to see the other troll on its back with thick roots wrapped around its wrists and ankles. It howled as the fire elemental continued to burn it over and over.

The dwarf ran over to it and stabbed the sword down into the creature's head. The troll shuddered and then lay still.

Wild Forest Troll dies.

Skill increase: *Fire* **magic +1%.**

You gain 35 experience. Experience to next level 1145.

"Nothing like a little exercise before bedtime to help you sleep," he muttered, letting all of his magic dissipate.

14

———————

It turned out that dead trolls stank worse than the live ones. Even after dragging the bodies away, the campsite reeked of dead trolls and they were forced to abandon it. Before they left, Yuliana was able to heal them all but both Ethan and Nia's jerkins were shredded. When they returned to Castlehaven, Ethan would need to look into new armor for all of them.

The group was forced to march another hour in the dark before they found a suitable campsite. By the time they got there and set up, there was no time to practice sparring and he was too tired to work on his magic.

The sudden appearance of the trolls and the ferocity of the ensuing fight had Ethan both exhausted and wired at the same time. He started at every twig breaking and every strange animal sound. He wanted nothing more than to sleep but forced himself to stay awake until his watch was over. Even when he finally fell asleep, his dreams were plagued by monsters.

The next morning, Ethan woke to the smell of roasting

meat. He sat up and looked around. Nia, Par'karr and Ainslee were sitting around the fire. On the fire was some sort of animal on a spit. It had already been skinned and Ethan didn't recognize the shape.

Looking around, he saw that Yuliana was still sleeping too. Luna sat protectively next to her. The big cat stared at the cooking meat, her nose continually sniffing the air.

He yawned and Par'karr looked over at him and grinned. "Ethan awake. Good. Almost time to eat!"

"Why didn't someone wake me?" he asked, wiping the sleep out of his eyes.

"You and Yuliana used a lot of magic yesterday," the dwarf replied. "Nia thought it would be better to let you two sleep as long as you could."

Ethan looked at the foxling. "Thanks!"

"If it were not for you two," she replied. "We would all have died. I have never faced a creature like that. Weapons did not harm it."

"Oh, they harmed it," Ainslee chuckled. "It just didn't stay harmed. The cursed things healed up almost as fast as you could hurt them."

"*Fire* hurt them." Par'karr grinned. "Good thing Ethan have strong magic!"

"I'd drink to that," the dwarf said sourly, "if I had any more mead."

"We all did our part," Ethan replied and stood up. He was sore and his chest felt tight where the troll had slashed him. The healing magic hadn't completely restored him, and he had three scars across his chest where the troll had clawed him.

"You do not need to be modest." Nia gave him a hard

look. "If it was not for your magic, those trolls would have been feasting on our corpses. You are a strong alpha."

Unsure what to say, he shrugged and sat down by the fire. As he did, he heard the movement from the elf's bedroll and turned to see her push herself up. "I'm sorry. I have overslept."

"It's okay." He smiled. "They let us sleep in."

"Oh." The elf started to return his smile but broke into a yawn. She quickly covered her mouth. "Sorry."

"It's okay." He grinned. "You still have some vegetables?"

The elf stretched and nodded. "Yes, I have the care roots and the potatoes of sweetness."

"Carrots," he chuckled. "And sweet potatoes."

"Car-rots," she repeated. "Yes, I have the carrots and sweet potatoes."

Nia announced that the food was ready and the rest of them cut slices of the mystery meat while Yuliana crunched down on a carrot.

As they ate, Ainslee showed him the sword he had heated up the previous night. It was warped and the edge was gone. "Won't be good for much until it's reforged."

He made a face. "Sorry."

"Better a ruined sword than ending up in the belly of one of those trolls." She shrugged. "Are they from your world? Is that how you knew about the fire?"

"There are no trolls on *Earth*," he replied with a shake of his head. "But there are stories and legends of them."

"Well, they definitely aren't from my world," the dwarf replied. "I've never even heard stories of things like that!"

"I have never seen creatures such as them either," Nia said bitterly, rubbing her hand across the scarred wound on her arm.

The group lapsed into silence as they retreated to their thoughts and finished their meal. After eating and packing, they continued their journey eastward. Nia took the lead, keeping an eye - and nose - out for any more trolls.

They continued following the winding road as it cut through the forest. The road crisscrossed with a river, sometimes on the right and other times on the left as they went over small bridges and sometimes just stones in the river where it was shallow.

Was that how the trolls had found them? Had the creatures just been coming to get water from the river and stumbled upon them? If the river was the only source of water around the area, it made sense that it would be popular with the local wildlife.

Luckily, they saw no more monsters, though the group did run across a variety of wildlife. There were deer, bears, wolves and even some of the strange reptilian turkeys. They all fled as soon as they saw or heard the group.

Around lunch time, Nia shot a deer and they cooked the venison over a fire and ate their fill. As before, he enjoyed the venison and wished he could take some with him. It seemed such a waste to leave so much meat.

Ethan thought about how people from medieval times preserved food. He knew from his research of medieval culture for his role-playing games that they either dried the meat, salted it or both. They definitely didn't have refrigerators, let alone freezers to keep it from going bad.

He was making a mental note to buy some salt when they made it back to Castlehaven when he remembered one of the first bits of magic he'd done on this world. It was shortly after he first awakened and realized he was on an alien world or inside an alien video game.

A group of kobolds had attacked them, and one jumped on top of him. Without really understanding what he was doing, Ethan had frozen the kobold to death using water magic. Could he do the same thing with cooked meat? Could he freeze it and preserve it?

It used water magic, which was the only one of the four elements he hadn't had the chance to rank up yet. Now, he just might get that chance. Excitedly, he sliced a large piece of meat from the spit and held the hot piece of meat between his hands. He burned slightly but he felt the heat inside the meat and tried to draw it out.

Skill increase: *Water* **Magic +1%.**

It worked. Steam rose from his hands and he could feel the meat getting cooler and cooler. Ethan continued to focus on drawing it out until the piece of meat was cold and hard between his hands.

Skill increase: *Water* **Magic +1%.**

"What're you doin'?" the dwarf asked, her brow furrowed as she looked at the meat in his hands.

Skill increase: *Water* **Magic +1%.**

Ethan grinned and tossed the frozen venison steak to Ainslee. She caught it and whistled. "Loki's balls, that's cold!"

"You have frozen it solid," Nia observed. "You can...eat it that way?"

"No." Ethan shook his head and grinned. "But with it frozen, it won't go bad. We can keep the meat for days."

Par'karr walked over to the meat and touched it with his finger. "Very cold! You sure it not go bad?"

"On my world, we have a thing called refrigeration," he explained. "We cool meat and vegetables and they last longer."

"But it will melt in a few hours," Nia said. "Will it not go bad then?"

"Longer, I think." He thought back to the Fourth of July when he'd meant to cook himself a steak but had forgotten to take it out of the freezer the night before. He removed it from the freezer that morning and by dinner, it was still frozen. He'd ended up nuking it in the microwave to thaw it and then cooking it. "It can stay frozen for at least 12 hours, probably longer."

Par'karr and the women exchanged looks. Almost as one, they shrugged. It was obvious they didn't really understand or believe him. He'd have to prove it. "Fine, cut me a few steaks and I will freeze them and bring them with us."

Nia gave him a skeptical look. "If we eat bad meat, we will get sick."

"Don't worry," he said. "I'll be the guinea pig."

His companions looked at him, confusion written all over their faces. He sighed. "It's an expression on my world that means, I'll test it out."

Nia shrugged and walked over to the deer carcass and began slicing more steaks from it. When she was done, the foxling walked over and held out six pieces of bloody meat. "Here."

Ignoring her skeptical expression, he grabbed the rough sack [C8]the baker had given him when he'd purchased the bread. He laid the sack out on the log. One by one, he took the steaks from Nia, froze them and set them on the sack.

When he was done, he wrapped the sack around and froze them.

He placed the sack of frozen meat in his backpack and then shouldered it. Within minutes, the cold of the frozen meat seemed to permeate the cloth of the backpack against his skin. He shivered. "Cold!"

Nia rolled her eyes. "I will not clean up after you if you eat bad meat and get sick."

"And don't expect me to either, wizard-boy!" the dwarf said between mouthfuls of food.

"Fine," he grumbled and shivered again. "Let's get going!"

"I'm not done yet!" Ainslee protested.

Ethan ignored the dwarf and took his backpack off. He adjusted the location of the frozen meat. He placed his bedroll between his back and the meat. He then shouldered his backpack again and after several minutes, he nodded. "That's better!"

The dwarf stuffed as much of the meat into her mouth as she could, then took the spit with the remainder of the meat. She put the spit over her shoulder like a caveman carrying a club. Ainslee stopped when she saw everyone staring at her. "What?! I'm hungry and there's no reason for it to go to waste!"

After they shared a chuckle, the group resumed their marching order and continued west down the road.

15

Around late afternoon, Yuliana stopped the group and signaled them all to crouch down and be quiet. The elf tilted her head left and right for almost a full minute of tilting before pointing down the road. "People are coming. I hear them talking. They have carts and animals."

Nia sniffed the air while Ethan and the others looked down the road, but it disappeared to the left a hundred yards away. Ethan thought about what she had just said. People, animals and carts. A patrol? A caravan?

"Can you tell how many?" Ethan asked. The people on this world, with a few exceptions, hadn't been particularly welcoming or friendly. Now a group of people with unknown intentions were headed straight for them. Some caution was in order.

The elf signaled for quiet again for several seconds. "Maybe four or five men talking, but there may be more who are silent. From the sounds, I think maybe a dozen animals."

"Let's get off the road," he told them.

"Why?" Ainslee asked. "You think they're trouble?"

"I'd prefer to avoid any trouble," he replied. "We can go into the woods and observe them. If it looks safe, we can always approach them."

"Oh, because a group of people coming out of the woods doesn't look suspicious," the dwarf snickered.

"Good point," he conceded. "We can come out after they pass and call out to them."

The dwarf rolled her eyes.

Nia's ears went back as she fingered her collar. "Perhaps it is wise to avoid notice for now."

"Fine! Fine!" the dwarf retorted, throwing her hands in the air.

No one else argued so Nia led them off to the right side of the road. She had spotted a thicket of bushes fifty yards into the forest which made a good hiding spot. The shadows of the forest would make spotting them from the road difficult, but their own view of the road was unobstructed.

They all settled behind the bushes. Once they were quiet, Ethan could hear the creaking of wagons. A few minutes later, the first of the wagons rolled into sight. And it was a wagon, not a cart. Thus far, he had only seen two-wheeled carts on this world, but this was definitely a longer, four-wheel wagon.

The cart was drawn by a team of four horses that looked like the horses from *Earth*. No, not horses. Zebras. Only instead of white with black stripes, they were green with brown stripes.

Pulling his eyes away from the strange zebras, Ethan could make out two men sitting on the front of the wagon. He couldn't see any details of the men, but he did notice something about the wagon. It wasn't an open wagon. It was some sort of cage.

Were there animals in the cages? Ethan remembered all of the farmers and craftsmen setting up shop between the walls of the Castlehaven. Is that what these men were doing? Bringing livestock into the city to sell?

Three more wagons rounded the bend, each nearly identical to the first. But as they got closer, Ethan realized that his first assessment had been wrong. Very wrong. The men driving the wagons weren't farmers.

Ethan saw that all of the men wore black tunics and an orange dog, and a fiery eye embroidered on them. Under the tunics looked like some sort of armor, maybe leather armor. He could also see that the men wore longswords strapped to their waist. These weren't farmers, they were warriors.

The real shock came as the first wagon passed them and he could see inside the cage. It wasn't livestock in the cage. They were humans. No. As he strained his eyes, he could see the slighter features and long tapered ears. They were elves!

He felt a hand squeeze his arm and looked over to see Yuliana staring wide-eyed at the elves inside the cages. She looked at him, her face a combination of rage and hope. Her jaw was set and her gaze intense as she whispered to him. "These are elves. My people. We have to free them!"

Looking to the faces of his companions, he saw they all wore hard expressions. They had heard Yuliana and one by one they nodded. He knew none of them liked the idea of slavery and it looked like they were in agreement that they needed to do something. They all looked at him expectantly.

He nodded his understanding and looked back at the road. The second wagon was passing, and Ethan realized he needed to think quickly. There were four wagons with two guards per wagon. It was five versus eight. Although, he could summon his elemental, which would bring it to six versus eight.

Multiple scenarios began to flash through his mind as he considered the odds and the tools at their disposal. Unfortunately, the guards were an unknown. He had no idea what level they were and what their fighting capabilities were. For all he knew, they could be level 50 with vorpal swords of smiting wizards.

Ethan remembered his encounter with the kobold medicine man. He'd used air to choke out the kobold wizard from afar. Could the same thing work in this situation? Maybe they could free the slaves without even a fight. It was worth a try.

"We'll let them pass," he whispered to the others. "And then attack from behind."

His companions stared at him expectantly and he realized they were waiting for the rest of his plan. He sighed quietly. "I'm going to use magic on them."

Par'karr grinned and nodded enthusiastically. The women gave him mixed looks but one by one, they nodded too. All except Yuliana, who looked worriedly at him. "You will not hurt the captives, will you?"

He shook his head and gave her a lop-sided grin. "Don't worry. No fireballs."

Patiently, they waited until the final wagon had passed them, then snuck from the forest to come behind the row of carts. The carts moved slowly, so it was easy for Ethan to move into range. Luckily, the wagon had no rearview mirror and the guards were too bored to look behind.

Closing in on the back of the wagon, he came within range of Analyze and checked out both guards.

```
Derryck
    Human
    Swordsman
    Level 7


Oleg
    Human
    Swordsman
    Level 6
```

As he scanned them in his HUD, several of the elves in the cage stirred. The elves twisted their heads to look at him. Their eyes were haunted and devoid of hope. He could see that each of them had a collar, similar to the one his companions wore.

He put a finger to his lips to signal them not to make any sound that might alert the guards. The elves would see him use magic, but he hoped that saving them would buy their silence. Channeling his air magic, he grabbed both men by their throats and squeezed.

```
You crush Derryck for 7 air damage.
Derryck is choking.
```

SKILL INCREASE: Air magic +1%.

```
You crush Oleg for 9 air damage.
    Oleg is choking.
```

SKILL INCREASE: Air magic +1%.

Channeling air at two different targets was more difficult that he had anticipated but still easier than levitating himself. The two guards clutched at their throats, desperately trying to ease the pressure.

You crush Derryck for 8 air damage.
Derryck is choking.

SKILL INCREASE: **Air magic +1%.**

YOU CRUSH **Oleg for 7 air damage.**
Oleg is choking.

SKILL INCREASE: **Air magic +1%.**

The men began to thrash around, and Ethan was afraid it would get the attention of the guards on the wagon in front of them. He looked to Nia and Ainslee but kept his voice low. "See if you can knock them out or hold them down until they pass out."

You crush Derryck for 9 air damage.
Derryck is choking.

Skill increase: Air magic +1%.

You crush Oleg for 9 air damage.
Oleg is choking.

Skill increase: Air magic +1%.

His two companions nodded and rushed forward. Ainslee ran up, hopped onto the wagon and pulled Derryck completely off the wagon. The guard hit the ground hard and then the dwarf jumped down on top of him. Nia, on the other hand, leaped onto the wagon and, with a few blows to the front and back of his head, caused Oleg to go completely limp.

Ethan released his air magic and quickly ran forward to see if the guards in front of them had noticed. Thankfully, they seemed blissfully unaware. Ethan checked his stats.

Mana: 32

It had taken more *Mana* than he thought. He might run out before he got to the last set of guards. So be it. He'd use *Stamina* if he had to. It was still better than fighting these guards outright.

Ethan moved quickly up to the back of the next wagon and performed the same maneuver.

```
You crush Jurgen for 9 air damage.
   Jurgen is choking.

Skill increase: Air magic +1%.

You crush Darcel for 6 air damage.
   Darcel is choking.

Skill increase: Air magic +1%.
```

This time, Nia and Ainslee didn't have to be told. They both rushed up to the front of the wagon and grabbed the men, pummeling them until they stopped moving. Once their bodies went limp, Ethan released his magic and checked his stats.

Mana: 20

He frowned as he realized he'd have to use *Stamina* for the last two guards. He checked his current *Stamina*.

Stamina: 19

Ethan's frown deepened. Between sleeping in the wild and hiking all day, his *Stamina* was less than a third of his maximum. Hopefully, he'd have enough to do what he needed to.

Moving up to the next wagon, Ethan did the same trick. Once again, both men clutched at their throats. Only this time, as the man on the left moved around, he could see that it was actually a woman.

You crush Karson for 7 air damage.
  Karson is choking.

Skill increase: Air magic +1%.

You crush Pruet Tattersall for 9 air damage.
  Pruet Tattersall is choking.

Skill increase: Air magic +1%.

Ethan began to feel guilty that he was choking a woman

but then the woman grabbed the bars and turned herself around. She caught sight of Ethan, with arms outstretched, and Nia and Ainslee racing towards the front of the wagon. The woman dropped her hand down to an amulet around her neck and Ethan got a really bad feeling. And then the world went black.

You are blinded.

Everything was dark. He blinked his eyes, but the darkness persisted. Unable to see, he couldn't direct his magic and without a target his spell dissipated. Panicking, he cursed. The woman had cast some sort of spell on him, he was sure of it. He cursed again as he turned in every direction, unable to see anything.

"Attack!" he heard a hoarse voice call out. "Attack!"

He heard grunts of pain somewhere. It sounded like Ainslee and Nia. They were in trouble. They were in trouble and he was useless. His pulse raised as he moved in circles, feeling at the air with his hands.

"Ethan okay?" a familiar high-pitched voice said from his left. Ethan started and turned towards Par'karr's voice.

"No," he said. "I'm blind. I can't see anything."

"Blind?" the kobold echoed.

"The woman," he said. "She's a spellcaster of some sort. I'm pretty sure she cast something at me. Summon your rabbits and have them attack her."

"Okay," the kobold responded.

"I'm blind!" he heard Ainslee's voice call out. "I can't see!"

Ethan cursed again. Things were falling apart very quickly. Whatever magic that woman possessed, she could apparently cast some sort of blindness spell - and cast it more than once. All the woman would need to do was blind them all and then the swordsmen could just cut them down.

He needed to think of something fast. Ethan couldn't see, which meant he couldn't direct his magic. But there was something he could do. He hoped.

He'd seen through the eyes of his elemental once before, when he'd scouted the kobold cave. Ethan wasn't sure if it would work this time, but he didn't know what else to try. He used some of his remaining *Mana* to summon his fiery weasel elemental. Next, he focused on seeing through the elemental's eyes.

It worked. He could see the thing looking at him, waiting for orders. Mentally, he had it turn around and scan the area.

The woman was stalking towards Nia with a steel-tipped mace in her hand. The foxgirl was not focusing on her but was sniffing the air. She stepped away from the woman, seemingly able to smell where the woman was.

Commanding the elemental to swing its head around, he saw that Ainslee was swinging wildly in the air all around herself as one of the guards tried to circle around her. He could hear the dwarf cursing and promising to cut off various parts of the man's anatomy, but she was as blind as Ethan.

Looking beyond, he could see the remaining two guards hurrying towards them from the first wagon. They were being hounded by Par'karr's demon rabbits, but the guards were keeping them at bay with their swords.

Rabbits or no rabbits, once they reached Nia or Ainslee, the women wouldn't stand a chance. They'd slaughter them. He cursed and tried to think of a way to slow them down.

"Yuliana, can you still see?" he asked loudly.

"Yes," she said. Her voice came from behind him.

"Root the guards from the first wagon," he ordered. "Don't let them reach us."

"But..." she started.

"Just do it!" he said more forcefully but then reined in his voice. "Trust me."

Trusting her to do as asked, Ethan had the elemental look around. As it swung its head around, Ethan saw the woman closing in with Nia but the foxgirl lashed out with her staff, nearly catching the woman in the head. Surprised, the woman hopped back, looking for an opening.

"I forgot you foxlings are little more than beasts," the woman snarled and tried to sidestep around Nia. The foxgirl, continuing to sniff, circled with her.

He heard a grunt of pain and commanded the elemental to turn back to Ainslee. The dwarf was slashing with one sword now, her left arm hanging limply at her side and covered in blood. The guard who was stalking her was moving in behind her to finish her off.

Ethan knew he needed to act quickly and was going to block the blow with air until a better idea occurred to him. He reached out with his magic and was happy to find that he could target through the elemental's vision. He focused on the blade of the sword and then willed it to bend. Just like his dagger, it resisted but he poured more *Mana* into it and the sword groaned.

The guard, who must have sensed something, looked down at his sword. Unable to take the strain, it ripped itself apart violently just like his dagger had.

You critically pierce Karson for 25 damage.

The guard fell back, a bloody mess. The remaining

shards of his weapon fell from his ruined hand as he staggered backwards, screaming in pain.

Through the elemental's eyes he saw the woman snap her head towards the man and then turn her attention to Ethan. She raised up her left hand with the amulet in it, obviously preparing to cast some other spell.

Ethan beat her to it. Pulling from his *Stamina*, he used air and ripped the amulet from her grasp. The chain that held the amulet around her neck gave only the briefest resistance before it snapped. The amulet went flying towards Ethan and stopped in front of the elemental.

The thing was metal, gold and silver, in the shape of a fiery eye. With a thought, he sent it flying back at the woman. Right before it reached her, he pulled at it with his *Earth* magic. The amulet exploded in the woman's face.

You pierce Pruet Tattersall for 11 damage.

The woman screamed as shards of metal pierced her face and neck. Whatever magic she'd been focusing through the amulet dissipated as it was destroyed and, like someone had turned on a light switch, Ethan could suddenly see again.

Blinking, he saw Nia close the distance with Pruet. The foxgirl brought the staff low, sweeping the woman's legs out from underneath her, and then brought the other side of the staff around and smacked the woman on the head. She went down and didn't move.

Karson dies.
   You gain 35 experience. Experience to next level 1110.

Ainslee had run the guard through with her short sword before staggering back. Yuliana rushed past Ethan and healed the dwarf, who looked like she could barely stand.

Further back, the remaining two guards were hacking at the demon rabbits and the roots that bound their feet. They screamed curses as they did, promising to kill Ethan and his friends slowly. Ethan looked down at the fiery weasel. "Kill."

The final two guards didn't last long.

16

After they finished off the guards, they quickly bound the unconscious ones. Ethan's intention was to question them once they regained consciousness. Unfortunately, once they released the slaves, the elves went into a frenzy.

The enraged elves grabbed rocks and sticks and proceeded to beat the helpless guards to death. And it wasn't just the men. The women attacked with just as much ferocity as the men - more even.

His group were so shocked at the display, by the time they moved to intervene, new messages in his HUD told him the people were dead.

Derryck dies.
You gain 35 experience. Experience to next level 1075.

Oleg dies.

```
    You gain 30 experience. Experience
to next level 1045.

    Jurgen dies.
       You gain 30 experience. Experience
to next level 1015.

    Darcel dies.
       You gain 30 experience. Experience
to next level 985.

    Pruet Tattersall dies.
       You gain 40 experience. Experience
to next level 945.
```

They might have continued beating the corpses but Ethan managed to squeeze in between them. He'd regained just enough *Mana* to activate his *Elemental Armor* and burst into blue flames.

The elves jumped back. They were obviously still angry but they knew enough not to attack a man engulfed in flames. Most of them had seen some of what he could do and since they didn't know he was almost completely out of *Mana*, they backed off.

"Enough!" he said loudly and glanced back at the bodies. Vacant eyes stared back at him and he wondered if he should feel sorry for them. Considering they were hauling slaves to a temple where they would be sacrificed, he couldn't muster any sympathy. "They're dead."

The crowd of elves muttered, casting wary glances at Ethan. One of the elves, a woman who looked only slightly older than Yuliana, stepped forward. "We owe you a debt of gratitude but I for one would like to know what you plan to do with us? And what are you? A warlock? Channeler? What dark demons do you answer to?"

Without thinking, Ethan instantly scanned the woman.

```
Manai Treefeather
    Elf
    Herbalist
    Level 4
```

"I'm a wizard," he replied, causing another chorus of mutterings in the crowd. Ethan didn't know if it was safe to tell so many people his little secret but he was just too tired to care at this point. He let the flames die. "And all we wanted to do was free you from the slavers."

"Slavers? Ha!" a male elf laughed mirthlessly.

"They are no slavers," Manai spat. "The priestess and her men, they are from the temple of Hel!"

Ethan let out a whistle. A priestess of Hel. Just great! Now he and the others were guilty of killing priests of Hel, a religion which apparently had no problems with sacrificing people to their dark goddess. Just freaking great.

He looked down at the tunics. Now that he was closer, he could see that the symbols were that of a fiery eye over a flaming dog. He remembered Pruet's amulet. It had been in the shape of an eye. At least now he knew what to look for, and what to avoid.

There was no way an attack like this would go uninvestigated and unavenged. He knew nothing about Hel or her temple, but he doubted they were the forgiving type. Not only had he killed their men and their priestess, he'd denied them nearly fifty sacrifices.

The herbalist seemed to read his mind. "Why would you help us and put your own lives at such risk?"

Ethan hadn't really thought that far ahead. He'd seen the slavers and, with some prompting from Yuliana, had done what needed to be done. Now, he was second guessing himself as he realized the implications of what he had gotten himself into.

"We did what needed to be done," he said plainly, looking at Yuliana.

"And now, like us, you will be hunted," the elf replied grimly. "They will not cease looking until they have found us and taken us to their temple."

Frowning, Ethan looked around at the faces of the elves. Their expressions were both defiant and accepting. They would fight, but they expected to lose. He wondered just how powerful the temple of Hel had become. And to what lengths they would go to avenge their dead and recover their sacrifices.

The scar on Ethan's chest itched and he absently scratched it. Then he froze and looked down at his chest. The trolls had given him that scar and they would have been more than a match for his entire group if they hadn't had fire. What if...

Grinning, he turned to his companions. "We need to hack these bodies into pieces and make sure blood gets all over these wagons!"

His companions didn't move a muscle. They looked at him like he had gone mad. He sighed. "We need to make this look like a troll attack!"

Nia tilted her head but then a smile spread across her features. "Yes, that might work."

The other elves all looked at each other and at him, obviously confused. Ethan waved them to the north side of the road. "You all will need to make for Moonpoint. That's to the north."

Murmurs broke out among them, but Ethan raised his voice. "We're going to make this look like a troll attack. If we're lucky, they'll assume the trolls ate most of you. If they do, they won't pursue you."

Manai gave him a hard stare but nodded; she called out to her people and began speaking to them in hushed tones. They seemed to be considering his suggestion. At least, he hoped they were.

While she did, Ethan called his group over to him. When they gathered around him, he laid out his plan. "We need to make this look like a troll attack. First, we need to cut the horses or zebras, or whatever they're called, loose. Next, we need to break open all of these cages and turn a few of them over. Hopefully the elves will help with that before they go."

He looked for confirmation that they understood him before continuing. "Once we do that, we need to wipe the footprints from this area and then leave just the ones we want. We need to make it look like...hmm... four trolls attacked this caravan. I think that would be enough to over-whelm them."

Nia raised an eyebrow. "But there will be no troll prints. That will make the story hard to believe."

"Ah," Ethan said, raising a finger. "But there will be! And claw marks!"

Nia and the others looked at him in confusion. "I need three or four large rocks and, Nia, do you remember what the troll prints look like?"

"I remember what they smell like." Ainslee smirked.

Nia nodded. "I do."

"Can you draw them on the ground?" he asked hopefully.

"Yes," she replied, eyes narrowed. "But drawn tracks will convince no one."

Ethan grinned again. "That's where the rocks come in!"

After explaining the rest of his plan, the others went to work. The elves helped push over two of the wagons and then used rocks to smash the wooden bars. It took a while to do it with rocks, but the holes looked rough enough to have been done by trolls.

In two of the wagons were chests full of supplies and a small coffer of coins. Ethan insisted that the elves take both with them and none of his companions objected. Manai accepted the supplies and the money graciously and had some of the elves carry it into the woods.

While the elves helped out, Yuliana took the opportunity to talk with them. Ethan had given her a list of things to ask them and the elf had questions of her own. Of course, now that she had found other elves, Ethan wondered if Yuliana would go with them when they left.

If she did, he realized he'd be sad to see her go. Over the last few weeks, Ethan had grown close to all of his companions. They'd literally saved each other's necks multiple times. To him, it had created a bond. But now that bond might be broken.

Putting those thoughts out of his mind, he had the rest of his companions gather some branches with leaves. He remembered seeing this in a movie and hoped it really worked. Rubbing the branches against the ground, erasing the existing tracks.

At least, that's what they started to do before Par'karr came up with the idea of tying small branches to the tails of his demon rabbits. Once they had, the kobold gave them a toothy grin and directed the rabbits around the area, erasing the existing tracks.

Once the area was cleaned of tracks, he asked Nia to draw the troll tracks. Taking two of the larger rocks, Ethan placed them next to Nia's sketches of the tracks. Then, using his *Earth* magic, he shaped them to fit the tracks. When he was finished, he had two troll-foot-size slabs of rock.

"Do we just drop them around the area?" Nia asked, looking at the large stones.

"Not quite." He grinned and motioned to Ainslee. "You're the strongest. Step on the rocks, one foot on each."

Eyeing him warily, Ainslee stepped onto the rock troll feet. Ethan smiled. "You're about to become Bigfoot."

Once again using his magic, he caused the rock to encase the dwarf's feet until she wore a pair of troll-shaped rock boots.

"What did you do, wizard-boy?!" she said. "I can barely move!"

"Hey." He shrugged. "You're the strongest. All you have to do is just walk around the entire area."

"You're going to owe me some mead for this, wizard-boy," she snorted and then began to slowly plod around the area.

Finally, came the gruesome task of hacking up the bodies. Ethan had them remove clothes from some of the bodies while leaving them on others. He also left some larger pieces, to plant even more evidence.

Using another rock, Ethan shaped it into a clawed hand, using the marks on his chest as a guide. He then raked it across the larger parts to leave large claw marks across them. They weren't perfect, but he hoped that by the time anyone found the bodies, they'd have deteriorated enough that no one would suspect they were fake.

It was dark when they finished and Ethan admired their handiwork by torchlight. "Not bad."

"You are a sick human," Ainslee said, but nodded. "But I have to admit, it looks like anything but a human attack."

"It is not perfect," the foxgirl said, scanning the area. "But to an untrained eye, it may suffice."

"I'm counting on the elements, other animals and nature to obscure the rest," Ethan countered. "Anything out of place will hopefully be chalked up to scavengers and the heat."

Nia shrugged. "It may work."

Sighing, Ethan turned as Yuliana and *Mana*i approached. The herbalist stared hard at the scene around them and then turned to him. "Do you think this will work? That the temple will not come after us?"

"I hope not," he replied. "If nothing else, it will buy you time while they figure out exactly what happened. I suggest you make your way north to Moonpoint as fast as possible. Avoid any towns or farms and if you do have to cross any populated areas, go at night and in small groups - don't let anyone see you in a large group."

The herbalist looked confused. "Small groups?"

Nia spoke before he did. "If they are looking for a large group, you must look like a small group. You must be what they are not looking for."

"That makes sense," *Mana*i agreed.

"Will you leave now?" he asked.

"The longer we stay, the more risk we are in," she said. "Few people travel at night, but it is not completely unheard of. We will head north by the moonlight."

"Are you leaving with them?" Ethan asked, turning to Yuliana.

His companion started and then looked from him to

*Mana*i and then to the group of elves further into the forest. Her expression was unreadable but she shook her head. "I will stay with you."

Ethan smiled and let out a breath he hadn't realized he was holding. He felt a great sense of relief, though he wasn't sure exactly why. "Glad to hear it."

"We will bid you farewell," the herbalist said. "There is no way we can ever repay you for what you have done, but if you are ever in Moonpoint, you will always be welcome in our homes."

*Mana*i raised a hand to Yuliana, palm facing her. Yuliana mirrored her gesture, her own palm an inch from the herbalist. They then moved their palms together in a circular motion, completing a circle before dropping their hands to the side.

"Farewell, young one." *Mana*i smiled.

"Farewell," Yuliana said and then watched as the other elf turned and walked back to the waiting band of elves. When she got there, they all turned and performed the same gesture at Ethan's group.

Not sure what to do, Ethan emulated their gesture, bringing his hand up, palm towards them and moving in a circle. The elves seemed to approve. They smiled and then turned and disappeared into the night.

His group was silent for a long time and then Ainslee interrupted the silence. "Anyone else hungry?! I'm starving!"

17

They were all hungry and tired, but Ethan insisted they put as much distance as possible between them and their staged "troll" attack. They had yet to see anyone traveling by night, but he wasn't willing to take the chance.

In the end, they left behind all of the equipment save for the coins that the individual guards and priestess were carrying and two other things. The first was a half dozen vials of green liquid, which once he identified, Ethan knew they had to take along.

```
Potion of Stamina Restoration
    Type: Potion
    Range: Special
    Damage: N/A
    Durability: 1 of 1
    Special: Drinking the entire vial
restores 10 points of Stamina
immediately.
```

These potions were as good as gold in Ethan's book, especially when travelling. Since they had yet to be able to restore more than half their *Stamina* while sleeping on the road, these would be invaluable if they ran into a protracted fight.

He needed to find out how these potions were made and learn how to make them himself. If MMORPGs had taught him anything, it was the importance of consumable items like potions to give you the right boost when you needed it.

The second item he took was something they'd almost missed. It was a Chymera stone and it had been inside the amulet he had shattered.

```
Chymera Crystal
   Type: Crystal
   Range: N/A
   Damage: N/A
   Durability: 2 of 2
   Special: Allows a wizard to channel
or   store   Mana   to   create   magical
effects or magical items.
```

His acquisition of a second crystal excited him. He'd earned the Enchantment ability when he'd leveled up wizard but hadn't been able to explore that ability since he only had one Chymera crystal and wasn't going to risk damaging it. Having a second crystal opened up a world of possibilities.

As for the other items, like the armor and weapons, Ethan had been adamant about not taking anything that could be traced back to the priestess or the temple guards. He'd argued with Ainslee for nearly a half hour about the swords until she finally relented. The last thing they needed was to be seen with something that was recognizable as belonging to the temple. It would only cause unwanted attention.

After an hour of walking in the dark, Nia spotted a campsite and they quickly made camp. Since it was so late, the foxgirl didn't have time to hunt. Instead, Ethan used his magic to defrost the meat he'd frozen earlier and everyone except Yuliana enjoyed some venison.

Ethan had wanted to ask Yuliana about her conversations with the elves, but he didn't get the chance. As soon as the elf finished up her dinner of carrots, she lay down in her bedroll and fell fast asleep. His questions would have to wait.

THE NEXT MORNING they continued east along the road. As they walked, Ethan dropped back to walk next to Yuliana. She smiled at him and he returned it. The elf gave him a knowing look. "You want to know about the elves."

He nodded. "Did you learn anything from them?"

"A few things," she said and her voice held a tone of sadness. "The elves of this world have been here for generations. Thousands of years. None of them were brought here like we were."

"None of them?!" Ethan asked incredulously. When he had learned that elves lived for centuries, he felt sure some of them would have stories of abductions like theirs. Now she was saying they'd been born here and the elves had been here for thousands of years. He wasn't sure what to think.

Ethan had been sure some of the elves would have been brought here in the last few hundred years. He had been counting on talking to other abductees and comparing stories, maybe even find out if they knew something about why they were brought here. Now he was no closer to unraveling the mystery of his abduction than before.

"They do not serve groves here," she murmured. "None of them. They live like humans, in villages."

Ethan saw a tear run down her cheek and on impulse he reached out a finger and caught it on his finger. She looked up at him and he gave the elf a reassuring smile. "Don't worry. We'll keep looking. Someone on this world must know what's going on and maybe even a way home. Or how to contact the beings that brought us here. Maybe we'll find other elves who care for groves."

She nodded and turned back to the road, but the look in her eyes told Ethan she didn't believe it.

He wished he'd had time to talk to them himself. If they had truly been in this place for thousands of years, they could have had all sorts of knowledge. But making the attack on the slavers look like a troll attack had been the priority. The last thing they needed was the temple of Hel after them. They had enough problems without looking over their shoulders.

Resuming his place in their marching order, Ethan brought up his character sheet and looked at his current stats.

Strength: 10
Agility: 13
Hardiness: 15
Intellect: 23
Intuition: 15
Charisma: 12

```
Health: 30
  Mana: 56
Stamina: 29
```

His *Health* and *Mana* were back up to full but, as usual, his *Stamina* hadn't regenerated past 50%, and already he was down a point. Now, he knew there was a way to restore more *Stamina* by using potions. But there were so few of them. Ethan needed to figure out how to make the potions himself.

Bringing up his skills, the only two that seemed remotely related to potions were Herbalism and Healing. Was there a potion-making or alchemy skill? If so, he needed to learn it and rank it up as high as possible! He'd never been a crafter in any of the MMORPGs he'd played, but it looked like that would all be changing.

The thought of crafting suddenly reminded him of his gaming buddies, Wyatt, Hunter and Gage - especially Gage. Gage had always been the group's crafter. He'd enjoyed that part of the game almost as much as the combat and questing.

Ethan wondered how his friends were doing and realized he genuinely missed his buddies. Things in this new world had been so hectic since his arrival, he'd barely given his old life any thought. But now that he thought of them, he missed them and wished he could share his adventures with them. They would have thought it was a blast.

He remembered Hunter had just broken up with his girl-friend right before his abduction. Ethan had meant to call him and check on him the next day. That hadn't happened. Now it would probably never happen.

What must they think happened to him? Did anyone even know something had happened to him? Ethan assumed work would have tried to reach him. Had any of his friends checked up on him? Had they sent the police to check up on him? Was he now a missing person back on *Earth*?

"Ethan," Nia snapped, waking him out of his thoughts.

"Yes, sorry," he said as he turned to the foxgirl.

"The farms." Nia rolled her eyes and pointed to the left and right. "Do you think we should avoid them?"

Ethan glanced around and saw that Nia was correct. They had entered an area with farms. Even more surprising was how much of the forest had been cleared away as fields. Then again, they were coming up to the village on his map named Timberwell. Perhaps it was a lumber town.

Bringing out his map, he looked it over. As he remembered, their path went right through Timberwell but there were no notes indicating anything else about the town. It was the only village between them and their destination. They could try to avoid it, but he knew some of the farmers had already seen them. It might look suspicious if someone questioned the farmers about a group that they later found avoided the city.

"Keep going and act natural," Ethan said quietly. "And don't bring up the caravan unless someone asks us. Everyone remember the story?"

Ainslee groaned. "We remember! We passed them last night, right before we made camp. They continued on. We never saw them again."

"Exactly," he said. "As far as we're concerned, they are fine, and on their way to Castlehaven. In fact, we tried to ask for any news and they were rude."

"How do you know they would have been rude?" Yuliana asked.

"I've never met a slaver," Ethan admitted, "but I imagine them as miserable, rude people."

"Probably. After all, their job is to enslave people and take them to be sacrificed," Ainslee snickered.

"Speaking of slaves." Ethan cleared his throat. "Remember, Nia, Yuliana and Par'karr, you all are supposed to be slaves. I'm not sure what that means but act as subservient as possible, don't look anyone in the eye and stay near me or Ainslee at all times."

Nia's face flushed and it looked like she was about to say something, but Ethan held up a hand. "You are not slaves. This is just an act so we don't have to fight off everyone who might want a chance at owning one of you."

"They would learn a hard lesson if they tried," Nia fumed.

"I know they would," Ethan answered honestly. "You'd tear them apart. But then people would notice that and notice us. Stories would start about a human, a dwarf, an elf, a kobold and a fierce foxgirl."

"So?!" Nia retorted. "They should fear us."

"It makes us noticeable," he argued. "And that's not what we want. We want to be forgotten quickly. It makes us harder to track."

Walking up to her he looked down at the petite but fierce warrioress. "Can I count on you?"

The foxgirl bit her lip and didn't answer for a full minute. Finally, she seemed to deflate a bit and let out a heavy sigh. "Yes. I promise I will not thrash anyone - even if they greatly deserve it."

He suppressed a chuckle and nodded. "Just stick near us and everything should be fine. Hopefully, we will be in and out of the village before anyone has a chance to notice us."

"We are going to stay overnight, though," Ainslee blurted out. "Right?"

Having already expected the request, Ethan nodded. He knew Ainslee really just wanted to get some mead, but they could also use a good night's rest in a real bed. The coins they'd taken from the slavers would be more than enough to cover a night's lodgings and a good meal.

Ethan noticed all eyes were on him, waiting for his response. He grinned. "Oh yeah, tonight, we will sleep in real beds."

18

It was dusk by the time they walked into the town of Timberwell. It had taken some effort - and a few increases in Diplomacy, but Ethan had convinced Yuliana to tell Luna to stay outside Timberwell. The last thing they needed was to alarm people with a mountain lion walking through town.

The druid wasn't happy, but she had eventually agreed. Yuliana told Luna to be careful and avoid the people around the town and then meet them on the eastern edge of the town. For her part, the mountain lion seemed to understand and padded off into the forest.

With the mountain lion gone, the group entered the town. Ethan thought of it as more of a town because he guessed it was four times the size of Hawkshead. Given the large swathes of treeless fields they'd passed coming into the town, he guessed this was a lumber town.

They walked through the town getting curious stares. The stares lingered on Nia, Yuliana and Par'karr more than Ethan or Ainslee. They weren't overtly hostile, nor were they friendly. They seemed more apathetically curious than anything else.

Groups of men and dwarves roamed the streets and by their dress and general build, Ethan guessed they were lumberjacks. As they passed, they shamelessly ogled the women. Some of them went so far as to give a few catcalls.

Nia simply glared at them, while Yuliana turned beet red. Ainslee, on the other hand, seemed to revel in the attention and went so far as to flex her large biceps for some of the men. Ethan noticed her arms were larger than most of the lumberjacks.

When Ainslee caught him looking at her, she shrugged. "What?! I'm as dwarven as the next woman. Who knows, maybe I'll get a little action tonight."

Ethan snapped his head back around, desperately trying NOT to imagine the dwarf "getting some action." It wasn't that Ainslee was unattractive. He just wasn't into women who could bench press more than he could. A lot more than he could.

He laughed softly to himself. Actually, considering his only exercise before being abducted had been carrying around a computer tool bag, the list of women who could bench press more than he could was probably a high percentage. But was that the case anymore?

He'd lost his little beer belly and his arms and legs were much more toned now, most likely from all of the walking he'd done since arriving on this world. Yet despite this, his Strength score hadn't increased.

Would he need to physically work out or lift weights to gain a point of Strength? And what about *Intellect*? Through skill ranks, he'd gained several points of *Intellect*, but he didn't feel any smarter.

Of course, *Intellect* could be more than a measure of intelligence. It could mean memory or ability to solve problems or speed of thought. Who knew what the aliens meant when they'd created the stats. Maybe they meant something completely different to the aliens.

Focusing his mind on the task at hand, he surveyed the shops and homes they passed. He was keeping his eyes open for an inn. The women were starting to garner more and more attention and the sooner they were indoors, the better.

The group followed the road east past closed shops and homes, to a main square of sorts. Encircling the square were a caravan of wagons, each loaded with trees. Most likely the caravan was headed for Castlehaven tomorrow.

The "troll" attack would be discovered in a day or so and then some sort of investigation would begin. He and his companions would be gone by then but given the amount of attention the women were receiving, they would not go unnoticed.

Hopefully, whoever saw it would believe that it was a troll attack and that would be the end of it. If not, then he was sure his group would be remembered and probably questioned. He sighed. They'd have to cross that bridge when and if they came to it.

Just past the town square were two large buildings on opposite sides of the street. They were both three-story buildings, built in what Ethan knew as the Tudor style on *Earth*. Painted wooden signs proclaimed one to be the Silver Axe Inn and the other to be the Felled Tree Inn.

Townspeople, mostly lumberjacks if Ethan guessed correctly, hung out at the entrance talking and singing. The doors to both establishments were open and Ethan and the others could see that the large, lamp-lit rooms were packed.

Loud, raucous noise wafted from the open doors of both establishments. It was singing, off-tune singing, that was punctuated by the occasional cheer.

Ainslee rubbed her hands together, a mischievous glint in her eye. "Now this sounds like my kind of place."

"Ainslee," he said sternly but then lowered his voice. "Remember, we have parts to play. You and I are the slave owners."

"Bah." The dwarf brushed off his concerns with a wave of her hand. "It'll be fine. I'm just going to have a few meads. Maybe a little dancing."

"Dancing?" Nia asked, suddenly perking up. Her previously sour mood was gone. Ethan remembered that when they'd first met, she had mentioned that she was a dancer.

"I do hear flute music," Yuliana commented, tilting her head left from right. She pointed left, to the Silver Axe. "From that one. There is music from the other, but I do not know how it is being created."

Ethan strained to hear over the chorus of off-key voices but couldn't make out instruments from either location. He shrugged. "Which one?"

"The one with the dancing," Nia said enthusiastically, pointing to the Silver Axe.

"Come on," roared Ainslee and charged off for the door. "Let's go!"

Reaching the open door, the stout dwarf pushed her way inside and disappeared from view before the others could reach her.

As Ethan and the others neared the door, the men and dwarves standing near the door sneered. "No slaves allowed inside!"

Gauging by their large physiques and simple clothes, he

knew they must be workers of some sort. Perhaps lumber-jacks or farmers who had come into town for a good time. They moved to block Ethan and his companions.

Ethan and the others halted a few feet from the men and he quickly scanned them all in his HUD.

```
Alan
    Human
    Lumberjack
    Level 6

Blacwin
    Dwarf
    Lumberjack
    Level 4

Elias
    Human
    Lumberjack
    Level 5

Giles
    Human
    Lumberjack
    Level 6

Munderic
    Dwarf
    Lumberjack
    Level 7
```

It had been Alan who had spoken. The man had long

brown, unkempt hair and large beard to match, along with a tanned, craggy face and nose that looked like it had been broken several times. The man had to be at least six feet and a half feet tall and was nearly as broad as the door. Ethan guessed he was the leader.

"He should leave the slaves out here with us," snickered Giles, leering at Yuliana. "We'll take good care of them."

Giles was young, maybe eighteen or nineteen. His flushed face was pock-marked and his eyes were just a little too small for his face. When he grinned, Ethan could see he was missing a tooth on his left side. While smaller than Alan, he was still taller and broader than Ethan.

The others laughed, evil grins spreading over their faces that left no doubt as to what they had in mind. He saw Nia tense and take a step towards the men. He quickly shot an arm out blocking her path.

Nia shot him an angry glare but he turned and gave her a meaningful look. His message was clear: stick to the plan. With a huff, she stepped back.

"Aw, looky there." Blacwin laughed. "I think the fox wants to play."

"I got something she can play with!" roared Munderic and grabbed his crotch. "Come on, foxy! You can play with this!"

The others burst into laughter just as a portly man pushed through them. He was middle aged and balding, with a trim beard and a puffy face. The man was tall, though not quite as tall as Alan. Like the lumberjacks, he was broad but while the man might have once been muscular, much of it had turned to fat.

Norman

Human
Innkeeper
Level 5

"What's this now?!" the innkeeper sputtered. "What goes on here? Are you blocking patrons, Alan?"

"We were just telling them the rules," Giles answered. "No slaves inside. Ain't that right?"

Norman turned and looked at Ethan and then at the elf, the foxgirl and the kobold. He frowned. "They're right about that, traveler, no slaves inside. Especially not kobolds."

"Stinkin' kobolds," Elias sneered.

"I told him we'd take care of them for him," Giles chuckled but stopped when the innkeeper glared at him.

"They'll have to stay in the barn," the innkeeper said and the lumberjacks smiled wickedly. Ethan could see that they were already making plans to have their way with the women. He wasn't about to allow that.

"What if I pay extra?" Ethan suggested.

"Rules are rules!" Giles sneered.

"Shut up, Giles," the innkeeper snapped but shook his head. "Sorry, traveler, those are the rules. No slaves allowed."

Ethan fumed at the thought of Nia, Yuliana and Par'karr having to sleep in the stables. He'd rather go back outside the village and camp, than have his companions treated so poorly.

"You heard him, whelp," Alan said, stepping forward. The man made to shove Ethan and without even thinking about it he activated *Elemental Armor*. Blue flames encased him in the blink of an eye and the big man quickly withdrew his hand. Alan and the others, even the innkeeper, all took a step back from him.

Cursing silently, Ethan berated himself for revealing his magic. Now there was no way they'd keep a low profile. These men would no doubt spread the word that a wizard, a foxgirl, an elf and a kobold were in town.

"Warlock," hissed Alan. Ethan saw both fear and disgust in his eyes. The man assumed he was a warlock. It was an understandable mistake considering the lack of wizards. And after meeting Charmine, he understood why these people might be fearful. That woman had been extremely disturbing and if all warlocks were like that, their reputation was probably deserved.

Ethan almost grinned. If these people expected a warlock, why not give them one. Better for them to think he was a warlock than a wizard.

"What's that?" Ethan said, letting his eyes go wild and looking over his shoulder, just as Charmine had done. "I should keep the slaves with me?"

Skill increase: Bluff +1%.

The men looked where Ethan was looking and obviously saw no one. They glanced at each other in confusion.

"But they said no slaves in the inn," Ethan said over his shoulder. From the corner of his eye, he saw the innkeeper shift nervously.

"What?" Ethan asked the imaginary voice over his shoulder. "I kill these men and burn down the inn?"

Skill increase: Bluff +1%.
Skill increase: Intimidation +1%.

"Kill?!" Giles croaked, his voice suddenly several octaves higher.

To better sell his bluff, Ethan made the little balls of flame used as light sources appear over the heads of each of the men.

`Skill increase: Bluff +1%.`
    `Skill increase: Intimidation +1%.`

The moment he did, Giles lost control of his bladder and a large wet spot spread across the front of his trousers.

"Good sir warlock," the innkeeper squealed, voice breaking. His wide eyes looked up at the ball of flames hovering over the heads of the other men. "No need to be hasty!"

Ethan had to work hard not to laugh and instead made the smile on his face more manic, almost crazy. He looked at the innkeeper with wild eyes. "It likes the slaves to be with me!"

`Skill increase: Bluff +1%.`
    `Skill increase: Intimidation +1%.`

"They can be with you! They can be with you!" Norman stammered. "Please don't burn down my inn. Good sir warlock!"

The other men were staring wide-eyed and fearful at the balls of light above their heads. Tears were streaming down Giles' face as he stared up at the ball of flame and Ethan could just make out his words. "Don't kill me... don't kill me..."

Ethan wanted to feel sorry for the young man but given what he might have done to the women, it was difficult to muster any sympathy for him. Instead, he focused on his charade. He channeled his inner Nicholson, stopping just shy of yelling "Here's Johnny!"

"But the rules?!" Ethan said and caused the balls of light to drop an inch closer to the men. "Rules!!! It doesn't like the rules! It likes fire!"

Skill increase: Bluff +1%.
Skill increase: Intimidation +1%.

"No! No!" the innkeeper cried. "No! I changed the rules. I changed the rules. You and your slaves can stay in the inn. Just... no fire please. No fire!"

Ethan looked back over his shoulder and muttered under his breath. All the men were sweating now, even Alan, as they stared terrified at the balls of light above their head. He pretended to carry on a conversation for a few minutes, alternating between talking over his shoulder and giving crazy looks to the men.

Skill increase: Bluff +1%.

Finally he extinguished the balls of light but didn't let go of the *Elemental Armor*. He gave the innkeeper another crazy look. As soon as the balls of flame disappeared, the lumber-jacks darted off and ran down the street.

"It wants me to eat and sleep," he told the innkeeper, nodding manically. "Eat and sleep!"

Skill increase: Bluff +1%.

The innkeeper bobbed his head up and down vigorously.

"I will get you a room. For you and your slaves. Yes, good sir warlock. And have dinner brought up." The man stopped and looked at Ethan, still encased in fire. "But...uh... good sir warlock, perhaps you can... I mean... you are... on fire."

Ethan looked at himself, pretending to just notice the flames. He muttered over his shoulder and dismissed the *Elemental Armor*. He turned back to the innkeeper, all smiles. "It would like us to go to our room now."

Skill increase: Bluff +1%.

19

———

They followed the innkeeper through the tavern, up the stairs and to a simple wooden door. Norman kept glancing nervously behind him at Ethan, as if expecting the "warlock" to suddenly start flinging around fire. Ethan couldn't blame the man. The act had worked well.

With shaky hands, the innkeeper unlocked the door and pushed it open. Then turning, the man held out the key to Ethan as if he were feeding a viper. Norman was pale, as if he expected Ethan to burst into flames at any moment.

"Is... is this room okay?" Norman stammered. "I mean... is it okay, your warlock-ness?"

Ethan glanced in but the room was dark. He created two balls of light and sent them into the room. The action caused the innkeeper to flinch, probably imagining Ethan lighting the room on fire.

The room itself was large but only had a single, king-sized bed in it. Ethan frowned but realized the innkeeper had probably assumed that the women were his sex slaves -

literally. Unable to think of a graceful way to explain he needed two rooms, he nodded. "This will do."

He saw Nia open her mouth to say something but he cut her off with a meaningful look. Luckily, she seemed to trust him and closed her mouth. Luckily, Norman was too busy sighing in relief to have noticed the exchange. As Ethan took the key from him, the innkeeper quickly withdrew his hand.

"I...I, ah." The man stopped and swallowed, casting a glance at Ethan. "I will go bring food."

The innkeeper made to move past him but Ethan held up a hand. "How much for the room and the food?"

Norman shook his head. He was still pale and sweat beaded [CII]the man's balding head. "No charge. You can stay for free."

Ethan sighed and shook his head. "It says we must pay our way. How much?"

The man wiped a hand over his sweaty brow and then moved his fingers. "Uh... 1 gold for the room, 8 silver for the meals."

Fishing 2 gold coins out of his pouch, he handed them to the innkeeper. "Here. Please have the food brought up."

Just in time, he remembered Yuliana's food preferences. "And bring a plate of fresh vegetables and/or fruit."

The innkeeper bobbed his head up and down and then carefully slipped past Ethan and the women before practically running down the rest of the steps.

"We cannot..." Nia started to protest but Ethan put a finger to his lips and nodded to the room.

"Let's talk inside," he said quietly and went inside the room and gestured for them to follow.

The women hesitated but Par'karr walked in and dumped his pack in the corner. "Me like this room."

The women glanced at each other before following the little kobold into the room. Once they had, Ethan stuck his head out the doorway to make sure no one was around and then shut the door and turned to face his companions.

Both women had their hands folded over their chests and were giving Ethan hard stares. He opened his mouth to speak but the women beat him to it.

"Why were you acting like that downstairs?" Yuliana demanded.

"We cannot sleep in the same bed!" the foxgirl blurted out.

"Wait? What?" Ethan said, confused. Both women had spoken at the same time and he hadn't caught what either had said.

"We cannot sleep in the same bed!" Nia snarled. "It is not proper. You are not my alpha and my alpha has not commanded me to sleep with you!"

Yuliana looked back at the bed, seeming to notice it for the first time, before she turned red and snapped her head back to Ethan. "We are sleeping in the same bed?!"

Ethan let out a breath and leaned back against the wall. He suppressed a smile as he thought of the irony. Story of his life. No woman wanted to share a bed with him. But in this case, it hadn't been on his mind. He had already planned to let the women share the bed and he and Par'karr would sleep on the floor.

"No," he told them with as much force and sincerity as he could muster. "You and Yuliana can have the bed - though you may need to share it with Ainslee too if she comes back. Par'karr and I can take the floor."

"Me like floor," Par'karr nodded and tapped the floor with his foot. "Nice and hard!"

"We just need to make people think that you are my... you know, slaves," Ethan continued. "There's less chance they'll bother you."

The women seemed to consider his answer. Yuliana blushed slightly, probably at the idea of people thinking she was a sex toy for a warlock. Nia didn't look pleased and muttered softly under her breath before she finally nodded slightly.

"Who were you talking to in the street?" the elf asked. "It looked like you were speaking with someone we could not see."

"Remember I said there were other magic-users?" he asked and waited for Yuliana to nod. "The warlocks make pacts with extra-dimensional creatures, what we - or I - would think of as demons. These demons give them power but they can also communicate with them. The warlock I met in Castlehaven talked like that to her demon, so I did the same to make them think I was a warlock."

"It was very...disturbing," the elf admitted.

"I know the feeling," he agreed. "Ainslee and I were a little freaked out when we first met a warlock."

Nia narrowed her eyes and put her hands on her hips. She looked Ethan up and down, giving him an appraising look. "Would you really have burned down the entire inn to protect us?"

Ethan shrugged. "If it came down to that, yes, in a heartbeat. I wasn't about to let them try and have their way with you."

The foxgirl smiled and nodded but then crossed her arms back over her chest and gave Ethan a defiant look. "You still cannot sleep in the same bed as me."

"The innkeeper is coming back up the steps," Yuliana said. "I can hear his heavy footsteps."

Wanting to complete the charade, Ethan looked around the room. He lowered his voice to a whisper. "We need to sell this. We want the innkeeper passing the story around so no one else bothers you. Drop your packs and hop into bed. Pull the covers up so only your heads are showing."

The girls both narrowed their eyes. "Just do it, please."

Reluctantly, the girls did as he asked. They both slid their packs off, pulled back the covers and got into bed. At the same time, Ethan shrugged out of his armor and pulled off his tattered shirt. He looked down to see that he still bore the three talon scars of the troll.

A knock on the door sounded and Ethan waited a moment before opening it. It was the innkeeper with a wooden tray containing four plates of food, plus a plate of carrots, tomatoes and chopped cabbage. Ethan let the door swing open just enough that the innkeeper could see the two women in the bed.

"Thank you," Ethan said and took the tray from the man. "If you can bring up another round of mead for later - we will be thirsty."

Ethan gave the man a sly smile and nodded towards the bed.

Skill increase: Bluff +1%.

Ethan reached into his belt pouch, pulled out a few more silver and handed it to the man. "This should cover it."

"Yes, good sir warlock." The innkeeper bobbed his head up and down. "I will set them outside of the door for you."

The innkeeper looked past Ethan at the women and then back to him. "Do you... uh... require a bath? It is only 2 silver extra."

Ethan glanced back at the women and gave them a questioning look. They both nodded and he turned back around and handed the innkeeper 2 more silver. "Yes, that will be good."

"I will have the tub brought up and I'll start boiling the water." Norman smiled nervously.

"No need," Ethan said. "Just bring up the tub and cold water."

"Cold?" The innkeeper looked puzzled.

"I will heat it myself." Ethan gave the man an evil grin and made another ball of light appear near him.

"Yes, mister warlock, yes sir." The innkeeper gulped. With that, the innkeeper turned and hurried back down the steps.

Ethan watched the man and then shut the door. He placed the tray down on a small table in the room. "Come on, let's eat."

The women climbed out of bed and grabbed some food and some mead. They were still eating when there was a small knock on the door. Ethan went over and opened it a crack. It was two beefy men carrying a copper tub. Both were young enough and similar enough that he guessed they were the innkeeper's sons.

Ethan opened the door all the way and let the two young men carry in the tub. He pointed to the corner. "Put it over there."

They did as they were told and then lumbered out of the room. The biggest gave Ethan a curious stare before leaving. "We'll be back with the water."

It took the two lads twenty minutes and many trips to fill the tub with water. Finally, they were done and Ethan, unsure what constituted a good tip, gave them a handful of coppers.

"Thank you, mister warlock, sir," said the bigger one, and the pair quickly left the room.

Ethan walked over to the tub and, focusing his magic, was able to heat the water up by channeling heat into the water. He hadn't been completely convinced it would work or how much *Mana* it would take but soon the water was nice and hot.

The women had started to look a bit nervous about the bath until he told Par'karr to retrieve their rope. Ethan had the women tie it across the corner and then they hung one of the blankets from their bed roll across the rope, creating a makeshift privacy screen.

"Who's up for a bath?" he asked.

All three of his companions spoke up at the same time.

20

———

Nearly three hours later, the music had stopped and the general noise from the downstairs had subsided. Most of the drinkers had probably been lumberjacks and they'd most likely be up at dawn. Whatever the reason was, Ethan was glad it was quiet.

It was finally Ethan's turn in the copper tub. He had insisted the women go first and then Par'karr. Now it was his turn and as he slowly lowered himself into the hot water, he felt human for the first time since arriving on this world. Back on *Earth*, he'd always taken showers, never baths. But as he sat in the tub and the hot water seemed to soak into his sore muscles, it felt amazing. He made a mental note to get one for his house back in Hawkshead.

Just as his tired and aching muscles were starting to relax, there came a heavy pounding at the door. He started, splashing some of the water out of the tub. He craned his neck, trying to see past the curtain.

In his mind, he imagined the town guard standing outside

the door, ready to arrest him for threatening to burn down the inn. Or maybe it was the lumberjacks, come back for revenge. He started to stand up so he could grab his breeches.

He heard groaning from the bed. Both Nia and Yuliana had gone to bed after their baths and had been sleeping. Apparently, the pounding at the door had woke them.

"Make it stop," Yuliana groaned sleepily.

"Are you in there?" came Ainslee's slurred voice as the pounding continued. "Let me in. I need to get some sleep."

"Tell the dwarf to stop making such a racket," Nia said groggily.

Ethan relaxed slightly behind the makeshift privacy curtain and sank back into the tub. "Par'karr, can you let Ainslee in."

He heard footsteps moving to the door and then the door open. Then he heard a crash. He waited for a long moment before Par'karr's head popped around the sheet. "Dwarf sleeping in doorway."

Ethan sighed. "She passed out?"

Par'karr nodded his little head. "Too heavy for Par'karr to move."

"Give me a moment," Ethan said.

Standing in the tub, Ethan reached down and grabbed one of the blankets from his pack. He stepped out of the tub. He shivered at the temperature difference, coming from the hot water to the cool air of the room. He wrapped the blanket around his waist and tucked in the end so it stayed up.

Stepping out from behind the curtain, he saw Ainslee lying face first on the floor in the doorway. As he looked down at her, she began snoring even more loudly than normal. To his left, he saw that Nia and Yuliana were sitting up in bed, glaring at the dwarf.

"Why must she resort to such debauchery?" Nia growled.

Ethan was too irritated to answer. Not that he had an answer. After all, the four of them had barely spoken about their own worlds. For some reason, Ethan found that odd. He also found it odd that he rarely thought of his own world either, except in passing.

Stopping in front of the dwarf, Ethan thought hard about the time since he'd arrived. He hadn't really thought of home much at all. He hadn't even missed most of the conveniences of *Earth*. He'd barely thought of his friends. Even now, as he actually tried to think of things from his past, his mind wanted to wander.

Had the aliens done something to him - to all of them - that made them forget, or at least not think about, their home worlds? He had no idea how the aliens could do that, but then again, he had no idea how or why he had a HUD in his head either.

Who knew what technology the aliens possessed? Could they be tapped into their thoughts? Maybe even be manipulating them in real time? That was a terrifying thought.

He wanted to entertain the idea longer, but Nia cleared her throat behind him. "Are you two going to leave the dwarf in the doorway or move her?"

Looking over his shoulder, he saw the annoyed women staring back at him. Ethan gave them an apologetic smile and turned back around. As he did, he struggled to remember what he'd just been thinking about. He shrugged. It couldn't have been too important. Maybe he'd remember it later.

Bending down, he grabbed the dwarf and tried to lift her up. He swore. The dwarf was much heavier than he thought.

"See! Ainslee heavy," Par'karr nodded.

Groaning and rubbing his back, Ethan nodded in agreement. The dwarf was much heavier than he thought. She must be all muscle and maybe even have denser bones. He stood up and stretched to the left and right to work out the kink in his back.

Looking down at the dwarf, he grimaced. He wasn't about to throw out his back trying to lift or drag the unconscious woman. Then he'd be in pain all day tomorrow. He motioned to the kobold. "Stand back."

Par'karr did so without question and looked to Ethan. "Magic?!"

"Magic," Ethan agreed.

He'd been using *Mana* all night to heat the water but it was never much and there was enough time in between for it to mostly regenerate. To be sure, he brought up his HUD and checked his stats.

Mana: 33

Given his own experiments at lifting himself and other objects, it was more than enough. Just in case, he left the HUD up so he could monitor his levels.

Taking a deep breath, Ethan reached out with his magic. He wrapped up the dwarf in tendrils of Air and lifted her up. It was tougher than he thought and he watched his *Mana* drop by 5 points.

Skill increase: Air Magic +1%.

He backed up and willed the air to move the dwarf with him. The unconscious Ainslee floated out of the doorway and into the room. As she did, Par'karr grabbed the door and pulled it closed.

Keeping the dwarf suspended was not nearly as taxing as picking her up in the first place, so Ethan kept holding her in the air. He looked at the dwarf and frowned. Her pack was gone. "Is her pack out in the hallway?"

Opening the door again, Par'karr stuck his head out and looked both ways. The kobold withdrew his head. He closed the door and then turned and shook his head. "No pack."

Ethan cursed. They'd have to buy her a new one if she lost it. He looked down at the dwarf's waist. The scabbards were there but the short swords were gone as well. He cursed louder.

"What is it?" Nia groaned irritably.

"Her pack and her weapons are missing," Ethan snapped.

"Money?" Par'karr asked.

Ethan massaged his temples with his left hand as he shook his head. "Par'karr, check her pouch."

The little kobold walked over to the floating dwarf and looked around. He found the pouch and shook it. It didn't make a sound. Par'karr looked closely and stuck his claws into what appeared to be a hole. Looking back at Ethan, he shook his head sadly. "No money."

Clenching his teeth, Ethan considered dunking the dwarf headfirst into the tub. Unfortunately, the dwarf was so drunk, she might not even wake up.

"Yell at her tomorrow," Nia yawned. "Let her sleep on the floor."

"Can she use your bedroll?" Ethan asked.

"No!" the foxgirl hissed. "It will stink like dwarf forever!"

Par'karr laughed and even Ethan couldn't fully suppress a snicker. "Ainslee doesn't stink. Just like she doesn't snore."

He heard Nia and Yuliana both chuckle.

"She can use mine," the elf said.

"Thanks, Yuliana," he said, gesturing towards Yuliana's pack. "Par'karr, can you grab it?"

The kobold ran over to the pack, pulled out the bedroll and laid it on the floor next to the bed. When he was done, Par'karr hopped back. "Done!"

Ethan willed the *Air* to move the dwarf to the bedroll and then began to lower her to the bedroll. As she brushed by him, her hand caught on the blanket. One moment, he was covered from the waist down, and the next moment he was standing completely naked.

Yuliana gasped and her face went beet-red. Nia stared at him, her eyes roving down his torso. A mischievous smile played across her face and she arched an eyebrow. "Are all humans so... big?"

Feeling vulnerable and humiliated, Ethan blushed furiously. He intended to dive for the curtain but suddenly there was a jerking sensation, and everything went topsy-turvy.

One moment he was in the room in the inn and the next he was falling through a strange tunnel-like kaleidoscope of color. First, he moved down, then sideways, then backwards. As the colors washed around him, he could see the characters on his HUD change and morph, becoming unreadable.

From the corner of his eyes, he saw flashes of images. There were planets and solar systems, galaxies and black holes. There were other things too, but Ethan couldn't make them out. Each time he turned his head to look more closely, the images dissolved away into the kaleidoscope of colors.

He wasn't sure how long he was in the tunnel or how many images flashed by, but one moment he was flying through the tunnel and the next he was yanked out of it.

In an instant, he appeared in midair, two feet above the tub. Falling, he splashed down into the tub, causing water to splatter everywhere. Incredible exhaustion suddenly overcame him, and he struggled to pull his head out of the water.

His HUD was still up, and the characters were once again readable. Striving to stay awake, he read the new messages.

You have gained: Aether Magic.
  Skill increase: Aether Magic +5%.

Mana: 1
  Stamina: 1

Both his *Stamina* and *Mana* had been almost entirely depleted. And what was Aether Magic? He felt exhausted and completely drained; it was an effort of will just to keep his eyes open. Whatever had just happened, it had taxed him almost to his limit.

"Ethan?!" came Nia's voice. It was immediately followed by a similar cry from Yuliana.

Par'karr's head poked around the curtain again and he grinned and waved. "Ethan in tub!"

There was the sound of feet on the floor and then the curtain was thrown to the side, revealing the women's faces. Both women looked worried, possibly even afraid.

"What happened to you?!" Nia demanded.

"Where did you go?!" Yuliana echoed.

Ethan was still dazed. He blinked his eyes to stay awake. He felt like he'd just pulled an all-nighter without coffee. It was a struggle just to keep his eyes open and to focus on what they were saying.

"What do you mean?" he asked groggily. "What happened? How did I get into the tub?"

"You disappeared!" Nia exclaimed. "We were...uh... looking at you and then you just disappeared."

"You popped!" Par'karr nodded.

"Popped?" Ethan said. His head was starting to hurt now and he rubbed his temples. "What do you mean?"

"There was a popping sound and you disappeared," Yuliana said, her face still flushed. Ethan saw her eyes flicking away, but then coming back to look at him.

Suddenly remembering he was naked, he brought his hands down to cover his lower half. He didn't feel his face flushed and guessed his body didn't even have the *Mana* to be embarrassed.

Nia chuckled, the mischievous grin coming back to her face. "Why bother? It's not like we did not see it a moment ago?"

Ethan felt like he should be more embarrassed, but he was simply too tired. He felt the tiredness creeping in on him. Still, he tried to make sense of what had happened. "How long?"

"How long, what?" Nia asked in confusion.

"How long was I gone?" he wondered. He wasn't sure how long he was in that strange kaleidoscope tunnel. Was it minutes? Hours? Days? He wasn't sure.

"I do not know what you mean," Yuliana said, her brow furrowing. "One moment you disappeared and the next there was a splash."

"A moment? Are you sure?" he asked, confused. He'd definitely been in that strange tunnel for more than a moment.

Nia nodded. "There was a pop and you disappeared.

Then, almost at the same time, there was a pop from behind the curtain. Then the splash."

His addled mind tried to make sense of what she was saying but already the sounds were growing distant. Blackness started to close in on the edges of his vision. He needed rest. Sleep.

And then the blackness closed in on him and he knew no more.

21

Ethan groaned softly as he woke up. His head hurt. It felt like he had a hangover. A really bad hangover. He shifted and realized he wasn't on the floor. He was in a bed. He could feel the soft mattress beneath him, an actual pillow under his head and unfamiliar covers on top of him. Then he realized that he could feel all of that because he was completely naked.

Snapping his eyes open, Ethan looked around. Light blinded him, cutting through his brain like daggers of fire. Wincing, he narrowed his eyes to slits. Slowly, he looked around. He was in a room. A somewhat familiar room.

His addled brain remembered the events of yesterday and last night. He was in the room in the inn. And light was streaming in the window. That meant it was morning.

A snore immediately to his left nearly caused him to start. Ethan twisted and saw the edge of the bed. Looking over and onto the floor, he saw the sleeping form of Ainslee. She was on a bedroll. His addled brain vaguely remembered her passing out in the doorway and having to put her on the bedroll.

The bed shifted and Ethan realized someone else was in the bed with him. Remembering he was completely naked, he felt his face and neck growing warm. His mind raced as he tried to imagine who it was: Yuliana or Nia. He actually found both women attractive and the idea of being naked in bed with them began to get him excited.

And then Ethan twisted his head to the right and saw the yellow-eyed lizard-headed kobold staring back at him. Par'karr grinned. "You awake!"

Suddenly feeling both embarrassed and awkward for getting excited, he sat up quickly. This proved to be a mistake as a thousand tiny fireworks went off in his brain. Bringing his hands to his head, he squeezed his eyes shut.

Through the pain, Ethan felt dizzy and dehydrated. His mouth tasted like sandpaper. If he didn't know better, he'd swear he had gotten completely wasted last night. But he knew he hadn't. Nothing so mundane. Instead, he had memories of the bizarre kaleidoscope tunnel and teleporting from the side of the bed to the tub.

Yes, he realized. That's what had happened. He'd actually teleported somehow. Beam me up, Scotty! And yet, unlike in shows and comics, it hadn't been an instantaneous experience. At least, not for him. It had been a ride through some sort of... tunnel.

He remembered Nia saying it had been instant, or nearly so. One moment, he'd disappeared with a pop and the next moment, she'd heard another pop and then a splash as he appeared over the tub. That had been what they'd seen. But that hadn't been his experience.

For Ethan, it had been seconds - maybe even minutes. He'd been in some sort of tunnel. Or at least, it had appeared to be a kaleidoscope tunnel of rainbow colors, swirling and mixing with images of planets and galaxies.

He paused in his thoughts as he repeated his previous thought: a tunnel of rainbow colors. Was that like a rainbow bridge? Was that something like the Bifrost from Norse legends? He wouldn't even have remembered it except for the deluge of recent superhero movies, including the one about Thor, the god of Thunder.

Had he experienced some sort of wormhole? What had that scientist in the movie called it? An Einstein-Rosen bridge? Ethan didn't pretend to understand the physics involved in it. He was a computer guy. He understood logic and circuits. All he knew was that something had happened and he had gone from one spot to another spot.

Ethan thought back to the various science fiction books he'd read. He tried to remember his science courses as well. He racked his brain for something he remembered reading a few times. Something about Einstein's theory of special relativity.

He thought he remembered. The closer one got to the speed of light, the more time slowed down. Is that what had happened? Somehow, he entered or created some sort of wormhole and while he was inside it, time moved differently? What had seemed like minutes to him had only been a fraction of a second for everyone else?

"Are you okay?" Yuliana's voice jarred him from his thoughts.

Ethan opened his eyes a slit to see Yuliana and Nia sitting up at the foot of the bed. Both looked disheveled, as if they hadn't gotten much sleep. And yet, both women had concern written all over their features.

"I'm...not sure," he replied honestly. He wasn't sure. He felt drained and fatigued. More so than he'd felt since arriving on this world.

"You blacked out," Yuliana said. "We couldn't wake you."

"I think I remember that," he groaned. The last thing he remembered, he was in the tub. After that, everything was a blank until this morning. He didn't even remember dreaming. Curious, he brought up his HUD. His eyes went wide and he nearly choked as he saw his stats.

```
Strength: 5
  Agility: 5
  Hardiness: 5
  Intellect: 10
  Intuition: 5
  Charisma: 5

Health: 10
  Mana: 30
  Stamina: 20
```

"What?!" Nia said in alarm. "What's wrong?!"

"My stats," he gasped, not understanding what had happened. "They've all been reduced to 5's... except *Intellect* - that's a 10!"

Nia and Yuliana exchanged looks and the elf nodded. "Your breathing was very shallow for several hours. We were worried you would not wake up."

Ethan had a bad feeling and scrolled up through his messages. Sure enough, he found what he feared.

Warning: *Mana* at 0. Channeling more *Mana* than you have available can cause temporary or permanent injury.

```
You have gained: Blood Magic.


Overchannel Active.


You have temporarily lost a point of
Strength.
    You have temporarily lost a point of
Agility.
    You have temporarily lost a point of
Hardiness.
    You have temporarily lost a point of
Intellect.
    You have temporarily lost a point of
Intuition.
    You have temporarily lost a point of
Charisma.
    Skill increase: Blood Magic +6%.
```

The system messages went on, showing that he had lost points in all of his attributes. The teleportation had cost more *Mana* than he had available - a lot more. The Overchannel ability had kicked in and had converted his attributes into *Mana*.

What Blood Magic was or why he had gained and increased in it, he wasn't sure. It sounded ominous.

He checked his *Mana*, *Health* and *Stamina*.

```
Health: 10
    Mana: 30
```

Stamina: 20

They were all at maximum, but the maximum values had decreased significantly. He now only had 10 *Health* and 20 *Stamina*! Ethan swore and the girls' expression became even more concerned.

"What?" Nia asked.

"Because my stats are all reduced, my health, stamina and *Mana* are all down. I have 10 health now!" he retorted.

Ethan ground his teeth and swore again. He hadn't tried to teleport or even intended to teleport. And yet, somehow, he had. Now, because of the damage, he was effectively a weakling until his stat damage healed.

"Ethan lucky," Par'karr said.

"Lucky?" Ethan growled, turning to the kobold in disbelief. "How am I lucky?"

"Use too much magic," the kobold answered and made an explosive gesture with his hands. "Medicine men blow up or die. Ethan lucky. That not happened to him."

Taking a deep breath and letting it out, Ethan nodded. "I guess being a weakling for a couple of weeks is better than blowing up."

Ethan realized the kobold was right. He remembered the kobold mentioning something along those lines before. Ethan guessed he was lucky in that respect. Things could have gone worse. Much worse.

"Will you be okay?" Yuliana asked him.

He turned to the women and nodded. "Yes, but it will take a week or two for me to get back to where I was. And I'll probably have to take it easy. I have less than half the stamina I had before."

"So, what do we do?" Nia asked.

"Let's stay here another day and night," he told them. "It will give me a chance to rest up."

Yuliana nodded her agreement. "Good, you need your rest."

Another snore sounded and Ethan looked down at the still-sleeping dwarf. "Nia, can you go down and tell the innkeeper that we will be staying another night and that we'll need food and mead brought up to us. Also tell him that the dwarf and I are having a disagreement and that she will need her own room, right next to ours."

Nia looked down at the dwarf, confused. "She will want her own room?"

Ethan smiled and shook his head. "No, but this way we'll have two rooms. One for you girls and one for us guys. Then we'll all have a bed." He flashed her a grin. "Unless you two want to share with me?"

Yuliana blushed slightly and shook her head, but Nia gave him a dismissive gesture. "I know you desire me, but it cannot be. I am bound to my alpha."

Ethan opened his mouth to tell her he had just been kidding but she waved away his reply. "No arguments will persuade me. This is the way."

Not wanting to start an argument, Ethan nodded while suppressing a smile. "Well then, let's get two rooms so all of us can sleep in beds... just, not together."

"That is acceptable." The foxgirl nodded. "I will go inform the innkeeper."

Ethan swore as he remembered the caravan that was supposed to leave today. He tried to get out of bed, but everything ached and he stopped. "Par'karr, look out the window and tell me if the wagons are gone."

"Okay." The kobold nodded happily and hopped off the

bed. He went over to the window and looked out. "No wagons. They gone."

"You are thinking of the priestess and her warriors," Nia guessed.

"That's exactly what I'm thinking of," he replied. He had originally only planned to stay a day. By the time word of the "troll" attack would have gotten back to the town, they would have been two days gone. Now, it would be only a day. "Maybe we should leave today instead."

"No!" both women said at once, the sound causing Ainslee to snort in her sleep.

"You must rest," Yuliana said in a tone that did not invite debate.

"Yes, you should rest," Nia said, though slightly less passionately than the elf. Hers was the cool tone of pragmatism.

"Fine," Ethan relented. "But we leave tomorrow morning."

Yuliana looked at Nia and made a small gesture with her head and eyes. The foxgirl shook her head and then the elf shrugged.

"What's going on?" Ethan asked, eyes narrowing.

"Nothing," both women said at the same time. Their tone indicated there was definitely something.

"Come on," he insisted. "Out with it."

"We were just wondering," Nia said, her manner uncharacteristically shy. "If you were... uh..."

"Just spit it out," he said, and then realizing they may not understand the figure of speech, rephrased it. "Just tell me what you want."

Yuliana gave Nia a small nod and "go ahead" gesture.

Letting out a breath, the foxgirl rolled her eyes at the elf.

"We were both wondering if you were feeling well enough to do the hot water bath magic again."

Unable to help himself, Ethan burst out into laughter. Unfortunately, that caused the fireworks to go off in his head again, but he managed to nod. "Sure. Just let me eat and drink something first."

22

Ethan spent the rest of the day alternating between sleeping and heating up water for the women to take hot baths. Heating water took almost no effort and little *Mana*, so he didn't mind. He also ate. He ate a lot. His body craved both food and drink and he ordered two meals for himself at each meal.

Around midmorning, Ainslee finally woke and immediately wanted to go back down and resume drinking. Then the dwarf learned about the hot baths and demanded that she get one too. By that time, the other two had gotten their baths so they let Ainslee take her turn.

This continued the entire day, with the innkeeper delivering food and mead to the rooms in regular intervals and Ethan mostly sleeping. Even the noise from the tavern didn't stop him from getting extra sleep.

The next morning, Ethan felt much better. He checked out the information in his HUD.

`Strength: 6`

```
    Agility: 6
    Hardiness: 6
    Intellect: 11
    Intuition: 6
    Charisma: 6


Health: 12
  Mana: 32
  Stamina: 24
```

All his stats had regained a point and his *Health*, *Mana* and *Stamina* reflected that, but he was still much weaker than he had been. He would need to be careful. That was especially true with his *Health*.

Everyone except Ainslee was ready to go at first light. The women had needed to roll the dwarf off the bed to wake her. When she did wake, she was grumpy and snapped at anyone who spoke to her.

Luckily, her pack had been found by the innkeeper the day before and returned to her, but all of her coins were gone. Maybe that would teach the dwarf not to party quite so hard.

While Nia and Yuliana were waking Ainslee, Ethan and Par'karr paid the innkeeper and bought some bread and cheese for the road. By the time the women came downstairs, they were ready to leave. Even the dwarf's spirits were instantly lifted when she saw the hand keg of mead, he'd bought for her.

"If I wasn't so thirsty," the dwarf said as she hoisted the hand keg onto her shoulder, "I'd kiss you. It's like the old saying, the way to a woman's heart is through her mug!"

Ethan had never heard of that saying but knowing of the dwarf's proclivity to drink, he wasn't surprised by it.

The group left before the lumberjacks had finished piling into the inn for breakfast. Ethan would have liked to have stayed an extra day or two, but time was ticking. By now, the caravan would have reached the "troll" attack and would have sent someone to report back to the town. He wanted to be long gone before they arrived.

They headed east and were quickly joined by Luna. How the cat had known when and where to find them, Ethan wasn't sure, but Yuliana was happy to see the big cat. The cat, for her part, seemed equally happy to see the elf.

Thus reunited, they all marched on. For over an hour they passed farms along the eastern road. After that, it became a thick forest with only a narrow road for them to follow.

Ethan was able to keep up but not nearly as easily as before. He became winded much more quickly and struggled to keep pace with the others. Despite his weakness, he forced himself to keep going.

According to his calculations, it was still four more days to the mountains. Once they hit the mountains, the map had them turning north along the base of the mountains. From there, it would be hard to gauge how long it would take, as the terrain would be rougher than they'd encountered so far.

WHEN NOON CAME, they stopped along the river and Ethan gulped down handfuls of water. As before, the water helped to restore his *Stamina*. But like before, water only restored him to half his maximum. With his lower *Stamina* score, that gave him only 12 *Stamina*.

While he didn't really see a difference when he had gained or lost *Intellect* points, the *Stamina* loss was more tangible. He'd been feeling like he had progressed since arriving on this world. He was leaner and had been able to walk all day before this incident.

Now, he felt like he was in worse shape than he had been when he had arrived here. It was frustrating - and exhausting.

He wished he could figure out a way to use magic to help make things easier. He'd considered levitating himself but with his lower *Mana* level, he was loath to use any magic at the moment. If they got in a fight, he'd need every bit of *Mana* he could muster. That meant he would have to keep walking.

After a meal of bread and cheese, and some wild berries they'd found, the group set off again. As they restarted their trek, Nia spotted dark clouds coming over the mountains from the east. Storm clouds. Stopping the group, she pointed them out.

"There is a storm coming," she said. "I do not know how the storms are on this world, but on my world, clouds like that would mean a bad storm."

"Great!" huffed the dwarf. "We're going to get drenched!"

"It's only water," Yuliana pointed out.

Ainslee muttered something under her breath and looked at the incoming dark clouds.

Ethan looked on as well and sighed. He was barely keeping up now. He doubted he could keep up if they were trudging through mud.

"Storm look bad," Par'karr said from behind him. "We find shelter!"

Nia narrowed her eyes and looked from the kobold to the coming dark clouds. "Do you really feel we should find shelter?"

The kobold bobbed his head enthusiastically. "Storms bad. Not get caught outside. Lightning! Boom!"

As if to punctuate Par'karr's statement, a thick bolt of lightning flashed off in the distance, hitting the side of the mountain and causing an explosion of rock from the mountain face.

"Thor's hammer!" Ainslee swore. "Did you see the size of that lightning!"

They all stared silently before exchanging glances. It was clear none of the others had seen lightning that powerful before. None of them except the kobold, who was the only native of this world.

Par'karr nodded vigorously, his eyes wide. "Very bad! Not get caught in open!"

Nia hissed and looked around. "There is no shelter here!"

"We'd better find some!" Ainslee growled. "Because those clouds look like they're moving quickly!"

They turned to watch the clouds and Ethan realized she was right. The clouds were moving faster than seemed possible. Given the little bit of wind, the clouds looked to be moving unnaturally quick, at least by *Earth* standards. But who knew what was normal on this world?

Yuliana turned to him, eyes worried. Even Luna seemed to sense the coming storm. The cat's ears were back, and she kept rubbing herself against the elf. "Can you make a shelter like you did before?"

Ethan remembered the last time he'd tried to make shelter. He'd done it, but it had used up more *Mana* than he'd had and left him in a similar state like he was now. He shook his head. "No way. The last time I didn't have enough mana and it burned through my stats. This time I have even less mana."

"We need to find cave!" the kobold urged. "Hide in cave until storm gone!"

"Where do we find one?!" the dwarf demanded, looking around at the forest to either side of them. "There's nothing but trees!"

They all looked around. Ainslee was right. The terrain was hilly, but there was nothing but trees to either side of the road. There was no telling if there were caves around or not. At least, not from their current vantage point.

"I have an idea," he told the group and sat down cross legged on the ground. Using his *Summon Minor Elemental* ability, he summoned an air elemental. It used up a good amount of his remaining *Stamina*, but hopefully it would be worth it.

Skill increase: Air Magic +1%.

The air elemental appeared, once again taking the form of a hawk or a raven composed of swirling air. As he had done once before when he scouted out the kobold cave, Ethan reached out and into the elemental's mind. When he blinked, he was seeing through the eyes of the air elemental.

Skill increase: Clairvoyance +1%.

Commanding the elemental to take flight, Ethan became momentarily dizzy as the creature quickly circled upward. In a moment, he was looking down at his party from above the trees. The air elemental circled higher and he was able to see the surrounding area.

As he expected, it was almost completely forest as far as the eye could see. But there were patches where the trees broke. One such patch was a small lake to the north, maybe 10 or 15 miles away. It looked like the river forked further east and fed into it. Another area to the north was a hilly, craggy area. There were large boulders and downed trees that covered a swath of the forest nearly a half a mile wide.

Looking south, he spotted a clear area a few miles away and commanded the air elemental to fly that direction. It took only a minute for the elemental to get him to a vantage point where he could see the area better. He instantly realized it could be what they were looking for. More importantly, it was close enough that they might make it before the storm hit.

The area was a cliff of sheer rock that looked like a hill had simply been shaved away with a giant axe. At the bottom of the rock wall was a field of huge, moss-covered rocks and boulders - the remnants of the rest of the hill. Some sort of earthquake, mudslide or other natural disaster had split the hill years or decades ago and now it might be just what they needed.

The air elemental flew even higher, giving him a literal bird's-eye view of the area. From several hundred feet up, it looked like that split hill was their best and closest option. Nothing else seemed remotely close.

Then his vision was spinning as the air elemental was tossed around like a rag doll. He felt the elemental's panic as an incredibly powerful gust of wind pulled the elemental along with it to the west.

Ethan commanded the elemental to fly lower but the

poor thing was rolled over and over as the mighty winds buffeted the elemental. Ethan stayed with it for only a minute longer, his stomach starting to lurch as the world spun around him through the creature's eyes. Then he jerked himself back into his own body.

Gasping, Ethan severed the connection with the air elemental. As he did, he willed it away and felt a sense of relief as it faded back to wherever it had come from. He blinked his eyes as he readjusted to his normal vision and looked up.

Up there, several hundred feet up, the wind was near hurricane speeds. No wonder those clouds were approaching so fast. Ignoring the new messages in his HUD, he looked around at the others.

"Did you find something?" Ainslee looked down at him hopefully.

Ethan pushed himself to his feet with a groan. "To the south, a few miles, there's a cliff. It's the only thing that seems remotely like it might provide shelter."

"We go now!" Par'karr said, pointing to the clouds. "Storm here soon!"

The clouds were closer now and they were just starting to actually be able to hear the boom of the lightning. The group didn't need any additional encouragement. Turning south, they followed Ethan into the forest.

23

T he wind had picked up and the dark clouds were almost upon them when they made it to the split hill. The booms of thunder had steadily gotten louder and closer and now sounded as if they were right on top of them. In addition, the wind was much stronger. It wasn't nearly as bad as the higher altitude wind, but it was enough to make normal talking difficult.

Ethan glanced around as they entered the clearing. It was just as he'd seen it from above. To the north was a small ridge, what remained of the hill. It dropped off into a sheer stone and dirt wall that was forty or fifty feet tall.

A small valley of sorts covered the dozen yards from the north part of the hill was the south part of the hill. The southern part had partially collapsed and was only half the height of the northern hill. If it had been sheer at one time, it was now worn and covered with vegetation.

Glancing at the small valley between the hills, Ethan could make out the large boulders he'd seen from the sky. All were the size of elephants and lay scattered in clusters around the area. If they were going to find a cave, this was their best bet.

"Fan out," he yelled over the wind. "Look for any caves."

Ainslee looked at him dubiously, her mouth twisting. "You really expect to find a cave in this?"

"Just search and be quick!" Nia hissed.

The dwarf made a face but did as she was asked. The rest of the group spread out too, looking at the hill faces, boulders and even vegetation. They searched for any caves or even something to provide them cover.

After ten minutes, they gathered in the middle of the valley. He already knew there were no caves. someone would have called out if there had been, but the disappointed looks confirmed it.

"I told you," Ainslee said smugly.

"We try." Par'karr shrugged, wrapping his little arms around himself to stave off the wind. "Storm will get bad!"

Ethan grimaced. He hadn't actually seen a cave here from the sky, but this had been the closest area that looked like it might have them.

"Too bad you can't make one of those shelters," Ainslee mumbled.

"I told you," he retorted. "I didn't have the *Mana* to do it then - not without almost dying - and I have even..."

Ethan trailed off as he looked around. On the way to Castlehaven, he'd literally formed a shelter out of nothing but ground. He'd used *Mana* not only to move and shape the earth, but also to harden it. What if he just reshaped rock, like he did with the flint arrowheads and creating the stone troll claw and feet? He didn't remember it taking much *Mana* at all.

"What is it, Ethan?" Yuliana asked, tilting her head.

"I might not be able to make a shelter like before," he replied as he approached the northern face. "But maybe I have enough mana to carve out a small cave - sort of like when I created the shelter."

"Don't remind me." Ainslee rolled her eyes. Then her expression became curious. "You can do that? Without bringing down the rest of the hill?"

"I have no idea," he replied. "But the alternative is weathering it huddled up next to a tree or one of those boulders."

"No!" Par'karr shouted. "No trees! Lightning hit tree! Bad!"

"Oh, right," Ethan muttered as he vaguely remembered reading that somewhere. Standing under a tree was bad during a lightning storm.

"If you can do something, you should try now," Nia said, casting a glance skyward. "We do not have much time."

Nodding, Ethan walked over to the north face. He already knew he could manipulate stone and earth. The question was: what was the most efficient use of his *Mana*? He checked his stats quickly.

Mana: 23
   Stamina: 3

His *Stamina* was extremely low from walking and then from summoning the elemental. He'd need to completely rely on his *Mana*. But how to use it? He'd have to focus solely on shaping the stone. No strengthening or anything else, just shaping.

Ethan walked over to a space between the northern rock face and a large boulder that stood six feet. He grinned as an idea came to mind. Looking back at the others, he waved them back. "Stand back a bit. I think this will work, but just in case... best to be out of the way."

His companions all took several steps away from him and Ethan nodded before turning around. Keeping his HUD up so he could keep an eye on his *Mana*, Ethan reached out to both the rock from the top of the boulder and the rock on the side of the cliff.

> **Skill increase: *Earth* Magic +1%.**
> *Mana:* 22

Slowly, channeling *Mana* into them, he willed them towards each other. At first, they didn't want to move, but he pushed more *Mana* into them.

> **Skill increase: *Earth* Magic +1%.**
> *Mana:* 19

The stone groaned but it began to move in an odd, almost liquid way. The rock from both surfaces flowed together and began to form what would become their roof.

> **Skill increase: *Earth* Magic +1%.**
> *Mana:* 17

He reached out for more of the rock and brought it together, forming at first a three-feet-wide roof, then five foot, six feet and finally an eight-feet-wide roof.

> **Skill increase: *Earth* Magic +1%.**
> *Mana:* 13

Eight feet was as long as the boulder, so he couldn't make it any deeper. He'd made the roof slanted, so water would run down it to the back of their stone shelter. Now he just needed a back.

He began repeating the process but this time, he shaped the rock to form the back of their shelter. He channeled more and more of his *Mana*, willing and shaping the stone as it groaned and protested.

Skill increase: *Earth* Magic +1%.
**   *Mana*: 5**

Breathing heavily, he stepped back and looked at his handiwork. What had been a six-feet space between a boulder and a sheer rock face was now a cozy six-foot-wide by eight-foot-long stone shelter.

And, the water shouldn't run over the sides, it should run backwards and run down the slight slope of the valley.

Ethan frowned and tilted his head as he looked at the valley. It did slope. And if it rained and water flowed down into this valley, it would go from west to east, or, right into their shelter. He swore.

"Ethan okay?" Par'karr asked.

"Not bad, wizard-boy," the dwarf said as she walked over to him.

"Yeah," he said glumly. "Except the water will flow right into the cave entrance. Why didn't I see that before!"

"Make pallet," Par'karr offered. "Like in kobold tent. *Water* flow under."

"A pallet?" Ethan asked, confused. The only pallets he was familiar with were the ones in stores. And they had no planks, no nails and no hammer to make any.

The kobold struggled to find the words and seemed to give up after a few seconds. Instead, Par'karr looked around and, finding several sticks, went about putting two sticks on the ground parallel to each other, then stacking more on top. He looked up and grinned. "See, water go under."

"Yes." Nia nodded. "We do something similar in the rainy season."

"Well, what are we waiting for?!" Ainslee bellowed. "Everyone start gathering logs and sticks! Now, people!"

Everyone rushed to obey. Whether they were actually listening to the dwarf or feeling the first drops of rain, he wasn't sure.

"Wizard-boy," she snapped. "While we gather logs and stuff, you go into your cave and make some holes for the water to flow out of on the back side, otherwise the cave'll just fill up."

Ethan snapped his head in the direction of the cave he'd created. Looking at the back, he realized she was right. He'd not only created a cave, he'd created a dam. There would be no place for the water to go and it would soon become a swimming pool.

Chiding himself for being stupid, he went back into the cave. Channeling most of his remaining *Mana*, he formed small holes in the bottom of the back of the cave wall, where the stone met the dirt.

Skill increase: *Earth* **Magic +1%.**
   ***Mana*: 2**

Wiping sweat from his brow and breathing heavily again, he dropped his concentration just as his companions began to drop off large sticks. Par'karr came bounding over and waved him out of the cave.

Then, one by one, the little kobold began laying the thickest branches on the ground, forming four parallel rows. Next, he took the eight next largest branches and laid them on top of the bottom row so that they were perpendicular. Finally, he laid the thinnest branches close together on top of the second row. Then, Par'karr took the blankets from his bedroll and laid them across the sticks, forming a platform of sorts.

"This best Par'karr can do," the kobold said as he stepped away.

"Not bad, little guy." Ainslee nodded. "We've got about a six-inch clearance. If the water gets higher than that, we're going to get drenched. But it's going to be a cold night. No way to start a fire on blankets."

Nia, who had been inspecting the kobold's handiwork, looked up. "Perhaps there is."

The foxgirl bounded up and raced around the valley before picking up a large rock. She brought it back and set it down in the middle of the pallet. "Can you make this stone as flat and wide as possible?"

Understanding dawned in Ethan and he checked his *Mana*.

Mana: 2

With only 2 points of *Mana*, he wasn't sure if he wanted to risk it. He'd burn up more stat points if he went too low. He started to shake his head but stopped, looking at his *Stamina*.

Stamina: 3

"I'll try," he told them and crawled into the cave. If he used too much *Stamina* and passed out, at least he'd already be in the cave. Forcing himself not to channel *Mana* through the crystal, he instead willed the stone to flatten.

As Ethan felt his *Stamina* leave him and felt the lethargy creeping in, the stone became as flat as a pancake. It spread out so that it was three feet by three feet. Enough room to build a small campfire.

Skill increase: *Earth* Magic +1%.
   Stamina: 1

Letting go of the magic and collapsing onto the pallet, Ethan smiled. "How's that?"

Before anyone could answer, the sky opened up and the rain began to come down in sheets. Par'karr and the women squealed and rushed into the cave and out of the wet.

Only once they were all in did Ethan notice that they had a "firepit" but nothing to burn. He looked up at the women and smiled. "Who wants to run back out and get some wood for us to burn?"

24

The storm was fully on them a few minutes later. Day turned into night as the dark clouds blotted out the sun. But every few minutes, night became day as thick bolts of lightning crashed to earth all around them.

Rain, intermixed with hail, pounded down all around them. Ethan was quickly thankful for Par'karr's pallet as water poured down the cliff, into and then through their cave. If it weren't for the kobold's idea, they'd be up to their ankles in mud.

The storm was easily one of the worst Ethan had experienced. He'd never actually been in a hurricane, but he imagined this was what it felt like. The rain and hail seemed to shoot into their cave nearly horizontally, soaking them all to the bone.

There was no more talk of a fire. With the wind and the rain whipping into the cave, they could only huddle under their cloaks in the back of the shelter - shivering and wet.

"How... long... do... these... storms... last?" Ainslee said, teeth chattering. She had her cloak and bedroll wrapped around her.

"Depends," Par'karr replied. "Sometimes hours. Sometimes days."

"DAYS?!" the dwarf sputtered and the kobold flinched.

"Sometimes." The kobold nodded quietly.

Ainslee growled something unintelligible but they all shared looks of concern. If this storm lasted for days, they'd be trapped in their little cave with no food, other than the few pieces of cheese they had left and soggy bread.

With the lightning strikes as powerful and frequent as they were experiencing, none of them would risk going out into the storm. Par'karr had been right. The storms were dangerous. If he hadn't warned them, who knew what might have happened.

Crack! As if it was reading his thoughts, a bolt of lightning struck a tree near them, splitting the tree and setting it on fire. The group watched the flames for a few seconds before they were extinguished by the rain.

Crack! The flames had just died out when another bolt struck the tree next to it, splitting it and setting it on fire. Ethan blinked back the afterimage and stared at the tree. "What are the chances of..."

Crack! Before he had even finished his sentence, another tree a few feet away was struck. This time, the tree burst into flames and toppled over.

"Thor's Hammer!" Ainslee gasped.

"Is that natural?" Yuliana breathed.

"I have no idea. I guess if there's a charge in the same general area there would be multiple strikes." Ethan shrugged. Even as he said it, he couldn't remember hearing about so many strikes in the same area.

Another lightning strike cracked from just behind them, the thunder rocking them. Ears pressed completely back, Luna whined and buried her head harder into Yuliana's lap. Ethan smelled ozone and shivered as the hair on his arms stood up. He looked to see the women's hair was starting to stand up as well.

That strike had been close. Too close. The charge in the air was palpable. Then another boom sounded behind them, momentarily deafening them even as it shook them and their pallet.

"That one was very close," Nia said.

Ethan's ears were ringing so loud, he could barely make out what the foxgirl had said. Instead he just nodded. That's when he caught the blue glow coming from his pouch. It was faint, but in the darkness of the storm he could just make it out.

Slowing opening his belt pouch, he looked inside. He could see the two Chymera crystals in the pouch, scattered among his coins. Both were glowing bright blue, just like when he channeled *Mana* into them. Except he hadn't channeled *Mana*.

He quickly brought up his HUD and verified his stats.

Mana: 15

His *Mana* had regenerated more quickly than he thought, but he knew he wasn't channeling any into the crystals. So why were they glowing? Was it some sort of residual from his earlier magic?

Another lightning strike cracked nearby. He was staring at the Chymera crystals when it happened and saw the glow in the crystals intensify. Had the lightning just charged them? His HUD was still up and he looked again at his stats.

Mana: 21

His *Mana* had just jumped up 6 points! Was that from the lightning strike? But how was that even possible? Unless. What if it was lightning? What if it was raw mystic *Mana*? Did that mean this was some sort of magical storm?

He nudged at the crystals with his will and unlike when he normally channeled *Mana* into them, now he sensed that they were full of *Mana*. He thought about trying to focus the *Mana* already in the crystal into a spell but quickly dismissed the idea. If the storm was charging it, who knew what actually trying to use magic would do. It could turn him into a lightning rod.

Another crack and then another and suddenly his *Mana* was back at his current maximum of 32. Then another and another. His *Mana* didn't increase any further but the crystals got brighter with each strike.

How much *Mana* could the crystals hold? And for how long? Could he store *Mana* in one or both of the crystals to use later? He remembered his Enchantment ability and suddenly wished he knew more about it.

Books! He needed books on magic and enchantment. He needed to figure out how all of this wizardry worked. At times, he felt like he had only touched the tip of the iceberg and there was still so much he might be able to do.

Ethan was thinking so hard about the books, that it took him a few minutes to notice that things had gone quiet. When he did, he looked up. It was still raining, but now there was no sleet and the cracks of thunder he heard were now heading south.

"Are we past the worst of it?" Yuliana asked, stroking Luna's head. The big cat's ears weren't pressed quite so hard against her head and Ethan guessed that was a good sign that the storm was moving past them.

"Let's hope so," growled the dwarf.

"Worst over," Par'karr said.

"Are you sure?" Ethan asked the little kobold.

Par'karr bobbed his head. "Storm never come back. Once lightning gone. Storm go soon."

"Considering how quickly it was upon us," Nia commented, "hopefully it will be gone just as quickly and we can resume our journey."

"Or we could just stay here," Ainslee suggested and then gestured to the cave. "We have shelter here."

"We should continue on," Nia stated, looking at the dwarf. "We should put as much distance as we can between ourselves and the town."

Ethan checked his *Stamina*.

Stamina: 4

Unlike his *Mana*, his *Stamina* hadn't been recharged by the storm. He wouldn't get far before collapsing.

"It might be best if we stayed here for now," he told them. He hated to appear to be the weak one, but dropping over on the trail would look even weaker.

The foxgirl flashed him an annoyed glance, but then she tilted her head and her face hardened. "You have used up too much magic."

Ainslee and Yuliana both looked over at him. The elf gave him a once over. "You do look really tired."

Fishing something out of her pack, the foxgirl pulled out a pewter mug and held it outside to collect water. In a few minutes, she pulled it back in and then thrust it at Ethan. "Here. Drink. Restore your stamina."

Nodding, Ethan took the offered mug and drank down the water. He repeated the process several times before his *Stamina* was back up to 12. While he drank, the others followed suit, restoring their own *Stamina*.

By the time the group had restored all the *Stamina* they could by drinking water, the storm was moving past and the rain had become a drizzle. To the east, they could see the sun shining. Nia was right, it was time to resume their journey.

It took them over an hour to make their way back to the road. The rain and lightning had all but washed away the trail they'd followed to get to the clearing. Mud and fast-moving drainage streams forced them to find ways around some of the obstacles.

When they finally did make it back to the road, Nia hissed and stopped them just before they left the forest to step onto the road. "Wait!"

They all paused and watched as the foxgirl sniffed the air for several minutes. After a minute, Nia motioned for them to stay put and she crept forward to the edge of the road.

Ethan watched the fox girl look back and forth on the road and they all mirrored her action, not really knowing what to expect. Then Nia knelt by the muddy road, staring at it for long minutes. Finally, she crept back to the group.

"What is it?" Ainslee asked worriedly. "Dragons?"

"Dragons would be flying, not walking." The foxgirl

rolled her eyes. "No, the scent is faint and the tracks are obscured by the rain, but I am sure it is the striped beasts we encountered with the wagons."

"Horses?" Ethan asked. Technically, he thought they might be zebras, but close enough. "With more wagons?"

His first thought was that it was another slave caravan. The elves hadn't mentioned any elves left in their village or another caravan, but perhaps they hadn't known.

"Yes, wagons," she said. "And they came from the town, they were not going to it."

"From the town?" Ethan frowned. That made no sense. There hadn't been any caravans in town headed this way.

"Yes." The foxgirl nodded. "They came from town and there were three wagons and six of the horse beasts. They were moving quickly."

Ethan let his frown deepen. Three wagons? Who could that be? If there had been another caravan in town, surely they would have seen it. And if it had arrived after they left, why hadn't it spent the day in town to restock?

"How come you didn't smell them before?" Ainslee asked with hands on hips.

"They were not here before," Nia snapped. "They rode past us after we left the road."

"After?" The dwarf screwed up her face in confusion. "You mean... during THAT storm?!"

Nia looked towards the dark clouds, still visible in the distance. "Yes."

"They crazy!" Par'karr squeaked.

"Maybe they had no choice," the elf said quietly and all eyes turned to her.

She smiled nervously with everyone looking at her. "We were nearly caught unaware and if it hadn't been for Ethan's magic, we would not have found a safe spot. Perhaps they were caught by surprise as well."

Ethan nodded. "That could be. But I wonder who they were."

"If we walk quickly," Nia suggested, "we may be able to catch them."

25

Only an hour later, Nia's earlier statement proved to be prophetic. The group came upon wagons. Or, at least, what remained of them.

Bodies of horses and men lay scattered across the road, along with the burned husks of wagons. Judging by the scorch marks, Ethan guessed the nearest wagons had taken a direct lightning strike.

Even as he examined it, he saw an alert in his HUD and checked. He'd gotten a skill increase.

Skill increase: Forensics +1%.

He screwed up his face in confusion at the skill and the increase. He remembered getting the skill weeks ago but it hadn't come into play since then. He guessed trying to figure out what had happened qualified as Forensics.

Ethan guessed that normally the carts would have travelled side by side, but these two were next to each other. Had the one in the middle been struck first and the other tried to go around it? It might have been trying to escape and tried to go around the other wagon when it was struck as well, just like those adjacent trees they'd seen struck.

Skill increase: Forensics +1%.

As he walked around the wagons, he could see that there were actually two blackened bodies in the back of the nearest two wagons. Even though the rain had washed away most of it, the smell of burnt flesh still assaulted his senses.

"It looks like both the wagons were struck by lightning," he thought aloud. "There were people in the back and they must have gotten the full brunt of the lightning and died instantly."

Skill increase: Forensics +1%.

He looked at the bodies of the horses and men nearby. "The ground and wagon were wet and probably carried the charge to the other men and the horses."

Skill increase: Forensics +1%.

Ethan walked to the furthest wagon, which was almost a hundred yards further on the road. The wagon had ended up on its side, blocking the road.

There were no scorch marks on this wagon and there was no one in the back. But the two horses were lying dead, still hitched to the wagon. The driver had probably seen the other two get struck and made a run for it. Somehow, the wagon had overturned.

Ethan looked and found an area where the dirt was

partially melted. He pointed down at it. "It looks like lightning struck here and probably sent electricity through the wet earth and into the animals. But where are the men?"

`Skill increase: Forensics +1%.`

Nia came up to stand next to him, sniffing the air. The foxgirl looked right and then left, her brow furrowing. "Their scent is faint, but there is another scent in the air. I do not know what it is."

There was suddenly movement from all sides as creatures burst from the forest. The monsters looked like huge snakes, arching up like cobras. The difference was, these things had human-like chests that sported two muscular arms. In their humanoid hands, they held stone axes.

There were four of them. Two coming at Ethan and Nia and two more coming at Ainslee, Par'karr and Yuliana. All of them had coppery-colored scales with rings of different sizes and colors around their tails.

He quickly sized them up in his HUD.

`Slitherstride Hunter`
    `Naga`
    `Hunter`
    `Level 5`

Ethan had fought nagas in various role-playing games but usually they were just snakes with human heads. These things were more like snake men with their large chests and arms. Hissing, the creatures lunged forward at them.

Backpedaling away from the charging naga, Ethan raised his *Elemental Armor*. He felt the *Stamina* drain out of him as he did and grimaced as he saw that his *Stamina* was already low.

Stamina: 4

With only 4 *Stamina* left, he wouldn't be able to summon his Minor Elemental. Ethan swore and brought up his staff in a defensive position. Remembering that he only had 12 *Health*, he knew that he'd need to avoid getting hit at any cost.

The naga hunter was on him then, swinging its axe down at his head. Ethan barely managed to dodge to the side and avoid the creature's powerful blow. The creature's tail whipped around as if to trip him or even possibly curl around him but stopped at the last moment. The creature narrowed its serpentine eyes and its forked tongue out several times.

Taking advantage of the naga's moment of hesitation and its seeming fear of fire, Ethan sent a bolt of fire into the creature's face.

You burn Slitherstride Hunter for 7 fire damage.

Skill increase: *Fire* magic +1%.

The naga hissed in pain and reared back. Ethan reached with *Earth* Magic and softened the axe head. If it had been metal, he could have made it explode but in this case it was just a sharpened piece of flint and became soft enough that it fell out of its binding.

The naga saw the axe head fall and brought the shaft up

in front of its face in confusion. As it did Ethan sent another bolt of fire into its face.

You critically burn Slitherstride Hunter for 13 fire damage.

Skill increase: *Fire* magic +1%.

The thing hissed again and slithered back several feet, clawing at its scaled face. Ethan took the opportunity to check out his companions.

Nia seemed to be holding her own but her opponent did not look injured at all. Even as he watched, the thing struck out with its mouth open and fangs exposed. The foxgirl nimbly dodged to the side and brought her staff down on the back of the snake-man's head. The naga snapped its head back and shook it several times before swaying back and forth, looking for an opening.

Glancing over to Yuliana, Par'karr and Ainslee, he saw the dwarf was bleeding from several wounds and moving slowly. The naga she faced off was also bleeding from several wounds, but it looked as if the dwarf had taken more than she'd given.

Par'karr's demon rabbits were hopping all over the other snake-man as it tried to lash out with its tail and axe at the nimble little creatures. The demon rabbits were too quick, deftly hopping back, over and around the frustrated naga's attacks even as they continued to drive their horns into the creature's scaled body.

Yuliana was between the kobold and the dwarf with Luna next to her, growling protectively. The elf reached out to heal Ainslee but she jerked to the side before Yuliana could finish. The naga had struck at her deliberately to make her move. They must understand healing magic.

Ethan wanted to finish off his naga so that he could help the others but he needed to check his *Mana* first.

Mana: 23

He'd used up a third of his *Mana*, so he'd need to be careful. He didn't have *Stamina* he could fall back on if he ran out.

The naga came at him again, wielding the axe handle like a club. He considered using fire again, but remembered that *Earth* snakes tended to hibernate in the winter, or at least, became more lethargic. Hopping back, Ethan used his *Water* magic to pull the heat from the creature.

You freeze Slitherstride Hunter for 11 cold damage.
> **Slitherstride Hunter is Slowed.**

Skill increase: *Water* magic +1%.

The effect was almost instant as the creature's shoulders seemed to slump and its head sagged forward. The naga's eyes became unfocused and even its tail, which had been swishing back and forth, slowed visibly. The snake-man stopped its advance and blinked in confusion.

Mana: 21

With his naga distracted, Ethan reached out and did the same to the other three nagas with the same effect. Immediately, their movements slowed, and they hesitated in confusion.

Mana: **15**

"I slowed them!" he yelled. "Hit them with everything you've got before they recover!"

He turned back to his naga to see the thing starting to retreat slowly. For a moment, he thought about letting it go. Then he imagined the naga and its friends bursting into their camp in the middle of the night.

No. He couldn't allow it to get away, recover and ambush them later. He knew he couldn't kill it with his staff. Nia had been hitting her naga more often and harder than him and it was still standing. He had to use something else.

Looking around, the only thing nearby was the naga's axehead. He screwed up his face as he thought about the best way to use it. Then he got an idea.

Reaching out, he reshaped the axehead into a large spike. Picking the spike up with Air, he hurled it into the back of the naga's head with as much force as he could.

```
You   critically   pierce   Slitherstride
Hunter for 19 damage.
   Slitherstride Hunter dies.
   You gain 50 experience. Experience
to next level 895.

Skill increase: Air magic +1%.
```

The creature collapsed onto the ground and Ethan reached out with Air and pulled the spike free. He turned to Nia's naga, ready to send the spike into it but hers was not retreating. It had curled its body around the fox girl and was crushing her. Its mouth was opened and poised to strike down with its fangs at Nia's exposed neck.

Not hesitating, Ethan sent the spike in through the creature's open mouth and up into its brain.

```
You critically pierce Slitherstride
Hunter for 23 damage.
    Slitherstride Hunter dies.
    You gain 25 experience. Experience
to next level 870.

Skill increase: Air magic +1%.
```

The naga's head snapped back and the thing's body simply collapsed onto the ground. Nia was still in its coils, but he could see the foxgirl trying to push the thing's body off.

The other two were in retreat and Ethan sent the Flint Spike of Naga Slaying, as he had just named it, after them. He took down the one that Par'karr and the rabbits were chasing. He sent the spike through the back of its skull and the creature toppled over, body twitching as the demon rabbits continued to attack.

```
You critically pierce Slitherstride
Hunter for 19 damage.
    Slitherstride Hunter dies.
```

You gain 25 experience. Experience to next level 845.

Skill increase: Air magic +1%.

The last one seemed to realize what was happening and tried to move faster but Ainslee barreled into it from the side, rocking it with the impact.

The naga pivoted and struck down at the dwarf's face with its open mouth. Surprised, Ainslee managed to get her left arm up in time to take the blow. The naga's fangs sank into the dwarf's arm and she screamed.

The naga pulled its head back, preparing to strike again but the Flint Spike of Naga Slaying slammed into its eye and embedded itself deep in the creature's brain. The naga convulsed once and then fell back.

You critically pierce Slitherstride Hunter for 20 damage.
  Slitherstride Hunter dies.
  You gain 25 experience. Experience to next level 820.

Skill increase: Air magic +1%.

"Poison," Ainslee choked, dropping to her knees and cradling her left arm. "I'm done for."

Yuliana rushed over to her and her green light began to envelop her hands. Just before she touched the dwarf Ethan cried out. "Wait!"

Unsure, the elf hesitated. She looked down at the grimacing dwarf. "I must heal her."

"Do you have some spell or ability that can cure poison?" he asked frantically. He remembered MMORPGs and role-playing games that poison and disease were usually treated differently than normal wounds. You had to cure them separately. What if that was the case here? What if Yuliana's magic healed the bite wound, sealing the poison inside?

"I do not know what you mean?" the elf responded, both concern and confusion wrinkling her forehead. "I need to heal her."

"Wait!" Ethan hissed. He swore as he rushed over to Ainslee. He remembered some first aid he'd learned, or maybe he had just seen it in movies. He couldn't remember now.

"Why are you waiting?!" the dwarf said through clenched teeth. "Heal me already!"

"No," he said, trying to sound as confident as possible. "We have to remove as much of the poison as possible."

"How-" The dwarf bit down her reply as pain seemed to wrack her. "How do you... propose we do... that?"

Ethan wasn't completely sure how it worked, but in the movies, they sucked out the venom. He reached and grabbed her arm. The dwarf seemed too weak to resist.

"Whatever... you're... going to... do," the dwarf muttered. "Do... it quick... I can't... feel... my arm."

Ethan swore. That probably meant the poison was moving up her arm. He quickly grabbed the rope from his pack and tied it tightly around her upper arm like a tourniquet to prevent any more poison from getting into her body.

Skill increase: Healing +1%.

Ripping the sleeve on her shirt, he exposed the fang

marks on her forearm. Hoping he was doing the right thing, he wrapped his lips around the wounds and began sucking.

Skill increase: Healing +1%.

Warm blood filled his mouth, a strong coppery taste and he fought the urge to retch. There was also something in the taste. Something strong and bitter. He pulled away and spit it out, once again having to stop himself from retching.

Skill increase: Healing +1%.

Clamping his mouth on the wound again, he sucked again, this time tasting more of the bitterness. He also started to feel his mouth go numb. That must be the poison. Maybe it was working.

He spit and repeated two more times before his mouth was too numb to continue sucking. Ainslee had passed out. At least, he hoped she had passed out and wasn't dead.

Skill increase: Healing +3%.

Ethan's mouth and tongue were completely numb and when he tried to tell Yuliana to heal the dwarf, his words were unintelligible. Luckily, the elf knew what he meant and the green glow of her healing magic surrounded the dwarf.

"I've healed her all I can," Yuliana said as she removed her hands from the dwarf.

His mouth and tongue were still numb so Ethan nodded.

The dwarf's face was cold and clammy and covered in sweat. Her breath was shallow but steady. Ethan didn't know any symptoms of poisoning or how long it might take someone to recover. Plus, anything he might have known would certainly be suspect given the sheer size and alien nature of the naga.

All they could do now was wait. Wait and hope that the dwarf recovered.

26

Despite the unconscious dwarf, Nia insisted they move on after ten or fifteen minutes. "That was most likely a hunting party. That means there may be more."

"How do we move her?" Yuliana asked.

"Dwarf heavy." Par'karr nodded.

Ethan nodded too, his mouth no longer numb but was now tingling with the all too familiar pins and needle sensation he felt when his arm or leg fell asleep. He tried talking but his words were slurred. "How...far...we... go?"

Nia shrugged. "We do not know where their hunting grounds are. So we should move as far as possible."

Ethan cursed. He was at his weakest at the moment, with his stat loss. He hadn't been able to lift the dwarf before the stat loss. There was no way he'd be able to do it now that he was so much weaker. He looked around to see what they had to work with.

It became immediately apparent that the only things they had were the wagons and whatever was on the bodies of the dead men. "Spread out and search the wagons and the men. See what, if anything we can find that might be useful."

The group did but there wasn't much. The wagon that had overturned had a basket of jerky and several bundles of wrapped cheese. They also found several blankets for the men to sleep on and, of course, several axes. The only other things were the wagons themselves.

Ethan did search the bodies of the creatures but like so many others, there was no loot. Not even a coin purse or a piece of jewelry. That part, at least, wasn't like the normal MMORPGs or role-playing games. In those, nearly everything dropped loot.

Unfortunately, Ethan wasn't an engineer, nor was he MacGyver. He couldn't just make something useful from a bunch of wagon parts and a stick of gum - even if he had gum. In the end, the only idea he could think of was to create a makeshift stretcher using two saplings they cut down and two of the blankets that they tied to the saplings.

They all took turns drinking at the river and filling their water jugs. It was late in the day and this would be the last bit of *Stamina* he could restore by drinking water. After this, only rest would restore it. He really needed to learn how to make some sort of potion of *Stamina*. *Health* potions and *Mana* potions wouldn't be bad either, if they existed.

Since Nia was the best fighter and Par'karr was too short to effectively carry the stretcher, the job fell to Ethan and Yuliana. The two of them together managed to lift up the litter and, after stuffing several blankets on their shoulders, placed the ends of the litter on their shoulders.

It was difficult for the two of them, but not impossible. Carrying the heavy dwarf between them, they followed Nia down the road, with Par'karr bringing up the rear.

The group walked until dark, Nia adamant about getting as far from the site of the attack as possible. When they could no longer see well, the fox girl called a halt. She looked around the area, her eyes better than any of the others.

"I do not know if there is a better place to camp," Nia told them.

Groaning as they bent down, Ethan and Yuliana lowered the dwarf to the ground. They set her down gently. Ainslee didn't stir. Her chest still moved, but otherwise the dwarf had shown no other signs of life.

Interestingly, he noticed that unconscious as she was, Ainslee did not snore. Assuming she recovered, he wondered if he could poison her every night - just a little. He smiled at the thought but then chided himself. He shouldn't make jokes when he had no idea if she would recover.

Pain in his shoulders quickly distracted him from his thoughts of poisoning the dwarf. Massaging his shoulder, Ethan stretched his neck left and right. Remembering the foxgirl's question, he looked around. "We could camp in the trees, but I don't know that it buys us any additional protection."

Nia considered his words and looked to either side of the road. "We should camp in the middle of the road then. Even if they sneak up on us, they must break cover to attack."

Stifling a yawn, Ethan nodded. He was exhausted and he didn't want to walk anymore. And he really didn't want to carry the dwarf anymore today. His legs, arms and shoulders all ached.

He looked back at Yuliana. Like him, the elf was breathing heavily. Perspiration beaded her forehead and she alternated rubbing her shoulders. She looked as exhausted as he felt but the elf hadn't complained the entire time.

"Then you two rest while Par'karr and I gather wood for a fire," she told them and then motioned for the little kobold to follow her.

The elf dropped down into a sitting position and her mountain lion came over to rub against her. Yuliana scratched the big cat's chin absently, but her eyes were unfocused. "You okay?"

Yuliana looked up and he could see the exhaustion in her usually flawless face. She tried to smile, but it didn't reach her eyes. Ethan thought the elf could fall asleep at any moment.

"Why don't you lay out your bedroll and grab some sleep," he suggested.

The elf seemed to remember her pack and shrugged weakly. She chuckled softly. "I'm not sure if I can move my arms."

Ethan knew how she felt. His own pack was still on his back and he let it slide down off his shoulders. Her eyes were half closed, and he thought she might fall asleep where she sat.

His *Mana* had regenerated during the walk and he reached out with air and gently pulled the straps of her backpack down over her arms so that the backpack slid to the ground. The elf was momentarily confused but then looked at Ethan and gave him another weak smile.

Skill increase: Air Magic +1%.

Continuing to use air, he opened her pack and pulled out her blankets. He laid them down on the ground next to her and then gently picked her up, causing her to squeal as she left the ground. Moving her over the blankets, he lowered her slowly to the ground. Then he used a last bit of air to wrap the blanket around her.

Skill increase: Air Magic +1%.

She looked over at him with her green eyes and gave him a smile. This time, the smile reached her eyes. She started to speak but yawned. She looked slightly embarrassed but smiled again. "Thank you, Ethan."

Then she shifted slightly under the covers and closed her eyes. The mountain lion, who had watched Yuliana float in the air, padded over to the elf and lay down next to her. Snuggling her head into the nook of the elf's arm, Luna stared at Ethan for a long moment before slowly closing her own eyes.

Ethan looked over to Ainslee, still on the pallet. The dwarf's pack was strapped to her legs and, groaning, he crawled over and untied her pack. Since he was right there, he opened it and pulled out her blankets instead of using magic. He spread them out them near Yuliana and then, using Air, picked up the dwarf and placed her on the blankets.

Skill increase: Air Magic +1%.

With both the women tucked in, Ethan crawled back over to his own pack, spread his own blankets out and lay down on them. He normally took the first watch. As exhausted as he was, it was going to be a very long watch.

He laid his head down on his blankets for a moment to

rest his eyes and the next thing he knew someone was shaking him awake.

"Ethan," came Par'karr's voice. "Your turn."

Ethan blinked awake. "What? Did I doze off?"

"You asleep when we come back," the kobold said. "Par'karr let Ethan sleep. Me take first watch."

Yawning, Ethan sat up and nodded at the little kobold. "Thanks."

"Ethan tired," the kobold replied. "Ethan needed sleep."

"I did," he chuckled softly. "About 24 hours of sleep."

"Want Par'karr take second watch?" the kobold offered.

Looking at the kobold's face, Ethan could see the fatigue in the scaly features. He shook his head. He was starting to wake up and he felt he owed it to the little guy for taking the first watch and letting him sleep. "No, bud, I got it. But thanks!"

The kobold nodded tiredly and then walked over to his bundle of blankets. Par'karr lay down and threw a blanket over himself before closing his eyes.

Ethan was tired and his muscles ached, but he managed to keep himself awake and keep the fire going until it was time for the next watch. Having fallen asleep without eating anything, he was famished and dug through the packs for some of the jerky they'd taken from the loggers.

His watch was, thankfully, uneventful. No snake-men, tentacled creatures, dragons or anything else bothered them. When it was time for the next watch, he woke Nia and then promptly fell back asleep.

When he awoke the next morning, it was to the sound of dwarven snores. Ethan blinked awake and sat up. He looked over to where the dwarf lay, apparently sleeping regularly.

The sun wasn't quite up yet, and he saw Yuliana sitting by the fire with Luna's head in her lap.

The elf looked over at him and he could see bags under her eyes. She nodded towards the dwarf. "I healed her several more times, but it didn't seem to do anything. Then, about fifteen minutes ago, she started snoring."

"That's probably a good thing," he said and then flashed the elf a smile, "for her. Maybe not so much for us."

Her stomach growled at that moment and she flashed him an embarrassed smile. "No berries, nuts or edible plants around here. I looked."

Ethan yawned involuntarily and stretched. "I'm up now. If you want to take Luna and go look a little further, I'll keep an eye on things here."

Yuliana's stomach growled again, and she gave him another embarrassed smile. "I think my stomach wants me to do just that."

"The stomach never lies," he replied with a grin.

Luna whined quietly as the elf stood up. She continued lying by the fire for a moment until the mountain lion realized that Yuliana wasn't going to sit back down. Then the big cat got to her feet and sat back on her haunches, looking from Yuliana to Ethan.

"I will be back shortly," she said and, motioning to Luna, strode off into the forest.

A few minutes after the elf left, Ainslee's snores became a snort and then muttered something incoherent. When Ethan turned to check on the dwarf, she was propping herself up on her side, blinking as she looked around the still-dark camp.

Focusing on Ethan, the dwarf smacked her lips. "Is it breakfast time?"

27

Ainslee's body might still be weak, but her appetite was not. The dwarf ate all of the bread, the cheese and the jerky before Nia had returned with a breakfast of rabbits to cook.

The others just stared at the dwarf as she literally ate everything they had. Considering what had happened to Ainslee, none of them wanted to say anything. Most likely the dwarf needed the extra calories. Even so, Ethan hated to see all of their backup food gone. There might come a time when they would need that.

"What?" Ainslee muttered with a full mouth as she looked up and saw everyone staring at her. "I was hungry!"

Nia turned back to the fire, suddenly interested in the rabbits on the spit. Yuliana looked down at Luna, whose head was in her lap and busied herself with scratching the cat. Ethan just shrugged and bent down to pack up his bedroll.

Par'karr just nodded and smiled. "Ainslee have good appetite!"

The dwarf snorted and looked around. "So it doesn't look like we're in the same place. I take it we beat the snake men?"

"Naga." Par'karr nodded.

"Yeah, whatever," Ainslee replied. "I don't really remember much, other than being bitten. Where are we? How did I get here?"

"We are several hours' journey from the site of the naga attack," Nia said as she rotated the spit. "Ethan and Yuliana carried you."

"Well, thanks for not leaving me behind." The dwarf looked between Ethan and the elf and smiled. For the first time since he'd met her, Ainslee's smile seemed genuinely warm.

She held up her forearm that Ethan had bandaged with pieces of one of the blankets. Ainslee looked to Yuliana. "I guess you healed the poison?"

The elf finished chewing some berries she had found and shook her head. Yuliana pointed to Ethan. "It was Ethan. He stopped the poison from spreading and then sucked it out."

The dwarf's eyes went wide as she turned to Ethan. "You what?!"

"It's a medical practice on my world," Ethan responded, suddenly feeling embarrassed. "You have to suck the poison out before too much of it gets into the bloodstream."

"How come you didn't die?" the dwarf asked in confusion. "I mean, it was poison. And you sucked it."

"I didn't swallow, I spit," he snickered. When no one reacted to his crude sexual innuendo, he sighed. Apparently, that didn't translate for his companions.

At times, he really did miss his gaming buddies. They would have gotten the joke. Sure, they would have groaned at the 12-year-old humor, but they would have gotten the joke, at least. "I spit it out. But, it did make my mouth go numb for a while."

"It made you not snore!" Par'karr offered happily.

Ainslee narrowed her eyes. "I don't snore."

"The rabbit is ready," Nia interrupted, saving them from an argument.

The group ate the two rabbits quickly, with Nia insisting that they get on the way. Ainslee moved slowly but insisted that she was able to walk on her own. Neither Ethan nor Yuliana argued with the dwarf. They were both still sore from carrying the dwarf the previous day.

As soon as they were all packed, the group continued their journey down the road. This time they kept a sharp eye out for berries and nuts. Yuliana had found only a handful of berries earlier and was still hungry.

Ethan noticed Ainslee was puffing as she walked along, which he assumed was due to the lingering effects of the poison. Part of him felt bad for the dwarf, but the other part didn't feel quite so bad as he was dragging too.

Checking his HUD again, he had actually gained another point back in all of his stats.

```
Strength: 7
   Agility: 7
   Hardiness: 7
   Intellect: 12
   Intuition: 7
   Charisma: 7

Health: 14
   Mana: 34
```

Stamina: 14

He groaned as he looked at his stats. At least he had slightly more *Health* and *Stamina*. Ethan's *Mana* had also regenerated to maximum - at least, his current maximum.

Not for the first time, he wished there was some way to accelerate the healing of his stats. It was one of a thousand questions he needed answers to. Ethan hoped he would learn some of the answers in the guild library.

Just before lunch time, Nia stopped the group. They immediately went on alert, hands going to weapons. The foxgirl sniffed the air, tilting her head to the side. "There is something sweet, this way. It smells like...honey."

"Honey?" the others echoed.

"They make mead from honey," Ainslee offered brightly.

Ethan snorted. Somehow, things seemed to always end up coming back to alcohol with the dwarf.

"Yes." Nia nodded. "It is very rare and highly prized on my world. I have only tasted it a few times, but it is sweet beyond description."

"I can barely hear the bees over the sound of the river." Yuliana nodded and pointed to the left. "At least a hundred yards that way."

"Honey good," Par'karr said with a toothy grin. "But hard to get."

"Hard to get?" Ethan asked, looking down at the kobold.

"Bee sting painful." He grimaced.

Ethan looked over at the others then back at Nia. "Let's check it out."

The fox girl nodded and led them off the road to the left. They had passed over a bridge earlier so once again, the river was on their left. When they reached the bank of the river, the group looked for some way to cross.

The river was at least twenty yards across and looked deep enough that they couldn't see the bottom. There were no stones they could use to traverse the river. Nor was there any other way Ethan could see to get across. "Looks like we'll have to swim."

"Yes," the foxgirl agreed and began to strip off her pack.

Ethan shrugged and slipped off his pack as well. It wasn't like there was anyone on the road or nearby to take it.

He noticed that neither Ainslee nor Yuliana had removed their packs. In fact, both looked extremely nervous.

"I'll just wait here," the dwarf said hesitantly.

"As will I," Yuliana said.

"Can you not swim?" Nia asked.

He glanced at the foxgirl to see she had stripped down to her underclothes. Ethan didn't realize he was staring until he saw her glance his way. When she saw him gawking, she gave him a knowing smile.

"You may close your mouth," the foxgirl snickered.

"Oh.. I... uh.." he sputtered and felt his face grow warm.

"I know you want me," Nia said. "But it cannot be. You are not my alpha."

Had there been a tone of regret in her last words? Ethan struggled to come up with a response to the foxgirl but luckily was saved by Ainslee.

"I can't swim," the dwarf snapped. "On my world, the oceans are lava, not water. And we don't go swimming in them! About the only water we do get are the hot springs. They're too shallow to swim in. Some of the towns have lakes, but they're not common. Personally, I've never been to one."

Nia turned away from Ethan and looked at the elf with a raised eyebrow. "And you?"

"I do not like deep water," the elf replied, her eyes shooting to the river before coming back to the foxgirl. "I will stay here."

"Par'karr ready," the kobold said, and they all turned to see that the kobold was completely naked.

"Um, Par'karr," Ethan said. "I think you can keep your loincloth on."

"It get wet." The kobold shook his head.

"Alrighty then," he said, exchanging glances with the foxgirl. Nia just shrugged and pulled a dagger from her sheath. Seeing that, Ethan took his own dagger and stuffed it into his boots.

Leaving Ainslee and Yuliana to watch their packs, he and the others swam across the river. Unlike Ethan, who had learned to swim at the YMCA, both the kobold and the foxgirl seemed to only know how to doggie paddle.

Carrying his boots in his left hand and keeping them above the water, he did a single breaststroke. Yet even with his single-armed breaststrokes, Ethan quickly outdistanced them and found himself alone in the center of the river. It wasn't until then that it occurred to him that there could be anything in the river. Piranhas. Alligators. Sharks, for all he knew. Pushing himself to swim faster, he made it across before the others.

Once all of them were on the opposite bank, Ethan slipped on his boots. Par'karr never wore shoes but Nia had been wearing boots. Now she was barefoot, but if it bothered her, she didn't show it.

The group followed her as she moved slowly through the trees and he tried not to get distracted by the view he had of her backside. At least, the part of her backside that the tail didn't hide. There was no denying the foxgirl had an incredible body.

Ten yards into the forest, Ethan began to hear the bees too. They moved closer and he began to see bees flying around the forest. But of course, these couldn't be normal bees. No, he sighed. They were giant bees.

The bees that buzzed looked like *Earth* bees but were easily the largest he had ever seen. If he had to guess, he would say they were four or five inches long.

"Those are very big bees," Nia commented. "I've never seen them that large."

"Big bees," Par'karr agreed with wide eyes. "Bigger than Par'karr see before."

They found the hive a few minutes later. The hive was six feet tall and five feet round. And it was swarming with the large bees.

"I would risk getting the honey if these were normal-size bees," the foxgirl whispered. "But these bees. Too many stings may be fatal."

Beside them, Par'karr nodded his head. "Too many bees kill. Big bees kill more! Use smoke. Make bees leave."

Ethan remembered that from somewhere, maybe a YouTube video. The beekeepers smoked out the beehives before getting the honey. Ethan looked around at the dense foliage. If they started a fire here, the entire area could go up. "I don't know if we can do that and not burn down the entire place."

Nia pouted, making her look incredibly cute. She saw him staring again but before she could say anything Ethan waved her off. "I know... I know. You're taken."

She nodded but then looked hopefully at him. "Can you magic it?"

Ethan looked at the hive and all the bees. He could use air to probably pull the hive down if he really wanted, but he didn't think the bees would leave. They'd probably just get really agitated and attack anyone nearby - which was them.

His best bet was to use his fire elemental armor. He wasn't sure if it would kill the bees if they touched it, but the heat alone should keep them at bay. Then he frowned.

The heat might actually burn their wings off, if it didn't kill them outright. They might be giant bees, but they were still honeybees. Then he thought of his *Earth* armor. It seemed to give him some sort of damage resistance. Would that work? If it didn't work, things were going to get really painful for him.

Earth or fire? Kill the bees or not? Ethan wasn't a cruel person at heart and the idea of burning off the bees' wings for no reason didn't sit well with him. He decided to try *Earth*.

Ethan pulled up his HUD and checked his *Stamina*.

Stamina: 8

He sighed in disgust. Using the armor would drop him down to 3 *Stamina*. He shrugged. At least the river was nearby, and he could drink water until his *Stamina* was restored.

"I'll use my elemental armor," he told them and pulled out his knife. "But if I were you two, I'd go back to the river and wait there. If this does work, they're going to get really angry at me."

The two nodded and ran off back towards the river. "Here goes nothing."

With his knife in hand, he activated his *Earth Elemental Armor*. Ethan watched as his skin was completely covered in stone. He actually hadn't been sure it would work. The last time he'd used it, he'd been next to a cliff wall. But then again, he could use his fire armor without a fire near. He shrugged. Magic.

Stepping out from behind the tree, he began walking towards the hive. Bees buzzed around him but didn't seem to pay him much attention. When he reached the hive, he took a deep breath. It was the moment of truth.

Taking his knife, he began cutting a two-feet-by-one-foot section of the hive. Immediately, the buzzing became frantic and agitated. He felt bees hitting him. Then the messages began to scroll by on his HUD.

```
Giant Bee pierces you for 0 damage.
   Elemental armor (Earth) absorbs 5
points of piercing damage.


Skill increase: Earth magic +1%.


Giant Bee pierces you for 0 damage.
   Elemental armor (Earth) absorbs 5
points of piercing damage.


Skill increase: Earth magic +1%.


Giant Bee pierces you for 0 damage.
   Elemental armor (Earth) absorbs 5
points of piercing damage.
```

Skill increase: *Earth* **magic +1%.**

The messages began to scroll by as more and more bees attacked him. He had no idea how much damage was being blocked by the armor, but he had never established whether or not the damage reduction had a limit.

He quickly finished cutting away the honeycomb, seeing the soft honey inside. He looked down at it, checking it in his HUD.

```
Queen Bee Honey
    Type: Honey
    Duration: N/A
    Effect: 1 serving of honey provides
0.6 of your nutritional needs.
    Other: Queen Bee Honey has unique
healing properties. A single serving
can restore all Stamina, Mana and
Karma. It also restores Health at the
rate 5 Health per serving. In
addition, each serving restores a
point of ability damage.
```

Ethan gawked at the description and was almost too slow as a bee tried to enter his open mouth. Clamping it shut, he turned and ran towards the water. The bees followed him for a dozen yards before breaking off.

He slowed and scrolled through his messages. The bees had attempted to sting him dozens of times. Ethan stopped and read a message that he'd almost missed with all the bee stings.

You have reached Rank 3 in *Earth* Magic.

+1 *Intellect*.

Making sure there were no bees around, he grinned. Not only had he managed to get something with healing properties, he'd also ranked up *Earth* Magic. Excitedly, he ran back to tell the others about the honey.

28

After a bit of testing, Ethan determined that a "serving" size of the honey was roughly a portion of the honeycomb the size of his fist. Par'karr and each of the women took one serving, leaving them with six additional servings.

Just as the description stated, it restored their *Stamina* completely to its maximum. That in itself would have been great, but it also seemed to heal whatever lingering poison effects Ainslee was feeling as she seemed back to her normal self after finishing her portion.

Ethan went last. They had discussed it and Par'karr and the women insisted that he eat the remaining servings to restore his lost stat points. He argued against it and in the end, agreed to eat four of them and save the other two, in case they needed them.

Once it was settled, he brought the first piece of honey-comb to his mouth and bit into it. Sweetness and flavor exploded into his mouth and he let out an involuntary groan of pleasure. It had been almost a month since he'd been on *Earth* and had some candy or anything nearly as sweet as the honey. When the honey hit his taste buds it made him tingle all over.

When he'd finished the honey, he checked out his stats.

```
You have regained a point of Strength.
    You   have   regained   a   point   of
Agility.
    You   have   regained   a   point   of
Hardiness.
    You   have   regained   a   point   of
Intellect.
    You   have   regained   a   point   of
Intuition.
    You   have   regained   a   point   of
Charisma.
```

He grinned when he saw that it had also healed his stat damage. Ethan also felt energized by the honey, like he'd just awaken from a restful night's sleep. It was an amazing feeling. He also felt completely full, as though he'd eaten a meal.

Eating the other 3 pieces, he waited for a moment and then checked his HUD again.

```
Strength: 10
   Agility: 11
   Hardiness: 11
   Intellect: 17
   Intuition: 11
   Charisma: 11
```

```
Health: 22
  Mana: 44
Stamina: 44
```

The honey had restored his stats. His Strength was now at its maximum. Most of the other stats were only a few points down. All except *Intellect*. With the point he had just gained from his increased *Earth* Magic skill, his *Intellect* score was 24.

It would take another week before he'd be completely healed. Unless he went back and got some more honey. But now that the bees were agitated, he wasn't sure if his *Earth* armor would last long enough to get him safely in and out.

"Go back and get some more!" Ainslee insisted, as if the dwarf had been reading his mind. But then again, considering some of the bland food they'd been eating lately, it wasn't really a surprise.

"Yuliana, can you tell if they're still agitated?" he asked the elf. Her hearing was uncanny and if anyone would know, she would.

The elf, who was licking the honey off her fingers, tilted her head. He saw her long slender ears twitch for a second and then she turned back to him. "The buzzing is louder and faster. I would say they are still agitated."

"Let's leave them alone for now," he said. "I have no idea how long my *Earth* armor would hold up against them if they're already upset."

"It worked before," the dwarf argued.

"Yes," he replied. "But before, they didn't start attacking until I started cutting into the hive. This time, they'd probably attack me on sight. That means more bites and more damage. If my armor failed, I'd probably die instantly from the sheer number of bites."

"Oh," Ainslee growled. "What about waiting until they calm down?"

"That could be all day," Yuliana said. "They are defending their territory and their hive now."

"Oh," the dwarf grunted but then shrugged. "Well then, let's mark this some way and stop here on the way back."

"No need to mark it." The foxgirl grinned. "I could smell it, remember. I'll know when we pass this way again."

"Then it's settled," the dwarf said, standing up and grabbing her pack. "Then let's get going. We need to cover some distance and make camp in time for Nia to find us a good dinner."

It was clear to all of them that Ainslee was back to normal. The lethargic dwarf who had been struggling along earlier was gone. The honey's amazing healing properties had done the trick.

He felt good that they had saved some of it for an emergency. Unfortunately, Ethan couldn't remember if honey would go bad. He hoped it didn't. And he did hope whatever healing properties it had didn't diminish over time.

THE GROUP RESUMED their trek eastward and walked for several more hours before small farms began to crop up. In each case, it had been burned to the ground with the bodies of livestock littering their yards. After the third one, they stopped.

"This might be the beginning of *Manai*'s village," Ethan

said as he looked around the ruined husk of the house. If so, that meant this was the work of the priestess of Hel and her men.

"Silvershade," Yuliana whispered.

"What?" he asked.

"Their village," the elf replied, "is called Silvershade."

"We're going to eat good tonight!" the dwarf bellowed happily and pointed. Following her finger, Ethan saw several pigs near a trough. These pigs must have escaped the slaughter but returned to the familiar setting they were used to.

"Yes! I will eat good too!" cried Yuliana and the elf bolted towards a group of small trees near the burned-out barn. Ethan scanned the trees and saw that they were pear trees. At least, he thought they were pear trees. Unlike the greenish pears he was used to, these were a dark crimson.

They followed the elf and began to pick the pears and fill their packs. They would make good snacks along the way and if nothing else, would give Yuliana something to eat for a few days.

The pigs walked over to them, possibly expecting to get fed. Ainslee insisted they take the pigs with them for dinner time. Ethan was hesitant but Nia and Par'karr were both salivating over them too so they tied them together with their rope and used it as a leash to lead them along.

Following the road, it only took them an hour to reach the village of Silvershade - or rather, what had once been the village of Silvershade. The entire village had been burned to the ground and the stench of burned-out wood permeated the air.

Silvershade had been slightly larger than Hawkshead, but not a single building stood untouched by fire. Some stone buildings still had walls standing but their roofs had been burned and had collapsed. Any building that had been built of wood was nothing but a burned-out husk.

As the group took in the desolation, Nia's nose twitched. She began sniffing around and then moved back to the group. She subtly pointed to what Ethan guessed had been an inn or tavern. It was one of the few buildings that had stone walls. "There are people in that one."

Ethan glanced at the building. The walls were blackened but still intact. Like the other stone buildings, the roof had collapsed and anything flammable had burned away - doors, shutters and even support beams.

"People like humans, elves or dwarves?" he whispered.

The foxgirl nodded. "Five scents and a... canine."

"Survivors," he said. "Maybe people who hid or managed to flee."

"And now they have nothing," Yuliana lamented.

Ethan handed his staff to Par'karr and stepped forward. "It's okay. We're here to help. We mean you no harm."

A twang sounded from the building and Ethan barely managed to raise a shield of air just in time to deflect an arrow.

Skill increase: Air magic +1%.

"Loki's balls!" a male voice said from inside the building. "It's a warlock!"

Ethan didn't take the arrow personally. Whoever the survivors were, they had obviously been through hell and would have no reason to trust them. He spread his arms in a gesture of openness. "I'm not going to hurt you. We saved *Manai* and the others from Hel's priestess and her goons."

There were whispers from the building for almost a

minute before the male voice yelled out, "You expect us to believe that? You have three slaves with you!"

"You're slavers!" yelled a girl's voice. He wasn't good with voices, but it sounded like an older girl.

"We are not slaves!" Nia bellowed defiantly.

"It is true," Yuliana said, stepping forward. "We wear the collars to avoid fights, but we are free."

"Par'karr no slave," the kobold joined in with the others. "Par'karr Ethan's friend."

Ethan looked down at the little kobold and grinned. He guessed they were friends at this point. They'd certainly been through enough together. Par'karr turned to him and gave Ethan a toothy grin.

"How do we know you're not just making them say that?" the male voice asked.

"How do you know I won't just cause all of the walls to collapse on you?" Ethan shot back. He sent a burst of air around the inside of the building, rattling burned timbers and shaking up dust.

"Ethan!" hissed Yuliana.

"It's okay," he whispered.

"No!" came the frantic woman's voice. "There are children!"

Another bow shot came streaking towards him but he was ready this time and caught the arrow with air.

Skill increase: Air magic +1%.

He spun the arrow around and sent it shooting at the building where it embedded itself in burned-out timber. "I know you've been through a lot, but if you shoot another arrow at me, I'm going to start to get angry. You won't like me when I'm angry."

"Now get your scrawny butts out here before we come in

there and get you!" yelled Ainslee, putting her hands on her hips. "And I won't be gentle!"

There were some more muffled voices and maybe some crying. Finally the male voice spoke up again. "Okay! We'll come out. Just don't hurt the girls! I was the one who fired the arrow. Just me, not the others."

The young male elf stepped out through the burned-out door to the building, holding his hands up. Ethan guessed he was the human equivalent of thirteen or fourteen. He had a medium build, a round, dirty face and bright-blue eyes. The young elf had long, blond hair that was now dirty with soot. His clothes were dirty and ragged but serviceable. "Just let the others go, please."

"We're not here to hurt you," Ethan said. "We're here to help you if we can."

"Yeah, sure," the elf quipped.

"It's true," Yuliana said. "We killed the men who did this to your village and freed your people. They are safe, on their way to Moonpoint."

"There's no way you can prove that." He smirked.

"No," Ethan said. "But if I really wanted to harm you or take you prisoner, I could. You saw what I did."

"Damn warlocks!" the elf hissed.

Ethan sighed. "I'm not a warlock, I'm a wizard."

"Ha! The wizards have been killed." He frowned. "There are no more."

"There's at least one," Ethan responded. "Do you know what the difference is between a wizard and a warlock?"

The young elf looked unsure. "Warlocks make pacts with demons. Wizards get magic from the gods."

Ethan tilted his head. He hadn't heard that before. Was that the common belief? Maybe the aliens were like gods to these people. "That's not the only difference. Warlocks can only use one element. Wizards can use all four."

To punctuate his point, Ethan shot a bolt of fire in the air, then picked the kid up slightly with air and caused a one-foot-tall slab of dirt to rise beneath him. He couldn't see anything to freeze with water magic, so he tried to make the air around the boy cold. The boy shivered as Ethan dropped him onto the slab.

```
Skill increase: Fire magic +1%.
   Skill increase: Air magic +1%.
   Skill increase: Earth magic +1%.
   Skill increase: Water magic +1%.
```

"Okay! Okay!" the kid yelled frantically. "You're a wizard! That still doesn't mean you're not a slaver."

"Do you have any doubt that I could rip that building down around the others and take them if I wanted?" Ethan asked. He wouldn't really do it, but he also didn't have time to coddle them. It would be dark soon and he needed to know what he was dealing with.

"No," the young elf said shakily. He glanced back at the doorway.

"So, tell them to come out already," Ethan insisted, putting some steel in his voice.

"Fine." The young elf's chest deflated, and he slumped. "Come on out."

Noises came from inside the building and then four young elves came out of the building in tattered, dirty clothes. The tallest looked to be just slightly younger than the male elf but the others were all much younger. Ethan guessed they were between eight and four. They all looked skinny and ravenous. Clenched tightly in the arms of the youngest was a puppy.

Ethan smiled at them. "We just want to help you. And we can start by feeding you."

The kids all exchanged hopeful looks and Ethan's heart went out to them.

29

"What are your names?" Ethan asked, once all of them were out.

The young male elf looked to the oldest female and she shrugged. He turned back around, his face skeptical. "I'm Thadran. This is Kelene, Nelea, Cathea and the smallest is Telina."

Thadran called them out in order of oldest first, with Kelene being the oldest girl and Telina being the youngest. Each nodded their heads as their name was spoken.

"And this is Buttons," Telina said, holding up the puppy. Telina was the smallest, with unkempt brown hair and a ragged green dress. He thought maybe she was four.

"Nice to meet you all." Ethan smiled. "I am Ethan, this is Ainslee, Nia, Yuliana and Par'karr."

"He's a kobold," Cathea said warily. The next youngest, possibly five or six, also had brown hair but it was pulled in a ponytail. The resemblance between her and Telina was so great, Ethan guessed they were sisters.

"Yes," Ethan agreed. "But he's a nice kobold."

Par'karr bobbed his head up and down and gave them a toothy grin. "Par'karr is nice!"

The kids exchanged looks but looked dubious.

"Are there any others?" Ethan asked. No one had moved yet. The kids still stood in the same place as they had when they came out and neither Ethan nor any of the others had made a move towards them. The last thing he wanted was to spook the kids and send them running off.

Once again, the two oldest, Thadran and Kelene, exchanged glances. Kelene shrugged.

"It's just us," Thadran replied. "We've been on our own since..."

The young male trailed off but Kelene gave him a hard, defiant look. She had fiery red hair and looked similar to Thadran. They might be brother and sister or cousins. She wore a soot-stained dress that was longer than the younger ones. "Since they came and took everyone away!"

"I'm sorry," he said honestly. "But we really did kill the priestess of Hel and her henchmen and free the other elves. They're headed to Moonpoint."

"Without us?" Telina whimpered, lip quivering. The child hugged the puppy to her chest. The little dog wagged its tail and licked her face.

"I don't think they knew you were still alive," Ethan told them. He looked to Yuliana for confirmation. "They didn't mention that we should look for you."

Yuliana nodded. "I fear they thought you perished in the fires."

"We almost did," Thadran said. "We were hiding in Mrs. Stoneoak's basement. When the fire started, we thought we would die..."

"But there was a hole the possums had dug last winter,"

Kelene finished. "We broke the boards and climbed out. Thadran was almost too big - he got stuck."

Thadran glared at Kelene but she was unfazed. "We managed to get out and then we hid in the forest."

"What have you been eating?" Ainslee asked, looking around the burned-out village.

"Whatever we could find," Thadran said quietly.

"Which isn't much," Cathea said. The oldest two gave her a hard look but she rolled her eyes. "It's true!"

Thadran nodded, glancing at the pigs the group had with them. "Food's been a bit scarce. What they didn't slaughter, they burned."

Seeing the kids eyeing the pigs, Ethan looked to Yuliana questioningly. He had thought all elves were vegetarians like her. But the way the kids were looking at the pigs, he half expected them to pounce on them at any second.

The elf moved her head close to his. "That was another thing I learned. The elves of this world do not follow the ways of my world. They eat the flesh of animals in addition to that which is provided by the land."

That explained the hungry look in the elven children's eyes. "Did you check the farms?"

The children exchanged looks. Thadran shook his head. "We kept hoping they were coming back, and we wanted to be here if they did."

Ethan sighed. They had the hope of children not used to the hard realities of life, but he understood their desperate need to cling to hope. Part of him still hoped that he could get back to *Earth*. The other part knew it was probably never going to happen.

Sliding his pack from his shoulder, he opened it,

revealing the large red pears and saw the children's eyes grow large and hungry. "We can cook one of the pigs tonight..."

"Two," interjected Ainslee.

"...two of the pigs tonight," he continued, rolling his eyes at the dwarf. "For now, here are some pears."

The kids started to take a step forward but stopped and cast a questioning look at Kelene and Thadran. The two nodded and the kids hurriedly walked over and tentatively picked out a pear. Even the older elves eyed the pears with hungry eyes and took theirs. They all began voraciously biting into the fruit.

"Are any of you injured?" Yuliana asked. "I can heal."

The kids all shook their heads and Ethan took the time to scan them all in his HUD.

```
Thadran
   Elf
   Commoner
   Level 1


Kelene
   Elf
   Commoner
   Level 1


Nelea
   Elf
   Commoner
   Level 0
```

```
Cathea
   Elf
   Commoner
   Level 0


Telina
   Elf
   Commoner
   Level 0
```

He wasn't surprised. They had no classes, other than the catch-all commoner class. Obviously, they were all too young yet. Or perhaps not skilled enough. He still didn't know exactly how picking a class worked for people without a HUD.

Turning to the others, he talked to his companions in a hushed tone. At his suggestion, Ainslee and Nia went off to slaughter the pigs and get them ready for the fire. Par'karr went to find wood to build the fire and Ethan and Yuliana stayed with the kids.

The children each ate another pear before the pig was ready. When Ainslee declared the pig ready, the children eagerly lined up to get a slice of pork. To their credit, Ethan noted that Telina and Thadran allowed the smaller children to get their portions before the older ones.

When they were all eating, Kelene looked around at Ethan and his companions. "What are you going to do with us?"

Ethan considered the question. He'd been thinking about it a lot since they'd found the kids. He really only saw two choices for the time being. Either they left the kids here to fend for themselves, or they took them with them.

There were risks for both. If they left the kids in the village, there was no telling what would happen to them. At some point, someone else could come into the village or monsters or wild animals might come into the village.

On the other hand, if they took the kids with them, they'd be responsible for them. If something attacked them, the kids would be in harm's way. His companions would have to worry not only about fighting the monsters, they'd need to worry about defending the kids.

He looked around at his companions. Their expressions made it clear they were leaving it up to him. Ethan sighed. He was okay with being the leader of a group of adults. After all, it was their decision to follow him. But being responsible for a group of children? That was pressure he didn't need.

"Much of that depends on you," he said. "We won't make your choice for you. You'll have to decide whether you want to stay here or come with us. But if you come with us, there will be rules you have to follow. And those rules aren't up for debate."

"What kind of rules?" Kelene asked, eyes narrowed. Ethan was beginning to see that Kelene, though younger than Thadran, might be the leader of the group. Or at least, the most outspoken.

"First, you have to do what we say," he told them.

"But..." Kelene started but Ethan cut her off with a raised palm.

"That one is not up for debate," he interrupted sharply. "We've fought two-headed dogs, slithering things with tentacles, trolls and more. In combat, I need to know that all of you will follow our orders TO THE LETTER. If not, I'm not going to risk our lives and yours."

He paused and looked from child to child, emphasizing

his point. The children looked around at each other and then looked at Kelene. Ethan chuckled inwardly. He had been right. Even Thadran deferred to her.

"What else?" the fiery elf demanded.

"That's the big one," he said. "The other rules, we'll make up as we go along."

Kelene crossed her arms across her chest. "You expect us to just accept whatever rules you make up?"

"Yes," he said. "Because any rules we make up will help keep you alive."

Ethan gestured around. "How long do you really think you can survive here? Assuming more priestesses of Hel don't come? A week? Two weeks? If you come with us, we're all putting our lives on the line to protect you and feed you. If you can't do something as simple as follow rules, then I don't think any of us should risk our lives for you."

Skill increase: Bluff +1%.

The HUD, or whatever controlled it, realized he was bluffing. He just hoped the kids didn't. There was no way he was about to leave them here to die. Ethan wasn't about to have that on his conscience.

The kids all looked to Kelene again, who seemed to squirm under Ethan's gaze. He hadn't wanted to sound cruel, but he needed these kids to listen to him - especially during combat. He hadn't been exaggerating. It could cost them their lives - or the life of one of his companions.

Finally, Kelene seemed to reach her decision. She locked eyes with Ethan. "Fine. We'll follow your rules, if you take us with you."

"Good choice." Ethan smiled. He didn't like the games he had to play with the kids, but he also knew it was for their own good. Leaving them here would be a death sentence. If not for the older kids, definitely for the little ones.

"Fine," he said. "Then we will take you with us."

The smaller kids smiled broadly, but Kelene and Thadran didn't seem quite as happy. Ethan guessed they knew their power was coming to an end and that they'd have to follow him and the others. Maybe he could use that to his favor.

"Then the second rule is that I, or one of the others, will give orders to Kelene and Thadran. And they will give orders to you." Ethan pointed to the three youngest. When he saw Telina still holding Buttons, he smiled. "And, Telina, you'll be responsible for relaying those orders to Buttons."

The little elf smiled, looked at the puppy, and nodded.

"Good," he said and looked around at his group. "Then I say we get some sleep soon and get started as early as possible."

Ethan looked between Thadran and Kelene. "Is the building we found you in the most defensible building?"

"The old tavern? It has the best walls and most of the floor is intact," Thadran replied. "The roof collapsed and blocked the back entrance and there's an old table we can move over the door to block it."

"Perfect!" Ethan said. "Then we sleep in the tavern tonight. It should make watch a little easier."

With the tough decisions made, the group finished up their dinner of roast pork. As usual, Ainslee ate a double - perhaps even a triple - share, but there was plenty to go around. The extra, Ethan used his water magic to freeze for the next day.

When everyone was done eating, they all went to the remains of the tavern and set up their camp. Each of them took blankets from their bedroll and laid them out for the children. It made resting slightly more difficult for all of them. Yet, when it was his turn to finally get some rest, he slept better knowing the kids all slumbered soundly.

As Ethan drifted off to sleep, he wondered if he had made the right decision. Only time would tell.

30

———————

The next morning, Ethan woke to a cold nose pressed against his face, followed by a small, wet tongue against his cheek. Opening his eyes, he found Buttons' head close to his own. As he blinked the sleep from his eyes, the dog wagged its tail and licked him.

"I'm up," he chuckled at the puppy and looked around.

Par'karr was up and stoking the fire, getting it ready for breakfast. Ethan yawned and scratched the little puppy on its head before pushing himself out of bed. Walking over to Par'karr, he squatted down next to the kobold.

"Any trouble?" he asked, warming his hands by the fire.

The kobold gave him a toothy grin. "No trouble."

"I'll get some more wood," he told Par'karr and then left the tavern. First, he found a place to relieve himself. The act reminded himself that this wasn't a simulation - or it was an extremely detailed simulation. Then walked around the village, examining the empty husks of the burned-out buildings.

The priestess and her goons had done a good job. Most

of the buildings were just piles of charcoal. Considering how much of it was burned and the degree to which it had burned, Ethan wondered if they had brought barrels of oil with them. Did that mean they'd always planned to burn the village?

He clenched and unclenched his fists as he thought of the cruelty of the priestess and her henchmen. If this was how all of the priests of Hel were, the whole religion could die as far as he was concerned.

Slavery, human sacrifice, looting and wanton destruction. Some of the worst things from his own world and now he found those same things here. Maybe evil was universal. It was a discouraging thought and he was in a foul mood when he returned with his armful of firewood.

"Can you thaw the meat?" Ainslee asked him as soon as he walked into the tavern. "I'm starved and they're still hard as a rock!"

Nodding, he set the wood next to the fire and went over to his pack. He retrieved the pork he'd frozen the previous night and systematically thawed them using a little fire magic. It was easy. And apparently too easy for him to get any skill gains.

He did take a moment to check his stats.

```
Strength: 10
   Agility: 12
   Hardiness: 12
   Intellect: 18
   Intuition: 12
   Charisma: 12

Health: 24
```

Mana: 46

Stamina: 23

His stats had healed another point and now both Strength and Charisma were back to their normal levels. The other stats, except for *Intellect*, would be back to normal in a few days. *Intellect* would take almost a week.

Ethan wished he would have taken more honey. He could have been back to normal if he had a few more doses. Then again, he might not have made it back alive from a second trip to the bees' nest.

He planned to get more when they passed back that way. He'd need to shape rocks into containers, so he had something to carry it back in. If he remembered correctly, honey didn't go bad and its healing properties made it invaluable.

Everyone was up by that point and they all ate pears and pork for breakfast. Afterwards, they packed up and got ready to move out. Thadran had his short bow and a quiver of maybe a dozen arrows, while Telina carried Buttons. None of the other kids had any belongings.

"Do you have anything else you wish to bring with you?" Ethan asked the kids.

They looked at each other and then back to him, shrugged and shook their heads. He shrugged.

"Alrighty then," he said. "Let's get this show on the road."

When everyone looked at him uncomprehendingly, he sighed. "Let's get moving."

~

THEY PASSED MORE BURNED-OUT farms to the east of the village. They didn't find any more livestock around the village that had survived. As they followed the road, Nia grabbed Ethan by the arm and pointed to the ground.

"Wolves," she said, pointing at some tracks that crossed the road. "A large pack. Maybe ten or twelve. Their scent is not fresh, but it crosses several times. They have been coming back to this spot for days."

Looking around the area, Ethan turned back to the others. "Be on your guard and keep the kids between us."

His companions put the kids in the center and moved to surround them. To their credit, the kids didn't cry or whimper, they just moved together in a tight circle. The two oldest stepped out slightly, giving the youngest kids even more protection.

They continued on, not stopping to check out any of the farmhouses, except the last one. Like their earlier encounter, the final house had several pear trees. They took the time to fill up their bags before continuing on.

They passed over three bridges as the river snaked through the area east of the village. As they were passing over the third bridge, Nia held up a hand. She sniffed and her ears went back.

"What is it?" Ethan whispered.

"Something very... strong," she said. "I have not encountered its scent before."

Ethan's imagination started to run wild but only for a moment. The crack of branches sounded, and an enormous humanoid stepped out of the trees.

The newcomer was huge! The creature was twice as tall as a man, maybe twelve feet tall. Like the trolls they had encountered, this one had long, thick arms that dragged on the ground and shorter, under-sized legs, like a gorilla. In fact, Ethan had first thought it was a giant gorilla, except that its head was wrong. It was more human, though its nose and mouth were disproportionately large.

The thing roared and the children screamed. Ethan quickly glanced behind to make sure they weren't being flanked by another one. Nothing. At least, not yet.

"Par'karr," he ordered, "take the kids to the other side of the bridge. If we fall, run into the woods with them!"

"Okay," the kobold agreed, wide-eyed.

Nia looked over at him. For the first time since he met her, her face showed worry - and maybe fear. "Ethan, I do not know how to fight a creature like this. There is nothing like this on my world."

"We have giants," Ainslee said, moving up to his other side. "But they ain't that ugly!"

The enormous creature strode forward, its determined strides bringing it quickly near them. Ethan tried to think of some tactics from his MMORPG or roleplaying experience, but game tactics just didn't seem adequate against a real creature this size.

He remembered a gray wizard's fight against a fiery demon on a bridge. In that case, the wizard had caused the bridge to collapse beneath the creature, sending it tumbling into the abyss.

Ethan looked over the edge of the stone bridge. It was barely above the water. Even if he ripped the bridge out from under the creature, it would fall five or six feet at most. Certainly not enough to even break a leg, let alone kill it.

But maybe he didn't need to kill it. Maybe there was some other way to deal with it. He smiled as an idea came to him and motioned to the others. "Go back to the other side of the bridge. Stay there while I try something."

"Ethan..." Yuliana started.

Holding up a hand, he flashed her a lopsided grin. "Trust me."

The women exchanged glances but moved back towards the children. As they did, the creature watched them move away. It grunted loudly and quickened its pace, bellowing as it did. It reached the bridge and started across.

"You shall not pass!" Ethan yelled out in his best wizardly voice. He held his staff in his right hand but would like to have held a magical, elven-crafted sword in his other hand like the famous wizard had.

The gigantic creature paused and looked down at him, as if just noticing him. It blinked and tilted its head. Ethan took that moment to scan it.

Forest Ogre
   Ogre
   Hunter
   Level 10

Ethan swore silently. An ogre. That made sense but up close and in-person, they were much more intimidating than any ogre in his MMORPGs. And stinky. The ogre's heavy musky smell seemed to permeate the air around it, almost making him gag.

Then there was the fact that it was level 10. Almost 5 levels above him. This wouldn't be easy, he realized. If it were possible at all.

The creature narrowed its eyes and let out a deafening roar before charging. It moved astonishingly fast for a creature of its size and Ethan barely managed to work his magic. He reached out and caused the stones of the bridge to move aside suddenly, forming a hole large enough for the creature to fall into.

The ogre's momentum worked against it and it wasn't quick enough to stop before it slid into the hole. The ogre fell through the hole in the bridge and ended up with its feet and hands in the water of the river. A look of shock came over the creature's face and before it could do anything, Ethan sealed the hole around the ogre, essentially locking it in place.

He could feel the amount of *Mana* flowing out of him and brought up his HUD.

Mana: 32

He still had a decent amount, but he wasn't done. Next, he reached into the water directly beneath him and ripped all of the heat from it. He felt more *Mana* leave him, but he heard the crack of ice as the river directly below the bridge froze solid.

Mana: 27

Realizing it was trapped, and probably cold too, the ogre bellowed and began struggling. Ethan heard the ice cracking below as the ogre began twisting and moving. The bridge groaned too, and he wondered if the thing could tear it apart with its sheer strength.

His plan had been to immobilize it and then let Ainslee, Nia and himself kill it while it couldn't move. Given the groaning and cracking sounds, it didn't appear that his trap would hold the ogre that long.

Cursing, Ethan looked around for a rock large enough to

form into a spike of ogre slaying. He should be able to use the same tactic he used on the naga, if he could find a stone large enough.

The ogre continued to rage against his restraints, growling and howling as it tried to wiggle free. The bridge shuddered and more cracks came from below.

"I need a rock! A big rock!" Ethan yelled but then cut himself off.

He shook his head as realized he had all the stones he needed. The entire bridge was stone. In fact, he didn't even need to form a spike and shoot it through the air like he had with the nagas. Focusing on the rock around he realized he could just form large spikes out of the existing rock.

"Look away, child! Look away!" he yelled and then, with maximum effort, he caused foot-wide spikes of rock to erupt from the stone of the bridge, into the ogre's chest.

```
You pierce Forest Ogre for 29 damage.
   You    pierce    Forest    Ogre    for    23
damage.
   You    pierce    Forest    Ogre    for    26
damage.
```

The creature bellowed in pain and stopped struggling for a moment as it looked down uncomprehendingly at the spikes that came out of the bridge itself, piercing its chest. It whined for a moment before Ethan drove another large spike directly into the back of its neck.

```
You critically pierce Forest Ogre for
49 damage.
   Forest Ogre dies.
```

You gain 100 experience. Experience to next level 720.

The ogre's eyes went wide for a second before the life left its eyes and its body convulsed. After a minute, the twitching stopped, and the ogre was still.

"Loki's balls!" came a voice from behind him.

Ethan turned to see all the kids staring wide-eyed at the ogre. He looked at his companions and gave them a "you were supposed to be watching them" look. They glanced between Ethan and the dead ogre and shrugged unapologetically.

"Not bad," came a new voice from behind him.

Startled, Ethan spun, already channeling *Mana* and ready to unleash it on whatever new threat had appeared.

But instead of a monster, Ethan saw an old man on the other side of the bridge. No, he corrected himself as he spotted the long, tapered ears, not a man - an elf.

The elf had gray hair and a short gray beard. He was dressed in green pants and tunic over which he wore a simple gray cloak that had been stained with use. Around his waist was a wide leather belt from which hung a number of pouches and a knife.

But the thing that caught Ethan's attention was a glowing blue crystal atop the man's staff, which he held in his right hand. The staff was held like a walking staff and not at all threatening, but if it was what Ethan thought it was, then it didn't matter how the staff was held.

"My name is Michalus Moor," the elf said, "and like you, I am a wizard."

31

———————

No one moved for a long minute. Ethan and his companions just stared at the old elf on the opposite side of the bridge. Finally, he heard heavy footsteps behind him and knew it must be Ainslee.

"Well Mr. Wizard-Elf," the dwarf shouted. "You could have helped out!"

The wizard raised an eyebrow and chuckled. "It didn't appear as if your young wizard needed any help. Handling an ogre single-handedly is no small feat."

"He still could have helped," the dwarf mumbled from behind him.

"What do you want?" Ethan asked, still not moving. He didn't know what to think of this newcomer. Worse, he'd used up most of his *Mana* killing the ogre. If it came to a fight, he wasn't sure he would fare well against a real wizard.

"For one," the elf answered, "I'd like to know your intentions with the children. Do you intend to make them slaves as well?"

"As well?" Ethan asked.

"You already have three other slaves," Michalus replied. "Or do my old eyes deceive me?"

"We are no slaves!" Nia hissed.

The elf looked skeptically from the fox girl to Par'karr and finally rested on Yuliana. Ethan knew he was looking at their collars.

"They're not slaves," Ethan told him. "They're my friends. They just wear the collars because right now, it's dangerous to be a certain race with the law the way it is."

"True enough," the wizard replied and then turned his gaze back to Yuliana. "Is this true? Are you free?"

"I am free." Yuliana nodded. "And we freed the elves of the village who were captured by the priestess of Hel. They are on their way to Moonpoint."

The wizard let out a sigh of relief and nodded. He smiled slightly and the blue glow from his staff's crystal dimmed. "That is good to hear. I scouted Silvershade two days ago via magic and saw what had happened. I was coming to investigate when I ran into your group."

"That's the real reason you didn't help, isn't it?" Nia asked with narrowed eyes. "You thought Ethan was a slaver."

Michalus shrugged. "I admit the thought did cross my mind. Had he fallen, I would have intervened to help the rest of you."

"Gee, thanks," Ethan said snarkily.

"So now what?" asked Ainslee, crossing her arms over her chest.

"Well," the wizard replied thoughtfully. "Since there is no pressing need for me to visit Silvershade at this time, I will return to my home. I think it would be best if you accompanied me."

Ethan wasn't sure if the man was making a suggestion or

giving an order but he didn't care. The chance to talk to another wizard was too good to pass up. There were so many questions he had.

He turned to his companions who were all looking at him to see what he would say. Ethan gave them a smile. "I say we go with him."

Ainslee frowned, arms still crossed over her chest. He leaned down to her and whispered, "Maybe he'll have some mead."

Skill increase: Bluff +1%.
   Skill increase: Diplomacy +1%.

The dwarf's face brightened. "You really think so?"

Once they accepted his invitation, the wizard crossed over the bridge and checked on the kids. All smiles, he asked them questions about the attack and what transpired. Although Michalus had been intimidating earlier, with the kids, the wizard seemed more like an uncle or grandfather in his manner.

He asked the children questions for about ten minutes before standing up, patting the head of Buttons and turning to the rest of the group. "We should begin our journey. It is a day and a half walk to my home." Michalus glanced back at the small kids. "Perhaps a bit more."

Ethan frowned as he realized that meant they would lose at least another three days from reaching their goal to retrieve the tomes from the library in Patheos.

Then again, the entire point of the quest had been to become a member of the Order of the Scroll so he could read the books and learn more about wizardry and the world they were on - and possibly a way home. Now he had a chance to talk to an actual wizard.

Michalus glanced at him curiously. "Is this a problem?"

"No," Ethan replied. "It's fine. We were on our way to Patheos to retrieve some tomes for the Order of the Scroll in Castlehaven. But it can wait."

"Patheos?!" the elf hissed. "They sent you to Patheos?"

Suddenly wary, Ethan nodded. "Why? Is there a problem?"

"Let's get started on our journey back to my home and we will talk as we go," the man suggested.

"Good idea," Ethan agreed and turned to his companions. "We're going to follow Michalus to his home. Same thing as before, let's keep the kids between us."

"We can follow the road east for the rest of the day, and then cut north. It's slightly longer but I think it will be easier on the kids," the wizard said. "But before we do, perhaps you should set the bridge back to the way it was – or at least make it passable?"

"Oh, right," Ethan said and turned back towards the bridge. He used fire magic to melt the ice and then used *Earth* magic to open the hole wider. The ogre's body slumped further into the hole and Ethan tried to lift it with air but stopped just before he did. He felt drained and checked his HUD.

Mana: 4

He turned to the wizard. "I'm out of mana, I'll need to wait until it regenerates."

Michalus shook his head. "No need, I think I can manage from here."

The wizard raised his staff and the crystal at the top glowed bright blue. Ethan watched as the ogre's body slowly moved out of the hole and onto the bridge itself. He then watched as the stone bridge reformed itself into a similar shape that it had been in.

Ethan grinned. When he watched someone else do it, it all looked like magic. When he did magic, it was different. He could actually sense the threads of elemental *Mana* as he shaped them to do his bidding. It seemed more cause and effect. Watching Michalus do it, it just looked very... magical.

"That required more mana than I thought," the wizard gasped. "I'm actually surprised you were able to do all of it."

Ethan looked at him with confusion. "It did use up most of my mana."

"I would think so." The wizard nodded. "How long have you been practicing wizardry?"

"About a month and a half, I think," Ethan replied.

"A MONTH AND A HALF?!" Michalus said incredulously, mouth falling open. "And you were able to accomplish that?"

"It's been a very busy time," he replied. "I've had a lot of, how should I say it, on the job training."

The wizard waved his reply away. "Who taught you the basics? Who did you study under?"

"Uh." Ethan grinned sheepishly. "I picked it up on my own."

"On your own?!" the elf repeated, eyes wide. "Surely, you are joking."

"I'm not joking," he replied. He grinned as he fought the urge to add "...and don't call me Shirley."

"This is incredible!" the elf exclaimed, looking him up and down.

"Yah, yah," Ainslee butted in. "It's great and awesome and everything. Can we get moving?"

The wizard looked momentarily annoyed but then smiled and nodded. "Right you are, my dear. We should get started. Come, follow me."

They began walking, with Ethan and the wizard in the lead, followed by Nia, then the children with Par'karr and Yuliana on either side. Ainslee brought up the rear. As they walked, the curious wizard began to bombard Ethan with questions.

Continuing to walk, Ethan held up his hand. "Listen. This may sound weird, but this might help explain things. Have you ever heard of people coming here from other worlds?"

The wizard stopped suddenly, forcing everyone to stop as well. The man looked at Ethan with narrowed eyes. "Are you trying to tell me you are an offworlder?"

Offworlder? Ethan hadn't heard that term before, but his answer was promising. Maybe he knew something about how they had gotten here. "I am. We all are, except Par'karr."

Michalus glanced between the companions and then back to Ethan. "When? When did you arrive?"

Ethan thought back and tried to calculate the days but failed. So many things had happened and with no routine and no real delineation of the weeks, he wasn't sure. Based on what he remembered, he related his best guess. "About six weeks or so."

The wizard resumed their walk but was silent, a thoughtful look on his face. "Interesting. That corresponds with some readings I picked up."

"Readings?"

"Yes." The old elf grinned. His tone became almost

conspiratorial. "Portals are a bit of an obsession of mine. I've made a device to register portal activity."

"Portals?" Ethan asked. He had assumed they had been beamed down from some alien spaceship in orbit. This idea of portals was new to him. Was that how the aliens "transported" people, with portals?

"Yes," the wizard said excitedly. "It's a type of Aether Magic..."

"Oh yes," Ethan said, both groaning and blushing at the memory. "I got that skill in Timberwell. I teleported from one spot in the room to another. I think it almost killed me."

"You what?!" the wizard sputtered. The elf stopped and stared at Ethan wide-eyed. "You've actually USED portal magic?!"

Ethan took a step back from the wizard, who had a crazed look in his eye. "I don't know about portal magic, but I did teleport according to the women."

"He went from in front of the bed," Nia interjected from behind them, "to the tub."

"Naked!" Ainslee yelled and then, seeing the kids look at her, flushed a deep crimson.

"Remarkable!" the old elf exclaimed. "Can you demonstrate it?"

Ethan shook his head vigorously. "Not a chance. I did it by accident and I think it nearly killed me. As it was, my Overchannel kicked in and drained all of my stats."

Michalus looked disappointed but nodded and resumed walking. "From my research, it takes enormous mana to open a portal. You are most fortunate not to have died or burned yourself out. I've heard of an ability to utilize your very essence to power spells. Overchannel. Yes, that was it. And you managed to gain that ability. Interesting."

"So, you've never opened a portal for yourself?" Ethan asked.

"Odin's missing eye, no!" the elf said. "I've studied them for close to two hundred years, but I've never mastered the skill to open one big enough for a person! Where did you learn it from?"

"I learned by doing," Ethan said. "By accident."

The old elf just shook his head. "I don't believe I've ever heard of someone discovering portal magic by accident."

"Probably because they died," Ethan said bitterly, "like I almost did."

"That is very possible," the wizard said, thoughtfully. "That would make a lot of sense. Either they died when they completed it or didn't have enough mana to complete it and died in the inbetween."

"The inbetween?" Ethan asked, not likely the sound of it.

"I, and other wizards, have theorized that there is a place between the world," he said. "And you traverse this place."

"The rainbow bridge," Ethan muttered, remembering the strange kaleidoscope of color he had travelled through.

"Yes!" Michalus retorted excitedly. "You... you saw it?"

"I did. For me, the journey was maybe thirty seconds or maybe even a minute," he replied, remembering the strange experience. "But to the women, it was instantaneous."

"It's true then!" He grinned. "The theory is true. There is an inbetween."

"The Bifrost," Ethan whispered, remembering the Norse name for it.

The wizard tilted his head at Ethan. "Yes, the Bifrost. Some earlier writings refer to it as such. But how do you know that?"

"It's a long story." Ethan smiled at the man. As they

continued their walk, they continued questioning each other.

32

After they began walking, the old wizard looked him up and down, forehead wrinkling. "I didn't notice it before, but now that I look for it, I don't see the crystal in your staff."

"Oh," Ethan answered sheepishly. "I just keep it in my belt pouch."

"In your belt pouch?" The wizard looked at him as if he'd just said the most ridiculous thing and Ethan felt his face grow warm.

"Uh, yah," he said and fished out the two Chymera crystals from his pocket. "Once I found that I didn't need to actually see the crystal to focus my energy through it, I kept it in my pocket for safe keeping."

More creases appeared in the wizard's forehead and he looked up to the top of his own staff where a large crystal was intricately bound to the top of the staff. "Well, I suppose that's true. I had heard of other wizards, from the south, who kept their crystals in rings, amulets or even crowns. But I haven't met any other wizards who didn't carry a wand or staff."

Ethan smiled wryly. "Now you have. I'm just glad to have taken it from the kobold wizard. Until then, I was using my stamina."

"You did what?!" the elf asked, wide-eyed.

"When I first started doing magic," Ethan explained, "I didn't have a crystal and didn't even know how to channel energy through it."

"And you managed to pull the energy for the spells from your own body?!" The wizard shook his head. "My boy, I am surprised you survived. We, wizards I mean, know that you can take your own body energy and convert it directly into magical energy, but it takes a huge toll on one's body. Only the most desperate wizards would attempt it."

"Why?" Ethan asked, though he thought he already knew the answer.

"You can keep pushing your body's energy into a spell, well past your physical endurance," Michalus replied. "Push too much and you will fall unconscious. Push too much, too quickly, and you will die... sometimes very painfully and slowly as all of your organs shut down."

Ethan swallowed. He hadn't really thought twice about using his *Stamina* in the early days. In fact, that was the only way he could work magic at all. Now, knowing what he did, he cringed at how close he'd probably come to killing himself.

Another question popped into his head. "Why do wizards need to focus their energy through crystals?"

The old wizard nodded approvingly. "Excellent question. We don't truly know the answer but there are a variety of theories. The most accepted of which is that the energy we are able to generate as wizards resonates at a certain frequency, but to tap into the universal energy that surrounds us all it needs to be at a different frequency."

Ethan nodded. To him, it sort of made sense. It was like an analog to digital converter. An older computer that only had a VGA port needed a special adapter to display on a newer HDMI monitor. Without that adapter, the two signals were incompatible. Maybe it worked in a similar way - converting magic from one frequency to another.

"So then why can we channel stamina into magic?" Ethan asked.

"Ah." The old wizard smiled. "Excellent question. It would seem that the energy that comes from our bodies operates at the same frequency. There is no need to change its frequency."

Considering the elf's answer, Ethan asked the next logical question. "So why are the two types of energy on a different frequency if they both come from inside us?"

Michalus chuckled softly. "Another excellent question. Not all wizards know or accept that our internal energy, stamina as you call it, can be used to power our magic. Those that do have boggled over that question for hundreds of years. I have never heard a satisfactory answer."

The way the old elf had said *Stamina* made Ethan remember another question he desperately wanted to ask. "Do you have a HUD, or heads up display?"

The wizard raised an eyebrow. "Heads up display?"

"Do you have a way of seeing words in front of you that are...uh... in the air?" Ethan explained.

"Interesting," the elf replied. "I have read of people who claimed something similar. A scroll in front of their eyes, I believe was how they describe it."

Ethan nodded. "Yes. That is how it might appear."

"Sadly, I do not know how to conjure such a thing, but I do know others have reported it." The old wizard shook his head as he answered but then gave Ethan a meaningful look. "The ones who claimed this also claimed to be offworlders."

"That's interesting," Ethan replied. And it was. Ethan had theorized that the HUD was something implanted by the aliens and if natives of the world didn't have it, that lent more credence to his theory.

"I thought so." Michalus smiled. "Perhaps some magic that you brought with you?"

He shook his head and then shuddered as the dream with the aliens flashed back into his head. There had to be something implanted in his head that allowed him to see the HUD. If so, why? What reason would the aliens have for implanting it? Or was he wrong and he really was inside some computer-simulated world - an alien MMORPG.

"You seem so sure," the old elf interrupted his thoughts.

"There is no magic on my world," he replied. "We have advanced science and technology, but no magic."

"Truly?" the wizard asked. "How can that be? Magic is a universal law!"

It was Ethan's turn to chuckle. "On my world, the only universal truths are science. We call them the laws of science or laws of the universe."

"What are these laws of science?" the old elf asked curiously.

Ethan screwed up his face as he tried desperately to remember back to his basic science courses. "Uh... there's the law of gravity, the law of relativity... uh... the law of thermo-dynamics... um... Osmosis?"

He trailed off as he wasn't sure how he could explain

some of the other laws or even remember their exact names. Funny how he could rattle off the 3 laws of robotics and the stats on nearly every monster in CastleBlaze or the tabletop RPGs, but couldn't remember all the various laws of physics.

Chuckling to himself, he shrugged. "Honestly, I don't really know them all."

Michalus made a dismissive gesture. "I understood gravity, but I have never heard of thermodynamo before..."

"Thermodynamics," Ethan corrected. "It's okay, I don't really understand them all myself. I have other, uh... more specialized talents on my world."

"Oh?" The elf perked up. "What sort of talents?"

"I fix computers," Ethan said without thinking and then, seeing the wizard's confused look, tried to explain. "I fix machines that do things for us."

"Like golems?" Michalus asked excitedly.

"Uh, no," he said. "So, golems are a thing on this world?"

"They were," the old wizard replied, "but the craft has been lost for centuries. And, what are... com-poot-ers?"

Ethan chuckled at his pronunciation. It wasn't the first time he'd heard the word computer pronounced that way. He thought about the best way to describe it. "It's like a huge library of books inside a small machine that can do certain things, like write a letter, keep financial records and even send messages."

He purposely neglected playing games, which was mostly what he used his computer for. That and watching funny cat videos that his friends sent him.

"Truly?" the elf asked. "That seems like magic."

"Technology," Ethan replied. "It's just a machine. Though to people who don't understand it, I guess it seems like magic."

"That's often the way it is with things people do not understand," the wizard agreed. "You can tell me more about the com-poot-ers later. But let's talk more about the Bifrost, as you called it."

The next hour went by quickly, with Michalus asking all sorts of questions about his experience in the Bifrost. He soon realized the old elf had an obsession with portals and the Bifrost. Ethan didn't mind though. It reminded him of some of his friends and their obsessions with roleplaying games or MMORPGs. Hunter even his own obsession with the tabletop miniatures and would spend hours painting them in excruciating detail.

Thoughts of Hunter reminded him of his other friends and his old life. More and more, he felt like his life on Earth was slipping away. It was if he were thinking through molasses when he tried to remember anything about his time before the abduction.

Once he started remembering his old life, he could remember the details, but it was almost as if something was running interference in his mind, trying to stop him from remembering anything before arriving on this world. Something the aliens did to him? Hadn't the women said something to that effect as well?

He shook his head as he realized Michalus was no longer next to him. He stopped and spun around. 'What?"

"Nia just said that we should stop. The children need a break," he said sheepishly. "I'm afraid my curiosity caused me to neglect checking on them until now. I apologize dearly."

"You are males," the foxgirl said without judgement. "It is to be expected. But it is lunch time. I will look for something we can cook."

"Hunt? Will that take a while?" the wizard asked.

"It will take however long it takes," she replied with a shrug. "You cannot rush a hunt."

"We have the pears," the old elf offered. "Why don't we just snack on those?"

"I do not eat prey food," Nia retorted sharply.

"Prey food?" Michalus asked.

Ethan leaned towards the old elf. "She only eats meat."

The wizard brightened. "Well then, perhaps you don't have to hunt."

Digging into his pouch, he pulled out a long piece of jerky and handed it to the foxgirl. "It's venison jerky. I made it myself."

Ethan's eyebrows shot up as he saw that the piece of jerky was too long to have fit into the small pouch, he pulled it front. Was that a... pouch of holding? At least, that's what it would be called in his role-playing games.

Before he could ask about it, Ainslee stepped forward, shouldering her way past the foxgirl. The dwarf smiled greedily at the wizard. "Would you happen to have any more jerky?"

"Of course, my dear," the wizard chuckled. "I had planned for a longer trip, so I have plenty."

Watching closely as Michalus reached into his pouch and bought out another piece of jerky, Ethan could clearly see that he had been right. The jerky was simply too long to have fit in the pouch. It was a pouch of holding! Did that mean the old wizard knew how to enchant items?

The elf caught him staring and pulled out another piece of jerky. "You want one too?"

Ethan took it without thinking and then pointed to the pouch with his left hand. "That's a magical pouch, right?"

Looking down to his waist, the wizard chuckled. "My Extendable Pouch? Of course."

"Did you make it?" Ethan said, his heart thudding with excitement.

"I did," the elf replied proudly.

"Can you teach me?" Ethan asked, trying not to make it sound like he was begging.

Michalus led the group up the road for the rest of the day. They ended up stopping a little before dark because the children were tired. Despite the offer of more jerky from the old wizard, Nia insisted on hunting. It took her less than an hour to return with a small deer.

After the group had eaten and settled down for the night, Ethan and Michalus sat around the fire discussing the making of magical items. Ethan listened intently to the old wizard as he spoke until it was time for his watch to begin. The old wizard offered to keep him company - at least for a while.

"It'll give us a chance to talk some more," Michalus had said.

"Yah," Ainslee grumbled sarcastically. "Because you two haven't had a chance to talk all day."

Ignoring the dwarf, he thought about magic items. In all of the MMORPGs and tabletop roleplaying games he'd played throughout the years, one thing was a constant: magic items. Magic items could make a weak party strong and a stronger party nearly invincible.

That was even the main goal of so many MMORPGs, keep grinding to get better and better gear. The better gear you got, the more powerful monsters you could kill and the better gear you got. It was an endless cycle, which kept players playing - and paying.

Now, the old elf was explaining how he created his pouch and Ethan was intent on every word. Most of the concepts were actually familiar to him - from roleplaying games. Michalus used Aether Magic to create the effect, in essence creating a small permanent portal in a chest in his house.

"Wait!" Ethan exclaimed and then immediately lowered his voice as one of the children stirred in their sleep. "Wait, so you HAVE created a portal."

"Oh yes," the wizard said with a dismissive wave of his hand. "Most advanced wizards have created small portals. But very few wizards have had the power to open one large enough for a person. I don't know of one alive today."

"So that's all you do?" Ethan asked. "Just create the portal and bind the magic to a Chymera crystal?"

"Is that all, he asks." The wizard scoffed. "Boy, it took me years to master the skills to make my pouch."

Ethan frowned as his spirit sank. "Years?"

"Years." The wizard nodded. "And several dozen destroyed crystals."

"Why?" Ethan asked. The wizard's description of what to do hadn't sounded overly complicated. Was there some aspect he wasn't understanding? Some piece the wizard wasn't telling him?

The old elf looked him up and down. "You have to use just the right amount of energy. If you use too much, the crystal explodes. If you use too little, the enchantment fizzles. Finding the right amount can take months... or years."

Ethan's frown deepened. His idea of arming his entire party with magical weapons and armor and bags of holding was quickly slipping away.

Michalus reached over and clapped him on the shoulder. "Don't worry, with enough practice I'm sure you'll figure it out."

"What about magical swords and armor? Can those be made?"

The old elf chuckled. "They can. You can harden metals and make them much stronger than normal metals. But it can only be done while the weapon is being forged. If you try to shape metal while it's hard..."

"It explodes," Ethan finished. "Yeah, I discovered that the hard way."

Lifting his shirt, he showed the old wizard the scars from where the dagger had exploded in his hand. He shuddered involuntarily as he remembered the pain. Ethan had been lucky Yuliana had been there to heal him.

The wizard nodded gravely. "You're fortunate. Many others died learning the lesson."

"Wizarding is dangerous work, it seems."

"It always has been. And over the last few years, it's gotten much more dangerous."

"Someone or something has been killing wizards."

"What have you heard?" the old wizard asked with a raised eyebrow.

"I heard someone, or something is going around killing wizards and sucking out their brains."

The old elf suddenly looked even older in the firelight. "What you say is true. No wizard has ever survived an attack by whatever or whoever it is. In many cases, people with the wizard were killed or left as little more than vegetables."

"And no one has seen what has done it? How is that possible?" Ethan asked. Even in a society with no surveillance systems and no cameras, he would have thought someone would have seen them.

"No one." Michalus shook his head. "No one who lived or was in any state to relay the information. There have been a few suspicious deaths at the same time as the wizard attacks and, if I had to guess, I would say the person or thing killed them too - probably to prevent the person from identifying them."

It was Ethan's turn to nod. He'd seen enough horror and crime movies and TV shows to know that was probably true. Unless the killer wanted people to know who he was for some reason, killing witnesses was par for the course in those movies. And whoever or whatever was doing these killings wanted to protect their identity.

"But why are they sucking out the brains?" Ethan asked. He had his own theory, but he wanted to see if there were any existing theories that matched his.

The old elf shrugged. "No one's certain but it seems to me like whoever or whatever is trying to garner the knowledge of the wizard by taking his brain."

"That was my theory as well," Ethan agreed. He could think of many creatures from roleplaying games that ate brains. Some could gain memories of the person whose brain they ate. He thought he even remembered a TV show where a zombie girl ate brains and got some memories of the person. "Are there any creatures on this world that eat brains and gain knowledge?"

Michalus shrugged. "Nothing that has been catalogued, but with offworlders arriving from time to time, who knows if a new type of creature arrived that does eat brains. Or, who knows if some dark entity was able to cross over into our universe through one of the warlocks."

"Is that possible?" Ethan asked, suddenly concerned. In most roleplaying games, demons were among the toughest enemies to vanquish. If such a creature was on this world, Ethan didn't want to meet it.

"Nearly three thousand years ago," the elf replied, "a demon crossed over into our world. The exact way that it crossed over isn't clear, but the thing was immensely powerful and wiped out cities. Blades didn't damage it and all, but the most powerful spells did nothing to it."

"And it ate brains?" Ethan shuddered.

"Not exactly," the elf replied. "It did seem to eat humanoids, that much is true. But it also seemed to suck the... essence... out of a person if it could touch them."

"But it's dead now, right?" Ethan prodded.

The old wizard nodded his head and then shrugged. "Yes... and no. The stories say a wizard, who to this day no one knows exactly who, used a portal to send the demon home."

Ethan did a double take. "A portal? Like the type of portal I opened?"

"Presumably," the wizard said with a meaningful look. "Remember that when you're trying to get to your tub next time. Portals don't just have to lead to our world. If you create a portal again, make sure you know where it leads before you recklessly jump into it."

Taking a moment to let the wizard's words sink in, Ethan's mind began to come up with all sorts of questions. "So, are you saying that if a wizard has enough energy, he can make a portal to anywhere in the universe?"

"Universe?" The wizard chuckled. "If a wizard had enough power, he could open a portal to other dimensions. But that would take an enormous amount of energy. More than any wizard alive has."

"But the wizard who opened the gateway to the demon realm..." Ethan started but the old elf shook his head.

"... died in the attempt," the wizard said soberly. "Had other wizards not been there to force the demon through, who knows what would have happened."

Another thought occurred to Ethan then. In roleplaying games, wizards usually had to know or have seen the location they were teleporting to. Did the same thing apply to portals? "Does a wizard have to have seen the place he wants to create a portal to? I would assume not, if someone opened a portal to a demon realm."

The old elf smiled. "Very good. The answer is no. At least, that is the prevailing theory. A wizard need only fix a place in his mind when creating the portal. The magic will seek out the closest match to that place. Sometimes, that might be another dimension."

Ethan considered the man's words. "So, if I imagined a place like this with a fire and cast a portal..."

"You'd most likely end up in this place." The wizard nodded. "But if you imagined a busy city street but didn't have enough detail that it was a specific place in a specific city, you would probably open a portal to the closest approximation of that street, whether it was Castlehaven, Moonpoint or some place on the other side of the world."

"When you created your portal for your pouch," he asked. "How did you make sure it went to your chest and not some other chest?"

Smiling, the old elf nodded. "Excellent question. The way I made sure it would go to my chest was to carve unique symbols on the bottom of my chest. That way, when I fixed a picture of where I wanted the portal to go, I knew only my chest had those symbols."

Ethan nodded. It was almost doing a web search on the internet. You could type in general criteria and maybe you'd find what you wanted. You might have to scroll down the results, but you might find it with general terms. But, if you had a specific web address, you'd go directly to that website.

If Ethan wanted to create a portal to a specific place, his best bet was to do what the old wizard had done - carve some sort of unique pattern into the place. Then he could always be sure.

Thinking of a video game that he had played, another idea came to him. "What if you carved a unique pattern into a stone and pictured the stone? Would you appear wherever that stone was? Even if it were moved?"

Michalus was silent as a thoughtful expression crossed his face. "I don't recall reading anything about that method, but it seems to me that as long as the pattern on the stone was unique and you focused on the pattern, your portal would go to wherever the stone was."

As Ethan imagined the possibilities, the old elf looked up at the sky. "I think it might be time for the next watch."

Looking up, Ethan nodded. Michalus bid him good night and walked over to his bedroll while Ethan woke Yuliana.

When he finally lay down in his own bedroll, he thought his mind was too full of ideas for him to sleep but shortly after his head hit the blankets, Ethan was fast asleep.

34

E than felt as if he had just closed his eyes when shouts woke him from his sleep. Sitting up and throwing his blankets off, he realized it was Par'karr shouting.

"Enemy! Enemy!" the little kobold shouted over and over again.

Heart racing, Ethan blinked as he looked around the camp. The small kids were starting to scream, and the bigger kids looked terrified. Nia was up with staff in hand, head darting from side to side.

Ainslee, Yuliana and Michalus were all struggling to get up. They were pushing themselves out of their bedrolls, but their eyes were unfocused.

"What is it?" Ethan croaked to the kobold.

Par'karr glanced over to Ethan, a worried look on his features. "Ogres."

"Ogres? How many?!" Ethan jumped to his feet, adrenaline kicking in. He'd gotten lucky with the single ogre and the bridge. It had made the perfect trap and killing it once it was trapped had been easy. Fighting multiple ogres, in the dark with no stone to help trap them - he wasn't sure they could handle that.

"Two, me think," the kobold retorted, pointing in front of him. "That way."

Following Par'karr's pointing finger, Ethan strained his eyes to see anything in the dark, but he couldn't make out shapes. He was about to ask the kobold if he was sure when Nia spoke up.

"Par'karr is right!" the foxgirl hissed, sniffing the air. "There are two! But only one is moving around to flank us."

"Ogres are nasty business," Michalus said, moving next to the foxgirl. "I can probably handle one." The old elf looked over his shoulder at Ethan. "Can you handle the other?"

Ethan swallowed unconsciously, his brow furrowing. He really had lucked out with the first one. He wasn't sure exactly how to handle one without something like a rock to contain it. His mouth went dry and he licked his lips. Then he nodded to the wizard.

"Good boy," Michalus said and turned back to the woods. "Yes, I see it moving around."

"What about me?" Ainslee asked, looking from Nia and the wizard to Ethan and Par'karr.

"You and Yuliana stay near the kids," he replied. "If the ogres get past us, you're all that stands between them and the kids."

The dwarf drew her swords and nodded gravely. Yuliana also gave Ethan a nod and the two of them took stances on either side of the kids.

Turning back to the forest, Ethan swore under his breath. Because of the fire, he had no night vision and couldn't see the hulking form of the ogre out in the woods. He looked down at the little kobold, who was shaking.

Ethan put a reassuring hand on the kobold's shoulder. "We'll make it through this."

The kobold looked up at him and grinned. "Ethan good wizard. Ethan kill ogre before!"

Forcing a smile, Ethan nodded, trying to give the kobold courage he wasn't sharing. He scanned the campsite and his eyes lingered over the stones that made up the fire pit. Channeling *Earth*, he reshaped six of them into, what he hoped, were spikes of ogre smiting.

Skill increase: *Earth* Magic +1%.

Using *Air*, he floated them over to him and laid them down next to him. The kobold glanced over and grinned again, seeming to have regained a bit of his courage.

Ethan had no idea if he could make the spikes work against the ogre, but he couldn't think of anything else at the moment. *Fire* would be another weapon, but there was so much wood around, he could end up setting the forest on fire and that could end even worse for them. Like usual, he'd have to play it by ear and improvise as things unfolded.

A roar sounded in front of them and a roar behind them answered. Then, Ethan could hear heavy footsteps and the sound of snapping branches as the two ogres charged.

Eyes wide, Ethan felt his heart thudding in his chest as the sound grew quickly closer. He still couldn't see so he summoned some of his glowing balls of light and sent them racing out into the darkness.

Fifteen feet out, they illuminated the enormous ogre that was charging towards them. It looked much like the other ogre, huge and brutish, but this one had two large, exposed breasts that marked it as a female. Female or not, it looked no less formidable than the one they killed. And it was charging right at them!

Par'karr saw it coming and a small whimper escaped him. The kobold made a gesture and three demon rabbits next to him crouched low, ready to spring. The rabbits were larger than any normal rabbit but still pitifully tiny compared to the ogre. Par'karr pointed a trembling finger and the three rabbits fearlessly charged off at the huge creature.

Ethan heard roaring from behind him, but he couldn't spare a glance back. He had his own troubles and he had to trust Michalus and Nia to do their part. Reaching out with *Air*, he picked up spikes and sent them speeding at the ogre.

Skill increase: Air Magic +1%.

The rabbits reached the ogre, leaping high into the air at the creature. The ogre swatted with one huge arm and managed to hit one of them, sending it flying into a tree where it exploded into smoke. Next to him, Par'karr flinched.

The other two demon rabbits hit the ogre at full speed, horns leading. The first one slammed into the ogre's thigh, burying its horn all the way into the creature's leg. The second demon rabbit was higher, driving its horned head into the thing's abdomen.

The ogre bellowed but it didn't halt its charge. Then the six stone spikes slammed into it. Ethan had aimed two at the ogre's head. Whether the creature had seen them or just by sheer luck, it had raised its arm and the two spikes embedded themselves in his forearm instead of its head.

```
You pierce Forest Ogre for 14 damage.
    You    pierce    Forest    Ogre    for    11
damage.
    You    pierce    Forest    Ogre    for    15
damage.
    You    pierce    Forest    Ogre    for    14
damage.
    You    pierce    Forest    Ogre    for    15
damage.
    You    pierce    Forest    Ogre    for    12
damage.


Skill increase: Air Magic +1%.
```

The other four had been aimed at center mass, hoping one would puncture the creature and hit a vital organ. All four did hit the creature, but one hit the creature's arm in the bicep and the other three hit in the chest and abdomen.

The creature bellowed in pain. It faltered in its charge, stopping long enough to swipe down with a tree trunk in its uninjured arm. The ogre-sized club knocked both demon rabbits off it, causing them to hit the ground with such force that they both burst into smoke.

"Rabbits!" Par'karr cried.

Ethan knew they could be summoned back, but he didn't know how long it would take once they were killed. Nor did he have time to ask. The ogre started forward again, though this time favoring the leg that the kobold's rabbits had hit.

Ethan quickly checked his *Mana*.

Mana: **35**

He still had a good chunk, but he wasn't sure if he should pull out the spikes and go for a head strike or try something else. But what?

Getting an idea, he caused the spikes in the ogre's chest to liquify and run up along the creature's skin. He then caused them to spread over the ogre's huge face before solidifying back into solid stone in a bubble of stone around the creature's head.

Skill increase: *Earth* Magic +1%.

The effect was immediate and satisfying. Its face covered in a bubble of stone, the ogre was unable to see or breathe and began to panic. It stopped and began frantically pawing at the stone with its injured left arm.

As strong as the ogre might be, it couldn't pull the stone bubble off its head. Dropping the club, it used both hands to try and pull the bubble off its head. While it did that, Par'karr's rabbits reappeared and sped off towards the creature.

Reaching it, they once again leaped and embedded themselves into the creature's leg and abdomen. The ogre winced and slammed his fists down on the rabbits, reducing them to smoke.

Ethan thought about pulling the rest of the spikes out and attacking with them again, but other than making the creature more upset, the first round hadn't done much and the creature's head was now covered in rock, protecting it from further attacks.

Sparing a glance over his shoulder, he looked just in time to see the second ogre's club impact Nia and send her flying towards a tree. Reflexively, he reached out with air and caught the injured foxgirl. He moved her to Yuliana, who was already moving towards her with glowing hands.

Skill increase: Air Magic +1%.

Looking back at the other ogre, he saw that the creature's attack had cost it. Michalus, who was wielding some sort of glowing blade that looked straight out of Star Wars, stepped forward and sliced the creature's left leg just below the knee. The ogre bellowed in pain and fell over.

He made a quick mental note to find out exactly how the old wizard had created what essentially was a laser-sword, or perhaps it should be called a mana-sword. That would certainly come in handy in a fight.

A crash from his own ogre snapped Ethan's attention back. The creature had somehow grabbed its club and smashed the club against the side of the stone bubble. The force of the creature's blow shattered the stone into bits but also impacted the ogre's head.

The creature staggered from its own blow and then shook its head before fixing its gaze on Ethan and Par'karr. It let out a deafening war cry and then began limping towards them.

Mana: 26

His *Mana* was just over half from creating the stone bubble and catching Nia. The ogre was only a few strides away from them and he needed to do something quickly.

Suddenly, an idea from one of his role-playing games came to him unbidden. Ethan created two balls of light and sent them directly into the creature's face. The ogre skidded to a halt shied away from the balls. When the light just hovered in the air, the ogre reached out to poke one of the balls but the light had no real form and it couldn't touch it. It grunted and began to move again when Ethan moved the two balls of light directly into the creature's eyes!

Skill increase: *Fire* Magic +1%.

The balls of light did not damage, but had the desired effect. With the light directly in its eyes, it was effectively blind. Dropping the club again, the creature clawed at its eyes, desperately trying to remove the balls of light.

The ogre was distracted with the light. Ethan sent out Air and yanked the creature's injured leg backwards as hard as he could. The action had the effect he hoped and the ogre fell forward with a large crash.

Skill increase: Air Magic +1%.

Next to him, Par'karr finished summoning his demon rabbits again. He looked at the kobold. "Go for the eyes! Go for the eyes!"

The ogre started to push itself up but Ethan used Air to grab the ogre's club, lift it above its head and then bring it crashing down again, snapping the thing's head back into the ground.

You crush Forest Ogre for 23 damage.

Skill increase: Air Magic +1%.

The ogre growled and lifted its head again, eyes still covered with the balls of light. It never saw the demon rabbits as they leaped forward and buried their horns deep into the thing's eyesockets. The ogre shuddered and then its head dropped onto the ground.

Forest Ogre dies.
You gain 50 experience. Experience to next level 670.

He looked down at the wide-eyed kobold and smiled. "Good job, Par'karr! You killed it!"

The kobold gave him a toothy grin. "Me did!"

But the two of them could only spare a moment. They both spun and looked for the other ogre. Ethan saw the glowing blade come down on the other ogre and then watched its head roll away. Michalus limped away from the dead ogre and then collapsed onto the ground with a groan.

Nia was back up, though she wasn't moving nearly as fast as she normally did and seemed to be wheezing. She strode slowly to the wizard and knelt down next to him. Yuliana was moving towards them, obviously ready to heal them.

Ethan started towards them and looked to Ainslee and the children. "Everyone okay here?"

"Aye." The dwarf nodded and the kids all bobbed their heads, looking at Ethan and Par'karr wide-eyed.

"Good, let me check on Michalus," Ethan said and then hurried over to the wizard's side. The old elf was on his back arguing with Yuliana.

"Heal her first," the wizard demanded. "I'll keep. But she might have a punctured lung. She needs it more."

Seeing Ethan approach, Yuliana looked up at him questioningly. He looked from the old wizard, who was obviously in pain, to Nia, whose face was contorted in pain as well but who was also wheezing and holding her left side.

"Do as he says," Ethan told her. "Heal her first."

Nia started to object but Ethan held his hand up. "When one wizard tells you to do something, you strongly consider it. When two wizards tell you, you just do it."

The foxgirl rolled her eyes but nodded. Yuliana moved to Nia and the green glow of her healing magic surrounded the injured woman.

Ethan looked down at Michalus. The wizard grimaced as pain shot through his body. He looked up at Ethan and forced a smile. "Caught a glancing blow from the club that broke my leg. I guess I'm not quite as quick as I used to be."

"Quick enough to kill the ogre," Ethan pointed out. Then, he remembered he'd seen the old wizard moving. "How were you still standing with a broken leg?"

The old wizard smiled. "I used air to create a brace. Hurt like hell, but I could move it enough to finish the fight."

"Not bad for an old guy," Ethan joked.

Michalus grinned. "Not so bad yourself for an untrained young pup."

By then, Yuliana was done healing the foxgirl and turned her attention to the old wizard. It took several healings but Michalus was able to stand on his leg again when she was done. They all walked back to the fire and sat down.

Having just been in a life and death struggle, none of them could sleep. No one except Ainslee. A few minutes after they had gathered around the fire, their conversation was interrupted by the dwarf's loud snoring. Looking over, they saw the dwarf had crawled back into her bedroll and was fast asleep.

35

The next day, everyone was tired. Everyone except Ainslee. The dwarf had slept through the rest of the night, snoring the entire time. Even when Ethan and Michalus had moved the bodies of the ogres far enough away from the camp to avoid predators, the dwarf had kept on snoring.

After breakfast, the group had continued their journey with the old wizard leading. Several healings through the night had completely healed his leg, but Ethan noticed the elf still walked with a slight limp.

He ran his hand over his chest, remembering the scars from the trolls. It seemed to Ethan that, unlike in his MMORPGs and tabletop roleplaying games, healing couldn't always fix them back to 100%. At least, not right away. Perhaps some injuries could never be healed back to pre-injury status.

He wondered if that was more proof that he was actually here, on a different planet, instead of in some super high-tech video game. Or was it further proof that the level of detail of the virtual world the aliens had created was far superior to anything created on Earth? He didn't know and perhaps never would.

As they walked, he moved next to Nia. The foxgirl had been hurt from being hit with the ogre's club. Ethan was no medic, nor had he had anything more than basic first aid courses, but he guessed she'd had broken ribs at best, a punctured lung at worst. He'd seen her coughing since it happened and was sure something was wrong. "How are you feeling?"

"I am fine," Nia replied quickly.

Ethan nodded but he could see beads of sweat on the woman's forehead. That in itself told him something was wrong as the warrior-woman never seemed to sweat except occasionally in combat.

Nodding, he continued to walk next to her. He knew Nia was in pain. It was obvious to him. But he knew better than to press a woman when she didn't want to talk about something. It never worked out well for him.

"If you think we should stop," he started in a low voice and she gave him a sharp look. He smiled and continued. "For the kids, of course. Just let me know."

She glared at him for a moment before letting it drain away. She gave him a brief smile and nodded before turning back to stare off into the forest.

Ethan was about to fall back into his normal spot when she spoke softly. "Those ogres. They followed us."

"Followed us?" Ethan said with alarm and then lowered his voice. "They followed us? Are you sure?"

She nodded. "They had the scent of the dead ogre we killed yesterday. Either they found it, or they knew it."

"But how did they follow us? Are they following our

scent?" he asked.

The foxgirl shook her head and twisted to look back at the children. She winced as she did so but then quickly masked her pain. She looked from the children to Ethan. "Our trail is easy to find."

"Do you think there will be more?" he asked. Considering the last fight, he wasn't looking forward to facing any more. Especially if there were more than two of them. They'd barely handled two. Had there been three, Ethan had no doubt they'd all be dead.

"I don't know," she whispered. "But we should choose our campsites with more defense in mind."

"That's a good idea," Ethan agreed. "Something like a cave or other natural feature that will let us control where our enemies come from."

She nodded. "Yes. Last night, they flanked us because we camped in the open. It was a foolish mistake. Especially with children."

"If we don't reach the wizard's house by late afternoon, a couple hours before we would normally stop, start looking for any defensible spots," he told her. "If we find one, we can always stop early."

The foxgirl looked at him, nodded again and then resumed her hard stare ahead.

Ethan resumed his position next to Michalus. "How much further to your home?"

The old wizard looked over at him. The man's face looked haggard from lack of sleep and probably whatever pain was causing him to limp. "I had thought we might reach it this evening, but now I suspect we will not get there until tomorrow unless we walk into the night."

"No." Ethan shook his head. "I don't think any of us are in

any condition to push ourselves. If we get attacked again, I want us to at least be able to defend ourselves."

The elf nodded wearily. He suddenly seemed so much older than he had only yesterday. "That is probably the wisest course of action."

That decided, the two of them continued to discuss how the wizard had created the laser sword last night. Michalus explained that you could combine the elements to create some interesting effects. In the sword's case, he had combined fire and air to create a fiery, but razor-sharp blade.

Ethan had tried several times as they walked but couldn't quite get it to work. He finally gave up when his *Mana* got low, realizing he was too tired to really concentrate.

Instead, he asked the old wizard about the creation of magical items and how to bind magic to an item using a Chymera crystal. According to the elf, the concepts seemed straightforward. But that was how things were. The theory was usually the easiest part. The actual application of the theory was where all the problems happened - as he had just learned with the flaming blade.

They stopped for lunch and ate a meal of jerky and fruit. The two youngest kids didn't want to get up after lunch but after some whispered words from the two oldest, they quietly got to their feet.

Ethan couldn't say he blamed them. He was tired too. By his calculations, after taking the first watch, he'd only gotten two hours of sleep before the attack. He checked his stats again.

```
Strength: 10
  Agility: 13
  Hardiness: 13
```

```
Intellect: 19
Intuition: 13
Charisma: 12


Health: 24
  Mana: 23
Stamina: 21
```

On the plus side, his stats had all gotten better. *Strength*, *Agility* and *Charisma* were completely restored. Unfortunately, his *Stamina* was still pitiful, never going above half, and his *Health* hadn't regenerated. Probably from the lack of sleep. Now, even his *Mana* was low from attempting the flaming blade.

Ethan was tempted to eat some of the honey but knew it would be better to keep it in case of an emergency. He did make a note to stop at that hive and take as much of the honey as they could carry on their way back to Castlehaven.

A few hours before dark, Nia brought them to a stop. She called Ethan over and gestured for him to follow her down the embankment they'd been hiking along. At the bottom, he saw what she had obviously spotted from the top. A cave.

"Good catch," he told her and flashed her a smile.

"Let us hope that nothing has claimed it," she said, bringing her staff up and sniffing the air. "There are some strange smells coming from the cave, but I do not know what they are."

He held out a hand as she stepped towards the cave and she glared at him. He returned her look with a glare of his own. "Let me light it up first. That could cause anything in there to come running out. It's probably better to fight it in the open than in its own lair."

The foxgirl nodded curtly and moved off to one side of the cave. Ethan followed her example and bringing up his own staff, moved to the other side.

When they were both ready, Ethan summoned his balls of light and sent them flying into the cave. It took only a moment before a cacophony of sounds exploded from the cave as dozens of angry, screeching bats came pouring out of the cave.

`Skill increase: `*`Fire`*` Magic +1%.`

They both ducked down as the swarm flew around the area. Ethan summoned some balls of actual fire at the entrance to prevent them going back in and after several minutes, the bats flew off into the trees.

"If this is their home, they will be back," the foxgirl said, once the bats were gone.

"Maybe," he replied, "but if we build a fire in the entrance, the flames and smoke might keep them away."

The two of them explored the cave and found that it was large enough to accommodate their entire group, though the floor was covered in bat droppings. Ethan used Air like a giant sweeper and quickly pushed them outside. It wasn't perfect, but it was as good as it was going to get.

Skill increase: Air Magic +1%.

Nia walked outside and cupped her hands to her mouth to call up to the others but Ethan stopped her. He had seen her favoring her side and knew something was wrong. "Wait!"

Nia hesitated and looked at him. "Something is wrong. I can tell. What is it?"

The foxgirl narrowed her eyes at Ethan. "Nothing. I am fine."

"You're not fine," he argued. "I can tell you're hurting. I'm not a healer but I do have some knowledge from my world that might help. Tell me what is wrong and perhaps I can help fix it."

"I am fine," Nia growled between clenched teeth.

"No, you're not," he said, his voice becoming heated. "It's obvious. Something with your right side."

The foxgirl's eyes darted down to her ribs and then back to Ethan. Her tone became dangerous. "I am fine."

"No, you're not," he said. To prove his point, he prodded the area of her ribs she'd been favoring all day and she yelped.

Skill increase: Air Magic +1%.

The foxgirl's eyes went wide with pain, then with anger and, snarling, she leaped at him. Ethan had been expecting something like that and caught her wrists and ankles in Air, effectively trapping her. She struggled against him, but he'd lifted an ogre. She was no match for his magic - at least, until his *Mana* wore out.

Skill increase: Air Magic +1%.

"Let go of me!" she snarled. "Let me down now! I will kill you!"

"No killing!" he said. "Remember, I am not prey!"

Her face grew red. "I will beat you! I will make you regret this!"

Ignoring the struggling foxgirl, he walked over and ran a

hand over the area of her ribs he'd poked earlier. She was snarling and fighting, but he still saw her flinch. More importantly, he felt a large lump.

"Your rib," he gasped. "It healed wrong."

Nia stopped struggling, though she still glared daggers at him. "What do you mean?"

"I'm no medic," he said. "But it feels like the bone of your rib healed wrong when Yuliana healed you."

"It will heal," she said, though her voice lacked conviction. "It will just take more time."

"No." He shook his head and brought his face level with hers. "That's the problem. It's already healed. It just healed wrong. It could be rubbing up against your lung for all we know."

The foxgirl went slack in her bonds and let out a heavy sigh that might have been a soft whimper. She coughed and then spat. Ethan saw that the phlegm was bloody. His eyes opened wide. "Nia! What the hell?! It's poking into your lung?!"

"There is nothing that can be done," she said. "I have seen other warriors with this affliction. It cannot be fixed. It will kill me eventually."

He gently lowered her to the ground and released the bonds. He was ready to take a beating from her but the foxgirl didn't move. He frowned. On Earth, a doctor would be able to fix that. At least, he thought they could. Wouldn't they just re-break the bone, set it and let it heal the right way?

Skill increase: Air Magic +1%.

There had to be a way.

36

"Yuliana!" he yelled up. "Can you come down here!"

"What?! Why?!" Nia growled. "She has already done what she can. As you said, it has healed wrong."

"Right," he agreed. "But maybe, if she knows what's wrong, she can fix it."

The foxgirl was silent until Yuliana joined them. Ethan quickly explained the situation and the elf looked shocked. "Nia, I'm so sorry. Let me try to heal it the right way."

Moving to Nia's side, Yuliana summoned her green healing magic and moved it over the injured area. She did this for nearly a minute before backing away and shaking her head. "I still feel the lump. It didn't work."

"I told you," the foxgirl said sharply, glaring up at him.

Ethan cursed. If only he were a doctor, he might know how to break it and set it. Still, he wasn't sure how he'd keep it in the right position long enough for it to heal, other than a full-body cast. That much he could do. He could use stone to make a cast, just like he'd manipulated the stone around the ogre's head.

An idea struck him like a bolt of lightning and he looked at the women excitedly. "I have an idea! But hold on!"

Looking up to the group at the top of the embankment, he yelled up. "Michalus, can you come down please!"

"Now what?" the foxgirl growled.

"Well," Ethan started. "Bones are made of calcium. Calcium is a type of mineral. Rocks are minerals and I can manipulate them. What if I can manipulate bones since they are basically minerals!"

The two women looked at him with blank faces, clearly not understanding. He sighed.

"What's going on down here?" the old wizard said as he approached. "Is Nia injured?"

"She is," Ethan said, ignoring the glare from the foxgirl. "Her rib healed wrong and it's poking into her lung."

"Oh my," the old elf said. "You poor thing."

"I have an idea," Ethan said excitedly. "Bones are made of calcium, which is a mineral, much like rocks. I can manipulate rocks. Can I manipulate bones?"

Michalus looked at him like he was crazy. "Bones aren't rocks."

"No," Ethan said. "But they're composed of the same type of material. That's what makes them hard."

The old wizard looked doubtful and Ethan realized he was talking science to someone who had never taken a science class and had a medieval understanding of the world.

The theory was sound though. At least, in his mind. He just needed a way to test it. He held up his own hand and concentrated. When he manipulated stone, he'd almost been able to "feel" it and then bend it to his will. He'd never focused on a person's body though.

Using his *Earth* magic, Ethan focused on his hand. At first, he didn't feel anything but as he concentrated, gradually began to sense the bones in his fingers. To make sure, he moved his fingers and his awareness of them moved as well.

Skill increase: *Earth* Magic +1%.

"I can sense the bones," he told them excitedly.

"Really?" the old wizard said with interest. "That would be remarkable if we could manipulate the very bones of a person."

It was true. Ethan could sense it, but it was almost as if there was interference. Something that was actively trying to block his senses. He explained what he was experiencing to Michalus.

"Interesting," the elf replied thoughtfully. "A creature's body is protected by its own flow of energy. Its own magic, if you would. It's much harder to manipulate something inside a person than something in the world around us."

"But not impossible," Ethan said.

"Not impossible," the wizard agreed.

Ethan couldn't just try it out on Nia, not in the shape she was in. He could do more harm than good. He had to try it on something else first. With no enemies around, that meant trying it on some unsuspecting woodland creature and he just couldn't bring himself to do that.

It was one thing to inflict harm on someone or something trying to harm him. It was something completely different to just torture or injure an animal for a bit of scientific research. Steeling himself, he knew what he needed to do.

"Yuliana," he called to her. "Can you come here and get ready to heal me."

The elf approached and looked at him. "What do you mean?"

Ethan said nothing. Focusing on his little finger, he channeled *Earth* and snapped the bone. Then he screamed. He'd thought he was ready for the pain, but it was so sudden and so sharp he had taken himself by surprise.

You crush YOU for 6 damage.
Skill increase: *Earth* Magic +1%.

The elf reached for him but he gritted his teeth and shook his head. "Not yet."

The finger was at an unnatural angle and if it healed like that, the finger would be useless. He focused through the pain, reached out to the bone and pulled it together. He sensed he could force the bone back together, just like he combined stones to make the bubble around the ogre's head.

Skill increase: *Earth* Magic +1%.

He hesitated. Ethan knew there was more than just bone. There was marrow, ligaments, tendons and who knew what else. Surely healing magic would do a better job than he would just fusing bone together.

"Heal it now!" he gasped through gritted teeth, as he held the pieces of bone together with his own magic.

Cool magic ran through him and he actually sensed the bones going back together at the same time he felt both pain and relief. It was an overload of emotions and sensations and he nearly collapsed.

He flexed his fingers and wiggled them. Thankfully, they all worked. Including his pinky finger, even if it was a bit stiff.

"That was stupid!" Nia hissed. "Why would you break your own finger!"

"Because I wasn't about to test it on you," he shot back. "I had to know I could do it and I just proved that I could."

The foxgirl's eyes went wide. "You proved you could break a bone! What do you plan to do with that?"

"The only way to fix your rib is to re-break it," he told her calmly.

Nia stared at him disbelievingly. "You wish to help me by breaking my rib again."

"Yes," he sighed. "If I break it and then hold it together the right way, Yuliana can heal it correctly.'

The foxgirl continued to stare at him incredulously.

"They do this all the time on my world when something doesn't heal correctly," he said. Ethan wasn't sure about "all the time" but did know it was a thing. No need to share that detail though. "Trust me, Nia."

Nia from Ethan down to her side and then back, brow furrowed. He could tell she was debating her decision, weighing the options. Finally, she sighed. "If you can fix this, then do it. I am no good like this."

Ethan nodded. He walked over to her and began to focus his magic. He reached out and sensed her ribs, making a mental picture of them. He could sense how the rib was wrong. As he suspected, the rib had been broken, but instead of the two pieces healing correctly, they'd healed at an angle. This caused a piece of the rib to go inward, towards what was presumably her lung.

He moved his awareness to her other ribs, noting how they went together. It looked like some of her ribs had been cracked and hadn't quite healed normally but nothing nearly as bad as what the troll had done.

If he broke the rib and then connected the pieces while Yuliana healed it, that should repair the damage. Or, at least, it should prevent any further damage.

"I know the problem," he told her. "As I thought, it did heal wrong."

"Can you fix it?" Nia asked. Her tone was both cautious and hopeful.

"I think so," Ethan let out a breath. He thought of his own finger and flinched. "But it's going to hurt. A lot!"

"Just do it," she said, gritting her teeth

Ethan turned to Michalus. "Can you bind her in Air? If she moves while I'm doing this..."

"No!" the foxgirl growled. "Only you!"

"But I..." he started but she glared at him.

"Only... you," she repeated, her tone brooking no argument.

Giving the old wizard an apologetic look, he turned to Nia. "Lie down, with your arms out."

The fox girl did as he asked and Ethan wrapped her in a cocoon of Air. "Try to move."

Skill increase: Air Magic +1%.

Nia grimaced as she struggled for several seconds. "I cannot."

"Good," he said. He'd need to remember the cocoon trick

during combat. It was basically a hold person spell. Ethan turned to Yuliana. "Be ready to heal her."

The elf nodded and knelt down beside the foxgirl. "I am ready."

Taking a deep breath, Ethan once again opened his senses to the bones in Nia's body, focusing on the rib. He ran his magic into the bone, ready to do what he needed. He looked to Nia, who nodded. Ethan broke the rib.

Skill increase: ***Earth*** **Magic +1%.**

Nia howled in pain, her body spasming against the Air. Ethan held the Air while moving the pieces of the bone into the proper alignment. As he moved them, the foxgirl tried to buck and squirm and he could only imagine the agony she must be going through.

Skill increase: Air Magic +1%.
Skill increase: ***Earth*** **Magic +1%.**

FINALLY, the pieces were in alignment. He glanced at Yuliana. "NOW!"

Immediately green healing energy flowed from the elf to Nia and the foxgirl gradually stopped squirming and finally went limp. She lay on the ground panting, face covered in sweat.

Ethan could sense the rib was healed correctly and let go of his magic as well as the Air surrounding Nia.

He moved over to Nia's side and took her hand. "Are you okay? How does it feel?"

The foxgirl twisted and then took a deep breath. "It is better. It no longer hurts." Nia looked into his eyes. "I will not forget this. You are a strong alpha."

"That was remarkable," Michalus said from behind him. "I've never read about a wizard doing healing before."

Ethan smirked. "Technically, I didn't heal anything. I just broke the bone. Yuliana did the healing."

"Ah." The old elf nodded. "True. But you actually fixed a bone that had healed incorrectly. That is no small feat."

Shrugging, Ethan stood up and pulled Nia to her feet. She took a deep breath and grinned.

Michalus cleared his throat and gave Ethan a sheepish glance. He looked down at his own leg, the one he'd been favoring all day. "I wonder if perhaps there was something you might be able to do for my leg."

Ethan took a deep breath. "Let's get camp ready and give my energy some time to recharge and I'll see what I can do."

37

———————

The group made camp in the cave, making sure to set the fire just outside the entrance. Nia, who was now feeling much better, managed to shoot several green, white and blue pheasants for dinner. Once they were cooking, Ethan pulled Michalus and Yuliana away from the camp so he could examine the old wizard's leg.

This time, Michalus insisted that Ethan explain everything he was doing and how he was doing it. The old wizard even wanted to know where Ethan had learned so much about physiology.

"Biology class." Ethan shrugged and was then forced to explain about high school and college and some of the various classes he studied.

"So, you did study?" Michalus asked.

"Science," Ethan answered. "Not magic."

When it finally came down to examine the wizard's leg, Ethan did see that not one but two of his leg bones were not quite right. He had forgotten that there were two bones in the lower leg but now he remembered the calf and the forearm both had two bones. Unfortunately, it appeared that both of the bones in Michalus' calf were somewhat deformed. "Where did the ogre hit you?"

Skill increase: *Earth* Magic +1%.

The wizard pointed to his lower leg and winced. "It got me good too. The leg was at a bad angle before Yuliana healed it."

"Yah." Ethan nodded. "It looks like the bones healed wrong." He turned to Yuliana. "It doesn't appear that your magic sets bones when you heal. If someone breaks a bone, we should set it before you heal."

"Set the bone?" Yuliana asked.

Ethan smiled. "Just call me over and I'll do my best. I should be able to manipulate the bone back into place using magic."

"What about me?" Michalus asked. "Can you do something?"

Taking a deep breath, Ethan nodded gravely. "I can, but it's going to hurt. It's going to hurt a lot. There are two bones that need to be fixed. I'm thinking I should break both at the same time."

The old wizard blanched but nodded.

Ethan looked between the two elves. "Are you both ready?"

"Yes," Yuliana and Michalus said at the same time.

"Take off your belt and bite down on it when I do the break," Ethan told the old wizard. Then he turned to Yuliana. "Remember to wait for my signal."

Once Michalus had the belt in his mouth, Ethan wrapped the wizard in Air from his hip down to his foot. He didn't think it would matter if the rest of him moved, but the leg would need to stay in place.

Skill increase: Air Magic +1%.

"Here we go!" Then, once again Ethan played the wacky doctor game and channeling his *Earth*, he grimaced in anticipation of the elf's pain and broke the bone.

Skill increase: *Earth* Magic +1%.

Michalus bit down hard on his belt, groaning loudly into the leather. His eyes rolled back into his head and then he collapsed bonelessly on the ground.

Ethan cursed. He wanted to check the elf for a pulse but knew he needed to set the bone first. He quickly manipulated the bones where he thought they should be and then signalled Yuliana. "Now!"

The green healing glow surrounded her hands and she moved them across the wizard's leg. As she did, Ethan reached over and felt for a pulse in the old elf's neck. It was there. He was alive, just passed out.

When Yuliana was done, they shook the wizard awake. It took a minute, but the old elf finally regained consciousness. Blinking, he looked from Yuliana to Ethan. "Did it work?"

"You tell me," Ethan said, standing. He reached down and, grabbing the man's hand, pulled him to his feet.

The wizard shifted his weight and then took several steps. He looked over at the two of them and smiled. "Yes, I think that feels better. It's a bit stiff but I don't have the pain each time I put weight on it."

"Great!" Ethan said, happy to be done playing doctor. "Now, let's go grab some food before Ainslee eats it all."

The group ate, with Yuliana eating the last pear, and then everyone turned in for the night. Ethan was physically exhausted, but his mind was whirling with everything that had happened recently. Part of him felt good about being able to help Nia and Michalus, but another part of him was terrified.

He felt like he had no idea what he was doing. He had been a computer tech and a gaming nerd. Now he was able to sense bones, break them and reset them. It was both exciting and completely overwhelming at the same time.

And then there were the fights. He was totally out of his league with all of these fights. Ethan had survived the ogre fight mostly by sheer luck. And like any luck, it would run out eventually.

Nia's words about the ogres following them had him worried. He knew nothing about ogres, or any other creature on this crazy planet. More than ever, he needed access to the Order of the Scroll's library.

After all, that's how he'd learned about computers and fixing them. He'd studied. Well, he'd studied and practiced. As he thought of practice, he remembered his failure with the *Mana* sword.

That seemed like a useful thing to be able to do so he spent the remainder of his watch practicing creating one. In the end, he didn't manage to create one, but he did get increases in both Air and *Fire* magic.

You have reached Rank 3 in Air Magic.
+1 *Intellect*.

You have reached Rank 3 in *Fire* Magic.
+1 *Intellect*.

He knew the extra *Intellect* would help with his *Mana*. And the more *Mana* he had, the more he could do. Taking the small victory, he woke up Par'karr for the next watch and then went to bed.

THE NEXT MORNING, Nia could find no prey in the area, so they left the campsite hungry. The kids complained but Michalus assured them they would be at his home by midday and that he had plenty of jerky and preserves. The kids seemed to be excited at the prospect, so they stopped complaining and instead began asking "Are we there yet?" every five minutes. After an hour, Ethan thought he preferred their complaining.

Then, halfway through the morning, they found a large patch of raspberries and the group ate their fill. All except Nia, who refused the prey food.

Once the group had eaten their fill, everyone's spirits were lifted, and their pace quickened. The terrain became hillier and the hike became more difficult. Yet, with full bellies, no one complained.

Ethan noticed that now that most of his Hardiness had healed, it was much easier to keep up. Added to the continued walking and he was actually starting to develop some actual stamina, not just "game" *Stamina*.

Before coming to the world, he would never have been able to hike for days. Ethan had spent most of his days in a car, driving to clients, and then sitting or hunched over their computer as he troubleshooted issues, fixed or replaced hardware or re-installed applications.

He knew Yuliana had been in a similar situation. She tended a grove and her walking was confined to just her grove. Now both of them were walking all day, every day it seemed. They kept their brisk pace until, as the old wizard had said, they reached a log cabin just at midday.

It was worn but well kept, with a large porch area that covered the front of the house. The area around the cabin had cleared, and flowers had been planted and tended around the house. As he peeked around the back, he could barely make out a large garden behind the cabin.

"Welcome to my humble abode," the wizard said, gesturing at his home.

"Finally!" Ainslee sighed. "I thought we'd never get here! What do you have to eat?"

The old elf chuckled. "Lots of vegetables in the garden and I do have quite a bit of jerky left."

Going to his door, the wizard paused, and Ethan heard a bolt slide open from the opposite side of the door.

Ethan gave the wizard a curious look. "You opened the bolt using air, didn't you?"

"I did." The old elf smiled. "I learned that trick when I returned from hunting and realized I'd ripped a hole in the pouch with the key."

"And you don't have to see it?" Ethan asked, impressed.

"I know this place so well; I can envision every part of it with my eyes closed." He smiled. "And that's all it takes. Just knowing where to apply the air."

"Good to know," Ethan nodded. It was actually very good to know. In the past, he'd had to see or sense where he wanted to move things with Air. It was interesting to know that he didn't actually need to see something. But then again, since he'd gotten to this world, he hadn't been in one place long enough to memorize every nook and cranny.

They all entered the wizard's home, which immediately became very crowded. The area closest to the door was divided into a kitchen with a fireplace on one side and a dining area on the opposite side, complete with a wooden table. The far end of the room had the old elf's bed in one corner, and a bookshelf and small desk in the other corner.

It would have been cozy for just the wizard and perhaps one other person. With Ethan and his friends, plus the kids, it was packed.

"As you can see," the wizard said sheepishly, "it wasn't meant to accommodate so many visitors at once, so I'm afraid some of you will have to sleep on the porch."

Ethan shrugged. "That's fine. It's probably more comfortable than the ground."

"Or the cave floor." Ainslee nodded. The dwarf looked around the kitchen area before turning to Michalus. "So, about that food..."

Chuckling, the patient old wizard smiled and walked to the kitchen area. On the shelves in the kitchen, he grabbed a large clay jar and carried it over to the table. "Here's more jerky."

Then, walking back to the kitchen, he opened another large clay jar and pulled out two small loaves of bread. Replacing the lid on the bread jar, he grabbed a smaller jar from a shelf above and took it to the table. "And here is some bread and some homemade strawberry preserves."

Nia made her way over to Ethan and leaned up. "This will not be enough food. I will go hunt."

Without waiting for a confirmation, she slipped out the door with her bow. Ethan watched her disappear out the door and then turned back to the table, where the children had gathered to get strawberry preserve sandwiches. Ethan wondered if they had peanut butter in this world. He could really go for a peanut butter and jelly sandwich.

Once the children were all eating, Michalus motioned for Ethan to join him near the door. The old wizard opened the door and smiled. "Let's talk about magic."

38

―――――

Ethan and Michalus went outside and sat in the two wooden chairs on the old elf's porch. The wizard stared out into the woods for a long time without saying a word and Ethan left the elf to his thoughts.

It wasn't easy. He had so many questions about magic and so far, Michalus was the only other wizard he'd met - unless he counted the kobold witchdoctor. The kobold wizard had been trying to kill him, so Ethan didn't exactly count him among his friends.

Reaching out with *Fire* and Air, he once again tried to form the energy blade that Michalus had shown him. As had happened previously, a yard-long gout of flame appeared near his hand. When Ethan tried to combine it with Air, it flashed and dissipated.

Next to him, Michalus chuckled. Ethan let out an exasperated breath and turned to the wizard. "What am I doing wrong?"

The old elf smiled at him. "Don't feel bad. As far as I

know, I'm the only one who ever managed to create these fireblades."

"So, you've taught others?" Ethan asked.

Michalus looked wistful. "Many years ago, when I was active with the Order of the Scroll, I did show it to some of the other wizards."

Ethan raised an eyebrow. "You were a member of the Order of the Scroll?"

"Still am, technically," he said, his voice tired. "But I've been out here for over a hundred years, trying to master portal magic."

"A hundred years?!" Ethan whistled. "And you still haven't mastered it?"

"Well," the old wizard chuckled. "I haven't been working on it the entire time. More like tinkering. I even invented a device that picks up portal activity."

"That's right." Ethan remembered the elf mentioning that earlier. Michalus had said he'd detected Ethan's teleportation. "What kind of device? Can I see it?"

The old wizard smiled with a twinkle in his eye. "I was hoping you would ask. I'm quite proud of it."

Returning his smile, Ethan gestured back to the house. "Lead the way."

A sly look came over Michalus' face. "It's not in the house."

Ethan looked around, he only saw the cleared-out area that was the man's yard, plus the forest beyond it. He furrowed his brow. He'd been back to the garden but there was nothing back there. "Where then?"

Smiling broadly, the old wizard stood up and motioned Ethan to follow him around the back of his house. Curious, Ethan followed him. Michalus led him to a barren patch of earth that looked like it had been neglected. Stopping a few feet from the patch of earth, he gestured. "It's right here?"

Ethan furrowed his brow again, not understanding what the man meant. And then he saw it. A leaf floated down from a tree and glided across something he couldn't see. The motion was so unnatural that there had to be something there. Something invisible. He turned to the old wizard excitedly. "No way! You have an invisible workshop?"

The old man glanced at him, frowned and then glanced at the space where Ethan had seen the leaf move across the invisible structure. Michalus put his hands on his hips. "How do you even know what I did, let alone figure it out so quickly?"

"On my world," Ethan replied sheepishly, "there are stories of invisibility. Some very well-known stories. I saw a leaf move unnaturally across what I'm guessing is the roof and I guessed."

The old man rolled his eyes, sighed and threw up his hands. "Of course, you did."

"Sorry," Ethan said, though he wasn't really sorry. He was excited that he'd actually seen real invisibility - something that only existed in books, movies and TV shows. Ideas of making a magical ring that made him invisible suddenly played through his head. He grinned.

Michalus looked Ethan up and down and smirked. "You don't look very sorry."

Ethan shrugged. "If I hadn't known that something was here, I probably wouldn't have guessed it. I mean, I was here picking things out of your garden and I didn't notice it. None of us did."

The old wizard smiled and nodded. "I was watching

earlier to see if anyone would notice it. You're really the first people I've had here since I enchanted the workshop."

"How did you do it?" Ethan asked but held his hand up. "Wait! Don't tell me!"

His mind kicked into full problem-solving mode, just like it did when he was troubleshooting computer issues. He thought about it logically.

The old elf had to be bending light around the object. That much was clear. He'd already said he couldn't create a man-sized portal, so portal magic was out. *Fire* and *Earth* didn't make much sense. *Water*? Possibly. *Water* refracted light. But it couldn't just be *Water*. Air too? To keep the *Water* magic suspended? "Air and *Water* to refract the light around it?!"

The old wizard just eyed him for a long moment without saying a word. Then he sighed. "You know, a person could really learn to hate you. How did you figure that out? It took me years!"

Once again Ethan shrugged sheepishly. "It's more science from my world. People have theorized about doing something like that with the technology we have but no one has ever managed to accomplish it."

Michalus snorted. "Well, I should be thankful for that, at least."

"Did you invent this too?" Ethan asked.

The wizard shook his head. "No, this is actually a commonly known spell among wizards."

"Really?" Ethan asked, surprised.

The elf nodded but then his face became grave. "Back when there were wizards."

Ethan nodded solemnly. He looked at the wizard. "Do you know who or what's been killing them and why?"

Michalus sighed and shook his head sadly. "Many theories, each one as unlikely as the next."

"Oh?"

"At first, I thought it might be enemy cities, killing off their opponent's battlemages. But then it became too widespread. Even small-town wizards began to die."

"And no clues?"

"To be honest, I haven't really looked into it. By time the stories reached the village and I heard about them, so many wizards were already dead. I retreated back to my home and haven't been back in over a year. If I hadn't seen the village burned down, I wouldn't have left at all."

Ethan raised an eyebrow. "Does anyone else know you're here?"

"No one living," the elf replied sadly and then looked up at Ethan. "Except you and your friends."

"I wonder if that's what has kept you alive so long?" Ethan asked.

"That would be my guess," the wizard replied. "But it's been tough, constantly looking over my shoulder, waiting for the assassin to show up. Some days, I spend all day in the workshop. I even sleep in there some nights."

"You think it's an assassin and not a group - like the priestesses of Hel?"

"The church of Hel isn't popular in many city-states. I don't think they have the resources for such a large scale, systematic killing."

Remembering one of the more gruesome details, Ethan posed the question to the old man. "What do you make of the brains missing."

Michalus took a deep breath, his face troubled. "I don't know, but I fear it is nothing good."

"You don't suppose whoever or whatever is killing the wizards is extracting their brains to gain their knowledge?" Ethan asked. It seemed like the thing from movies or TV, or fantasy books. Then again, so did magic, monsters and alien abductions.

"I've never heard of any such magical ritual or a creature that did such a thing," the elf replied. "Other than the demonlord I told you of. And I think we'd know if another one was back in this universe. Though, with more and more warlocks, who knows what rituals they could have learned from other dimensions."

"So, it could be a warlock?" Ethan asked. Remembering the crazy warlock woman, Charmine, who had sent him on the quest for the Tomes, he wouldn't be surprised.

"I suppose that's possible," Michalus replied. "But there were fewer warlocks, channelers and summoners before the wizards started dying. Many people turned to the dark arts to fill the void left by the wizards."

"Seems like a motive," Ethan said, channeling his inner sleuth.

"Motive?" the elf asked, obviously confused. "No, I've never seen any warlock with the power to overcome a decently experienced wizard. They only have one element at their command. Any wizard worth his salt can counter them and attack with an element they can't counter."

"Interesting," Ethan said. "Does that mean wizards are more powerful?"

The wizard scrunched up his face in thought and then shrugged. "In general, that is true. But powerful warlocks can command a good amount of whatever element their patron is affiliated with, usually fire. In a straight-out contest, we might not be able to out-conjure them in fire, but our ability with other elements can overcome that."

"Good to know," Ethan said.

"Just be careful with warlocks, channelers and even summoners," the elf told him. "Their powers come from other dimensions, granted by beings with generally one goal - to enter this dimension and conquer it."

Ethan nodded. Seemed like a familiar storyline in many horror flicks. But that begged another question, one he'd been afraid to really explore. "So where do we get our powers?"

Michalus smiled and nodded. "A good question. I'm afraid I don't have a definitive answer for you. Some believe the gods granted us these powers. Others say we are born with the ability through some rare trait like two different-colored eyes. Some even believe it is a curse. The truth is: no one really knows."

"A curse?" Ethan asked, his forehead wrinkled. How could being able to do magic be a curse.

Michalus chuckled. "You're young yet. The older you get, the more you'll realize that our magic isolates us, sets us apart from the others. People will see you as someone who can make amazing things happen."

"And that's a bad thing?" Ethan asked.

"Maybe not at first," the old elf said wryly, "but people don't understand magic. They don't understand its limits. They put unrealistic expectations on you. Wizard, can you end this drought? Wizard, can you give us a better crop? Wizard, can you bring my son back to life? What do you mean no, wizard, do you mean you can't, or you won't?"

Ethan heard the pain in the wizard's last words and

wondered how many times that scenario had played out in his long life. He nodded. "I see your point."

"You're new to magic yet," the old man said. "You don't yet realize its true limits. But there are limits. We aren't gods."

Again, Ethan nodded. He'd never thought of himself as a god, but in a world of medieval technology, he could understand how people who could work magic might begin to think of themselves as gods.

He, on the other hand, was all too often reminded of his limitations with magic. He was far from being a god.

Michalus clapped his hands together and the old wizard's expression brightened. "Enough about that, let me show you my workshop... and my portal detector!"

39

___

The old elf walked to a spot on the ground, reached out and pulled something. When he did so, a door swung open. Ethan thought of it as a door, but as it opened, it continued to refract light so that Ethan could only see a shimmer in the air as it moved. It was almost like the predatory alien in that action movie.

As soon as the door stopped moving, it became truly transparent and impossible to spot. Ethan looked through the door at Michalus. "When it's moving, it's not quite invisible. You can see it shimmer."

"Yes," the wizard confirmed. "For whatever reason, invisibility never works quite as well when the target moves quickly. Slow, steady movements and it still hides you. Move fast and, as you pointed out, you get a shimmering effect."

"And you still leave footprints," Ethan offered with a smile as he remembered one of his favorite movies about the little halfling who had to destroy a ring of invisibility.

"Footprints?" The old elf tweaked an eyebrow. "I never thought of that. Yes, I supposed you would."

"And if you couldn't see footprints," Ethan suggested, "you could always hose the person down with water."

"*Water*?" Michalus asked, curiosity splashed across his features.

Ethan moved his hand until he touched a barrier. It was a soft barrier, made of Air he knew, but it felt cold to his touch. Probably the *Water*. As he touched it, the Air seemed to push his hand downwards. "The air pushes stuff down so it doesn't sit on top and give it away, right?"

The old wizard nodded.

"But it doesn't happen instantly," Ethan observed. "So water will be slowly pushed down the layer of air. The refractive nature of the water should cause it to be visible."

"Like sunlight hitting a brook. That's an interesting theory," Michalus said as he scratched his chin. "But I don't remember seeing any such effect on rainy days."

Ethan looked to the left to where a stone well sat between the workshop and garden. "Does that well have water?"

"Of course," Michalus said.

"Then let's do some experimentation." Ethan grinned. He channeled his *Water* magic down into the well and found the water. He willed the water to come rushing out of the well and hit the workshop.

Michalus opened his mouth to protest a moment too late. The gout of water sprayed off the top of the workshop and splashed all over the old elf, drenching him.

Ethan stopped the water immediately and flashed the wizard an embarrassed look. "Sorry."

The elf just stood there dripping and shaking his head. As he did, the elf muttered something too low for Ethan to hear.

Then the sunlight hit the water-soaked workshop and they both turned to stare. The entire workshop now glittered like a diamond, refracting and reflecting light in a dazzling pattern and outlining the entire structure in sparkling light.

"Beautiful," Michalus remarked, staring at the rainbow patterns. "Why have I not seen this before?"

Grinning, Ethan pointed to the two suns, once again shaking his head at the sight of the black hole in between them. "The sun's not out when it's raining."

The old wizard looked up at the sky, then back to the sparkling building. "It seems much more intense than a brook."

Ethan shrugged. "It might be some interaction between the water and the magic, since I assume it's refracting light too."

Michalus wrinkled his brow in concentration and Ethan watched as his clothes dried out instantly. He smiled. "That's better. Now, let's go inside."

The elf reached towards the invisible door and his fingers momentarily disappeared. Then, the door swung fully open and Ethan watched as his entire body seemed to disappear behind the invisibility field. All except a bit of his feet. Stepping around the door, he saw it led into a small building that looked like a large storage shed back home.

Michalus grinned proudly and stepped inside. "Welcome to my workshop. Come on in!"

Ethan followed the wizard into the small building. It was maybe eight feet by twelve feet and, like the house, made of logs. To the right was a large, messy desk filled with parchments and books. On the opposite side were two tables.

The closest table had something that looked like a copper gyroscope, but with six different concentric circles.

Embedded in each copper circle was a small, glowing blue crystal. Chymera crystals.

Ethan whistled. "Impressive."

The old wizard smiled. "Took me almost a hundred years to get it working."

"Wow." Ethan shook his head. Ethan couldn't imagine working on something for a hundred years, even if he managed to live that long. "That's a long time."

The elf smiled and shrugged. "On and off, over a hundred years, I should say. I almost gave up on it dozens of times but I always came back to it."

Ethan looked at the rotating circles, trying to divine their meaning and purpose. After a minute, he gave up and looked at the elf. "What does it do and how does it work?"

The wizard smiled and pointed to the circles. "Each circle represents fifty miles and each crystal is enchanted to point to portal activity. Major portal activity, not something like my pouch. If a portal goes off within fifty miles, like it did when you created a portal in Timberwell, the inner circle pointed to it. It stays pointed in that direction for a few days or until more portal activity is detected in the same distance."

"So, the innermost circle is anything within 50 miles, the second circle would be anything between 51 and 100 miles, and so on?" Ethan reasoned.

"Very good. That is precisely how it works." The elf nodded and pointed to the center circle, which was unmoving. "As you can see, the inner ring is still pointing to Timberwell."

Ethan nodded and took the elf's word for it. He'd need to look at his map to figure out exactly which way Timberwell was from his current location - if he even could.

"Why did you build it?" Ethan asked. "Not that it's not

cool, but I'm trying to figure out what it does for you. I mean, what's the use in knowing a portal opened 300 miles away?"

"Well, you see." Michalus looked slightly embarrassed but then let out a sigh and smiled nervously. "There is a theory that outlanders come to our world through the portals."

"Really?" Ethan asked, his curiosity piqued. As far as he knew, he'd been brought by aliens, but nothing said they couldn't use some sort of teleportation, or portal, technology to beam him from their ship down to the planet's surface. Perhaps their "beaming" technology worked like portals.

The old elf sensed his interest and his tone suddenly became more enthusiastic. "Oh yes! It's not a popular theory. Most people simply believe the gods bring them here for some reason or another. Far be it from me to blaspheme, but an old colleague of mine, Merlin, suggested that people were brought through portals..."

"Wait!" Ethan exclaimed. "Merlin?! THE Merlin? You know Merlin?"

Michalus looked surprised. "You knew Merlin?"

"He is a legend on my world. He's thought to be a fictional person," Ethan replied. His mind was reeling from the mention of Merlin and that he might be a real person. Could that really have been the Merlin from King Arthurian legends? How would that even be possible? "According to the stories he lived like... fifteen hundred years ago."

The old elf shook his head. "They couldn't be the same person. The Merlin I knew disappeared only eighty years ago..." He scratched his head. "Or is it eighty-one years ago?"

The real Merlin would have been long dead centuries ago, so they couldn't be the same person. Ethan felt strangely disappointed that they weren't, in fact, the same person. Too bad. "What happened to him?"

"He was studying portal magic too," Michalus explained. "That's how we met. He always claimed he was from Camelot but that city disappeared ages ago. Nice enough fellow. Human, like you..."

"Wait," Ethan interrupted again. "There's a Camelot in this world too?"

"Oh yes," the old wizard sighed. "Or rather, there was. It's long gone now."

"In our legends," Ethan said. "Merlin is associated with Camelot. Is there a King Arthur in Camelot?"

"King Arthur?" the old elf chuckled. "I believe there was a king with a similar name, long ago. We really haven't had a king for hundreds of years. Just the city princes. It's an unusual coincidence that there is a figure in your stories called Merlin and he lived in a city called Camelot."

"There are no coincidences," Ethan said, quoting one of his favorite movies. "Only the illusion of coincidence."

Michalus looked thoughtful. "An interesting hypothesis. Where was I... oh, yes. Merlin. He did have a keen interest in portal magic. He had some interesting theories as well. He stayed here for nearly a year, helping me with my device. Very helpful chap."

The old wizard gestured to the portal detector. "Come to think of it, this was actually his idea. Though I did help with and ended up perfecting the design after he left."

"What did he, and you, hope to learn from being able to detect portals?" Ethan asked.

"Merlin theorized that the portals were opening at fixed intervals," the elf replied. "But without some way to detect them, it was impossible to prove. It's impossible to rely on firsthand and secondhand stories, if there were anyone to actually see them arrive. And that's assuming the outlanders even lived."

Ethan remembered finding the corpses of other people when he'd first arrived and nodded. "When the women and I first arrived, we found some others, but they had been killed by kobolds. We might have been killed too, but we grouped together and fought them off."

The old elf scratched his chin, looking Ethan up and down. "Tell me, was it your idea to band together, one of the women's or a mutual idea you all came up with?"

"We... uh... I mean, I... um..." Ethan tried to remember the exact series of events that had happened. Had it been his idea? He thought so, but so much had happened and things had been very confusing then. "I think it was my idea."

"Interesting." He nodded. "From my own study of portals and outlanders, they do not quickly band together. Perhaps that's why so many of them die."

That gave Ethan something to think about. He remembered the first few fights and knew there was no way he would have been able to survive on his own. He doubted Yuliana would have either. Maybe Ainslee, and probably Nia. But by himself, Ethan wouldn't have survived. "You might be right."

Michalus nodded. "I don't know as much about outlanders as Merlin did, but I have run across many stories of them in my research of portals. Some of the ones who lived reported some strange things - like the hood you spoke of."

"HUD," Ethan corrected. "Heads up display."

"Yes, HUD." The elf nodded. "I thought I might be able to track down some outlanders with the portal detector, to get firsthand accounts. But the first time I got a strong hit was only a couple of months ago. Given the assassination of so many wizards, I thought it best to stay where I was - far from others."

The wizard sighed and turned his back to the portal detector. "I could talk all night about portals but let's talk about magic. I think you said earlier you wanted to learn how to enchant items."

Ethan nodded excitedly. "Oh yes, learning how to enchant items would be awesome!"

40

E than spent the next several hours listening to the old wizard explain the basics of enchanting items. It was both more simple and more complicated than he had expected but it really seemed to boil down to Chymera crystals.

The crystals seemed to function as both batteries and some sort of programmable processor. In his mind, he equated the programmable aspect to some sort of firmware on a computer. You could load a program into the crystal, and it stayed in the crystal until you overwrote it.

Michalus showed him the side of his pouch and Ethan could see six different crystals sewn into the pouch that caused the effect. He also pulled a chest from underneath the table and opened it up. Inside, were some sort of runes.

"This is the chest that Extendable Bag creates a portal to. I created these runes myself," Michalus explained. "They are unique. Or rather, unique enough that I can lock the portal onto them. That is why the portal always opens inside of the chest."

"Cool," Ethan grinned. He really wanted to create one of those for himself, but he needed Chymera crystals. Lots of Chymera crystals.

"Watch this." The elf smiled. He reached down, opened the pouch and stuck his hand inside.

Now that he knew what to look for, Ethan saw the crystals inside the pouch flare to life. The wizard reached into the pouch and then Ethan saw his hand appear inside the chest. Ethan looked from the pouch to the chest and back. He grinned broadly. "That is so cool!"

"And very handy." The elf nodded as he withdrew his hand. "But that's the largest portal I've been able to conjure."

"Can I create a portal to the chest," Ethan wondered aloud, "if I concentrate on the runes you created?"

Michalus looked down at the runes. "There's nothing to stop you from doing so. Two people could technically do so."

"So," Ethan theorized. "We could both create a portal to the same place and use it to pass messages or even items back and forth."

"I've heard of such things being done," the wizard admitted. "But even at the height of our power, wizards tended to be a solitary bunch. Many of the things we learn to do are fairly common, but many of us discover some unique things that we keep to ourselves."

"Like your *Mana* blade?" Ethan asked with a raised eyebrow.

The old wizard smirked. "Yes, and I like that... *Mana* blade. Seems fitting. Though to be honest, I have shared that with a few wizards."

"I still can't make one you know," Ethan confessed.

"I'd be surprised if you could. It took me years to master

that." The elf smiled. "Let me guess, you're trying to combine elements."

"Yes, but they don't really combine," Ethan admitted.

"They do combine," the old wizard chuckled. "But we just don't fully understand how. That's why you always focus on the result you wish to achieve, rather than the exact method."

Ethan furrowed his brow as he considered the wizard's words. As he thought back to it, he'd created effects based on his ideas of spells from MMORPGs and tabletop RPGs he'd played. He'd never really thought about the exact workings of the spells, just the end result.

Had he been overthinking things? Trying to use rational and logical methodology to deconstruct the spells. Was he getting in his own way?

Michalus seemed to see the confusion etched on his features. "To create a spell, you visualize it and then will it. The hard part is knowing the exact effect that you really want and being able to focus on it so that your will can turn it into reality."

Ethan blinked. "Wait, so I just visualize and will it?"

The old elf chuckled. "When you say it like that, you make it sound easy. But I think you know better than that."

Ethan backed out of the shed and faced away from the wizard. He imagined exactly what he wanted, drawing on the memories of the famous space movies he'd enjoyed - at least, the first trilogy. He wanted a handle of air and then a *Mana* blade. Then he willed it into being.

Nothing happened. Ethan frowned and looked at Michalus. "It didn't work."

The old elf put his hands on his hips. "You've been practicing magic for all of what, two months, and you think everything is just going to come easy to you?"

"Well, it kind of has so far." Ethan smirked. "I was kind of hoping it would keep going that way."

"You will find that as you attempt more complicated things the way you envision it becomes more and more important. Sometimes, you have to envision it differently."

"What do you mean?" Ethan asked, letting out a frustrated breath. "I thought you said you just envision it and then will it into being."

"That's true. But let's say you wanted to get water out of a well," the elf said with a meaningful look. "Suppose you envisioned hardened air bringing the water up. You would have gotten a different result than you did earlier. Or say you envisioned a rock inside the well becoming a bucket and bringing water out."

"You're saying you can envision the same task in different ways, each time getting a different result?"

"Yes and no," the elf said. "Sometimes, if the way you envision is not something the magic can make real, it will fail. Or, sometimes, it will work but will consume much more *Mana*. Finding just the right way to make it work so that it minimizes *Mana*, that is what true mastery is about."

Ethan frowned again. That was actually something he hadn't considered that he could be doing things but maybe not in the most efficient way. But how did you figure out the best and most efficient way? He thought he knew the answer, but he asked anyway.

"So how do you know the most efficient way?" he asked the wizard.

Michalus smiled. "I think you already know the answer..."

"Spells," Ethan finished.

"Spells," the old elf agreed. "That's why we share and write down spells. When someone finds what they believe to be the most efficient way of doing things, they share that with others." The wizard looked thoughtful and then gave him a sly look. "Mostly. As I said before, sometimes we wizards tend to keep a few things to ourselves."

"Do you have spell books?" Ethan asked excitedly. He was sure that being able to read another wizard's thoughts on the most efficient way of doing specific spells would help him improve his magic.

The old wizard shook his head sadly. "I'm afraid I no longer really needed them, so I left them in the care of the Order of the Scroll in Moonpoint some time ago. They may be still be there for all I know."

Ethan sagged. He wanted, no, he needed to learn more about magic. The talk of spellbooks had raised his hopes, only to leave him disappointed.

That did mean that retrieving the Tomes and becoming a member of the Order of the Scroll was more important than ever. Ethan needed access to their library and any spellbooks he could get his hands on.

Michalus seemed to notice his frustration. "Sorry, my boy, but I haven't needed my old spellbooks for several hundred years and you'll find that we mostly use the same spells over and over. But maybe I can give you some other pointers."

A half hour later, the wizard had explained the way he created the *Mana* blade in more detail. This time, Ethan listened and carefully paid attention. When the old wizard was done, Ethan thought he knew enough to do it. At least he hoped.

Walking back outside, he once again focused, but this

time he focused on what the elf had told him. Forming the handle first, out of air and then extending the air up and mixing it with the fire to form a blade.

Exerting his will, he felt something solid form in his hand and there was a snap hiss as a blade of brilliant white *Mana* appeared. He grinned ear to ear. Then he quickly checked his HUD.

```
Mana: 41

Skill increase: Air Magic +1%.
  Skill increase: Fire Magic +1%.
```

His *Mana* had dropped significantly and even as he watched, it dropped another point.

```
Mana: 40
  Skill increase: Air Magic +1%.
  Skill increase: Fire Magic +1%.
```

Ethan whirled the magical laser sword around and it gave a very satisfying sound, just like the laser sword in the space opera movies he loved. Then he released his will, and the sword simply vanished.

"Wow, I did it!" Ethan exclaimed and checked his HUD again. "But it still takes a ton of mana to maintain that."

"It does." The old wizard smiled knowingly. "Not something you want to pull out at every fight."

Suddenly a thought struck Ethan. "I can see my total mana and my remaining mana in my HUD. If you don't have a HUD, how do you and other wizards know how much mana you have total and how much you have left?"

Michalus cocked his head. "You just gain a feel for it after a while. But it takes some time. That's why it's not uncommon to find wizards who have burned themselves out, or worse, killed themselves. Having a way to know precisely how much *Mana* you have at any given time is truly a miraculous gift."

Thinking about it, Ethan couldn't help but agree. Just to prove he could, he created the *Mana* blade again, but this time, added a little touch of his own to it and charged the color of the blade to a pale blue. Now he could change his last name to Skywalker.

"Good job," the elf complimented. He ducked back into the workshop and came out a tiny black velvet pouch, which he held out to Ethan. "Here, take these."

Curious, Ethan reached out and took the pouch. He pulled the velvet pouch open and poured the contents into his hand. In his hand were a dozen Chymera crystals. His eyes grew wide. "For me?"

"Yes." The old wizard grinned. "You've been drooling over my portal pouch since I told you what it was. This should be enough to make your own. Just place them evenly inside your pouch. Alternate between a battery and a spell stone. There might be a few extra in there, just in case."

"Wow," Ethan said, still not quite believing his good fortune. "Thank you."

Michalus made a dismissive gesture. "It's nothing. I've been collecting them for a few hundred years. They're getting rarer, but every now and then you find a cache of them."

Ethan poured the crystals back into the bag and put the bag into his belt pouch. He looked back at the wizard. "What else can you teach me?"

The elf smiled tiredly. "Nothing more tonight. And I think we must part ways tomorrow. You need to continue on to the library in Patheos and I believe that I should take the children and lead them to Moonpoint, where they can be united with their parents.

"Patheos is not a safe place by all reckoning," Michalus stated as Ethan started to open his mouth. "And it is certainly no place for children. Leaving them outside is not an option either. There are things that prowl the area around the library. Terrible things."

"Terrible?" Ethan swallowed.

"At least, that's what the survivors claim." The elf winked.

"Wait," Ethan frowned. "I thought there were no survivors."

"No one who has entered the library has returned," he said. "But people, porters and such, who were left on the outside, some of them made it back."

"Should I just give up this quest?" he asked the elf.

"It will be dangerous," the old wizard said. "But if you keep your wits about you, you might make it."

"Are you sure you don't have any spell books I could read on the way there?" Ethan asked.

Michalus smiled and scratched his chin. "I'll tell you what. Once I reunite the children with their families in Moonpoint, I will come visit you in Hawkshead and help you create your portal pouch."

Ethan grinned and held out his hand. "Deal!"

The old wizard returned his grin and took Ethan's hand in a firm grip. He gave Ethan a wink. "If you survive."

41

The next morning, Ethan's group set off for the Patheos and the library of Daemonium, while Michalus and the kids set off for Moonpoint. The old elf had explained that the encounter with the ogres had made it clear to him that the kids needed to be taken to safety. The wizard didn't want to risk them on the trip to the library.

For their part, the children wanted to stay with Ethan and the women. When it was finally decided that they would go with the wizard, the smaller kids had cried, saying they would miss his group. Ethan had found it strange considering how little interaction they'd actually had with the kids.

If anything, Ethan was going to miss the old elf. There was so much more he wanted to learn from Michalus. Luckily, the wizard had agreed to come visit Ethan in Hawkshead after he had dropped the children off in Moonpoint.

Before they'd left, the wizard had told them to fill their bags with vegetables from the garden, as well as some apples from the apple trees in his backyard. At least, that's what he'd called them. And in his HUD, they identified as apples, but they were a dark purple in color and extremely hard.

His skepticism was laid to rest when Ainslee began crunching down on one, even as they packed their bags full.

"They're harder than normal apples," Michalus had told them. "But they keep longer. When I don't have jerky, I put these in my chest to keep me going. I recommend you save as many as possible until you reach the mountains. Once you do, you might not find much game."

"Why not?" Nia had asked.

"It's desolate," the wizard explained. "Very few plants. That means very few animals. Not even many predators because of the lack of prey. And then there are rumors of... creatures, as well."

"Creatures?" Yuliana asked with alarm.

"What sort of creatures?" Nia demanded.

"Descriptions vary." The old elf shrugged. "What they truly are, I have no idea."

"Great," Ainslee growled. "Just great."

Once both groups were set with food, they'd said their farewells, and each had headed a different direction. Michalus took the kids southwest towards Moonpoint, while Ethan's group headed due north towards the Mountain road. From there, they too would head west and follow the map to the library.

IT TOOK them a day and a half to reach the northern edge of the forest. When they did, they understood Michalus' warning about saving their food. Beyond the forest was a craggy wasteland of rock that culminated in tall spires of stone that must pass for mountains.

Behind him, Yuliana gasped. "How terrible! I've never seen such desolation."

Ainslee shrugged. "Actually, it reminds me of home, except there's no lava pools or volcanoes around."

"That's terrible," the elf remarked.

"That's home." The dwarf shrugged again.

"There is no cover," Nia pointed out. "We will be exposed. And Michalus was correct, we will find little game here."

"This place ugly," Par'karr commented and Ethan couldn't help but agree.

Ethan surveyed the vast stretch of wasteland before him and couldn't help but agree. Other than some patches of grey grass, there was no vegetation at all. He glanced at Yuliana and made a mental note to save his share of the apples and vegetables for the elf.

He looked west along the edge of the forest and then north to where he could make out the road several miles away. "Let's stay along the forest's edge as long as it runs parallel to the road."

Glancing at Ainslee who was about to take a bite out of an apple, he frowned. "Let's keep the food we have until we have no choice."

The dwarf looked at him and then to the apple, frowned and put it away. "Well, it's lunch time!"

"There is another problem," the foxgirl said, gesturing to the wasteland. "No wood."

Ethan looked out and cursed. She was right. There were no trees at all that he could see. No trees meant no wood. No wood meant no fire. He cursed again. "People traveling through this area probably come with wagons and bring their own supplies."

"That makes sense," Ainslee agreed. "We have to do the same when we cross the Barren Expanse. Sometimes, it takes two or three wagons, just for the supplies."

Ethan kicked at a rock and cursed. "It would have been nice if someone would have told us about this."

Ainslee snorted. "What? Someone like that looney warlock woman?! That lady had some serious bolts loose."

"Ethan," Nia said. "You make a fire. I will go hunt for something larger. You can use your magic to make it frozen and we can keep it with us. I need something other than prey food."

"Me too!" Ainslee bobbed her head up and down.

Ethan rolled his eyes at the dwarf and then nodded to Nia. Leaving her staff with them, the foxgirl took her bow from her back and ran back into the forest.

"I hope she gets a deer," Ainslee said wistfully as she licked her lips. "I could really go for some venison."

"The venison won't cook itself," he told the women. "Let's see if we can get a fire going."

The four of them scoured the closest part of the forest for some firewood, then made a fire just outside of the forest. Since the ground was mostly rock, Ethan thought about shaping it into something useful.

He checked his HUD, to see how his stats were looking.

```
Strength: 10
   Agility: 13
   Hardiness: 15
   Intellect: 23
   Intuition: 15
```

Charisma: 12

Health: 30
Mana: 56
Stamina: 22

After a night at the wizard's home and a night in the forest, he'd healed two more points in his stats. Now, only *Intellect* was low but that would heal up in a few days. Then, he'd finally be back to normal.

Since he had full *Mana*, Ethan used his *Earth* magic to create four stools for them. After the stools, he got an idea about the fire. With the abundance of stone, he formed it into thin lines, effectively creating a thin, stone grill.

He played with the shape several times until he settled on a circular outer grill around an open area in the middle, where they could use their normal spit. That would allow them to cook some filets and a shank or two at the same time.

"That magic stuff is pretty handy," Ainslee remarked as she watched him form the grill. "Still have no clue how it works, but anything that helps cook up a meal is useful in my mind."

Par'karr examined the grill closely, nodding. "This good for cooking."

The three of them watched the fire for a long time, each in their own thoughts until, after over an hour, Nia returned with a small deer over her shoulders. The group quickly went into action, repeating a now-familiar routine of dressing and cooking the deer.

As they did, Nia noticed his grill. She raised an eyebrow

at it. "Impressive. This will allow us to cook more meat at the same time?"

Ethan nodded.

"Very good." She smiled. "We should cook it all, even if it takes us longer. Then, you can make it cold..."

"Freeze it," he supplied.

"Yes," she agreed. "Freeze it. Then we take all we can carry."

"I'm all for that!" the dwarf said, slicing some of the meat into filets. "The more the merrier."

"We must conserve!" the foxgirl hissed. "You must control your hunger."

Ainslee became red-faced and for a moment Ethan thought she might try to throttle Nia. But Nia pressed on, gesturing to the woods. "I saw very little sign of prey. I believe this deer became lost and wandered the wrong way. We may not find another for days."

The dwarf blinked. "Days?!"

Nia nodded. "We must conserve what we have."

"What about small game? Some rabbits maybe?" Ainslee asked desperately.

"Par'karr send out rabbits," the kobold offered. "Maybe rabbits find something."

Nia just shrugged. "Do as you wish, but there is very little there."

Unfazed, the kobold summoned his demon rabbits and sent them hopping into the forest, presumably to hunt some food for them.

In the meantime, the rest of them kept an eye on the cooking venison. Unsurprisingly, the filets cooked first. It wasn't until Ethan went to try to flip them with his fingers that he realized he needed to create something else out of stone - a spatula. Grabbing a nearby rock, he did just that.

As he began flipping the steaks with the new spatula, Ethan was reminded of grilling out hamburgers with his family when he was younger. He realized he hadn't seen his mom or dad in over a month. And now he may never get to see them again.

Sure, he talked to his mom or dad once a week on the phone, but it wasn't the same. They were just a couple of towns away, but Ethan always seemed to have things going on. Now, it was probably too late.

"I think that one is burning," Ainslee said, snapping Ethan out of his reverie.

Flipping over the rest of the venison steaks, Ethan settled back and wished he had some way of contacting his parents to let them know what had happened and that he was okay. He swore inwardly. What would they think happened to him?

He wondered why he hadn't thought of his parents before. It wasn't like him. He talked to them every week. And then there were his friends. He rarely thought of them as well. It couldn't just be that they were always busy. Something else was going on.

Ethan thought he had come to this conclusion before, but he couldn't quite remember. It was like something was making him forget. Or, maybe forget wasn't the right world. Was something actively making it so that he didn't think about home?

What could do that? And why? He started to run through possibilities in his mind when Ainslee called out to him. "I think those are done!"

Ethan blinked as he looked over at her. What had he just

been thinking? He felt like it was important but now he couldn't quite put his finger on it. He tried to remember but then Ainslee's insistent voice cut through his thoughts. "It's done! Can you use your flat tool to take them off so we can put some more on?"

Shrugging, Ethan picked up his spatula and took all of the venison steaks off the grill so they could put new ones on. Something nagged at the back of his mind while he did so, but soon the delicious aroma of cooked venison was the only thing on his mind.

He and the others dug into the venison steaks, happy to enjoy the warm meal. They all knew it might be the last fresh meal they had for a while.

42

Par'karr's rabbits had returned in ten minutes, which seemed like the maximum length they could stay summoned. As Nia had predicted, they did not return with any small game. Unfortunately, that meant the foxgirl was right about this possibly being the last fresh meal they would eat for a while.

The group spent another two hours cooking the rest of the venison and Ethan froze several days' worth of meat. He guessed they had two more days of traveling before they would cut north to the library, then maybe another day to the library. They just might have enough to get back to the forest, unless they ran into trouble at the library.

Once all the food was done, they continued along the edge of the woods. Nia was right when she'd said they'd be out in the open if they marched along the road. At least traveling along the edge of the forest gave them some cover if they needed it.

The only issue was fresh water. The road ran along the only river they'd seen. Once their current water ran out, they'd have to walk several miles to the river to refill their water jugs. They'd be exposed at that point, but there didn't seem to be anything moving in the wasteland. Nothing at all.

"I find it weird that someone would build a library out here in this wasteland," he thought aloud. Ethan hadn't actually realized he'd spoken aloud until Ainslee answered.

"Maybe they wanted to keep it secret," Ainslee remarked from behind him.

"Libraries are where you're supposed to share knowledge," Ethan argued.

The dwarf snorted. "Not all libraries. Guild libraries, for instance, only allow guild members. And that Order of the Scroll library, they don't allow anyone but members."

"True," Ethan conceded. He was so used to public libraries back on Earth and being able to find almost anything on the internet. Even college libraries were open to the public to browse, even if you had to be a student to actually check books out. "But it's like they went out of their way to make it hard to get to the library."

"Why do you make something hard to find?" Nia interrupted.

"Because you don't want people to find it?" Ethan replied with the obvious answer.

"That makes you wonder what kind of information was in that library," Ainslee added, giving him a meaningful look. "Especially considering who asked for it."

The dwarf made a good point and it was something Ethan had considered. He didn't know what kind of information the Tomes contained, but he'd need to read them before handing them over. If they contained something dangerous, he'd have to figure out what to do at that point.

They walked in silence for another two hours before it

began to get dark. The group was getting low on water and would need to fill up before making camp. Nia cut away from the edge of the forest and made for the river.

The group reached the river just as the sun kissed the western horizon. Luckily, there was enough light to see a solution to their food problem. Fish. The river was teeming with them, as well as vegetation.

"Is that normal?" Ethan asked as they all looked into the river.

"Rivers are the source of life," Yuliana said. "They carry nutrients from the mountains down into forests. It is not unusual, even in so desolate a place, to find a pocket of life around a water source. They are..."

The elf stopped abruptly and looked to the far bank of the river. She pointed, backing away. "I hear something coming. And it is coming quickly."

Ethan followed the elf's finger and saw something large moving quickly on the opposite bank of the river.

"What is that?" the dwarf muttered next to him.

"It coming this way," Par'karr yelped. "We run!"

Nia sniffed and then wrinkled her nose. "It is pungent, whatever it is."

The foxgirl looked around quickly and then looked back to the water. "This may be its feeding grounds. We should back away."

The ground backpedaled quickly but the creature quickly reached the opposite bank. Now that it was closer, Ethan could see that the thing looked like a small dragon, though small was relative. It had to be at least twenty feet long from head to tail. But unlike the dragon they'd seen, this thing had no wings and had six or seven sets of legs.

"What in Odin's Beard is that?" Ainslee cried.

The creature let out a loud roar at them and then, crouching down with all of its legs, launched itself into the air at them.

They all scrambled back as the thing splashed down in the water, two-thirds of the way to them and then began to slither towards them like a water snake. They'd only managed a few steps backwards when it reached the shore and clawed its way up.

It was close enough now, that Ethan could analyze it in his HUD.

Balweer
    Level 10

The creature was level 10, like the ogres. But unlike the ogres, this thing was covered in dark-gray scales that seemed to match the wasteland around them. Except its belly, which Ethan noticed had pale-cream scales.

The balweer's body was serpentine, like the dragon they'd seen, and a forked tongue darted in and out of its mouth. It stared at them with yellow, slitted eyes. Its many legs twitched and tapped as it glanced between them. Its backs had tough-looking spikes that lined its spine, all the way down to its tail.

It took the thing only a few seconds and then it darted, serpent quick, directly for Par'karr. Ethan tried to use *Earth* to trap its feet but the creature moved too fast. Before he could pin it down, it was on Par'karr.

Luckily, Ainslee stepped between them and slashed her short swords at the thing's head. The blades bit into its snout, deep enough to draw blood and the creature reared back and roared in pain.

Nia leaped up, doing a somersault in midair and slammed her staff into the balweer's head. There was a large crack and her staff split, though the creature's head rocked to the side at the same time. She landed on the opposite side of the reptilian monster just in time to take a swipe from its tail that sent her flying backwards.

The creature tried to snap out at her, but three horned demon rabbits slammed into its neck. Distracted, the balweer turned its attention to the small attackers. Unfortunately, their horns did not penetrate the scaly neck and they dropped to the earth and scampered back to try another run.

Ainslee charged in, slicing at its neck and body with her swords, but like the rabbit's horns, her blades simply bounced off the monster's thick scales. The dwarf growled as she stepped back. "Its scales are like steel!"

"Ethan!" yelled Nia, who had regained her feet a dozen paces away. "Your staff!"

Understanding her meaning, Ethan tossed his staff to the foxgirl. The motion seemed to get the creature's attention and it lunged at him. He leapt out of the way and barely avoided the creature's open maw.

Rolling to his feet, Ethan willed the *Mana* blade to appear in his hand and with a snap-hiss, the brilliant blue blade appeared in his hand. Even as it did, he felt *Mana* draining out of him. He checked his stats.

Mana: 41

Knowing he wouldn't be able to keep the blade going for long, he slashed at the creature. The blow barely grazed the creature's neck, but he heard and smelt the sizzle of burning flesh as it cut through scales.

You critically burn Balweer for 11 fire damage.

The thing reared up and roared, its yellow eyes staring at the blue glowing blade. Nia took the opportunity to rush in and slam Ethan's staff against the creature's leg. The balweer didn't even flinch. The foxgirl slammed the staff against a different leg with a howl of frustration.

Ainslee slashed her swords against the scaled legs as well with little effect. Then the rabbits darted in and once again slammed their horns against the scaled belly of the creature. Once again, their horns didn't penetrate the hard scales.

Moving quickly, the creature twisted its body, bringing its tail around. This time, Nia leaped up and over the tail, and it instead slammed into Ainslee. The dwarf bellowed as she went rolling across the ground, losing her swords in the process.

The balweer seemed to want to lunge at the fallen dwarf but Ethan stepped protectively in front of her, blade out in front of him. The monster snaked back, out of range of the blue white blade.

Ethan took a moment to check out his *Mana* level.

Mana: 36

He burning through his *Mana* quickly. He wouldn't be able to maintain the blade indefinitely. They needed to find a way to finish off this creature before he ran out of *Mana*.

Remembering his elementals, he summoned the fire weasel and commanded it to attack. His *Mana* dropped again but the little elemental leaped onto the creature's neck. The balweer whipped its head around to snap at it but stopped just before it reached the fiery elemental and drew its head back. It then shook itself, sending the fire weasel flying.

Ethan cursed. The creature was too smart to bite the elemental and the fire elemental didn't seem to be able to latch onto the monster's scaly hide. So much for that idea. The only other thing he could do was try to get close enough to use his *Mana* blade.

Unfortunately, that seemed impossible to do. As he moved towards the creature with the blue-white blade, the balweer backed away. It seemed to understand that the *Mana* weapon could hurt it.

Ethan kept moving towards it and it kept backing away. Ethan backed it all the way to the water but the creature refused to retreat any further. Instead, it would move right or left rather than go back into the river.

Mana: 23

Ainslee, Par'karr, Nia and Yuliana were all behind him, waiting to see what he would do. Unfortunately, with his *Mana* so low, there wasn't much he could do. Soon, he'd run out and then his blade would disappear. At that point, the creature would probably attack them.

If only he could create more blades, one for each of his team. Then they'd have a chance. But it was hard enough to maintain concentration on one *Mana* blade, not to mention the *Mana* cost would be enormous.

At least, it would be enormous if the *Mana* blades were real. But what if...

"Everyone!" he called out. "Hold out your weapons! When they glow, I want you to start moving in on it. Don't attack, just move in. I want to see if we can scare it away."

"What do you mean glow?" Ainslee asked.

Instead of answering, Ethan used a tiny amount of *Mana*

to create his little balls of light. But instead of making the light in the form of a ball, he shaped it to fit their weapons. He also made the light much more intense, so it looked like his own *Mana* blade.

"Is this real?" Ainslee gasped.

"It's my ball of light," he shot back. "Just formed around your weapons."

"Now move forward and wave them around," he ordered.

Nia and Yuliana moved forward, twirling their staves while Ainslee slashed back and forth with her light-covered short swords.

The balweer's head moved from person to person, hissing. As they all moved forward, the creature backed into the water several feet. Then, as the group reached the edge of the shore, the thing turned and slithered back across the water. Reaching the other side, it roared at them. Then, it turned and ran off.

Ethan waited until it was several hundred yards away before releasing his focus on the *Mana* blade and letting it disappear. He left the glow on the other weapons. It took almost no *Mana* and no concentration, and he was afraid if he let it go, the balweer might come back.

"Everyone," he told them, "keep your weapons out. Fill up your water jugs and let's get out of here."

The group did as he said. Ethan joined them at the edge of the water but kept a wary eye out for the monster.

When they were all done, the group made their way back to the edge of the forest and set up camp. Even though it was several miles from the river, they kept double watch that night in case the creature came back.

Luckily, it did not.

43

The balweer had not followed them to the forest's edge, nor had they seen any other predators during the night. When morning came, they were all tired from the double watch duty. Ethan thawed some of the venison and the group ate in silence. He caught everyone casting wary glances back to the river.

"Do you think there are more of those creatures?" Ainslee asked as she finished her second deer steak. She was the only one who ate two but no one else complained. They were used to the dwarf's appetite by now and would rather watch her eat a second steak than listen to her complain all day.

"Let us hope not," Nia retorted. "One was nearly a match for all of us. Only Ethan's magic seemed to have any effect."

"I did get it in the jaw," the dwarf muttered, licking her fingers clean of any steak juices.

"It was crafty," Nia pointed out. 'And learned quickly. Once you cut it in the snout, did you notice that it kept its head up high, out of your reach? And once Ethan's glowing sword..."

"*Mana* blade," he corrected.

"...*Mana* blade," the foxgirl gave him a look of annoyance, "harmed it, it kept away from Ethan rather than confronting him directly. When we all appeared to have... *Mana* blades... it left."

"What does that mean?" asked Yuliana, who was finishing the last bite of her apple.

"It means it is no dumb beast," Nia replied. "It is intelligent. We must be very cautious if we encounter it again."

"Bah, just give me a couple of those light swords and I'll take care of it," Ainslee said dismissively.

Ethan frowned. "I can barely keep one *Mana* blade up. I'm not sure if I can manage two at the same time. And if I could, they wouldn't last long. Plus, I'm not actually sure I can hand off the blade."

The dwarf pouted but Nia hissed. "No! That is not the solution. Ethan must not run out of his magic. If he does, we have no defense against that creature. Had he not been there, we would all have perished."

Ainslee opened up her mouth to say something then closed it, shrugged and nodded. "I have to admit, I've never seen anything like that. I gave it some good whacks but those scales were like forged steel. Maybe stronger."

"Par'karr and rabbits not want to see lizard-monster again," the kobold announced. He had summoned his demon rabbits and was gently petting their fur.

Despite their odd appearance, the rabbits reminded him of Earth rabbits. Very large Earth rabbits, but they didn't seem to be aggressive unless the kobold ordered them to. Perhaps, like Earth rabbits, they were at the bottom of the food chain in whatever dimension they came from.

Ethan thought back to the balweer. It was definitely not at the bottom of the food chain. Most likely, it was an apex predator in this area. If not, Ethan definitely didn't want to meet whatever hunted balweers.

Those scales had covered nearly every part of its body, making the creature impenetrable to their weapons and, he assumed, the claws and teeth of other creatures. And yet, there hadn't been any large scales around its head. Was that its only weakness? Other than a magical *Mana* blade that drained his *Mana*.

He began thinking of MMORPGs and how sometimes creatures dropped special materials that could be used to forge special items - like dragon scale armor. He wondered if they could create some sort of armor from the creature's scales if they managed to kill one. Armor that was impenetrable to most weapons would certainly come in handy.

Of course, first they had to kill one. At the moment, that seemed like a herculean task, given the creature's size, speed and intelligence. But it was something he would keep in the back of his mind.

The group finished eating, packed up their gear and continued on. Normally, they would have filled their water jugs first thing in the morning, but no one even mentioned going to the river. Instead, they marched on along the edge of the forest.

They continued along the forest until just before noon. By that time, each of them had run out of water. It was time to risk another foray to the river. Nia realized it too and called them to a halt. She turned to the group. "We must get water. We cannot afford to be weakened by dehydration."

"You can say that again," Ainslee agreed. "I'm parched!"

"You should all stay here, and I will go fill the water jugs..." Nia started but Ethan and Ainslee immediately objected.

"No way I'm staying here like a nursemaid!" the dwarf bellowed. "I'm going with you!"

"Me too!" Ethan said. "I'm the only one who has a weapon that can hurt them!"

The foxgirl crossed her arms over her chest and glared. "I am the stealthiest. Strength of arms is not what we need. It did not help us before. I can sneak down, get the water and sneak back without being seen."

Ethan shook his head. "No way, if there's a balweer down there..."

"A what?" the group asked as one.

"The thing we fought," he replied. "It's called a balweer."

Ethan looked from person to person, seeing the blank expressions. "Wait. Are you saying none of you examined it last night with your HUD?"

Par'karr and the women looked around at each other. Par'karr, he knew, didn't have a HUD. He was a native to the world. But the others did. They should be examining everything they came across.

"I did not think of it," Nia said, looking slightly embarrassed. "It is not something that I am used to. And I find it distracting."

Ainslee just shrugged. "I forgot about it."

Yuliana looked at the dwarf and nodded, though she did look slightly apologetic. "I forgot about it too."

Ethan fought down his frustration. He reminded himself that the HUD and all of the classes and stats were something none of them had ever experienced before. Still, he found it almost infuriating that they didn't keep up with their HUDs, and probably not their leveling either.

He partially blamed himself. Ethan had asked about them and their abilities early on, but he hadn't done it in a while. He'd been preoccupied with other things - like surviving. He'd need to make sure he kept abreast of their levels, achievements and abilities.

Taking a deep breath and letting it out, he changed the topic back to getting water. "Nia, you should let me go. I have the *Mana* blade."

The foxgirl shook her head. "No, you are clumsy and weak. And noisy. Stealth is needed."

He was willing to give her the noisy comment; he grimaced at being called clumsy and weak. Ethan started to object, but he got an idea. Or rather, he remembered Michalus' workshop. Invisibility. The old wizard had said other wizards could do it and that they could make themselves invisible. Could he?

Focusing his mind, he envisioned what he wanted: bending light around himself to make himself invisible. Then, like creating the *Mana* blade, he willed it to happen. The result was instant and extremely satisfying - everyone in the group started.

"Ethan!" Par'karr screamed.

"Where'd he go?!" Ainslee gasped.

Nia looked alarmed, her nose immediately sniffing the air. She blinked and looked directly at him. Darn, she had a good sense of smell. She pointed to where he stood. "He is still there."

Yuliana nodded. "I can hear him breathing."

Trying to be quiet, he took several steps to the side. He also tried to hold his breath. He found it amazing that the elf could hear him breathing. He almost laughed as he thought how loud Ainslee's breathing must sound to the elf.

The foxgirl cocked her head, her fox ears twitching. She smirked. She turned towards his new spot, as did Yuliana. "And you are still noisy. And you leave footprints."

"Darn!" Ethan released the spell and Par'karr and Ainslee's heads snapped to him.

"Wait," the dwarf muttered, looking from where Ethan had been to where he was. "Was that more of that tele...telepot..."

"Teleportation," Ethan corrected and shook his head. "No, it's invisibility. I learned it from Michalus."

"So what?" the dwarf asked. "No one can see you but you're still there?"

"Exactly," he said. "And apparently, I still smell and make noise."

Ethan quickly checked his *Mana* to see how much he had used to power the invisibility.

Mana: 53

It was surprising little considering what he was doing, bending light. That wasn't something anyone on Earth had figured out how to do with technology, and yet it seemed an almost simple spell on this world. It was certainly far less than the *Mana* blade.

Yuliana stifled a giggle. "You are very noisy."

"And you still smell." The foxgirl nodded, winking at the elf.

"But let's face it," Ethan said. "If the balweer can smell, it's going to smell you as well. I might be noisy, but if it doesn't know what's making the noise, it won't know exactly what to look for."

Nia looked towards the water and back towards Ethan. "Fine. You may come. But only you!"

As she said the last part, she looked directly at Ainslee. The dwarf huffed and crossed her arms across her breasts. She made a face at the foxgirl. "Fine!"

The dwarf's face brightened suddenly, and she looked at Ethan. "Can you warm up some steaks before you leave?"

When the dwarf saw everyone glaring at her, she frowned. "What? I'm hungry. Why not eat while they're gone?"

Ethan looked at the river, several miles away. It didn't take much *Mana* to re-heat a few steaks. Whatever he used up; it would regenerate before they made it to the riverbank. "Fine. Let me do that while everyone is getting their water jugs out."

He quickly warmed up two steaks for the dwarf and one for the kobold. He looked to Nia. "You want one too?"

"No. I will have one when we return," she said. "It is not good to fight on a full stomach."

Ethan nodded, dropping the steak he'd been about to pull out for himself back into the pack. He scooped up two of the jugs. "Shall we?"

The foxgirl looked him up and down. "Are you using your magic?"

"I'll wait until we get closer," he said, not sure if he'd be able to maintain the spell for the several miles they'd have to traverse to the river. She nodded and then set off at a jog towards the river. Sighing, he followed after her. Why did she have to jog everywhere?

They jogged until they were within half a mile of the

river. Nia held up her hand, signaling him to stop. Ethan did so gratefully. While long hours of walking these past few months had given him the endurance to keep up with her, he was still sweating and puffing while she barely looked winded.

She turned to him and gave him a disappointed look. "Get your breathing under control and then we will sneak forward. Use your magic and stay as quiet as possible."

Ethan nodded and searched the far bank of the river as his lungs worked to suck in more air. It took him several minutes and then they moved forward. Ethan used his spell and kept his HUD up so he could monitor *Mana* use.

They crept forward. Ethan moved as quietly as he could but even he heard the small stones crunching under his feet as he tried channeling his inner ninja. Nia had dropped down to all fours and was creeping silently along next to him.

They were only a hundred feet from the water when he spotted two dust clouds heading towards them from the east and the west. The eastern one was maybe three hundred feet away while the western one was four or five hundred. Both were on the opposite side of the river and coming fast. "Company!"

The foxgirl froze and Ethan watched as the two dust clouds stopped a few seconds later. He could barely make out the closest shape but there was no doubt that it was a balweer. Most likely the other one was too.

"They have stopped," Nia whispered.

Ethan watched the two balweers closely. They seemed to be waiting, but on what? He needed to figure out exactly what was attracting their attention. Smell didn't seem likely. He'd noted earlier that the wind was actually coming from the north, towards them. That meant they were upwind from the creatures.

That left sight and sound. Could these creatures have better hearing than Yuliana? He supposed it was possible, but he hadn't seen any ears on the creature. There was an easy way to test it. He yelled, "OVER HERE!"

"What are you doing?!" the foxgirl demanded, snapping her head towards him.

The creatures began running towards them again and the foxgirl turned her head around to stare at them. "Look what you've done!"

It appeared that they might be attracted to the sound. But at the same time, Nia had moved too. She'd moved her head to look at him and then moved her head back. Could they actually see her? Or, like the T-Rex in that dinosaur movie, was their sight based on movement?

"Stay absolutely still," he told her.

Nia shook her head. "We must leave now! There are two of them!"

The monsters were closer now, the first one only fifty feet away.

"Stay still!" he ordered.

Eyes wide as the first balweer reached the edge of the far bank, Nia started to turn so she could run. The creature on the shore roared and leapt into the water, moving quickly.

Hoping he was right, Ethan tackled Nia to the ground, coming up on top of her. He pressed his body tightly against hers, his lips right at her ear. "Don't move."

Willing his invisibility to cover both of them, he stayed still as the balweer reached their side of the shore. The creature clambered out of the water and looked around with its huge head. Ethan saw no scar on its neck. That meant it wasn't the same one they'd found the previous night.

"I think its vision is based on movement," he breathed into her ear, carefully watching the creature for any sign that it heard him. "If we don't move, it can't see us." He purposefully didn't add "I hope."

He felt Nia's warm body against him and felt her heart thudding against him. They both watched the creature as it flicked its tongue in and out of its mouth, tasting the air.

Ethan checked his HUD.

***Mana:* 33**

Even covering Nia, he wasn't bleeding *Mana* nearly as fast as the *Mana* blade. He reached out with Air and shoved a rock about fifty feet away, near the shore.

Immediately, the creature spun and roared, rushing at the rock. It stopped a few feet from it, testing the air with its tongue, head moving back and forth. It didn't seem to be able to find the rock, once it stopped moving.

Ethan smiled. Its vision was based on movement. If they didn't move, it could see them. He whispered in the foxgirl's ear. "I was right. It sees movement. As long as my spell holds, we should be safe."

"That is good," she whispered, her breath hot in his ear. "But how long can you maintain your magic?"

"I'm not sure," he told her honestly. Plus, he had no idea whether the creature would leave or decide to hang out for a while. He needed a distraction. Ethan grinned. He knew just the thing. He summoned his air elemental, willing it to appear on the opposite bank.

Commanding the thing to stay low, but just above the

level of the balweers, he sent it flying off to the east. Immediately, the balweer near them spun around and roared, then dove into the water towards the air elemental. Ethan saw the other balweer head for it as well.

Ethan watched the two dust trails follow the elemental and get further and further away. Once he felt safe enough, he rose up slightly, his face nose to nose with Nia. "I need you to wrap your arms around me."

"What?!" she said, breath coming fast.

"I need you close so I can keep the spell around both of us. Wrap your arms around me," he told her.

She swallowed and did as he said, pressing herself hard against him. Ethan realized that his body was starting to respond to her body but there was nothing he could do about that at the moment. He needed her close to keep the spell around both of them.

Pushing himself up with her, he stood, and she wrapped his legs around his waist pulling her hips against his. She looked down and gave him a satisfied smile. "I told you that you wanted me."

Feeling his face flush, he ignored her self-satisfied smile and walked them to the water's edge. Bending down, he filled their water jugs one by one. The two of them kept their movements close to their bodies so they stayed inside the invisibility spell.

As soon as they were done, Ethan stood up and hurried back towards the forest. He managed to make it to the road before he was forced to drop the invisibility spell or start burning stat points again.

Once the spell dropped, Nia hopped off him. She looked him up and down, her eyes lingering on his hips a little longer than was comfortable for him, before looking him in the eyes. He saw mischief in her eyes, and she seemed about to say something. Instead, she spun and began jogging back to the forest.

Ethan watched her go, then, adjusting his breeches, hurried after her.

44

———————

When they reached the others, Nia handed out the water they had gathered, grabbed her pack and began marching along the forest. Ethan noticed she purposefully did not look at him the entire time. The others didn't seem to notice the strange tension between them. They accepted their water jugs and hurried after her, leaving Ethan to trail behind them in the back.

A few hours later, Ethan spotted the tall twin peaks that marked where they would need to turn north. After calling them to a stop, he brought out his map and made sure. He pointed to the two jagged spires and the small valley that ran between them. "That's where we're headed."

Everyone followed his gaze to the columns of rock that rose above the mountains around them. The group looked around at each other and then turned to Ethan. Ainslee was the first to speak up. "What about those lizard things?!"

Ethan frowned. He'd thought of that too. The creatures seemed to make the area on the opposite side of the river their homes and attacked anything that came into sight. To make it through the spires, they'd need to travel for hours on the opposite side of the river.

"I don't know," he admitted, looking out at the columns of stone. "We'll have to see how things are when we get there."

"Can you surround us all in your invisible spell?" Nia asked. It was the first thing she'd said to him since their encounter earlier.

"No," Ethan answered with a shake of his head. Although Michalus had made an entire workshop invisible, Ethan knew from his discussions with the wizard that he'd used many crystals to do so. Trying to maintain a field around all of them would be impossible. Or, if it were possible, would drain his *Mana* so quickly, it would be useless.

"And you cannot give anyone else your light blade?" she asked.

Once again, he shook his head.

Nia nodded grimly. "And none of our weapons have been able to harm them."

"Not even Par'karr's rabbits," the kobold lamented.

"I do not see how we can make it hours through their territory," the foxgirl told them. "They move too swiftly and can see from a good distance."

"Yah," Ainslee agreed. "We were watching, and those things came at you quickly once they caught sight of you."

"Once they caught sight of us," Ethan repeated, an idea coming to his mind. "But what if they couldn't catch sight of us? What if they can't see well in the dark?"

"Uh." Ainslee rolled her eyes. "We can't see in the dark, so it's a bit of a moot point, ain't it?"

Ethan looked at Nia. "She can see just fine in the dark."

Everyone turned to the foxgirl who shrugged. "I have led

night raids before. But we have no evidence that the creatures cannot see in the dark."

The group turned back to look at Ethan. He smiled despite the attention. "No, but I can test that tonight."

"Not alone!" the foxgirl snapped. "I will go with you."

"Oh?" Ethan raised an eyebrow.

"If you are wrong," she stated, "you will need me."

"Fine," he agreed, remembering the feel of her body underneath him. It was actually a very pleasant thought and he had to consciously prevent a smile creeping onto his face.

She hadn't spoken to him since they returned from the river. Now, suddenly, she was demanding to go with him. Would he ever understand women? He sighed. Probably not. He did smile inwardly as he realized Nia was right earlier, he did want her. He just couldn't have her.

"Good," Nia said. "Let us eat and continue on."

Thinking about supplies, Ethan realized they would need to restock before making their way to the library. That meant getting some fish. And getting fish meant getting close enough to the river that the balweers would see them. Unless Ethan's theory was right, and they couldn't see in the dark.

The group continued on for the rest of the day. As dusk came, they made camp near the trees again. Everyone ate in silence, the anticipation palpable.

He understood their concern. If the creatures could see at night, there was no way they could make it past the balweers. They were too quick to outrun and too invulnerable to fight. And that was just one of them. Even with his *Mana* blade, he didn't know if they could fend off two or more.

If it ended up that the balweer's eyesight was just as good

at night, then they'd have to turn around and give up on the quest. That meant not joining the Order of the Scroll and not getting access to the library.

He sighed. He really needed to learn as much as possible about this world and about magic. But he wasn't willing to risk everyone's life unnecessarily. At the moment, he felt it was an acceptable risk. After all, anything he learned would benefit all of them. If it meant trying to fight their way through balweers, the risk versus reward ratio suddenly wasn't so great.

They watched the fire for a while, each of them staring into the flames until it was almost time for first watch. Ethan was about to say something when Nia spoke up. "It is time."

Looking over at her, he nodded and stood up. Both of them had shed their packs and were ready to go. Ethan had no weapon, having let Nia keep his staff after hers had been broken, but he noticed the foxgirl wasn't carrying any weapons either.

"No weapon?" he asked with a raised eyebrow.

She shrugged. "Staves and swords cannot hurt the monsters. Why burden myself with unnecessary gear?"

She looked at the water jug in his hand and lifted her own. "We can fill these if we are able to get close enough."

"That's the plan." He nodded and turned to look into the dark. "You'll have to lead the way; I can barely see anything."

Reaching out, she took his hand and led him into the dark. He had no choice but to stumble after her, trying his best not to trip over stones. After a hundred yards or so, she stopped and let go of his hand. "Wait here until your eyes adjust from the fire blindness."

The two of them stood in silence as his eyes slowly

adjusted. He tried to think of something clever to say, but his mind was coming up blank. Instead he wiped his sweaty palms on his breeches and waited for his eyes to adjust.

Slowly, he was able to pick out more and more detail as his eyes adjusted to the dark. There was some light from the stars and the glow around the ringed planet, so he could make out general shapes, just nothing specific. "Okay, I can see a bit better."

"Good," she said and grabbed his hand again. "Follow and be quiet."

He did and the two made their way closer. It took a long time without light, much longer than previous trips to the river. Still, it was better to approach completely in the dark, rather than risk alerting any balweers with light.

Finally, they came within a hundred yards of the river. Nia paused, sniffing the air and straining to see beyond the river.

With the river so close, Ethan was able to make out the general shape of the river due to the reflection of the stars. He hadn't really looked up in the night sky, not without a nearby campfire, for some time. It was strange how even the stars looked so alien to him. How far must he be from Earth? Hundreds of light-years? Millions? Hundreds of millions? He had no way of knowing.

"I do not see any movement," she said in a low voice. "But that does not mean anything. They seem to appear from nowhere and get here quickly."

"Then you keep a sharp eye out," he told her. "And don't move a muscle if you see one come. Just whisper a warning."

"I will," she assured him. "Now, let us move closer and see if you are correct."

They crept closer, staying low to the ground. They covered half the distance and then paused as the foxgirl sniffed and peered into the darkness. "No sign of them yet."

"That's good." He smiled, glad Nia could see it in the dark.

The pair moved within one hundred feet and stopped. Ethan's heart was thudding in his chest and he was sure Nia and every balweer in the area could hear it. He strained his eyes and ears to pick up any trace of the creatures moving in to attack. But there was nothing.

"Anything?" he whispered.

"I do not see or hear anything," she whispered back. "Nor do I smell them nearby."

"Stay here," he told her. He barely made out the sharp look she gave him. "I'm going to move closer. I can throw up the invisibility spell if I need it - just warn me before one gets close."

"Fine," she hissed.

Ethan moved all the way up to the water's edge, alternating glances between the opposite shore and the foxgirl. She hadn't indicated anything was amiss, so he bent down and filled his water jug.

Replacing the cork stopper in his small jug, he motioned for Nia to move up. The foxgirl padded over and squatted next to him.

"Fill yours," he said and then looked out towards the far bank. He couldn't see or hear anything, but with his human senses, that didn't mean much.

He saw Nia replace the stopper in her own water jug. "It appears you are right. We have not been able to get this close before without attracting one or more of them."

"True," he said. "Assuming there are some balweers out there."

"This is true," she admitted. "This proves nothing if there are no balweers out there to see us."

He flashed her a grin. "Only one way to find out."

After sending the foxgirl back a hundred yards, Ethan summoned two balls of light on the opposite shore. He noticed that he couldn't will them any further and guessed that was the range of his spell.

He caused them to spin around each other for a minute before he heard it. It sounded like a small herd of cattle coming up fast. Looking out past the river, he caught movement in the dark. At least one balweer was coming!

Letting go of the light magic, he wrapped himself in invisibility. Almost immediately, the sound of the creature stopped. Ethan strained his eyes to see it in the dark but not moving, he couldn't tell the creature from the darkness.

Knowing he needed to test the creature's capabilities, he dropped the invisibility but stayed absolutely still. He listened. Nothing. He took a step to the right and then froze. Still nothing. He jumped up and down, stopped and waited. Nothing.

The creature's eyesight might be uncanny in the daylight, but apparently, it was as bad as a human at night. Maybe even worse. Ethan began backing away from the river. He kept a wary eye out the entire time, ready to cover himself with invisibility at a moment's notice.

Instead, he made it all the way back to Nia. The foxgirl punched him hard in the arm. "That was stupid!"

"We had to know!" he shot back, rubbing his aching arm. He looked at her in the dark. "Did it react at all when I was moving."

"No," she replied. "Not at all. It appears you were right. They have very poor night vision. This is something we can use to our advantage if we travel by night. Come, let us go tell the others."

Taking his hand, Nia led them back to the fire.

45

The group reached the spires around noon the next day. They stopped at the forest's edge, looking down at the river and beyond into the towering spires of rock that marked their trail. They would wait until dark to cross the river, which gave them some time.

Nia went into the forest to see if she could find any game while Ethan decided to summon his air elemental to do some reconnaissance.

Sitting down cross-legged, Ethan activated his elemental ability and then moved his awareness to the elemental with Clairvoyance. Then, ordering it to take off, he soared into the air and towards the spires.

From his vantage point, through the eyes of his elemental, Ethan saw that the road that paralleled the river intersected with a smaller road that veered north between the two spires. There was a simple stone bridge over the river.

Ethan also managed to spot holes scattered throughout the landscape on the opposite side of the river. Through the elemental's enhanced sight, he spotted the heads of balweers sticking out of the holes.

Flying around, he saw dozens of the balweer holes along the ten or so miles until the spires. Unfortunately, that seemed to be the limit of the elemental's sight. Even though he willed it further north, it wasn't able to go past a certain point. Either it was the limit of the elemental, or the limit of his Clairvoyance.

Dismissing the elemental, Ethan blinked and looked around. The entire group was looking at him, waiting for his report. He quickly related what he'd seen. When he was done, he stood up and stretched his legs, looking from person to person.

"So many, very scary," Par'karr said, petting one rabbit with each hand. The third rabbit was sitting contentedly in his lap.

"Can we get by so many?" Yuliana asked with concern.

"I believe we can move at night without much risk," Nia said. "But we will not be able to use any sort of light."

Ainslee crossed her arms over her chest. "You really think we can make it all the way to the spires in one night? With no light?"

"If we move quickly," the foxgirl said.

"And what do we do if we don't make it all the way?" Ainslee asked. Par'karr and Yuliana looked to Nia for an answer.

The foxgirl looked from face to face. "If we do not make it by daybreak, then we will need to remain absolutely still until dark."

"You're kidding," Ainslee chuckled.

"I am not," the foxgirl stated.

"That's not possible," the dwarf snorted.

"I have to agree with Ainslee," Yuliana said, her face even more worried. "I do not believe I could stay still for so long."

"I might be able to hide us," Ethan spoke up. He realized the conversation was going to quickly degenerate and he'd been mulling over ideas since he had dismissed the elemental.

"I thought you said your invisibility wouldn't cover us all." Nia looked at him questioningly.

"Par'karr want to be invisible!" the kobold said enthusiastically.

He shook his head. "That's not what I meant. The balweers gave me an idea. I may be able to dig us a hole, like theirs. If we're below their line of sight, they shouldn't be able to see any movements we make."

"Shouldn't be able to?" the dwarf scoffed. "That means you don't know if it will actually work."

Everyone looked to Ethan expectantly. He shrugged. "No, I don't know for certain. But there is a way to find out. I can go down there now and try it."

"I thought we were waiting until nightfall," Yuliana said, casting a glance towards the road and the wasteland beyond.

"WE will," he said. "I will go by myself."

"I should go with you," Nia protested.

"No." He shook his head. "I'll use invisibility to get to the other side, then dig the hole."

"You could make me invisible too," Nia retorted, "like you did before."

Ethan couldn't deny that the opportunity to press her body up against him appealed to him. If anything, it appealed a little too much. She was easily more attractive than any woman he'd ever dated. She was like a fitness model, lean and muscled but with an adorable face. He didn't even mind the fox ears and tail.

He shook his head to clear his daydreams. Like attractive Earth women, she was out of his league. Not the kind of woman who bothered with a lowly computer tech like him.

"Well?" Nia asked with a raised eyebrow, her hands on her hips.

"Fine," he gave in. "The two of us."

"Good." She nodded. "We should go immediately. We must know whether it will work during the daylight."

"Fine." He shrugged and, following her example, slipped his pack off his shoulders. No point in taking it with them if they were coming back. Also, no point in taking it with them if things went bad and they didn't come back.

"How long do you think it will take?" Ainslee asked as Ethan and Nia started to leave the camp.

Ethan grinned. "Concerned?"

The dwarf snorted. "Concerned you won't get back in time to warm up dinner."

"I'm touched," he replied, rolling his eyes.

"I'm just saying." Ainslee shrugged. "Maybe you could thaw some steaks now."

Nia took Ethan's hand and began to pull him out of the camp. "Come! We must hurry!"

"What about steaks?!" the dwarf yelled after them.

"Take a few out and set them in the sun. They'll thaw all by themselves," he yelled over his shoulder.

"They will?" the dwarf asked brightly.

"In a few days," he yelled with a big grin.

"A FEW DAYS?!" Ainslee yelled after them before erupting in some very unladylike curses.

Ethan and Nia kept moving and the dwarf's tantrum was

soon out of earshot. They moved at the foxgirl's normal pace, which was a light jog and Ethan fell in beside her.

The two of them jogged to the road and stopped. Nia seemed completely unfazed by the run, other than a light sheen of sweat. Ethan was puffing and fought for several minutes to get his breathing under control.

Once he could breathe normally, he sat down and summoned his air elemental to scout around. He sent it over the bridge and along the north road. There were three of the balweers within a few hundred yards of the road. It would be a good test.

He released the air elemental and looked up at Nia. "There are three of them nearby. You sure you want to come along."

The foxgirl didn't hesitate. "Yes."

He was glad to have the fierce warrior with him, but at the same time, he didn't like the extra responsibility. If things went bad, it would be rough enough to get himself out of trouble, let alone Nia.

"Then we'd better go," he said and held his arms outstretched. That had been the way they'd done it before: Nia clinging to him as if giving him a hug, her legs wrapped around his waist.

She rolled her eyes, stepped around him and hopped onto his back, wrapping her arms around his neck and her legs around his waist. "This is better. It will give you more freedom of movement and will not obscure your vision."

Ethan sighed and tried to hide his disappointment. All of what she said was true, but he had been looking forward to the more intimate front hug method.

When he didn't immediately move, she tapped him with the heel of her foot. "Come! We must go!"

Rolling his eyes, he willed the invisibility over himself. Ethan then jogged slowly towards the bridge. He kept a wary eye open for any movement. He also kept an eye on his stats.

Mana: 51

The invisibility would continue to drain him. He would need to be careful to conserve enough to actually make a hole. If not, things would get very dangerous, very quickly.

He jogged what he guessed was a mile before stopping. His *Mana* was down to half and he needed the rest to create the hole. Plus, despite the foxgirl being light, he was still jogging with her on his back and he was getting winded.

Looking around, he realized it was difficult to distinguish the road from the rest of the wasteland rock. The only difference seemed to be that it was slightly more worn than the smoother rock around it.

Ethan moved off the worn road and onto the smoother rock and squatted down. He lowered his voice. "Here goes nothing. If this doesn't work, I won't have enough mana to make us invisible for the return trip."

"Do it," Nia whispered in his ear.

Letting out a deep breath, he reached into the stone began to form a hole in it. He made it just long enough that he could fit into it and wide enough that they could lie down next to each other. He watched his *Mana* depleting quickly.

Finally, it was done. Looking down at it, Ethan realized it resembled a grave. He hoped the fact that they were essentially going to crawl into a grave wasn't some sort of premonition.

With Nia still on his back, he climbed down into the

hole. Once inside, he twisted so he was face to face with the foxgirl. He looked right into her eyes. "You ready?"

She gave him a slight nod. "Do it."

Crossing his fingers, he let the invisibility go. They both stayed absolutely still and listened. Ethan heard nothing. But then again, his hearing was subpar compared to Nia, let alone Yuliana.

"Do you hear anything?" he whispered.

Nia had a look of concentration on her face and her ears twitched left and right. She tilted her head slightly to one side, then the other. Finally, she made eye contact. "I do not hear them."

"Let's give it a few minutes," Ethan told her, trying to still his thudding heart. He half expected one of the creatures to appear overhead at any moment. But nothing appeared.

They waited for a slow count of 300, which Ethan hoped was about five minutes. He'd gained some *Mana* back and it was enough to summon his air elemental.

Ethan summoned it thirty feet straight above him. He willed it to immediately fly higher and circle around them in large circles. "I'm going to scout from above. When I tell you, make some movements so I can tell if they can see us. If I say still, stop whatever you're doing and be absolutely still."

"Okay," she whispered.

Moving his awareness to the air elemental, he looked down at their little hole. It looked small from so high. It was certainly smaller than the holes the balweers had dug.

"Make movements," he said back in his body.

Nia did and with the enhanced vision of the elemental, he could make out her moving her arms back and forth. Ethan immediately moved his gaze to the three balweers nearby. None of them moved. He smiled inwardly. It appeared that it worked.

They did a few more tests and found that nothing inside the hole attracted their attention. Even small things, like Nia moving her hands out of the hole, didn't attract their attention.

Ethan dismissed the air elemental and his awareness flashed back to his body. He grinned at Nia. "It works. We can use the holes to stay out of their field of vision."

"That is good," she said, but she was not smiling. She was biting her lip.

"Are you okay?" he asked, suddenly concerned.

"Ethan," she said, looking into his eyes. "We must talk."

46

Ethan suppressed a frown. He knew from experience that when a woman wanted to talk, it rarely turned out good for him. Unfortunately, they were stuck in the pit until his *Mana* regenerated. Whatever she was about to unload on him, he would have to take it. "What do we need to talk about?"

Nia took a deep breath. "You must be honest with me. Will you do that?"

He groaned inwardly. First, she wanted to talk. Now, she wanted him to be honest. Things had just gone from bad to worse. Women NEVER wanted you to be honest with them. They asked questions like: Does this dress make me look fat? Do you think that girl's pretty? Do I look old? And did they want you to tell them the truth, no way.

Still, there was only one answer when a woman asked if you would tell her the truth. "Sure."

The foxgirl nodded, as if that was the answer she had been expecting. He noticed that she was fidgeting with her hands and she looked down at them before rubbing them against her breeches. "Answer me truthfully. Will I ever get home?"

Ethan let out a breath he hadn't realized he'd been holding, feeling himself relax. He hadn't been sure of what she was about to ask, but that hadn't been it. They rarely talked about their homes any longer. Ethan barely even thought about his old life. It felt strange that he shouldn't miss Earth, but he was usually so busy just trying to survive that he didn't have time.

He considered her question. Would any of them get home? Did he even know where home was? He had looked at the stars in the beginning, trying to find any familiar constellations or stars but there had been nothing. Millions or even trillions of light-years could separate him and Earth.

It was the same with all of them. Whatever planets they had come from, he had no idea how they could possibly get home. At least, not with alien intervention. He assumed they had all been abducted and brought here. If the aliens had brought them here, then the aliens could potentially take them back.

Unfortunately, they had no way to contact the aliens, let alone a way to convince or force the aliens to take them back to their homes. Not unless there was something in the Order of the Scroll library about the aliens.

He looked at Nia, who was still waiting for an answer. He saw hope in her eyes, but also resignation and sadness. It was if she already knew the answer but wanted someone else to confirm it for her.

Sighing, Ethan reached over and took her hand. He looked into her big eyes. "No, I don't think any of us are going home."

She bit her lip and nodded, her eyes getting a faraway

look to them. Ethan allowed her a moment to process what he'd told her. While Ethan had tons of science fiction movies and TV shows to give context to what was going on, none of the women had that advantage. He could only imagine how terrifying it must be for all of them.

He waited for several minutes, while different emotions played over Nia's face. She seemed to be coming to terms with the situation or dealing with some inner turmoil. He remembered that, unlike him, she had a tribe. She hadn't really talked about it, but he did remember that she was married.

Hadn't she said she was like the 13th or 15th wife or something like that? Did she miss her husband? Did she have kids? It seemed like the topic of kids would have come up before, if she had. He couldn't imagine a mother not wanting to get back to her kids.

Nia looked up at him with a determined expression. She opened her mouth to say something but then shut it. Her brow furrowed as she seemed to struggle with something internally. Finally, she took a deep breath and looked intently into his eyes. "You must take me."

Ethan blinked. He wasn't sure he'd heard what his brain was telling him. "Excuse me?"

"You must take me," she said more confidently.

Involuntarily, Ethan wiggled back from her. Unfortunately, he only got a few inches before running into the side of their hole. His brain was desperately trying to figure out what she was asking of him, despite the fact that his body was already making some assumptions. "What do you mean - take you?"

She smirked and gave him a knowing look. "You know what I mean. I know you desire me."

"Woah!" he objected. "What about the married stuff?!"

"This is how it is done," she stated flatly. "The alpha of the new tribe takes the daughter of the chieftain of any tribe he conquers. She then becomes his wife. And the tribes are united under the new alpha."

Ethan narrowed his eyes. "And the father doesn't object?"

"The old alpha is already dead," she replied dispassionately, though he did see a brief glimmer of sadness pass over her features. "This is our way. If you take me, you will be my alpha and I will be your wife. Then you can allow me to fight for our tribe."

"Wait?! What?!" Ethan asked. His heart was thudding in his chest and the other parts of him were responding to the idea of having sex with the foxgirl.

She blew out a breath. "I cannot fight as I should. I am the daughter of a chieftain, but I was made Cha'to'mir'ta, seventeenth wife. I am not allowed to fight for the tribe. I am not allowed to kill, unless it is prey! I was not even worthy of my husband's attention!"

Her tone had gotten more and more angry as she spoke and she said the final words with a sneer. She had also revealed something he hadn't suspected. She was not happy with her lot in life. Nia didn't actually enjoy being a seventeenth wife.

Her face softened slightly, but was still full of determination. "You must take me and make me your wife. You must command me to fight for you. Then I can fight off these monsters without feeling like a child with a club!"

Ethan swallowed reflexively. He wasn't really sure what to make of this situation. On one hand, he definitely wanted to have sex with her. She was beautiful, despite the fox ears and tail, and he couldn't deny being attracted to her. More than that, she'd shown herself to be a loyal and fierce companion.

Part of him didn't feel he was in her league. Another part cringed at the idea that she thought of sex as marriage. Yes, that was it. The whole idea of having sex and suddenly they would be married. That was terrifying.

"Why do you hesitate?" Nia asked. Her voice was both angry and hurt.

"I... uh..." he started and then took a deep breath. "On my world, marriage is a serious commitment. We don't... uh... just marry the first person we have sex with. Um... I mean... some people do ... but I..."

She furrowed her brow. "Have you not seen what a good wife I would make? I am a good hunter, I can prepare food, and I am a good fighter."

He could tell she wasn't bragging, simply stating her qualifications. And he couldn't argue that she was all of that and more. But still, marriage. He'd never really thought about marriage, other than in passing. It was sort of like a bucket list item: get married, have kids, settle down. Unfortunately, he hadn't found a woman who he liked enough or gotten along with well enough to even contemplate marriage.

A thought occurred to him and he gave her a quizzical look. "Okay, let's say you would be a great wife. Why would you want me to be your husband?"

She looked at him like he was mad. "You are powerful. You are an alpha."

Ethan smirked. He thought of himself as many things but powerful and alpha weren't two of them. "No, really?"

She tilted her head. "Those are the reasons. You are a powerful alpha. You have magic. You single-handedly killed an ogre - no alpha on my world could have done that."

"Yeah, but..." he started but she didn't let him speak.

"You are cunning," she stated. "You know many things."

"But that's just..." he tried but again she did not let him finish.

"And you are loyal and brave," she said. "You do not turn your back on your companions, and you have never run from any fight!"

Ethan tried to object but realized that everything she had said was true. At least, from a certain point of view. Of course, many of the truths people cling to depend greatly on their point of view. Wise words from a master in one of those great scifi movies. She just made it all sound so much more heroic than it actually was.

She gave him a sly smile. "And you are not completely unpleasant to the eyes."

He rolled his eyes. "Gee, thanks. Well, you are not completely unpleasant to the eyes either."

"Ha!" she snorted. "I see you staring at my tail when you think I am not looking."

Despite himself, Ethan blushed. He also cursed inwardly. He really had thought he was being subtle too.

"Now," she demanded. "You must take me."

"I..." Ethan started but then closed his mouth. He was being stupid. A beautiful warrior woman wanted to be his wife on a world where there were dragons, ogres and balweers who wanted to kill him. Was he really going to find someone better matched to him? She had the martial prowess and he had magic.

His brain couldn't think of any more excuses and his body didn't want him to. He'd been thinking about his parents and their marriage of forty years. He hadn't been sure if he wanted to spend forty years with Nia. Then he realized, on this world there was no guarantee of living forty minutes, let alone forty years.

"Fine," he said and she gave him a lustful grin.

"Good!" She smiled and wiggled her body around, pushing herself away from him. "I will prepare myself to fight you!"

Ethan blinked again. "Wait?! What?! Fight me?"

"Yes! You must take me, but I am married," she said nonchalantly. "I must fight you off!"

Ethan gawked at the woman. "WHAT?!'

She rolled her eyes. "I am no honorless whore. I am Cha'-to'mir'ta! I must defend my honor!"

Feeling some of his excitement ebb, he just stared at the foxgirl. This proposition was sounding less appealing by the second. "So, you want me to force myself on you. Are you serious?"

"Yes." She nodded. "You must prove your dominance, and thus your right to be my husband."

"And you're going to fight me off," he asked. He'd already had her claws around his neck once, when he'd first arrived. He had no desire to test himself against the fierce foxgirl. "Like really fight me? No holding back?"

"Yes." She nodded enthusiastically.

He caught a lustful gleam in her eye as she said it and he was both repulsed and excited at the same time. But the idea of forcing himself on her was appalling and even the idea bristled against his upbringing.

But then again, she was asking him to. What was he saying, she was practically demanding him to do it. Did that make it okay? Was it forcing himself if she was telling him to do it? "So just to be sure, you want me to take you. You are honor bound to fight back, but you want this."

"I want this!" Her breath came out quickly and she nodded. "Now take me!"

Still uncomfortable with the situation, he nevertheless realized the foxgirl was telling him to do it. So, that made it more like roleplaying, right? She had to play her role and Ethan had to play his. It was kinky, but he knew some people did stuff like that. He took a deep breath. And she was telling him what to do.

He was glad his life wasn't a movie or a novel. If so, he knew there'd be trigger warnings out the arse for what was about to happen, despite it being consentual.

Not wanting to give his mind any more time to ratio-nalize a way out. Without another thought, he channeled *Air* and bound her wrists and ankles holding her in place. She struggled against the bonds but despite her strength, Ethan's magic was stronger.

He used the magic to undress her as she snarled and snapped at him with her teeth. He moved over her, and slowly lowered himself on top of her. Her breath was coming quick and her eyes full of lust but still she struggled.

Finally, he lowered his head down to hers. She snapped at him several times, each time allowing him to get closer and closer until finally she stopped snapping and he brought his lips down on hers. After that there was no more struggling.

He did quickly learn she had an animal side. He also learned that he did too!

47

Afterwards, they both lay panting on the bottom of the hole he had created. Nia was nestled in the crook of his arm with the sun beating down on their mostly naked bodies. He hadn't been able to get all of their clothes with his magic, but they'd managed anyway.

"Now I am yours," she murmured, fingering her collar. "Now I am Tal'Cha. First wife."

Suddenly she shot up and Ethan managed to grab her just before her head cleared the top of the hole and they were seen. She looked embarrassed for a brief second before looking down at him intently. "Do you have other wives? You did not mention any, but I must know if I am first wife, or what my new rank is!"

"Uh, no," he chuckled. "No other wives. You are my first wife."

He felt weird even saying it. Then again, what about his life over the last few months wasn't weird. And just like that, he was married. Or was he? He didn't even know the marriage laws on this world. Were they different in different cities? Could he make his own marriage laws in Hawkshead?

He looked up to see Nia grinning broadly.

"I am Tal'Cha." She bent down and kissed him hard. She broke away after a minute, rolled over and began to get dressed. He watched her lithe body as she did, no longer concerned about getting caught. After all, marriage had to have some perks.

The foxgirl saw him watching and rolled her eyes. "You males are all alike. Now is not the time for mating. It is time to get dressed and get back to the others."

Ethan sighed. They'd been married for all of like twenty minutes and already she was telling him what to do. But, she was right. They needed to get back and prepare to head out as soon as it turned dark.

As soon as they were both dressed, Ethan checked his *Mana* level.

Mana: 60

He was at maximum. Ethan smiled as he realized they must have been at it longer than he thought. Not that he was complaining. If they would have had more time, he wouldn't have minded a few more times.

All business, Nia slipped onto his back. He did notice that she held him a bit more affectionately than before, nuzzling her head into his neck. It made him excited, but he didn't mind one bit.

Covering them with invisibility, Ethan left the safety of their grave-like hole. He set off at a light jog down the road to the south. Neither of them spoke as he ran; the only sound was the sound of his own labored breathing.

They reached the bridge fifteen minutes later and a little way after, he dropped the invisibility and they separated. Nia didn't give him any time to catch his breath but set off for the others right away. After a shake of his head, and a glance at her backside, he jogged after the foxgirl.

When they entered the camp, Nia was barely breathing hard. Ethan on the other hand, collapsed against a tree.

"Well," Ainslee chuckled as she looked between them. "You're both alive. I guess that means it worked."

"It... worked," Ethan replied, still trying to catch his breath. "As... long... as we... stay... in the hole... we... should be... safe."

"I am first wife now," Nia declared to the others.

"You're what?" Ainslee asked, screwing up her face. Yuliana and Par'karr looked at the foxgirl curiously.

"Ethan has taken me," she stated, hands on her hips. "I am now Tal'Cha, first wife. If he commands me, I will now rain down death upon our enemies."

"You did what to her?" said the dwarf, turning on Ethan with an angry glare.

Ethan growled and waved his hands defensively. "WE... Nia and I... had sex. It was... her idea!"

Hands still on her hips, Nia nodded. "He took me and now I am his mate. He has no others, so I am Tal'Cha."

Ainslee, Yuliana and Par'karr looked from Nia to Ethan, then back to Nia and finally back to Ethan. The dwarf smacked her fist into her hand while glaring at Ethan. "Someone better start explaining what happened or someone's going to get a fist in their face!"

Ethan looked pleadingly at Nia, still trying to catch his breath. "Please... explain it to them."

Nia did explain it, but it sounded just as bad the next

time. Ethan ended up having to clarify several points each time the dwarf glared at him. Finally, everyone seemed to understand what had happened and that Ethan "taking" Nia had been at her insistence.

"So what?" Ainslee asked, brow furrowed. "You have sex in a hole, surrounded by monsters and boom! Just like that, you're married? That's really the way it works? A guy just forces himself on you and you become his wife?"

"No." Nia shook her head. "Not any male, the alpha of the tribe. That is how he makes you his. Other males must get his permission to mate. To do so without permission is to challenge the alpha."

"Freyja's White Breasts, what kind of cockamanie marriage is that?!" the dwarf said, aghast.

"It is our way," Nia retorted defensively. "How do your leaders choose their wives?"

"Well, first of all," Ainslee snorted. "Men don't choose nothing. Women do the choosing. Men are too stupid. Always thinking with that tool in their pants! Ha! Oh, and it's just one mate. You don't want too many men around, messing things up!"

"Women choose?" Nia said wide-eyed. "Are your women alphas?"

"Uh." The dwarf made a face. "Our leaders can be men or women. Just depends on who the clans elect."

The dwarf turned to Ethan. "What's it like on your world?"

Ethan shrugged. "Two people decide they want to make a life together and they either live together or get married."

Ainslee grunted and turned to Yuliana, who was looking off into the woods. "What about you? Do the men or women pick?"

"What?" the elf replied with a start. "Did you ask me?"

"Yah." The dwarf nodded. "On your world, do the men chose your mates or the women?"

"The families choose a mate that they believe will be suitable for you and support your grove," she said. "When two elves are joined like this, they both move to the larger grove and someone else takes over the old grove."

"You have no choice either?" Nia asked.

"No." The elf shook her head. "Though it is not as... violent as your method. We are told who we will be joined with. That has been our tradition for hundreds of thousands of years."

"Huh," the dwarf said and then looked to Par'karr. "How about you? How do kobolds choose who they will mate with?"

"Chieftain mate with the females," Par'karr replied with a grin. "That why it good to be chief!"

"Only the chief gets wives?" Ethan asked the little kobold.

Par'karr shrugged. "Not understand wife. But all females go to chief."

"It is similar to my people." Nia nodded. "The alpha gets first pick. The others are given to his most loyal followers."

"Chief not share," Par'karr said sadly.

Ethan looked towards the towering peaks. They didn't seem that far away, and in the light, they could reach them in a few hours. At night, following Nia and unable to see more than a foot or two in front of them, it would be a long, slow journey.

"We should start getting everything ready and maybe do some practicing with our eyes shut," he suggested.

The others nodded and they all gathered up their gear. Ethan warmed up some steaks and handed them out so they could eat and be ready to leave. Nia got his attention and tossed him his staff. Instead of the staff, he saw that she now wore two short swords.

He raised an eyebrow. "Have you been carrying those since the brigands?"

Nia just smiled and then finished packing her stuff.

They each gathered and packed some wood in their packs, so they had something to burn when they were in the wasteland. Without that, it would be cold, dark nights with no hope of seeing what was sneaking up on them.

Then they practiced walking in a line, each person's hand on the shoulder of the person in front of them. It took over a dozen tries before they worked out a system, but once they did, the group seemed to find their groove. By the time it got dark, they were ready to go.

IT WAS dusk when they walked down to the bridge, staying a good hundred yards south until it was dark enough. Ethan took the time to use invisibility to fill everyone's water jug. He then used a little magic to freeze a bit of the water, so it would stay cooler longer.

A branch of the river seemed to come down from the mountains to the north. It ran into the river they'd been following, just east of the bridge. That meant they'd have water as they headed north. The hard part would be filling up their water jugs along the way. It would be difficult without being able to see. Best to make the water last as long as possible.

Once Nia deemed it dark enough, which Ethan guessed was about 8pm or so, the group began their trek. Slowly and silently, the five of them walked along the road in the dark. They walked on for what seemed like hours before Nia brought them to a halt. As they caught up with her, she motioned them down.

"We will rest here for a short time," she said in a low voice.

"Warm us up a steak!" Ainslee whispered.

Ethan could make out his companions' general shapes, but not much more. Before he could answer or do anything, Nia hissed. "No! We do not know how acute their sense of smell may be. If they smell the meat, they could be on us within a minute."

"But I'm hungry," the dwarf insisted and Yuliana and Nia both shushed her.

"You will need to wait until we stop for the night," Nia told her. "Maybe until we reach the spires."

"Until we reach the spires?!" the dwarf said, a bit too loudly and everyone shushed her.

Nia hissed. "Do you wish to have those monsters attack us in the dark?"

The dwarf mumbled something unintelligible but remained quiet.

After a few minutes, Nia prodded them to resume their march. Once again, they continued their journey in the darkness with nothing but the shoulder of the person in front of them guiding their way.

The trek seemed to drag on and he watched his *Stamina* dropping. The earlier exertions hadn't helped either, both the running and the sex had sapped his *Stamina*. He smiled into the darkness as he remembered he and Nia rolling around in the pit.

The memories of earlier and daydreams of the next time

he might be able to get Nia alone kept him going through the night. They stopped several more times to allow their *Stamina* to regenerate before continuing.

Each time they had to listen to Ainslee complain about being hungry, but eventually she'd give up and fall silent. After a while, they move on again and the whole cycle would repeat.

When the first glow of dawn began to appear on the horizon, Ethan squeezed Nia's shoulder. He moved in close to her ear, trying to make sure he didn't smack his face into the back of her head. "Should I start digging the hole?"

The foxgirl stopped and turned to face him. She moved very close to him and he could feel her warm breath against his ear. "There is no need. We are here."

A few minutes later, the sun peeked over the eastern sky and the first rays of the new day illuminated the enormous columns of rock to either side of them. They had made it all the way to the spires.

48

———————

A fter Ethan used his air elemental to scout the area out for any balweers, the group took a much-needed rest. All of them were tired from the night's march but Ethan wasn't used to sleeping in the daytime. He wasn't sure he'd be able to fall asleep. Yet when his head hit his bedroll, he was out like a light.

Ethan awoke a few hours later. He had been so tired when he lay down, he hadn't been thinking of anything but sleep. Eyes still closed, he felt someone warm pressing against him.

Opening his eyes slightly, he was surprised to find Nia nestled next to him. Then he remembered, they were married according to her. He still wasn't sure how he felt about that, but she did feel good pressed up against him.

His movement must have woken the foxgirl, or she had been waiting for him to wake up. As soon as he moved, she rolled out of bed and sprang to her feet. Looking down at him, she nudged him with her foot. "Come! We must move out!"

Ethan groaned but noticed that others were stirring too. He nodded tiredly and pushed himself into a sitting position. He looked up at the pretty foxgirl. "Sleeping with me now?"

"I am Tal'Cha." She nodded. "My place is in your bedroll, unless you choose a different wife for the night."

Ethan smiled and raised an eyebrow at her. "Choose a different wife for the night?"

"You males are all the same." Nia made a face. "You have no other wives. Put it out of your mind!"

Everyone was getting up by that point and they quickly ate. After their rushed meal, the group headed north through the spires. The area beyond was all gray stone, with no balweers in sight. They still kept a wary eye out for any other creatures. Who knew what other creatures called this wasteland home?

THEY REACHED their destination just before dark. One minute, they were climbing an incline and the next they reached the crest and looked down into a valley full of ruined stone buildings. Ethan didn't recognize the architecture style. It didn't resemble anything from Castlehaven, Hawkshead or the villages he'd passed.

He stared out at the remains of the city. There was a lone building in the center of the desolation that was standing. The buildings immediately surrounding the lone structure were pulverized, while buildings further away were in various states of destruction, almost as if they were dominos that had been knocked over.

If this were Earth, he would have thought a bomb had

been dropped in the city. Except that single standing building that would have been ground zero. Of all the buildings, it was the one building that should have been completely obliterated. So why was it standing?

"Just looking at the city and seeing how well our journey has been so far," Ainslee scoffed. "I'm guessing we have to go in that building in the middle of all of these ruins."

Resting her hands on her hips, she turned to Ethan. "Am I right?"

"The map doesn't say." Ethan shrugged. "But you're probably right."

"What could cause such destruction?" Yuliana breathed.

"Dragon?" Par'karr murmured.

"I don't think so," Ethan said, looking at the destruction. "I'm not sure how a dragon would have destroyed so much while leaving that single building intact."

"If it wasn't a dragon, what in Thor's Hammer did it?" Ainslee demanded.

"Some sort of explosion," he told them. "Something that was centered on the building. Or, something that came from the building itself."

"What could cause such an explosion?" Nia asked.

"I don't know," Ethan answered. "Maybe something magical."

Ainslee whistled. "Can you do something like that?"

Ethan chuckled mirthlessly. "Even if I knew exactly how they did it, I don't have anywhere near that power."

"And we want to go down there, into that building when it might contain whatever did this?" Ainslee asked sardonically. "That's your plan?"

Ethan bit his lip. When she said it like that, it sounded like a plot of a bad horror movie: there's a haunted house where people go in, don't come out. And what do they do? Run away like normal, sane people? No. They go INTO the haunted house.

Was that what he was doing? He had literally been told that no one who had gone in had come out. And now he was about to go into certain death. Why? Just to get some dusty books so he could join a nerd club?

This was the point where any sane person would turn around and leave. But he knew he wouldn't. He couldn't. He needed access to that library if he was going to learn more about this world and more about magic. Then again, what use was that knowledge if he were dead?

"Listen," he told them. "I need to go in there and get those tomes. I need access to that library to find out as much about this world as possible. You all can stay here. You don't need to come."

Nia hissed at him. "I am Tal'Cha! I go where my mate goes!"

He smiled at her and nodded. He would certainly feel better with her by his side and he knew that there was no way he would be able to talk the stubborn foxgirl out of coming with him. Not if she thought it was her duty.

"Par'karr come." The kobold came to stand next to him. "Ethan Par'karr's friend!"

He looked down at the little kobold and smiled. Par'karr returned his smile and the toothy grin.

"I guess I'd better come along too. Without me, who knows what trouble you'd get into." Ainslee rolled her eyes. The dwarf shrugged. "Besides, if you don't come back, there's no way I'll get past the balweers."

Yuliana gave a start at the dwarf's words and looked back towards the spires off in the distance. She looked back at the group and seemed to deflate. "I must go with you too. Ainslee is right. If you do not come back, anyone left here will not be able to get past the monsters. We would slowly starve to death."

Ethan suddenly felt bad. He felt like he was forcing them to come with him against their better judgement. That was the last thing he wanted. He thought for a moment. "It will take more time, but we could take you back across the wasteland in the dark and leave you on the other side. If that's what you want."

The dwarf shrugged. "Can't say that'd be any better. The only one who's any good with hunting is... your wife." Ainslee said the last word with a curve of her lip and a glance at the foxgirl.

"Ainslee is right," Yuliana agreed. "We would not last long without the rest of you."

The dwarf seemed like she was about to object but then shrugged her shoulders. "Probably right. I ain't no good at hunting. And I certainly can't make those ice steaks."

"It is agreed," Nia stated. "We will all go with Ethan."

Ethan nodded but couldn't shake the feeling that he might be leading everyone to their deaths. He looked down at the building as the shadows lengthened. Looking to the west, he could see the sun had almost disappeared.

If he was going to be stupid enough to follow the horror movie tropes and walk into the "haunted house," he was at least going to do it in the daytime. "Let's sleep up here tonight. We can check out the library first thing in the morning."

The others quickly agreed. They might not have seen horror movies, but it seemed to be common sense not to go into the place that no one had returned from when it was dark.

They quickly made camp. Using some of the wood they brought, Ethan made a campfire. Digging into his pack, he took out some of the frozen steaks. He noted that they had a day's worth of steaks left. Using a bit of *Water* magic, he refroze the remaining.

"How many apples do we have left?" he asked, looking around the camp.

The four others quickly went through their packs and did a count. When all was said and done, they had twenty apples left. Ethan thought they should have more but more than once he had caught the dwarf munching on one.

He did some quick calculations. Nia didn't eat fruit, so the apples wouldn't help her. Ainslee could eat apples, but preferred steaks. He wasn't sure about Par'karr. But if he ate apples for two meals, that meant one more steak for Ainslee and Nia. He sighed.

"Toss me an apple," he said. "I'll eat that instead of a steak."

"You are the alpha," Nia objected. "You should have a steak!"

He gave her a smile but shook his head. "We're running low and I can eat apples. If I do that for two meals, that gives you and Ainslee an extra meal each."

"I'm fine with that." The dwarf grinned.

Nia flashed her a glare. "Then you can eat mine. I will go without."

"No," he said adamantly. "You are... Tal'Cha, and I have commanded you to smite my enemies. How will you do that to the best of your ability if you do not eat?"

The foxgirl growled and opened her mouth again but

Ethan held his hand up. "My people eat meat, fruits and vegetables. I'll be fine. It is... my way."

Nia shut her mouth and nodded. He wasn't sure, but he thought he saw a little pride in her eyes. Or maybe that was just firelight.

"Par'karr eat apple too," he offered. "Par'karr like apples."

"Are you sure?" he asked the little kobold.

"Yes," Par'karr answered, pulling an apple from his pack. "Par'karr like wizard's apples."

With the food choices settled, the group ate. The apple wasn't nearly as satisfying as the venison steak. He had to console himself with knowing that there would be more meals for Ainslee and Nia.

Hopefully, it meant Nia should lose only a single meal before they got back to the forest. Of course, that was if it only took them part of the day tomorrow to get the tomes. And all that was contingent on them making it out of the library alive.

Finishing up his apple, he prepared to take first watch as the rest of them lay down on their bed rolls. This time, Nia laid her bedroll next to his. His mind went back to their time in the hole and a grin spread on his face. The foxgirl caught him smiling and seemed to read his mind. She rolled her eyes and then laid her head down before giving him a wink and shutting her eyes.

Ethan wasn't sure what that wink meant, and he didn't have time to contemplate it. Instead, his mind went to the library and what dangers could possibly lurk there. He let out a long breath. Tomorrow was going to be a big day.

49

The group was up early the next morning. Giving steaks to Nia and Ainslee, he ate his own meal of an apple. It wasn't very satisfying but that was the way it had to be. Once everyone had eaten and they had packed up their camp, it was time to head to the library.

Moving through the empty city didn't pose much of an issue. They had to scramble over the ruined remains of the buildings, but they caused only a slight delay.

Ethan took note of the various buildings, trying to place the architecture. The buildings looked strange, like nothing from any Earth history he knew about. Of course, that didn't mean anything. With all of the alien species on this world, they could be - and probably were - from some other planet's culture.

But something bothered him. Like an itch in his mind. A sense of wrongness about the buildings, perhaps the entire area. It wasn't anything Ethan could place his finger on. Just a nagging sense in the back of his mind.

They were almost to the library when a terrible thought

occurred to him. What if the damage caused was from some sort of nuclear weapon? Could there be some sort of radioactive fallout? Were they all being exposed to lethal doses of radiation?

He racked his brain for the symptoms of radiation poisoning. The only symptom he could remember was losing your hair. But how soon after exposure would that happen? Was that why there was a wasteland around the city? Radioactive fallout?

Ethan stopped unconsciously as his mind processed the possibility. The others continued on a few steps before noticing that he had stopped. They turned back to look at him.

"Is something wrong?" Nia asked, eyes darting around and nose sniffing the air.

"I'm... not sure," Ethan said, his own eyes taking in the devastation around him. He was no expert on nuclear weapons, but he thought if this were nuclear, even a small-yield nuke would have taken out the entire valley in a huge fireball. "On my world, we have advanced weapons that could do damage like this. They leave behind... poison... in case people come back. The poison can last for years."

"Poison?!" Ainslee blanched.

"But looking around," he continued. "I don't think that sort of thing was used here. There's not enough destruction."

"Not enough?" Nia gasped. She gestured to the shattered city. "This is not enough destruction."

He shook his head. "The weapons I'm thinking of would have turned this entire valley into a charred pit."

Nia and Yuliana went pale. Ainslee just whistled while Par'karr bobbed his head up and down. "Like dragon."

Ethan snorted. "As strong as dragons might be on this

world, the weapons on my world could wipe out a hundred dragons."

The kobold looked at him wide-eyed.

"So, you do not think this poison you spoke of is here?" Nia asked, eyes narrowed.

Ethan brought up his HUD and looked at his stats. Other than his *Stamina* being a little lower from the walk, everything else looked normal. Even his *Intellect* stat had fully regenerated. There was no indication that he was being poisoned by radiation.

Shaking his head, he started forward. "No, just me being paranoid, I guess."

The others gave a last glance around before following him. He knew he had spooked them. Had he been able to fully explain radiation and radiation poisoning, he was sure they would really have been spooked. For now, he had to put that out of his mind and focus on the library.

They reached the library forty-five minutes later, stopping a hundred feet from the structure. Up close, the building was larger than he'd first thought. It was a round building, with no windows and a dome-shaped roof. From this side, there was no way into the building - just solid walls.

Ethan motioned them along the perimeter of the building until they found a set of double doors. The doors appeared to be made either bronze or brass, with large rings mounted at chest level to pull the door open.

There was some sort of stone geometric pattern molding around the outside of the doors. There were circles inside of triangles that were inside of squares. The pattern repeated along the entire molding. But that wasn't the most interesting thing.

In the middle of each of the circles was a glowing blue crystal. A Chymera crystal! It couldn't be just a coincidence that someone had embedded crystals around the door. Something about the door was enchanted.

"Don't touch the door," he warned.

"Why?" Ainslee asked. The dwarf looked from the door to Ethan and then back at the door. "They're just big bronze doors."

Ethan pointed to the glowing blue crystals. "It's enchanted. These are the same type of crystals that I focus my power through. They can also be used to enchant things."

"What sort of enchantment?" Nia asked. She eyed the blue crystals with wariness.

"I don't know," Ethan replied. He cursed himself for not asking Michalus how to tell what sort of enchantment was in a crystal. If there were enchanted items already in the world, it seemed like a very good thing to know.

What he did know was that bronze was mostly copper and copper was a great conductor. That's why they used it in circuit boards. If he were building some sort of electric or lightning trap, bronze doors would be a great conductor. Even the rings and the ring mounts were bronze.

Despite not knowing exactly how it worked, he could easily see that it would make a great trap. Any electricity sent into the door would find the path of least resistance to the ground. In this case, it would be the actual ground. Anyone touching the door, or the ring would become the circuit from the door to the ground, effectively electrocuting them.

"Everyone stand back," he said and the others quickly cleared the area. They all deferred to him when it came to issues of magic. Just one more reason he needed to learn more about it.

"I'm going to use magic to open the doors," he told them. "If I'm right, there might be a lightning discharge so make sure you're nowhere near the door."

They formed a semi-circle around the door and once Ethan saw that everyone was far enough away, he summoned some Air and pulled on the ring. The door started to move and as it did, Ethan saw lightning arcing between the two doors and heard his companions gasp. Other than lightning, they'd probably never seen electricity.

The electricity continued to arc between the doors until the door he was moving was about halfway opened and then it stopped abruptly. He let go of the door with the Air but as soon as he did, it began to slowly close again.

He didn't understand the mechanics of it but guessed there was some sort of spring mechanism or something along those lines that shut the doors behind them. Almost like a horror movie cliche.

He looked around for a suitable piece of rubble and then used Air to move it near the door. The effort taxed him, and he watched his *Mana* level plummet with the exertion of moving the large stone. Ethan used Air to pull both doors open and then shoved the piece of rubble between them, wedging them open.

"Are they safe now?" Yuliana asked.

"Only one way to find out," Ethan said and started walking towards the doors.

Nia rushed over to him and grabbed him by the arm in a tight grip. "No! You mustn't. I will go."

Ethan gave the foxgirl a smile and withdrew his dagger. He wasn't actually stupid enough to test it himself. "Actually, neither one of us will go."

Taking some water from his jug, he coated the blade.

Then, plucking the dagger from his hand with Air, he sent it over to the area between the two doors. He brought the tip down so that it touched the stone and waited.

If the current was going to arc, it should have arced to the dagger and then down into the ground. With the blade wet, it would have been the path of least resistance. But nothing happened. No arcing electricity. That meant it should be safe. Theoretically.

"It should be safe," he said, pulling the dagger back to his hand.

The foxgirl frowned and narrowed her eyes. "I will still go first."

"No," he said adamantly and saw her bristle. He tried to make his voice as soothing as possible. "There may be more traps. Magical traps that only I may spot. Just let me go first."

The foxgirl hissed and he could see her inner debate playing across her features. Finally, she nodded. "Fine. But I will be right behind you."

"Fair enough," he agreed. "But whatever you do, do not go pass me unless I tell you to. No matter what you see. Agreed?"

"Fine," Nia glared at him, obviously unhappy to be told what to do.

"That was lightning, right?" Ainslee asked. Her tone said she already knew the answer to the question.

"Not natural lightning," he replied. "But close enough."

"And that was obviously meant to be some sort of trap, right?" the dwarf said in the tone that was more statement than question. "You figured it would have gotten at least one person. If so, where are the bodies?"

Ethan, who had been walking towards the door, stopped in his tracks. He looked around the door. Now that he knew what to look for, he spotted several scorch marks on the stone beneath the door.

The electricity he'd seen wouldn't have been enough to incinerate a person. And even if it could burn away flesh, any metal items and probably bones would have been lying around. He looked all over the area and his companions began to do the same.

Everyone was looking around for any signs of bodies or any sorts of remains, but there were none. If people had died from these electric doors, there were no bodies or even signs of bodies in sight.

"Two possibilities really." Ethan frowned. He held up a finger. "One, they had companions with them and when they died, the companions took their bodies with them."

"Kobolds take bodies with us sometimes," Par'karr agreed. "Have big dinner later."

Ethan tried not to think about his little friend's comment and moved on to point two, holding up a second finger. "Two, something else came and took the bodies."

"Something?" Yuliana squeaked. "Like what?"

"I don't know," he replied. "But we should watch our backs. There could be something in these ruins that we haven't seen."

"Or something in the library that comes out," Nia said, peering in through the doors.

"Or that," Ethan agreed and tried not to think about what that thing could be. "Same advice. Everyone watch their backs."

Nodding, they gathered near Ethan and prepared to enter the library.

50

Ethan and the others peered into the library. In contrast to the destruction outside, the inside of the library was intact and fairly organized. The walls were smooth stone, just like the outside. The ceiling was high and had been painted with some sort of mural. The scene it revealed was one of what Ethan could only guess were humans, dwarves and other races intertwined with figures of what Ethan guessed were demons.

At least, Ethan thought they were demons. He wasn't sure what else they could be. The things had dark-red skin, were horned, winged and had hooves for feet. All they were lacking were pitchforks. Or was it devils who had pitchforks?

As he looked closer, he noticed that the demons seemed to be handing things to the other races. He couldn't be sure, but it looked like glowing balls of light. Ethan remembered what the channeler from the Order had said. Warlocks and channelers received their power directly from demons. Was that what the ceiling mural was supposed to depict? Demons giving power to those who wanted it?

Ethan summoned several balls of light. He sent them into the chamber, but they disappeared as soon as they moved through the doorway. He frowned. Was there some sort of anti-magic field in the room? If so, his magic might be completely useless.

The room itself was completely open and the walls were lined with bookshelves, most of which was empty. In a strange way, it reminded him of the Order of the Scroll's library. Arranged in a circle near the center of the room were sturdy-looking, polished wood tables. In the center of those tables was what appeared to be some sort of fire pit.

Along the far wall was a circular staircase that hugged the wall and led up to the second level. Because of the curve of the staircase, he couldn't actually see any part of the floor above.

"Wizard-boy," Ainslee said with a little trepidation. "Are those... bodies?"

All of their eyes were drawn to the bodies. There had to be at least two dozen bodies scattered across the room. Some were at the tables; others were on the floor. One was even against the stairs.

"I see dead people," Ethan whispered, unable to resist despite the morbid scene. None of his companions got the movie reference, of course, and once again he missed his gaming buddies.

"What killed them?" Ainslee gasped from his left.

Nia put a hand on his shoulder. "Are you sure you wish to go in there?"

"Not really," Ethan admitted as he looked from body to body. Something or someone had killed them. But what or who?

There was something strange about the bodies. They

didn't seem to be lying in ways that would indicate violent deaths. Had they been surprised? Was there some sort of poison or gas?

He thought back to his earlier idea of radiation. Could that be it? Could they have died of radiation poisoning? Were he and his group dying even as they stood here, doomed to a slow, lingering death?

Maybe it was something inside the room. Or someone. Was there some creature or some person on the second floor, waiting for them? He needed to know what was on the second floor, but he needed to know before he entered the building.

"Everyone back up," he told everyone. Then he took several steps away from the door and waited for the others to do the same.

Ethan sat cross-legged on the ground and held out his arm. After checking to make sure he had enough *Mana* and *Stamina*, he summoned his air elemental. Instantly, the wispy hawk-like creature appeared on his arm and he felt the sting of talons as they dug into his arm.

He used his Clairvoyance ability to switch his vision to the hawk and the world erupted into detail. Things he hadn't noticed before, insects moving in the rubble, a rat scurrying between broken buildings, all became crystal clear.

The balls of light he'd conjured had winked out as soon as he'd sent them through the door, but he was hoping the elemental might have more luck. He just needed it to last long enough so that he could see if there was some monster or being upstairs that was the cause of these people's deaths.

Commanding the air elemental to fly into the room, he winced as the creature's talons bit deeper into his arm as it launched itself towards the doorway. He watched through its eyes as it shot in through the doorway and then lights and colors exploded in his vision.

Ethan rocked back as scintillating colors assaulted his eyes. In the enhanced vision of the air elemental, it appeared that he was flying through an infinite tunnel of swirling hues of every color imaginable. He saw the scene for only a second or two before he was suddenly rocked back into his own body.

Gasping at the abrupt change, he blinked his eyes as if to clear the afterimage of the rainbow spectacle. He looked into the library to see if the air elemental had made it into the room. It hadn't. Now he knew why.

"Where air elemental go?" Par'karr asked from behind him.

"The Bifrost," Ethan muttered and pushed himself to his feet.

"The what?" Ainslee asked, screwing up her face in confusion.

"Like when I teleported before," Ethan replied, "back in the inn. I went through a rainbow tunnel when I went from one part of the room to the other. Some people in my world called that the Bifrost and I just saw the air elemental go into it."

Ethan walked to the doors. Careful not to cross the threshold, he looked around the doorframe until he found what he expected. Embedded into the door frame were dozens, perhaps hundreds, of Chymera crystals.

Grinning, he realized what it was. Someone had created a portal. If he was right, it was like a giant version of Michalus' portal pouch. And it was big enough to fit multiple people. Ethan marveled at how much *Mana* it would take to create a permanent portal so large.

Looking around at the devastation to the city around the library, he wondered if somehow the magic had caused some sort of feedback when they'd created the portal. Was that the reason for the devastation? He'd probably never know.

Still, he needed to test his hypothesis. Ethan reached down and grabbed a stone. Carefully, he tossed it through the doorway and watched as it instantly flew into the room and went skittering across the floor. But it didn't make a sound.

He nodded. Matter could pass through the portal, into the room beyond. And just like the women's description of him teleporting, it was instantaneous to anyone watching. He didn't understand why it seemed to take longer for someone actually in the Bifrost. Some sort of time distortion maybe?

"Why did you throw a rock into the room?" Nia asked from behind him.

"The door is a portal," he told them excitedly. "A very large portal. And I think I know why the people died."

"Why?" Yuliana asked and her question was echoed by the others.

"It's a one-way portal," he said. It made sense. People would walk into the library, not realizing it was a portal. Once they got to the opposite side, the portal either didn't exist or wasn't working and they were trapped in that room - wherever it was. The fact that no sound had come back confirmed it in his mind.

"One way?" Nia asked, walking over to him and looking into the room. "Why would anyone do that?"

Ethan looked around at the devastated city. "I'm not sure they intended to. This is a huge portal. It must have required a ton of magic to create. Somehow, I think they did something wrong or made a mistake that caused some sort of magical explosion."

The group looked around at the ruins. Ainslee whistled. "That's a lot of power."

"So, anyone who goes in there is trapped?" Ainslee asked.

He nodded. "I think that's why no one who's ever gone in has ever returned, but people who stayed on the outside made it back."

"This means, there is no way to retrieve the books?" Nia asked.

Ainslee glared at Ethan. "You mean we wasted all this time coming out here for nothing?!"

Ethan didn't immediately reply. His mind was formulating a plan. A risky plan, but one that just might work. Maybe. If it didn't, he'd be stranded in the library until he died.

"Maybe not," Ethan said.

"But you just said it's a one-way portal," Ainslee pointed out.

"That's true. But perhaps I can create a portal from the room, back to here," Ethan suggested. It was a long shot, he knew. Michalus had gone over the basics of enchanting and he thought he might be able to use the Chymera crystals the old wizard had given him to power a portal just large enough for him to crawl or dive through.

He knew the principles. He could make a series of unique runes on this side of the portal and then create a portal to those runes, just like Michalus did to create the portal pouch. Unlike the portal pouch, he would only need to create a temporary portal from the library to his runes.

"You cannot do this," Nia said sternly, planting her hands on her hips. "You could become trapped."

"I agree with the foxgirlly." Ainslee shrugged. "I say we turn around and head back. Forget about the books. Let's get back to that inn and have some more mead."

Ethan looked at Yuliana. The elf gave him a small shrug, but her face told him she didn't believe it was a good idea either.

"What about you?" Ethan asked Par'karr.

The kobold gave him a toothy grin. "Ethan good wizard. Ethan make portal home."

Ainslee and Nia both rolled their eyes but Par'karr ignored them.

"You cannot do this!" Nia insisted. "You are my mate."

Ethan opened his mouth to object but couldn't see any way that he would win an argument with the foxgirl. She believed they were mates, and that's all there was to it. Instead, he thought of an idea.

"What if I prove I can open a portal?" he asked.

"Without collapsing for a day?" Ainslee smirked and Nia's brow furrowed.

"Without collapsing," Ethan agreed. "If I can do that, then do we agree that I can go into the library and get the tomes?"

Nia bit her lip, her brow still furrowed as she looked from the library to Ethan and back several times. Finally, she sighed and nodded. Then her face became steely. "But I go with you!"

Ethan smiled at her acceptance until his brain processed her words. "Wait?! WHAT?!"

"I come with you!" she told him insistently. "Or you do not go!"

He looked to Ainslee for support, but the dwarf just chuckled. "You married her."

Cursing, Ethan walked around in circles for several minutes, trying to think of a way to prevent or convince the foxgirl from following him into the library without irrevocably damaging their relationship.

Finally, he threw his hands up in the air, realizing he had lost. He'd either have to take her with him or abandon the quest. "Fine, you can come."

51

Ethan spent the next three hours figuring how and then preparing to test his ability to create a small portal. It needed it to be large enough that he could dive through but small enough that it didn't overtax him.

He also had to prepare three symbols that were unique. For that, he chose combinations of geometric shapes and hoped that would serve his purpose. Then he spent over an hour loading *Mana* into three of the Chymera crystals. He was going to try and use them as batteries to augment his *Mana* level.

Even though he had, thanks to Michalus, figured out to load *Mana* into the crystals. Through a little trial and error, he figured out how to draw *Mana* as well. But it wasn't an easy process. He had to really concentrate to use it.

It was a shame he had to focus so hard. If not, he could have stored up tons of *Mana* for fights and then let loose with a torrent of spells. Ethan guessed that's why Michalus hadn't attached dozens of crystals to his staff to help in combat. He'd need to ask the old wizard the next time he saw him.

Ethan's first attempt to open a portal failed and completely drained one of the crystals, causing it to shatter. He realized he'd tried to pull too much *Mana* from it, much like he'd done to himself when he'd teleported.

The difference was the crystal had no other stats to pull from. When too much *Mana* was pulled from it, it shattered. Ethan realized that without his Overchannel ability and all of the stat drain it did on him, he would have suffered the same fate as the crystal. He would have died. It was a sobering thought.

His second attempt did manage to open a small portal to the three symbols, though he caused another crystal to shatter. He kept the portal open long enough for them to send Par'karr's rabbits through. The little demon-rabbits disappeared into the portal and instantly emerged next to the symbols.

"It actually works, wizard-boy?" Ainslee asked.

"It appears so." Ethan grinned, letting the portal wink out of existence. He felt drained and looking at his *Stamina* and *Mana*, he realized why.

Stamina: 4

Mana: 3

Opening the portal had taken a lot out of him. Ethan looked down at the shattered crystal. It had taken a lot from the crystal too. Too much. Grabbing his water jug, he drank the rest of the lukewarm water to replenish his *Stamina*. He didn't even spare the *Mana* to cool it.

"I need to go fill up my water jug," he told the group. "And then Nia and I can go into the library."

"You stay and rest," Nia commanded. "I will get us water."

"Par'karr go too!" the kobold said, his demon-rabbits hopping to his sides.

Nia nodded and the two of them gathered everyone's water jugs and jogged off, back out of the valley to the river. For some reason, the river flowed around the valley and not into it and Ethan guessed the former city must have gotten their water from wells instead. If so, there was no sign of the wells now.

While they were gone, Ethan considered the ramifications of what he'd done. He'd opened a portal from one place to another, much like the portal pouch Michalus had created. It was big enough for them to fit through, well everyone except Ainslee. He'd have to make it a bit larger for the broad dwarf to get through.

If he could set up symbols at different locations, with some preparations, they could travel places instantly! Beam me up, Scotty! That was exciting. He just needed to learn how to better control the pull of *Mana* from the crystals.

Ethan was down to four crystals now, no longer enough to make himself a portal pouch. He'd need to get more. But where? He immediately thought of the crystals on the doorway. There were a lot of them. Maybe he could take the ones from the electricity trap.

Unfortunately, he didn't understand enough about enchanting yet to risk doing anything to the door. For all he knew, the electric enchantment and the portal enchantment were linked. If he pried loose a crystal, it might cause the entire thing to fail. He couldn't risk that. Not yet, at least.

An hour later, Nia and Par'karr returned with water.

After making sure they had everything ready, Ethan and Nia prepared to go through the doorway. Before they did, Ainslee stopped them.

"Here," she said, holding out her water jug. The dwarf looked almost embarrassed. "In case you need it."

"You'll need it too," Ethan told her.

The dwarf shrugged, looking down at her feet. "I can always walk up to the river if I get thirsty. Who knows if you can get more water wherever this portal-thingy goes. Just take it."

The dwarf thrust the water jug at him and this time he took it with a smile. "Thanks, Ainslee."

"Yah, yah," she said and turned away.

Par'karr came running over with his own water jug and held it up to Nia. "You take Par'karr's water."

"I don't..." she started to reply but Ethan gave her a meaningful look and gave a subtle nod at the little kobold. She gave him an annoyed look but then smiled at the little kobold and accepted his water jug. "Thank you."

Par'karr grinned broadly. "Nia welcome."

"Do you want mine as well?" Yuliana asked, holding her water jug.

"I think we're good," Ethan replied and then looked at Nia. "You ready to go?"

"I am ready," she said. She had put the water jug in her pack and had her short swords out. He still wasn't used to seeing the foxgirl with the blades, but the way she held them, Ethan had no doubt she knew how to use them.

Ethan took a deep breath and gave a last look at the others. Turning back towards the portal, Ethan stepped through the doorway and into the swirling rainbow tunnel he'd come to call the Bifrost.

Colors swirled around him as he shot through the tunnel. Ethan turned his head to look behind him, trying to see Nia but she wasn't there. He briefly panicked but then remembered the strange time distortion that happened in the Bifrost. She may not even have entered the doorway yet.

Forcing himself to stay calm, he tried to look into the scintillating colors as he shot through the tunnel. They were swirling and merging with each other, but every now and then, he thought he glanced things in the colors. They were like images, but they went by too quickly for him to make out.

Suddenly, the rainbow tunnel was gone, and he was inside the library. He gasped for air and instantly regretted it. The smell of decay was all around, and he had to force himself not to retch.

A moment later, he heard Nia gasp and turned to see the foxgirl screwing up her face. She looked at him, her face a mask of disgust. "This place reeks of death."

"It's all the people who died," he replied, trying to breathe through his mouth. Looking past the foxgirl, he saw an archway they'd come through. But that was all it was, a stone archway. There was no exit. It was just a stone archway carved into the wall, lined with shattered Chymera crystals.

He walked past Nia, who spun to see where he was going. He put his hand on the stone wall but felt nothing but cold stone. He glanced around the archway, noting the shattered crystals. He also found a few that were still intact and made a mental note to pry them out before they left. "That explains why no one could leave. There's no exit. At least, not on this level."

Nia glanced at the archway and nodded, then looked towards the staircase. "We should check the upper level."

Ethan waved at the archway and Nia wrinkled her forehead. "Why are you doing that?"

"The others should be able to see us," he said. "They won't be able to hear us, but they should be able to see us, just like we could see the rock that I threw inside."

Shrugging, the foxgirl turned towards the library and gestured with one of her swords. "Let's find the books you need and leave. I do not like the smell of this place."

Turning from the archway, Ethan created balls of light and sent them to the opposite side of the room. Unlike his previous attempt from outside the library, this time the balls of light did not vanish but did as he willed.

With the entire library illuminated, they saw more bodies, stacked against the far wall. More victims of the library and its one-way portal.

Ethan started towards the bookshelves and light flared from a nearby pillar. He started and jumped back while Nia pivoted towards the light with a growl, swords pointed at the pillar.

"Hello?" he said but there was no reply.

Nia started to circle around, and he took another step backwards, preparing to wrap up any attacker in Air or cast a fireball. As he stepped back, the light went out. They both froze.

"Do you see someone?" Nia whispered.

Testing a theory, Ethan took a step forward and once again the light flared on. When he took a step back, the light went off. Automatic magical lights. Cool.

Nia eyed him warily. "Why are you smiling?"

"It's magic," he told her and walked to the pillar. He found multiple crystals embedded around the pillar. They glowed slightly and he could sense the *Mana* in them. He looked to Nia. "They're enchanted. They create light when someone is near."

Nia narrowed her eyes at him and stalked over to another pillar. Like the first one, it shed light. She hopped back and the light went off. She tried it several more times before looking at him and nodding.

Ethan grinned and started to walk over to the tables, but Nia hissed. "What are you doing?!"

"Looking for the tomes," he retorted.

"First," Nia chided him, "we look at the upstairs! There could be enemies. Just because that was magic, doesn't mean there may not be someone upstairs. We do not want them surprising us."

"Good point," Ethan admitted.

Nia was right. He assumed everyone in the library was dead, but that could be a very dangerous assumption. Ethan had also assumed that the people had died of natural causes, either dehydration or starvation. For all he knew, something had killed them and arranged their bodies so that they appeared to have died of natural causes.

"Let's go check it out," he told the foxgirl.

Nodding, Nia moved ahead of him. Stepping over bodies, she quietly crept along through the library to the bottom of the steps. When she reached the bottom of the stairs, she waited for Ethan to come up alongside her.

"I will go up," she whispered. "You stay here."

Ethan started to object but she hushed him with a stern look. "If something is up there, I will lure it down here. As it comes down the stairs, you can use your magic on it."

Unable to find any flaw with her plan, Ethan simply nodded.

Seeing him agree, the foxgirl turned towards the stairs

and slipped on to them. As she did, light illuminated the stairs. Nia hissed and hopped off them. She grimaced. "This will make stealth much more difficult."

Not waiting for a reply, she stepped back onto the stairs. Quiet as a shadow, she moved from one step to another in a crouch. Since the stairs curved around the wall, as she moved up, she moved out of sight, but he could track her by the light.

Ethan stood there for long moments, heart thudding and ready to cast a fireball or summon his energy sword. The moments stretched to nearly a minute with no sign or sound of the foxgirl and he began to worry.

Just as Ethan was about to go up the stairs after Nia, the foxgirl's head appeared at the top of the staircase. Her brow was furrowed but she didn't look as though she was worried about an enemy.

"Ethan," she whispered down to him. "You must come up and see this."

With a sense of foreboding, Ethan nodded and mounted the staircase. One by one, he began to climb the stairs to the second floor.

52

Following the staircase around the edge of the wall, he emerged up on the second floor. Glancing around, he found it almost identical to the floor below, including more dead bodies. "More bodies."

Nia motioned to get his attention. "Not them. That!"

She pointed her finger at the opposite wall and Ethan saw what meant. It was another staircase up. This library had another story. She gave him a confused look. "Didn't the building only have two floors?"

Ethan shrugged. While the building they had thought was the library had only two stories, they weren't in that building. They'd passed through the gateway into some place completely different. "This isn't the inside of that building. We're somewhere else. We might even be in a different part of the world."

The foxgirl frowned and it was clear she was having a difficult time wrapping her mind around the concept or teleportation and portals. His exposure to science fiction movies, comic books and fantasy roleplaying games gave him a theoretical understanding of the concepts. Unfortunately, how exactly it worked was beyond him.

"Where are we then?" she asked.

"I don't know," Ethan replied, looking around the second floor. Like the floor below, this floor was completely devoid of windows. This floor even had a similar mural to the one below, depicting demons handing things to men, dwarves and elves. "Maybe there will be windows or some indication of where we are further up."

"Fine," she said nervously. "Let us go up then but stay behind me."

"No problem," he replied. The foxgirl was faster and more experienced than he was. Even though it did chafe his sense of chivalry, his common sense prevailed. Besides, he could do his magic from in front or behind her.

They passed several pillars on the way to the other steps and, like the floor below, these too created light as soon as they stepped within five or six feet of them. He still had his balls of light and they didn't seem to set off the magical pillars.

He considered dismissing the balls of light but decided not to. He could still use them to illuminate the corners of the building without having to actually walk over. Ethan followed Nia to the steps. The foxgirl sniffed but made a face. She turned to him. "I can smell nothing but the stench of death."

Turning back around, she began to creep up the stairs. After a few steps, she motioned him to follow. Ethan began to climb the steps too, doing his best to be as quiet as possible.

The pair quickly reached the third floor, only to find it was identical to the first two floors. And like the previous two floors, it also had a staircase up. Nia turned to him. "How large is this library?"

Ethan looked up but couldn't quite see into the next floor. "Let's find out."

They cautiously climbed each staircase, finding that there were six floors in total. Each floor had an identical setup as the lower floors. They all had shelves along the wall, tables in the middle and each had bodies sitting at tables, lying on the floor or propped up against the shelves.

The sixth floor was different. It didn't have a staircase up, like the others. There was no floor above it. There was also no mural on the ceiling. Instead, the ceiling was a transparent dome, made of some sort of crystal or clear quartz.

Looking up, Ethan could make out the sky, but it wasn't the sky he was used to in their new world, nor was it the blue sky from Earth. It was a deep crimson sky with a huge red sun just starting to climb over the horizon. They weren't on whatever world the aliens had left them on. They were on a different planet!

"Is that the sun?!" Nia gasped.

Ethan swallowed, his mouth suddenly dry. He was trying to wrap his mind around the fact that they had traveled to another planet. Could magic really transport someone from one planet to another? Even if it could, how could the people of Par'karr's world even figure out how to do it?

He and Nia were still staring up at the large red sun. It really was enormous, taking up most of the horizon. Ethan thought it had to be a red giant. Either that, or this planet was much closer to its star than Earth was to the Sun.

"I do not like this place," said the normally fearless foxgirl. She looked around the room. "And why are there no bodies on this floor? Let us get your books and return to the others."

Tearing his eyes from the transparent ceiling, Ethan nodded and looked around the sixth floor. Nia was right. Unlike the other floors, the top floor had no bodies at all. Not only that, there were no shelves of books, just the tables and chairs in the center of the room, along with a large marble statue of some sort of demon.

Ethan eyed the statue warily. If this were a movie or even video game, that statue would come to life and attack them. They'd lower their guard, stop paying attention and then the statue would pounce. At least, if he was the game master and this was an adventure, that's what he'd do.

Walking over to the statue, Ethan conjured up his energy blade and in a quick strike, sliced off one of the statue's arms, then the other. He waited, ready to strike out again but the statue didn't move.

Nia gave him a curious look, arching an eyebrow at him.

Grinning sheepishly, he dismissed the energy blade. "Just making sure."

"Of what?" she asked, eyeing the severed arms of the statue.

"That it wouldn't come to life when we weren't looking." He smiled.

"Do statues do that on your world?" she asked.

"Sometimes," he replied, thinking of some movies and comic books where statues had come to life. "Sometimes."

Nia eyed the statue and then sniffed. After a moment, she shrugged. "I do not think it will come to life. Let's find the books you seek and leave this place."

Ethan couldn't help but agree but there was one small problem. He had no idea what the tomes looked like. He thought back to getting the quest back in the Order of the Scroll. Bringing up his HUD, he displayed the quest.

```
Retrieve the Tomes of Ashmedai I
    To join the Order of the Scroll, you
must    give    the    Order    a    unique
collection of knowledge. Retrieve the
Tomes of Ashmedai for Mertin Graystaff
of    the    Order    of    the    Scroll    in
Castlehaven.
    Tomes acquired (0/3).
```

"We're looking for 3 Tomes of Ashmedai," he told her as he read the quest on the HUD. "But it doesn't say what they look like."

He thought back to the conversation he'd had with Mertin. The channeler had said the books had been borrowed by one of their members and brought here to the library. Did that mean they might be on one of the bodies?

"We need to search the bodies," he told Nia. "One of the dead people should have the books on them."

Nia wrinkled her nose and bristled as she looked from body to body. "There are many bodies."

Ethan looked around. "You're right. But I don't want to stay any longer than we absolutely have to. Let's start on the floor below and we'll work our way down."

The two of them went downstairs and began searching the corpses. It was slow, disgusting work as the corpses were mostly dried, shriveled flesh and disturbing them usually sent up a cloud of dust that made Ethan want to retch.

They also found that almost half of the bodies had some sort of demonic features. The shriveled tails or bone-like horns marked them as channelers, like Mertin. Ethan wondered if the others had been warlocks. Or were they just normal people who had wandered through the gateway?

A search of the fifth floor didn't turn up the tomes, but they did find an exquisitely made long sword, three daggers and a shiny metal round shield. They also found a few necklaces and a handful of gold and silver rings, one of which had a Chymera crystal in it. Then there were the coins. Nearly all of the bodies had pouches or purses of some sort containing a mixture of coins. Some even had some loose gems.

Ethan didn't really have any qualms over taking items from the dead. It wasn't as if they were going to use them anymore. Nia didn't seem to have a problem either, strapping the long sword to her belt. When he looked over at her, she just grinned. She pulled out the blade and gave it some practice swings before replacing it back in the scabbard.

Ethan was about to suggest they go down to the next floor when he realized he was sweating. He wiped sweat off his forehead. Who knew that searching bodies was such hard work? He pulled out one of the water jugs and took a sip.

Replacing the water jug, he started to head for the stairs when he felt the sweat beading on his forehead again. He looked around. He turned to Nia. "Is it my imagination or is it warmer in here?"

The foxgirl sniffed and looked around the room. "You may be right. It does feel warmer."

Ethan jogged over to the staircase which led to the sixth floor and quickly ran up. Nia followed him and he heard her sharp intake of breath as they reached the top. It had taken them about an hour to search all of the bodies downstairs and in that time, the sun had risen completely over the horizon.

If he thought the red sun looked large before, it was gigantic now, taking up most of the sky above the horizon. Ethan also noticed that it felt decidedly warmer on the sixth floor. The sun was warming the air inside the library.

"The sun is so big," Nia murmured from behind him.

"Yah." He smirked. "And hot. And it's probably going to get much hotter."

"How hot?" Nia asked, her voice and face concerned.

"I have no way of knowing," he told her, glancing at the huge red sun. "But if it got this warm in an hour, I think that, by the time it is whatever passes as noon on this planet, this entire place is going to be very hot."

"We should go then," she insisted.

Ethan looked at the sun and then back to the foxgirl. He hated to miss out on a quest, but she might be right. If it got hot enough, they might find it very difficult to breathe. If that happened, they could pass out and die before the sun ever set.

He glanced down the stairs to where he knew the bodies lay. Was that what had happened to them? Even access to the library was not worth dying over. The problem was, he needed to charge up the crystals. That would take time. Ethan swore.

"What?!" she asked with alarm.

"I need time to charge up the crystals," he told her. "At least a few hours to charge one up, get my mana back, charge the next one and so on."

"Do we have that long?" Nia looked up at the red sun.

He shrugged. "I don't know but I should start charging them now. While I do it, you keep searching."

She nodded and, with a glance back at the large red orb, they both scrambled down the steps to the fourth floor.

O n the fourth floor, Ethan pulled out one of the Chymera crystals so he could charge it. He brought up his HUD so he could view his stats.

Mana: 55

His *Mana* wasn't at maximum because he had maintained the balls of light. He let them wink out and waited for his *Mana* to regenerate before charging up the crystals.

While he waited, he dismissed his HUD and helped Nia search the bodies. She actually found a book on one of them but it was not what they were looking for. It was a small, brown leather-bound book that looked more like some sort of journal. Ethan read the first page.

The personal journal of Merlin, Wizard of Camelot, Volume 71

Ethan blinked and read the line again. This was the journal of Merlin? He read it again. Yes, Merlin, Wizard of

Camelot! Heart thudding, he looked up at Nia who was staring at him with a bored expression.

"This is the journal of Merlin!" he said excitedly. "The Merlin!"

"Merlin?" she asked with an arched eyebrow. Her face became curious as she saw his excitement. "Who or what is a merlin?"

"On Earth," he explained, holding the journal out in front of him like it was made of crystal, "legends say he was the greatest wizard to ever live."

"And he wrote down things in the book?" she asked, head tilted. "Can it help us?"

"I don't know," he said, thumbing through the pages of the book. "I'd have to read it all."

Ethan took a breath and noticed the air was already feeling warmer down on the fourth floor. How hot would it get in here? And how hot would it need to become before they started to dehydrate? He frowned. "I'll have to look at it after we get out of here. My mana should be recharged by now. Let me charge up the crystals and then we'll find the tomes and get out of here."

Nia agreed and went back to searching the bodies. Ethan took out the Chymera crystal again and opened up his HUD. He was about to start charging it when he saw his *Mana* score.

Mana: **55**

"What the -?!" he said aloud.

Nia, who had been searching a body, raised her head and glanced around, her hands went for her sword hilts. "What is it?!"

Ethan checked his HUD again but he hadn't misread it. His *Mana* hadn't regenerated at all. It was the same it had been 10 minutes ago. He looked Nia in the eyes. "My mana isn't regenerating."

The foxgirl relaxed and rolled her eyes, letting her hands drop away from her weapons. "What does this mean? Why isn't it regenerating?"

"I don't know why it isn't regenerating," he told her. His mouth had gone dry but it wasn't from the warm air. "But if I can't regenerate mana, I can't charge the crystals. If I can't charge the crystals, I can't create a portal back."

Nia's eyes went wide. "We cannot leave this place?"

He swallowed. Ethan remembered how much stat damage he'd taken when he'd accidentally teleported in the inn. It had nearly killed him. And that had just been him and had only been a short distance. Opening a portal back to the symbols he carved, on another planet, would probably kill him.

He looked at Nia's worried face. Then he looked around at the dead bodies. Was this going to be their fate too? Doomed to die of dehydration or heat stroke?

The foxgirl seemed to read his face. Her face looked sad, but she quickly covered up the sadness with a steely expression.

"All warriors die," she said and looked around. "I would have preferred to have died in battle, defending my pack." She looked over at Ethan. "But I will die next to my alpha. My mate."

The foxgirl said it with such sincerity that Ethan couldn't help but smile. He doubted he would ever hear an Earth girl say that, certainly none of the women he'd dated. It was touching.

Suddenly the foxgirl's face brightened. "Can you drink water to restore it? We have lots of water!"

Ethan forced a grin and shook his head. "*Water* only works on *Stamina*."

He realized what he had just said, remembering he'd used *Stamina* to power his magic long before he'd figured out how to channel *Mana* through Chymera crystals. Then his spirits sank as he did the math. *Stamina* could only be recovered so many times per day and never went above half. He'd never be able to charge enough crystals with his *Stamina*.

Looking up at the beautiful foxgirl, he shook her head. "It's a really good idea, but even with all the water we have, I couldn't use enough of my stamina to fill the crystals I need."

Ethan walked over to one of the tables and slumped down in the chair. As he did, the nearby pillar burst into light. Annoyed, he looked over at the pillar and then back at the tabletop. Then his head snapped back to the pillar. The lights on the pillar. They were powered by crystals and some of those were "battery" crystals.

He thought back to Michalus' explanation of enchanting. A wizard could create a crystal that acted as a battery and held the mana to cast the spell. Somehow, the batteries recharged themselves, but the old wizard hadn't explained exactly how. Presumably that was one of the things he was going to show Ethan when he came to visit.

It didn't matter right now. All that mattered was that there was a source of *Mana* to tap. He glanced from pillar to pillar. There was a big source of *Mana* to tap. He turned to Nia with a big grin on his face.

The foxgirl saw his grin and her face instantly brightened. "You have figured out a way!"

He nodded.

She gave him a smug nod. "My mate is clever."

"I just saw what was right before my eyes." Ethan shrugged and pointed to the lights. "I can take mana from the crystals powering the lights. I think I can combine that to get enough to send us home."

"This will work?" she asked hopefully.

"I think so," he said, standing up from the table. "Go ahead and keep searching. I'll see if I can siphon mana from the lights."

Nodding, the foxgirl spun happily and began searching the bodies. Ethan smiled after her and then turned and approached the nearest pillar. He located the crystals and probed them with his own *Mana*.

He sensed the *Mana* in the crystals and could tell which ones were the batteries. He tried to pull *Mana* from one of the battery crystals, but it resisted. He frowned. Why was it resisting? He tried harder, willing the *Mana* to flow into him but still nothing happened. It was as if something was pulling the *Mana* back, keeping it in the crystal.

Probing the crystals again, he could barely detect tiny bits of *Mana* that flowed between the crystals. It was almost like an electronic circuit. A live electronic circuit. If that were the case, then maybe it was difficult to suck out *Mana* when the circuit was live, or in this case while it was magically generating light.

He backed up until the light went off, then tried reaching out and pulling some *Mana*. This time, it gave a bit but then snapped back. He swore under his breath. Why wasn't it allowing him to pull the *Mana* out if it were off?

Then it hit him. It wasn't off. The enchantment was never off. It was sitting there, monitoring for the presence of a person before turning the light on. Because it was constantly in a state of monitoring, it would never truly be off.

Still, the *Mana* had given a bit. Maybe if he drew harder, he could pull it out while it was in the monitor state.

Taking a deep breath, Ethan held onto the empty Chymera crystal in his right hand and closed his eyes. He reached out with all of his will and wrapped it around the core of *Mana* he felt inside the battery crystal. Wrinkling his brow in concentration, he pulled with all of his will.

The *Mana* moved, but only slightly. Then, he felt it pulling back, just like before. Exerting more willpower, he pulled harder and felt it give a little. He kept mentally pulling until he felt like a blood vessel was going to burst in his forehead. Just as he was about to give up, he felt the *Mana* snap out of the magical "circuit" with a jolt.

A message notification popped up on his HUD but he was too busy channeling the newly acquired mana into the empty crystal in his hand. He opened his eyes and saw that the small crystal was glowing slightly. He'd done it!

He reached into the crystal in his hand and tried to gauge how full it was. The feeling he got back wasn't encouraging. He'd only filled the crystal about 5% with all of his exertion. He looked around at all the pillars. It was going to be a grueling task to fill them all.

Wiping sweat from his brow, he pulled up his HUD to see what message he had received.

Ability gained: *Mana* Siphon

Mana Siphon
   Type: Wizard
   Cost: Special

```
Range: 10 ft
Duration: Special
Description: Wizard can pull Mana
from objects or people to channel into
a Chymera crystal.
```

Ethan read the description with interest, especially the part about pulling *Mana* from people. Did that mean he could load up Chymera crystals by borrowing *Mana* from the members of his group in the future?

He looked over at Nia, who was searching bodies. Like getting a new toy, he was sorely tempted to test out his new ability on Nia to see if he could use some of her *Mana* to load up the crystal. But he didn't know exactly how the ability worked. What if it harmed her? He shook his head. It wasn't worth it.

Turning back to the pillar, he reached out again to the enchanted crystals. The battery he had drained was beginning to fill back up somehow, but it would probably take it hours before it would be full again. Instead he focused on one of the other two battery crystals and tried to pull out the *Mana*.

There was a slight resistance and then the *Mana* shot towards him. Caught off guard, he had to quickly focus the magical energy into his crystal. Once it was loaded inside, he checked the crystal's power level. Now it was about 10%. Not bad. It would be easier than he thought.

At least, that's what he thought until he got a bit light-headed. He brought up his HUD and checked his stats.

```
Mana: 55
Stamina: 2
```

He cursed. Draining the crystals was using up *Stamina*. But how much *Stamina*? He hadn't been keeping track, so he had no way to know what each attempt was costing him. He cursed again. Couldn't he catch a break?

Reaching into his pack, he pulled out his water and drank enough to restore his *Stamina*. Then he tried again with the last battery crystal on the pillar. Once again, the magical energy came much more easily than the first attempt and he funneled it in his crystal.

He checked his stats again.

Mana: 55
Stamina: 29

The attempt had only cost him one *Stamina*. Was that because of his *Mana* Siphon ability? It had to be. That first attempt had been exhausting and had probably drained a ton of *Stamina*. But it appeared the latest attempt only used 1 point of *Stamina*.

If each attempt only took a single *Stamina*, it meant he could do another 29 attempts. If he got 5% with each attempt, that would be 145% more *Mana*. It would be enough to fill this crystal and most of a second. Then, he'd need to drink more water and that would restore enough *Stamina* to allow him to fill up three crystals.

He grinned and moved to the next pillar. They just might make it back to the others after all.

54

———

It took him around half an hour to fill up three of his crystals with *Mana* from the pillars. He was only guessing because he had no true way to tell time. Even if he had wanted to walk up to the top floor, he had no way of knowing how the movement of the red sun corresponded with the passage of time. The days on this world could be 24 hours, 48 hours or an hour, for all he knew.

During the time it had taken him to collect the *Mana*, the temperature had continued to climb. When they'd arrived, he had guessed it had been maybe in the high 60s. Now, it had to be in the high 80s or low 90s on the third floor and even hotter on the floors above.

He was concerned exactly how hot it might get in the library. Ethan doubted it would get hot enough to kill them, but it would get hot enough to dehydrate them quickly. It would be like being stuck in a sauna with no way out.

"But it's a dry heat," he snickered quietly.

Luckily, they should be gone long before they would dehydrate. He had the crystals. Now they just needed to search the second and first floors. Once they found the tomes, he would open up the portal and they'd get back to the others.

Ethan glanced around the room and saw Nia's foxtail sticking up from between two of the tables. He walked over to her and stood behind her for a moment, admiring the view.

"I know you are looking at my tail," she said without turning around. "This is not the time for love-play. We must find the tomes and leave this place."

"Find anything else interesting?" he asked, tearing his eyes away from her posterior.

She glanced over her shoulder just in time to see him looking away from her rear and smirked. "You males are all the same." She then held up a large leather belt pouch. "This has the crystals you use inside."

"Chymera crystals?" he asked, taking the pouch from her. She nodded and he started to get excited. Could this be another portal pouch, like the one that Michalus had created?

The pouch was made from thick leather. Unlike the simple pouch that Michalus had carried on his belt, this one had been dyed black, with the trim dyed red. The front of the pouch had been worked and had some sort of Celtic pattern etched into the leather. Whoever had created it had been a skilled leatherworker.

But it wasn't the outside that Ethan was interested in. He lifted the flap of the pouch and peered inside. The interior was empty, which was how Michalus' pouch had appeared. But like the old wizard's pouch, this one had Chymera crystals embedded around the inside of the pouch.

It certainly appeared to be a portal pouch. But where

would this one lead? Another chest like Michalus'? And what would be at the other end? Ethan stared at the pouch for a long moment.

"Is it a wizard pouch?" Nia asked curiously.

"It looks like it," Ethan said. Again, he wondered what was on the other end of the portal. Unfortunately, there was only one way to find out. Pushing the risks out of his mind, he knew what he had to do. Gritting his teeth, he reached into the pouch.

His hand didn't go far before it hit the bottom. He blinked and looked into the pouch. Ethan could see his hand inside. It was definitely inside the pouch and not through some portal.

He frowned and withdrew his hand. He tried again with the same result. He did see the crystals flare to life, but no portal formed for him to pass his hand through. Why didn't it work? Was it broken? Out of *Mana*?

Ethan scowled as a terrible thought occurred to him. What if portals couldn't be opened from this world? What if whatever was preventing his *Mana* from regenerating also prevented portals from forming? They could be trapped!

"What's wrong?" Nia demanded.

"I'm... not sure," he replied. "But the pouch doesn't work. It doesn't open a portal."

"It is broken?" she asked, glancing at the black and red pouch.

"I'm not sure," he replied, trying to decide how much to tell her. On one hand, he didn't want to worry her. On the other hand, if the roles were reversed, he'd want to know.

He sighed. "The portal pouch doesn't work and I'm wondering if it's because we're on a different planet."

She furrowed her brows, clearing not understanding the

implications. He couldn't blame her. He wasn't sure he fully understood them either. He put it as bluntly and as simply as possible. "It might not be possible to open portals from here."

Nia's eyes went wide. "Truly? We are... trapped here?"

"I don't know," he said. "And I won't know until we try to open a portal home. But because of the mana usage the portal takes, and the fact that my mana isn't regenerating, and since I already restored about as much of my stamina as I could today by drinking water... we'll only get one chance today."

The foxgirl considered his words and then looked up. He knew exactly what she meant.

"If we don't get out the first time." He nodded. "We'll have to spend the day here and pray we can survive the heat."

She brought out her water jugs. One was uncorked and she turned it upside down, showing it was empty. "I am already through one of them."

"Me too," he told her. "And about half of the second one. I need to restore my stamina a couple of times to siphon off the mana."

Nia thrust her full water jug at him. "Let us switch then."

Ethan waved his hands dismissively. He wasn't about to take her water. His sense of chivalry wouldn't allow him to.

The foxgirl turned around and stood up. She looked him in the eyes. "Ethan, you are strong in magic and strong in mind. But I am strong in body..."

He opened his mouth to protest but she put a finger to his lips. "You are the alpha, I will give my life for you. This is my way. Besides, you are the only one who can get us back to the world of the two suns. I do not know the portal magic. You must keep your strength up if we are to get back."

Despite not liking it, her logic was sound. He was the only one who had any chance at all of getting them back to the others. But he wasn't going to give in so easily. He pushed her water jug back to her. "You keep it for now. If the portal doesn't work, then we can figure out the water situation."

He gestured to the remaining bodies they had to search. "You finish up here and I'll go down and start on the next floor."

Nia held his gaze for a moment longer before nodding and putting her water jug back into her pack. He had a feeling that if he tried to renege, the foxgirl might force feed him the water. He suppressed a grin. That was probably exactly what she would do. And if the portal failed, he'd have no *Mana* left to defend himself.

Leaving Nia to finish the third floor, Ethan climbed down to the second floor. He did a quick walkaround, looking at all of the bodies. He caught sight of one body that seemed to be some sort of warrior. The person, it was impossible to tell if it had been a man or woman due to the age of the body, wore a chainmail jerkin and around his waist were two scimitars.

He checked both blades and both looked well maintained. Removing the belt from the body, Ethan took the belt, scimitars and scabbards and set them at the bottom of the steps. He had a feeling Nia would like them. If not, maybe Ainslee would.

Ethan wished he could use them. He hated always having to use a staff. But then again, he wasn't a dark elf and he didn't have a pet black panther named Guenhwyvar, so he probably wouldn't be as dashing as one of his favorite fantasy characters.

Returning to the corpse, he began stripping off the chainmail jerkin. As he lifted the body, he found that it had been lying atop a haversack. Curious, Ethan pulled it out from underneath the corpse and opened it up.

Inside, there were books, three large, leather-bound books. Wiping his sweaty palms on his breeches, Ethan pulled one out and looked at it. The leather was a rich, textured leather that had been dyed a deep crimson. The corners of the book had been reinforced with brass and a large pentagram was embroidered in the middle of the book.

Ethan's pulse quickened. Could these be the tomes he was looking for? He looked the book over, but found no other markings. There wasn't even a title stamped on the spine of the book. With no alternatives, he opened the book and looked at the first page.

Tomes of Ashmedai

Volume I

A Treatise for Contacting and Bargaining with the Demon Lord, Ashmedai

Written by Johann Faust

As soon as he read the text, a notification appeared in his HUD. He brought up the HUD and read it.

Retrieve   the   Tomes   of   Ashmedai   I Updated

   Tomes acquired (1/3).

If there had been any doubt that he had one of the tomes, it was now gone. He read the description again. The book was written by someone named Faust. Was that a coincidence? There seemed to be so many crossovers between Earth history and legends and this world. There was the Viking gods and goddess, Merlin and now Faust. How was that possible?

Putting the strange coincidence aside, the book seemed to be all about contacting and bargaining with some demon lord. In all the movies, books and TV shows, summoning, talking to or bargaining with demons never ended well. He didn't think anything good would come from reading this book. And definitely nothing good would come from giving these books to the warlock.

He started to doubt whether or not returning these books was a good idea. He hesitated before taking the other two books from the haversack. Just knowing these books were for contacting demons made him shudder.

Still, he'd come this far. Steeling his resolve, he pulled the other two books from the haversack.

Retrieve the Tomes of Ashmedai I Updated
    Tomes acquired (3/3).

Quest Complete.
    Retrieve the Tomes of Ashmedai I
    You acquired all 3 Tomes of Ashmedai.
    Reward: 500 experience, +250 reputation with Order of the Scroll
    You gain 500 experience.
    You gain +250 reputation with Order of the Scroll.

A new notification appeared in his HUD.

You have received a new quest "Retrieve the Tomes of Ashmedai II"

```
You have acquired the 3 Tomes of
Ashmedai. You can deliver them to
Mertin Graystaff of the Order of the
Scroll in Castlehaven to receive
membership into the Order. Or you may
destroy them to prevent them from
being used to summon Ashmedai.
    Deliver Tomes to Mertin Graystaff.
    Tomes delivered (0/3).
    Reward: 500 experience, +500
reputation with Order of the Scroll,
Membership in the Order
    Destroy Tomes.
    Tomes destroyed (0/3).
    Reward: 500 experience
    Accept quest (yes or no)?
```

Acquiring the tomes had finished the first part of the quest but had started a quest chain. The new quest gave him two ways of completing it. He could either deliver the books or destroy them.

Before he could think about it further, Nia came bounding halfway down the stairs. She was smiling. "You have found the tomes?!"

"How did you know?" he asked.

"The messages said the quest had been completed," she said and then caught sight of the scimitars at the bottom of the stairs. Her head shot to Ethan. "For me?"

He grinned. "If you want them."

She walked down the remaining steps to the scimitars and pulled them from their scabbards. After admiring them for a moment, she twirled them around as if she had been practicing with them all of her life.

She stopped and beamed at Ethan. "We have weapons like these on my world. They are part of a dance I learned."

Before Ethan could answer, she bent over, slid the weapons back into their scabbards and then ran over to Ethan and threw her arms around them. "They are wonderful! Are they my wedding present?"

"I... ah... um..." Ethan stuttered, unsure what to say to that. He hadn't even realized he was supposed to give her a wedding present. As he thought about it, he probably should have figured that out. But it had all been so sudden.

Since it appeared to be something he could rectify right now, he nodded and smiled. "Yes, they are. I hope you like them."

"Truly, I do!" she said before locking her lips on his own. They were both hot from the temperature, but he felt like he just got a bit hotter. After a minute, she broke away and stepped back. "Does this mean we can go back now?"

Ethan let out a sigh and nodded. "Yes, it does."

55

───────

Since they now had the tomes, there was very little reason to stay in the library. Part of him wanted to get out of the place as soon as possible. Yet, the gamer inside him wanted to search all of the bodies.

Once they left this place, Ethan had no desire to ever come back here. They needed to loot the place now. If nothing else, he wanted to collect any weapons and armor they could find, as well as any coins and valuables. Those were all things they could use now or sell.

Nia agreed to search the rest of the bodies while Ethan looked through the books on the bookshelves, trying to find any books on magic. He found none. Unfortunately, all of the books were written for channelers and warlocks.

Given the mural and the books, this must have been a library dedicated only to those who drew their powers from demons. Ethan wanted nothing to do with it. Growing horns and a tail or having some demon whispering in his head was not his idea of a good time.

After picking out dozens of random books from two

different floors, Ethan finally gave up. There were no books on wizardry or enchanting. Everything was about demons: channeling their power and making pacts with them.

Disgusted, Ethan gave up finding useful books and decided to join Nia down on the first floor. Not only were there no useful books, but it was now so hot on the third floor that he was sweating. He guessed the temperature on the third floor was close to 100 degrees. As he made his way down to the second and finally the first floor, the temperature dropped, but only by 10 or 15 degrees.

"Did you find anything good?" he asked the foxgirl as he came down the stairs.

Nia looked up and pointed to a table near where they'd first appeared. "A few weapons, more coins, some jewelry and some armor. I also gathered some waterskins that look serviceable."

Ethan glanced at the table and saw a small collection of items piled up. "Nice job."

Taking off his pack, he walked over to the table and began to toss in the jewelry and coins. He also grabbed a few daggers and some of the waterskins. When he was finished, his pack was full. Ethan grimaced. "We may need to toss the rest of the weapons and armor through the portal first, then jump through ourselves."

Nia, who had finished searching the bodies, came over with an armful of coins and some weapons. One of the weapons appeared to be a warhammer. He chuckled. "I know a certain dwarf who will probably like that."

The foxgirl nodded and let the items spill over the table. "Did you find any books?"

"No," he sighed. "They're all about demons. I think this was some sort of warlock/channeler-only library. I didn't look through every book but everyone that I did browse had something to do with contacting, bargaining with or drawing power from demons."

"Then you are ready to leave now?" she asked.

Ethan gave a last look around the library. He did wish he had more time to look through the library to see if there were books that he had missed. He hadn't even gotten to the fourth or fifth floors. Not that he wanted to ever come back, but if he could learn more about magic or this world, it might actually be worth it. But this place was so remote, coming back here would be a major pain.

He chuckled and Nia gave him a curious look. "Something is funny?"

"I was just thinking that if I ever wanted to come back here and search through more of the books," he replied with a wry smile, "this place is pretty remote. It would be a long journey to get back here."

Nia gave him a look of disbelief. "You want to come back here?"

He shrugged. "If I could find a book on wizardry, it might be worth it."

"You are right. This place is a long journey. It would be best not to come back," she said.

"Except." He grinned. "I might be able to open a portal to it. Assuming of course, I can actually open a portal to get us home."

"You can?" She arched an eyebrow.

"Maybe," he said and walked over to the archway where they had appeared. He focused some of his *Earth* magic on the wall and inscribed three more unique runes on it. These he based off of a combination of logos from fast food companies from Earth. That should be impossible for anyone to guess but easy for him to remember.

Stepping back, he admired his handiwork and committed it to memory. Nia came over to stand next to him. "You will use those to come back? Like the symbols you made before?"

"Exactly." He smiled.

"Then we are ready to go now?" she asked.

"I guess it's time to give it a try," he told her, his hand falling to the portal pouch on his belt. He wasn't 100% sure that he could open up a portal, but he had to try. The alternative was to join the bodies here.

Ethan reached into his pouch and brought out the charged Chymera crystals. Nia put her hand over his and pushed it down. Confused, he turned to the foxgirl and saw a lusty look in her eye.

"The journey is long, and we will not have any time alone," she said with a sly grin. Her voice had become husky and he knew what she was asking before Nia finished her sentence. "You are my husband and I wish to spend some time with you."

The foxgirl moved in but he grabbed her by the shoulders and held her at bay. Her eyes narrowed and her forehead wrinkled. He smiled at her and nodded at the archway. "Don't forget the others can see in."

Nia's head snapped to the side, even as she flushed scarlet. She twisted back to look at Ethan, her face bright red. "I did forget. Though it is not uncommon on my world. We often learn from watching others."

Before he could reply to that, she took his hand, pulling him to the steps and then upstairs to the second floor. Once there, she pulled him to a table and began to strip off her clothes. He watched her, once again fascinated by the woman's slim, athletic body.

Sooner than he would have expected, she was naked and turned to him. She rolled her eyes at him. "Are you going to stare all day or are you going to join me, husband?"

Ethan didn't need to be told twice.

AFTERWARDS, she lay in his arms on one of the long wooden tables. Both of them were covered in sweat, but not just from their previous activity. The room was getting hotter. If he had to guess, it was over a hundred already on the second floor. He wondered what temperature it was on the sixth floor. 140 degrees? 150 degrees?

Ethan stroked her hair absently as she sighed contentedly. He wasn't sure what she was thinking of, but he was worrying whether the portal would open. It wouldn't be long before it was over a hundred degrees on the first floor too. How long would they last in 140 or 150 degrees?

He brought up his stats to see how much *Mana* he had left.

Mana: **62**
  Stamina: **15**

Ethan sat up suddenly, causing Nia to groan. "What?!"

Blinking to make sure he was reading the HUD correctly; he double checked the numbers. "My mana is back to maximum."

Nia frowned at him, rolled her eyes and slid off the table.

She bent down and retrieved her clothes and began to dress. "I thought you said your mana was not regenerating."

Ethan sensed the foxgirl wasn't happy with him. He tried to give her a placating smile. "Sorry, Nia. It was just so surprising. But it's good! I was worried that if I didn't have enough mana, it may have burned up some of my stats."

The foxgirl stopped dressing and gave him a hard look. "And you did not tell me this?!"

He gave her a sheepish look. "I'm sorry. But in the end, it didn't matter. The only way out of here was for me to open a portal. I had to try whether or not it burned up my stats."

She nodded but her eyes were narrowed, and he could tell she was still sore at him. He checked his stats again to make sure his *Mana* really was full and then began dressing. He had just put on his boots when an unexpected thought came to him.

Many of the pagan rituals back on Earth involved sex. Some witches even claimed that sex powered their spells. Could it be the same way on this world? Could sex restore *Mana*? He looked at Nia and smiled.

"What?" she asked, eyes narrowing.

"I'm not sure," he replied, hoping he was right about sex restoring Mana. "But I think our sex restored my mana."

"Truly?" Nia asked with wide eyes. "It can do that?"

"I think so. But we may need to experiment to make sure," he grinned. That was an experiment he was willing to try. Repeatedly, if necessary. For science, of course.

By the time they were both fully dressed, Ethan felt like it was even warmer. Nia was panting, and it wasn't because of their lovemaking. She glanced his way. "It is very warm now."

"Let's try to get out of here," he told her and, taking her hand, went downstairs to the first floor.

They quickly gathered their stuff near the archway. Ethan brought out the Chymera crystals and held them in his hand. He glanced at the archway, remembering that there were still some unshattered crystals embedded in it.

Taking one of the knives they'd found, Ethan quickly went through and pried a total of two dozen intact crystals from the wall. He slipped them into his pouch.

Once that was done, he took out the three charged crystals and set them in his hand. They would help him power the portal. The larger crystal he channeled through was in his pocket but that didn't matter. As long as it was on his person, he could channel through it.

"You ready?" he asked Nia.

"I am ready," she replied. She had bundled the weapons in one of her sleeping blankets and held them against her chest.

"Assuming it works, I'll open the portal," he said. "As soon as I do, jump through it, just like we did before. I'll be right behind you."

The foxgirl clenched the bundle of weapons tighter against herself and nodded. "You had better come after me!"

Turning back to the archway, he held the crystals tightly in his fist. Technically, he could open the portal anywhere in the library, but doing it where they came in just seemed right. "Here goes nothing."

Once again, Ethan focused on the three symbols he'd created back in the destroyed city. He focused and then willed the portal to appear. He kept the image of exactly how large he wanted it. Just big enough for them to crawl through.

Nothing happened so he focused every ounce of willpower he had on the portal. He focused on pulling more *Mana* from the crystals, willing it to create the portal. It had to work. It had to.

And then a sparkling area appeared in the air in front of him. It expanded into a gateway and beyond he could see the symbols on the ground. He'd done it!

Then one of the crystals exploded in his hand and the image faltered for a second. He focused harder. "Go, Nia! Go!"

The foxgirl darted forward and dove through, appearing on the other side of the portal next to the symbols. Another crystal exploded in his hand and the image faltered again. He also felt his own strength draining away and knew it was now or never.

Lunging forward, Ethan threw himself through the portal and into the whirling colors of the Bifrost.

56

Ethan sped through the scintillating tunnel of color. Like before, it seemed like minutes that he was in the tunnel before abruptly he was rolling on the ground in the ruined city.

No sooner had he come to a stop when he heard Nia hiss and then the sound of swords being pulled from scabbards. Ethan looked around, trying to see what was going on. That's when he spotted them.

A dozen yards away were Ainslee, Yuliana and Par'karr. They were tied up and gagged, down on their knees. On either side of his companions were several men in familiar armor. Directly behind his companions were two women. The first he recognized instantly as a priestess of Hel. She was dressed nearly identically to the other priestess they had killed, but this woman was taller. The woman was in her late twenties or early thirties, with a strong jaw and long blond hair. If the woman was from Earth, he would have guessed she had Eastern European blood.

Standing next to the blond priestess of Hel was

Charmine Norton, the warlock who had asked him to retrieve the tomes. She wore the same sky-blue robes he'd seen her in last time, though these looked a bit road worn. The warlock cackled when she saw Ethan.

Luna was nowhere to be seen and he hoped the men hadn't killed the mountain lion.

"We've been waiting for you," Charmine chuckled, her voice manic and bordering on insanity. She muttered something to herself and then continued but suddenly she was screaming. "Now hand over the tomes!"

Ethan glanced at his bound companions. As he looked closer, he saw that their eyes were completely white. Anger surged up inside. What had they done to them?

"What's wrong with their eyes?!" he demanded.

The warlock chuckled again and glanced over to the priestess. The tall blond woman just grinned sadistically. "Hel is the goddess of the night. To the infidels, she brings endless night."

He saw the priestess finger her amulet as she spoke, and he remembered how the other priestess had been able to cast some sort of blindness spell using her amulet. Was that what this priestess had done as well.

"Give us the books or they die!" Charmine screamed. "Give them to us!"

Ethan chuckled. "You really expect me to believe that you will let any of us live if I give them to you?"

Charmine mumbled something unintelligible to herself for several minutes. As she did, even the priestess and her henchmen glanced at the warlock with concern. Ethan got the impression that they didn't trust her either.

But why were the priestess and her goons here at all? Had they found out about the others his group had killed? If so, how? There had been no witnesses and they'd left that elaborate - but plausible - ruse.

The priestess turned to Ethan, a grin plastered on her face. "You and your friends were promised to me. A wizard will make a particularly good sacrifice to Hel!"

Ethan smirked. So, this had nothing to do with their earlier incident. Charmine had made some sort of deal with the followers of Hel. She'd hired them as muscle, with their payment being Ethan and his friends.

He brought up his HUD and checked out his stats.

Mana: 11
Stamina: 6

He cursed silently. The portal had taken so much of his *Mana* and *Stamina*. He barely had enough to cast a few spells, let alone defeat a half dozen goons, a priestess and a warlock. He didn't even know what the warlock could do. And he'd doubted they'd let Nia and he go for a quickie to restore his *Mana*. Though he did smile inwardly at the thought.

He felt the stinging in his hand and remembered he was still holding a Chymera crystal in his hand. Two of the crystals had been destroyed but the third one was still intact. Unfortunately, he could sense it had been nearly completely drained. He didn't seem to have many options.

"Any plan?" he whispered to Nia.

"Fight," the foxgirl hissed back.

Ethan appreciated the woman's enthusiasm but one foxgirl and an almost out of power wizard against a warlock, a priestess and six goons seemed like suicide for them - and their companions.

"Enough stalling!" the warlock screamed. "Give us the books now or you will watch them kill one of your companions!"

Beside her the blond priestess, who had been playing with her medallion, nodded to one of the guards and the man took a step towards Par'karr. He moved his sword in front of the little kobold.

Looking at the woman's medallion, Ethan knew that inside it should have two Chymera crystals. There had to be a spell crystal and a battery crystal. That was how Michalus had explained that magical items worked. Yet when he reached out with his mind to the amulet, there was only one. But that one crystal pulsed with *Mana*. And that gave him an idea.

"Nia, follow my lead but be ready," he whispered. "And, in case I didn't say it before, you have my permission to smite my enemies."

The foxgirl flashed him a toothy smile but stayed at the ready.

Ethan raised his left hand in a gesture of surrender. "Okay. Okay. Don't hurt them and I'll give you the tomes."

Slipping his pack off, Ethan opened it and dug around for the tomes. He brought out one and set it on the ground. As he did, he heard a squeal of delight from the warlock, followed by some muttering.

Ethan found his water jug and pulled it out, taking a long drink from it.

"No drinking! Give me the other tomes!" demanded Charmine from behind him.

"Fine! Fine!" Ethan retorted and tossed the empty water jug to the side. "Just let me find them."

He pretended to rummage around for the second one but as he did, he first checked his HUD.

Mana: 11
 Stamina: 16

The water hadn't restored much *Stamina,* but it was something. He reached out and found the battery for the amulet. It was maintaining the blindness spell on his companions and was already weak. If he pulled the *Mana* out of it, the spells on his friends would fail. He just needed to make sure they didn't let the cat out of the bag.

"Yuliana," he whispered. The elf, with her superior healing, would be the only one who would hear him. "I'm going to suck the magic out of the amulet. Tell the others not to let on that you can see. Tell everyone to go face first in the dirt when I give the word."

He brought out the second tome and set it on the ground, looking over his shoulder as if to confirm the warlock saw it. As he did, he looked at the elf and saw her give a subtle nod. Good! She had heard him.

Turning back around, he pretended to be looking again. This time he reached out and pulled the *Mana* from the amulet's battery crystal, channeling into the crystal in his hand. With that done, he pulled out the third book and set it on top of the other two books.

Turning, he picked up the books and turned them around. He held the books above his head. "Here they are. All three of them!"

"Give them to us! Now!" screamed the warlock, spittle flying from her mouth. Her eyes bulged and she was breathing heavily. "Give them to us or we kill your friends!"

Ethan created a ball of flame in his free hand and moved it towards the books. "Let my friends go or I destroy the books right here."

He thought the veins in Charmine's forehead were going to burst as she seethed with anger. And fire writhed the warlock's hands. "I will utterly destroy you!"

"And you'll destroy the books too!" he countered.

Charmine muttered to herself for a minute before looking up. "Release the prisoners!"

The priestess gave the warlock a disbelieving look. "We will not! These are sacrifices to Hel. They are the payment you promised."

"Release them!" Charmine shouted again.

"Enough of this," the priestess sneered and pointed to the warlock. "Take them all. This one included."

The priestess moved her hand over her amulet and pointed at the warlock, probably expecting her spell to blind Charmine. Unfortunately for her, there was no *Mana* in the battery to power the spell.

More red fire filled both of Charmine's hands and then shot out at the priestess, engulfing the woman in flames. The blond priestess screamed for only a moment before there wasn't enough of her to scream.

Guards leapt away from the warlock, drawing their swords. They hesitated, swords out, unsure whether to attack the mad, fire-wielding warlock. And that's when Ethan yelled.

"Now!" he bellowed and watched as Ainslee, Par'karr and Yuliana all fell face first into the dirt.

Ethan, who had been using the time to focus the *Mana* in the crystal, focused all of the magic from it into the guards' swords and helmets. He willed them to bend and shift, knowing that the steel couldn't take the stress. There was a rending sound and the groan of metal and suddenly the swords and helmets exploded.

```
You critically pierce Roedrick for 23
damage.
    You critically pierce Roedrick for
37 damage.
    Roedrick dies.
    You gain 60 experience. Experience
to next level 110.

You critically pierce Sandrel for 24
damage.
    You critically pierce Sandrel for 39
damage.
    Sandrel dies.
    You gain 60 experience. Experience
to next level 50.

You critically pierce Aeron for 19
damage.
    You critically pierce Aeron for 27
damage.
    Aeron is Bleeding.

You critically pierce Torin for 21
damage.
    You critically pierce Torin for 28
damage.
    Torin is Blinded.
    Torin is Bleeding.
```

```
You critically pierce Grant for 24
damage.
    You critically pierce Grant for 39
damage.
    Grant dies.
    You gain 60 experience. Experience
to next level 3190.


You critically pierce Dar for 21
damage.
    You critically pierce Dar for 28
damage.
    Dar is Bleeding.


Congratulations!
    You have reached level 6.
    +1 Attribute Point.
    New ability: Specialization I.
    Note: Requires Action.
```

Three of the guards fell lifeless to the ground while the other three screamed in pain. Nia, quick as lightning, was already moving towards them to finish them off.

Charmine looked around at the decimated guards and then turned and looked wide-eyed at Ethan. She summoned red fire to her hands again but Ethan held up the books, now stacked nicely on top of each other.

"You want the books." Ethan smiled wickedly. "Let me give them to you."

With all the Air magic he could muster, he sent the first book soaring towards the warlock. Charmine's eyes went wide again as the book flew towards her. She let the flames in her hands die out so she could grab it but Ethan shifted the book's trajectory, sending it up over her hands to slam right into her face.

He heard a crunch as the woman's nose broke and the warlock blinked several times before she glared daggers at Ethan and summoned fire back to her hands.

"Ethan!" screamed Nia, who had just cut down another of the guards. Ethan registered the experience gains from the kill assists but only briefly. He didn't have time to pay attention to them at the moment.

The warlock raised her hands to send red fire at Ethan and that was when the second book hit her in the throat. Then the third book hit her in the forehead.

The fire in her hands instantly died out as she fell to her knees. Charmine clutched at her throat, coughing and gagging, trying to suck in oxygen.

That's when Luna bounded out of the shadows, leaped up and locked her jaws around the back of the woman's neck. With a savage twist of the big cat's head, there was a crunchy pop and the warlock's body went limp.

Charmine Norton dies.
   You gain 25 experience. Experience to next level 3105.

Possibly unaware the woman was dead, the mountain lion shook the woman's dead body like a ragdoll for several minutes before dropping it on the ground.

Ethan swooned, his *Mana* and *Stamina* nearly gone. He saw Nia cutting their friends free, even as three demon rabbits lunged repeatedly at the last guard until he finally collapsed onto the ground.

Aeron dies.

You gain 35 experience. Experience to next level 3070.

He sat down heavily on the ground, feeling light-headed. "Everyone okay?"

The rest of his companions signaled that they were. Nia rushed back over to Ethan and crouched next to him. The foxgirl threw her arms around him, hugging him tight. Her mouth moved close to his ear and in a low voice she whispered, "If you are low on mana, I know a way to restore it."

57

———

When it was clear that there were no more enemies, Nia ran off to get water for Ethan. He wasn't sure if it would actually restore any *Stamina* considering how much he'd had already today.

Yuliana healed the group of the few wounds they'd received, as well as Luna's wounds. The mountain lion had been shot with two crossbow bolts before Yuliana had told the mountain lion to run off.

Ainslee was busy stomping around and kicking the corpses to make sure they were dead. Even when they didn't move, she kicked them a few extra times, cursing them and their entire line for several generations.

Par'karr sat near him, scratching his demon rabbits. Stifling a yawn, Ethan looked over at the little kobold. "How did they capture you?"

"They sneak up." The kobold scowled. "Even elf not hear them. We all looking at portal. We waiting for you to come back. They make Par'karr blind first. Me not able to command rabbits. Then me hear dwarf yelling. Then elf."

The kobold rubbed his arms and Ethan saw bruises. "Then men come. Grab us. Throw us to ground and tie us."

"But Ethan save us." The kobold looked at him and gave him a toothy grin. "Ethan powerful wizard!"

Ethan returned his grin. "I'm just glad they didn't hurt you any worse."

The kobold wrapped his arms around himself and shivered. "Priestess taunt Par'karr. Tell him she kill Par'karr. Say Par'karr not worthy to be sacrifice."

"Luckily," he nodded grimly, "no one was sacrificed."

Ethan was feeling guilty for the lovemaking session with Nia. Maybe they would have been back in time to fight off the warlock and the Hel followers.

On the other hand, had they not found that sex restored his *Mana*, he probably would have been unconscious when he came through the portal. And that assumed that he made it through the portal at all. He could have passed out there in the library. Then they wouldn't have made it back at all.

He was still running over "what if" scenarios in his head when Nia came trotting back with the water. He gulped down the cool water and watched as some of his *Stamina* was restored, but not much.

As he had guessed, he had almost drunk his limit of water today. Only rest or sleep would restore his *Stamina* at this point.

"We should go," Nia told him as he continued to sip on the water. Despite it not restoring his stats, it was refreshing after the sweltering library. "It will be dark soon and we are too exposed here."

Looking around at the bodies strewn around the library, Ethan couldn't help but agree. "Let's check the bodies for anything useful and then we can get going."

The guards were a bloody mess from the exploding swords and helmets. Other than a few dozen coins, they found very little. Too little. As Ethan searched the bodies, he realized they had no packs, no food and no water.

"Did any of you see them take off packs?"

"What part of blind didn't you understand," the dwarf growled, kicking another guard's body. "We couldn't have seen a giant's arse if he was squatting over us!"

Ainslee stomped over to the priestess' charred remains and looked like she was about to kick it. She stared down at the blackened corpse and seemed to think better of it. Throwing her hands up, she stalked away and kicked another one of the guards instead.

Ethan stood up and walked around the library with Nia trailing after him. When he didn't find any discarded packs, he turned to the foxgirl. "Can you track them by scent?"

The foxgirl rolled her eyes at him. "Of course."

"Let's grab what we can here and then backtrack their trail," he told her, heading back to their own pack.

"A hammer!" shouted Ainslee. Ethan looked over to see the dwarf had found their bundle of weapons and items they'd taken from the library. He chuckled; he'd forgotten all about them in the fight.

Ainslee held up the hammer, showing it off to everyone. "Now this is a real weapon."

The dwarf swung it around several times and then frowned. "The balance is off. Obviously not made by a dwarf!"

Her frown didn't last long and soon she was swinging the hammer around and pretending to strike at enemies.

Ethan paused in front of the portal into the library and stared at it. He could still see all of the bodies and wondered how many more people might get trapped. How many more would die in that terrible place?

His conscience wouldn't let him just leave and allow other people, warlocks or not, to become trapped and die in that place.

"What are you doing?" Nia asked when he didn't move away from the portal.

"I need to destroy this portal," he said. "Otherwise, innocent people would get trapped in there."

"If they come for those books, then perhaps they should die in there," Nia retorted.

"But what about innocent travelers or explorers?" he asked her with a raised eyebrow. He remembered coming across a small skeleton. It could have been a halfling but it could have been a child. "What about an innocent family, maybe with children?"

The foxgirl bit her lip. "Fine. Do what you must."

Nia turned and began gathering their gear, leaving Ethan alone. He wasn't sure what to make of Nia's attitude, but he could ask her more about it later.

Ethan turned and faced the portal. He didn't look at the portal as much as he looked at the Chymera crystals that made the portal possible. He hated to destroy something that had obviously taken a great deal of time and power to create.

But he knew the portal had to be shut down. He didn't want anyone else dying in there and he also didn't want any other warlocks or channelers getting to it. He hadn't looked through many of the books, but if they were anything like the Tomes of Ashmedai, he wanted those out of people's hands.

Reaching down, he picked up a rock. With one last look

through the portal, he smashed the rock against several of the crystals. As expected, the crystals shattered and a moment later, the inside of the library disappeared, revealing the inside of the actual building.

He sent a couple balls of light into the room, revealing a bare, dust-covered room. It looked vaguely like the inside of the library, but it was devoid of tables or books. After his previous experience in the actual library, he wasn't even remotely curious about the inside of this building.

Instead he looked over the remaining crystals and smiled. He called over Par'karr and together the two of them pried dozens of crystals from the wall before Nia insisted, they leave. Stowing away his Chymera crystals, he joined the others and Nia began to follow their enemies' scent.

The trail led up through the rubble-filled streets and finally up the embankment, nearly a mile from the river. As they came up to the top of their climb, Ethan recognized something he hadn't expected. Horses. Eight of them.

The group stopped, Nia with her hands on her weapons and the other women looking wary. Only Par'karr seemed to know what they were.

"What are they?" Nia asked, scrunching up her nose.

"Are they... friendly?" Yuliana asked. The elf seemed fascinated by the horses.

"Can we eat them?" the dwarf wondered aloud.

"They're horses," he said and suddenly the horses began to whinny and stomp around. Ethan saw Luna come up next to the elf and guessed the mountain lion had spooked the creatures.

"Can you take Luna down the hill for a few minutes?" he asked.

Nodding, Yuliana headed back down the embankment and the big cat followed her.

Once the cat was gone, the horses seemed to calm again. Slowly, making calming sounds, Ethan walked over to the horses. He petted each of them, wishing he had an apple or sugar cube to give them - at least, that's what people fed them in the movies.

Once they were calm, Ethan searched through the packs on the animals and found both human food and some grain for the horses, as well as bedrolls. He grinned. At least they didn't have to worry about food now.

"How did they bring these beasts past the balweers?" Nia asked.

Ethan scratched his head as he thought about it but then the answer came to him. "The priestess probably used that blinding spell on any balweers that got close. Since they seem to rely so much on their sight, they were helpless." He looked back at the horses. "Plus, horses can gallop pretty fast."

"Oh," Ainslee said. "They're riding beasts."

"Yes," Ethan retorted, pointing to the leather saddles. He suddenly wished he knew how to ride a horse. But he was a geek, not a cowboy. "But I've never ridden them before."

"Par'karr not ride them either," the kobold squeaked.

"Maybe it's like riding a goat," the dwarf said. "That's what the knights ride. I mean, how hard can it be."

It turned out that it was much more difficult than any of them expected and night came before they had fully gotten the hang of the horses. They led the horses to the river and let the animals drink while they made their camp.

Once the horses had drunk their fill, Ethan used a bit of magic to shape a stone into something they could tie the horses to for the night. It took a bit of time and some coaxing from Yuliana, who the horses seemed to like, before the skittish creatures let Luna come near the camp.

After some time, the horses seemed to accept that the mountain lion wasn't going to eat them - though Ethan did catch the big cat eyeing them several times.

After a meal of jerky from the horses' packs, they all settled in for sleep. During his watch, Ethan brought out the Tomes of Ashmedai he'd retrieved from around the warlock. He wasn't sure why the woman wanted them so bad and he really had a bad feeling about reading them.

He looked at the quest in his inventory, thinking about how much he wanted access to the library at the Order of the Scroll. And yet, he couldn't shake how wrong the books felt and how wary he felt about giving them to the Order.

Cursing quietly, so as not to wake anyone, Ethan tossed the books into the fire. There was no explosion of evil fire or screams or any indication that they were anything but normal books as they browned, then blackened and finally caught fire.

He looked at the new message in his HUD.

```
Quest Complete.
    Retrieve the Tomes of Ashmedai II
    Destroy Tomes.
    Tomes destroyed (3/3).
    Reward: 500 experience
    You gain 500 experience.
    You gain +1 Fame.
```

Ethan hadn't been expecting the Fame and wasn't even sure what it did, if anything. He spent the rest of his watch wondering if he had done the right thing or if he'd just made a huge mistake.

Next, he brought up his HUD. He still had some character sheet housecleaning to do.

He took his unassigned point and stuck it into *Intellect* for the additional *Mana*. That taken care of, he looked at his new ability.

```
Specialization I
  Type: Wizard
  Cost: N/A
  Range: N/A
  Duration: N/A
  Description: The wizard may choose
to specialize in a specific skill of
magic. Specialized skills require less
magic and can create more powerful
effects.
  Note:     Specialization     skill     not
chosen.

Choose School of Specialization:
  Aether Magic
  Air Magic
  Earth Magic
  Fire Magic
  Water Magic
```

Ethan read the description and shrugged. The *Specialization* ability seemed to work the same way it did in the MMORPGs and other roleplaying games. It basically made a school of magic, or in this case skill of magic, more powerful.

He considered which skill would most benefit. *Air* was extremely useful for convert actions and was very versatile. *Fire* did tons of damage and his fireball had a good range. *Earth* had come in handy for shaping things and causing metal weapons and armor to explode. *Water*, he'd only really used to freeze meat so far.

Then there was Aether magic, or as he thought of it, portal magic. So far, he'd created only a couple of portals - one of which had completely laid him out. Yet of all the skills, Portal magic was the most fascinating and potentially the most useful. Without advanced forms of travel, the person who could move people from one place to another instantly had a decisive advantage.

After some debating, he ended up specializing in Aether magic. If nothing else, he really wanted to be able to make portal pouches for everyone. Since there was no inventory system like in MMORPGs, they needed ways to carry more. Plus, he already had ideas on how to expand on the portal pouch concept.

That done, he sat back and stared at the fire, thinking of things he might be able to do with portals. When his watch was over, Ethan lay down on the bedroll and fell asleep quickly. When the dreams came, they were no longer of him being chased. Instead, they were of Ethan hopping through portals to different places - and different planets.

58

———

The next morning, after spending some time figuring how to ride the horses, the group set off towards the spires that marked the edge of the wasteland. Ethan guessed that the warlock and the follower of Hel made it through the balweers by using the priestess' blindness spell on the creatures.

He briefly considered using the same technique when they realized they'd need to cross their territory, but the problem was the creature moved so fast, that once his spell wore off, the creatures could still catch up with them. Now that they had horses, that shouldn't be a problem.

Ethan had wanted to test it on his own, but Nia had insisted that she come with him. The two of them rode out until they attracted the attention of one of the creatures and then Ethan had used his light spell to blind it. Then they had turned around and rode back the way they came. By the time the blindness wore off, they were well away from the balweer and it didn't follow.

Once they reported back to the others, the group rode

through the wasteland. Every time they ran into a balweer, Ethan would blind it and they'd spur the horses into a gallop. With the horses' speed, it took them only a few hours to traverse what had taken all night on the way to the library.

After that, they stayed on the forest road until they reached the road back to Timberwell. The hunting was sparse until they cut back into the forest, but with the horses they made excellent time.

Despite the first couple of days being agonizing on his legs, Ethan was amazed at how quickly the travel went with horses. Within only a couple of days, they reached Timber-well. Falling back into his role as crazy warlock, Ethan secured two rooms and this time there was no trouble.

He and Nia shared one room while Ainslee, Yuliana and Par'karr shared the other. Once again, they had a tub brought up to the room. They all took turns taking hot baths, but this time Nia insisted that she restore his *Mana* between each bath. Ethan didn't object.

After several good meals, and Ainslee drinking herself into a drunken stupor again, the group set off for Castle-haven. Ethan knew he couldn't complete the quest and become a member of the Order of the Scroll. He still felt he needed to at least tell Mertin in person that the books were destroyed, as was the library.

Ethan would just leave out the part where he destroyed the books, the gateway to the library and killed one of their members. He didn't think the Order would retaliate against him if they found out he'd killed Charmine, considering she'd attacked them. But there was no need to put that to the test.

When they reached the outskirts of Castlehaven, the group rode into the woods, away from the road and prying eyes. Ainslee, Yuliana and Par'karr were at risk of being taken as slaves, despite the collars they still wore. Like before, it was best if they stayed outside the city. This time, in the off chance they were discovered, he asked Ainslee to stay with them.

The dwarf resisted at first but once he promised to bring back at least one hand keg of ale or mead, she quickly relented. He also promised to find some fresh vegetables for Yuliana, whose diet had been a sporadic mix of whatever berries and nuts they could find.

After receiving a parting kiss from Nia, he rode into Castlehaven and straight to the Order of the Scroll library. Tying off his horse, he went to the door. This time, no one was there to open the door for him, so he tugged it open and went inside the familiar structure.

There were very few people in the building but as soon as he entered the main library area, he saw a familiar face sitting at one of the tables. As he started towards Mertin, he stopped and looked around at the library, noting how similar it was to the library of Daemonium. It was eerily familiar, and he had flashbacks to all of the dead bodies in the library.

"Ethan?" Mertin asked, looking up from the book he'd been reading. "You returned?"

He smiled and walked over to the table Mertin was at. The channeler started to stand but Ethan gestured for the man to stay seated. Moving to the opposite side of the table, he slid into a seat opposite the man.

Mertin looked disappointed. "I take it you did not find the library?"

Ethan smirked. "Oh, we found it alright."

Mertin's eyes grew bright with excitement. "Was it where Charmine told you it would be?"

"It was," Ethan replied. "Though she neglected to mention the balweers that lived nearby."

The channeler slapped his head. "Balweers. That's right, I remember one of the survivors mentioning them now. I'm sorry, I had forgotten that detail. But you made it through?"

Shrugging, Ethan continued. "We made it through. Their eyesight is based on movement, so we went at night."

"Based on movement?" the man repeated. "How fascinating. I don't believe I've read that anywhere."

"We made it all the way to the library," Ethan continued. "But it was completely empty. There were no bodies or books inside at all inside the building we found."

"What?!" the man gasped. "People who witnessed others go in claimed to have seen many books, and a few bodies."

Ethan smirked, wondering why Mertin hadn't mentioned the bodies previously. The man did seem a bit scatterbrained, or had he done it on purpose.

"I examined the library doorway very carefully," he told the channeler, watching the man's face carefully for a reaction. "I think the door used to be a portal."

"A portal?" Mertin's eyes went wide. If he was faking it, he was a good actor. "A portal to where?"

Ethan had concocted the story on their way to the city. It had enough truth that he didn't feel too guilty telling it to Mertin. But he couldn't tell the man the real truth without revealing that he was a wizard. Technically, everything he'd said so far had been true, as proven by the lack of Bluff increases.

"The real library would be my guess," Ethan replied. Again, not a lie. He knew exactly where the portal had led and it was the real library.

"But how do you know it was a portal?" the channeler asked. "And not just some looters."

"I don't know if anyone can be completely sure at this point," he replied, choosing his words carefully. "But it looks like there are dozens of Chymera crystals around the doorway, some of which had been shattered or removed."

"No!" the man gasped; his face horrified. "The library is lost forever?"

Ethan nodded. "Either it has been completely ransacked by someone or the portal to the real library has been destroyed!"

A man near the bookshelves, garbed in blue robes shushed them. "Shhh!"

Looking chagrined, Mertin lowered his voice. "Are you sure?"

"When we left there, the building was completely bare and there was no sign of any books or that there had ever been any books," he replied.

"So, you do not have the Tomes of Ashmedai then," the channeler sighed. "A pity. Though perhaps it is for the best. Some say those books told how to open a portal directly to the plane of demons."

"Say what?" Ethan gasped. No one mentioned anything about portals to the demon world, or dimension or plane - or wherever they lived.

"What?" the man asked, confused.

"What was that about a portal to the demon world?" he demanded.

Mertin snorted. "It was only a rumor. A few people who had seen the books and could actually understand them, wrote about opening a portal to the demon plane to allow them to enter our world and grant us even more power."

Ethan knew his eyes were wide at the man's revelation. In what world was opening a demon portal ever a good idea.

Chuckling, the channeler waved off Ethan's obvious concern. "It was just a rumor. Besides the power needed to do that, even briefly, would be enormous. And it would require a wizard."

"A wizard?" Ethan perked up. "Why a wizard? Why not a warlock or channeler?"

Mertin nodded. "I know it may be difficult to understand for laymen. Wizards have access to all schools of magic, including Aether magic. To my knowledge, no warlock or channeler has ever been gifted with Aether magic, which is required for opening portals.. Either the demons themselves do not possess it, it is not something they can share, or it is not something they choose to share."

"Fascinating," Ethan nodded. And it was fascinating. That meant that only a wizard could have built the portal to the library building. He'd suspected it had been built by wizards because of the enchantment but this seemed like confirmation.

Mertin nodded but then frowned, his countenance falling as he looked at Ethan. "I'm afraid this means we cannot accept you as a member for now."

"I guess not," Ethan agreed. "Unless there's something else I can do to earn membership."

The channeler shook his head sadly. "Unfortunately, the rules are very specific. You must introduce new knowledge, or in the case of the Tomes, it would have been restoring lost knowledge."

"I understand," Ethan said and stood up.

Mertin stood too and held out his hand. "I'm sorry you wasted your time."

Ethan nodded. "Me too."

"If you recreate your research," the man said, holding out his hand. "We'd be glad to accept your application."

He shook the channeler's hand. "I'll bear that in mind. It was good meeting you, Mertin."

"You as well," Mertin replied. They shook hands for a moment longer and then let go. The channeler gave him a nod and then sat back down.

Ethan turned and left the Order. He hadn't been able to join and he hadn't gotten any new quests, so it had been a bust. There were two more items of business he needed to take care of.

Asking directions to the Mercenary's Guild, he found the large building and went inside. Several burly men in various types of armor sat around tables with mugs of ale or mead. They had been talking when he walked in but went silent as soon as they saw him.

A portly dark-skinned man in a leather-bound chair eyed him. Ethan eyed the man back.

Terry Pratchett
    Human
    Warrior
    Level 6

"What do you need, little man?" Terry asked in a gruff voice.

The trader they'd originally talked to, Athalia Brownlock, had said the only way to get a caravan coming back to Hawkshead was to get the mercenary guild to sign off that it was safe. At the time, they hadn't had the money to hire mercenaries. Now, with the money they'd gotten from the bodies in the library and the money from the followers of Hel, he did have enough.

Ethan smiled. "I need to hire a company of mercenaries to investigate the area around my village."

LATER THAT DAY, Ethan rode into the clearing where he'd left the others. Luckily, everyone was still there and there appeared to have been no trouble. Riding over to the other horses, he dismounted and tied off the horse with the others. As he did, he pulled a sack off the horse.

Ainslee came bounding over him, her face a mask of excitement and anticipation. "Did you get it? Did you get the mead?"

"I didn't," he replied, hanging his head. "We were a bit low on money."

"Low on money?!" growled the dwarf sourly. "What did you do with all of it?!"

"I hired some mercenaries to scout out the valley so we can restart the caravans," he replied. "And that was all the money..."

The dwarf muttered under her breath and turned away and began to stomp off.

"Except for these blacksmith tools I managed to find," he said to her back and the dwarf spun and stared at him wide-eyed. He patted a leather bundle tied to his saddle.

"Blacksmith's tools?!" she said, spinning around, eyes wide. A huge grin crept across her face. "You mean it?"

"I do," he said and pointed to the bulky leather bundle on one side of the horse. "I couldn't get an anvil. It was just too heavy and more expensive than I thought. We'd need a wagon to get one to the village."

"Of course, you do." Ainslee bobbed her head. She hurried over to the horse and began unstrapping the leather bundle.

Leaving her to it, he carried the sack over to Yuliana and handed it to her. "There should be enough apples and carrots in there to make it back to Hawkshead."

"Thank you!" The elf smiled.

"Did it go okay?" Nia asked, coming up to him.

He shrugged. "About what we expected."

"No membership," she said, it was a statement, not a question.

Ethan nodded. "No membership. But I did hire the mercenaries to survey the area, so hopefully caravans will start up in a month or two. Plus, I got Ainslee some black-smith tools."

Par'karr gave him a toothy grin. "Now what?"

He looked around at his companions and smiled. "Now, we go home to Hawkshead."

EPILOGUE

It skittered across the daylit countryside with its insect legs. Though smaller than the warrior caste, it nevertheless had the same forelegs, triangular head and killing mandibles. But unlike the warrior caste, it had wings and could fly short distances. This helped it find its target. Or run it down if it tried to escape.

This was a familiar area to it, as it had killed another wizard near recently. A kobold wizard - its single failure. The Queen had not been happy with its offering. This was a new thing to it. Normally the Queen was happy with the brains of wizards that it delivered. But this time, she had not been happy, which meant it had failed.

The Queen had immediately sent it out again, to the same area to find a different wizard. A wizard whose brain she desperately wanted. It didn't know why she wanted this particular wizard's brain so badly and it wasn't its place to even ask. The Queen commanded and it carried out her wishes.

Now it knew. The Queen had shown it that its prey was a

soft skin. One of the many pasty vermin that infected this world. It hadn't been given an exact image of the target wizard, but that was not uncommon. Sometimes the Queen did, and sometimes she didn't. It had enough to know that it was one of the soft-skins - not a kobold.

Stopping, it tested the air with its antennae. Its mandibles clicked together involuntarily as it picked up the scent of magic in the air. It had been following its prey for days, getting closer each day. Now it was close. Very close.

With the prey so near, its instincts urged it on. Moving swiftly through the trees, it rounded the crest of a hill and stopped. Its multifaceted eyes spotted something down in the valley formed between several hills. Its two faceted eyes rotated forward, and its vision zoomed into the spot where it had seen movement.

A moment later, it reappeared; the thing it had spotted broke cover between two trees. A soft skin! Its antennae moved forward, tasting the air. Magic. It could smell strong magic. It had to be his target: a soft skin with great magic. Its prey.

Bending at the thorax, it kept a low profile, even as it skittered sideways on its rear legs. It watched the prey as the soft skin moved between the trees. Its eyes rotated left and right, watching for any signs of others. There was none. The wizard was alone. Easy prey.

It circled around the prey trying to find the best avenue of attack. It would need to be careful, so it did not damage the wizard's brain. Nothing else mattered, only retrieving the wizard's brain for the Queen. That was what would make her happy.

Tasting the air again, it clicked its mandibles in anticipation. So much power. The Queen would be so pleased. This soft-skin wizard was much more powerful than the kobold wizard it had killed so close to this very spot.

Moving sideways as quick as it could, it got ahead of the prey. Then it paused, its right eye rotating skyward. Something was there, something nearly invisible, something magical. An air elemental. An elemental was circling above it.

Its left eye was still fixed on the prey, so it immediately noticed when the prey stopped moving. The prey slowly looked up the hill to exactly where it was lying low. It had been discovered!

Now that the need for stealth was gone, it darted forward, wings launching it into the air and towards the prey. With a buzzing of its wings, it glided towards the prey, antennae out and ready to counter any magic the prey might use to save itself.

Its multifaceted eyes caught movement above as the air elemental dove toward it. Its antennae rubbed together, creating a solid wall of Air just above it. It was nearly invisible except for a slight distortion but somehow the air elemental or the prey detected it and the magical construct veered off just in time.

The prey launched a ball of fire at it, but its antennae rubbed together again, and *Water* magic extinguished the fire before it was even halfway to it. It knew many ways it could have killed the prey then and there, but it needed the prey alive. It needed the prey's brain alive and intact.

Instead, its antennae rubbed together. It summoned fire to surround the air elemental, which was preparing for another attack. Within moments, the elemental had been neutralized and dissipated.

In the time it had taken to destroy the prey's elemental,

its glide had brought it within striking distance. Extending its forelegs to grab the prey and pull it in for the brain extraction, it prepared to strike. Instead, it slammed into a hastily constructed wall of air - similar to the one that it had just created.

Its thick carapace absorbed the shock, but the sudden jolt momentarily stunned it and it collapsed to the ground. A long, brilliant blade of energy appeared in the prey's appendage and struck out at it.

It managed to recover just in time to move its head to avoid having its head sliced in half, but the blade caught one of its antennae, severing it completely. It did not feel pain. The Queen had made it so that the distraction of pain did not hinder it. But it did feel loss.

Loss of one of its antennae prevented it from working magic. Without both of the antennae, it could no longer cast spells of its own, nor could it counter magic from the prey. It did not matter; it was still physically more than a match for any prey. That was how it had been created.

Moving sideways in a blur, it reached out with its left foreclaw to disarm the prey. This was a tactic it had used many times before but this time it had to be more careful. Normally, the prey carried weapons of metal or wood, and its carapace was proof against such weapons. This time, the weapon was one of magic.

It was inches away from slicing off the prey's appendage when its foreclaw hit an invisible barrier of Air, stopping its momentum. The barrier lasted for only a second, enough to stop the foreclaw, before disappearing. But that was enough.

The prey brought the energy blade in a small arc and severed its left foreclaw. The energy blade sliced off the fore-claw cleanly and cauterized the stump so there was no bleeding. Its left eye rotated down to survey the damage and it instinctively struck out with its right foreclaw, slicing the prey along its chest.

The prey stumbled back, one hand going to the wound across its chest. That hand was still clutching a wooden weapon, one with a blue crystal at the top. The prey didn't drop the wooden weapon, which it found curious. Yet, it didn't have time for idle thoughts.

It had wounded the prey and it was not sure how badly. If the prey died, the brain would be ruined, and the Queen would not get what she desired. She would be unhappy. It had to move quickly to get the brain. The Queen must not be unhappy!

With a sudden burst of speed, it raced at the prey. It intended to grab the prey with both forepaws, and hold it still, just as it had done to dozens of other prey. But in its haste, it had forgotten that its left foreclaw was missing.

Its right forepaw wrapped around the prey's left appendage, but with no left forepaw, the prey's right appendage was free. That was the appendage that held the energy blade. The prey moved the energy weapon and suddenly the world was spinning.

The world stopped spinning after a few moments, and it tried to focus its multifaceted eyes. Things came into focus and it realized it was on the ground. It tried to get up but neither its legs nor right forepaw responded. Then its eyes saw the prey staggering towards it, still clutching its damaged chest.

Beyond the prey was a body, but it was hard to see. Its eyes were not working well. The light was growing dim. It focused both eyes past the prey and onto the twitching body on the ground. It recognized that body and the missing fore-claw. The body lying on the ground was its own.

The world grew even darker as it struggled to understand what had happened. Its thoughts were muddled, and thinking was difficult. Some instinct told it that it was dying. Its life was coming to an end.

It felt no fear at death, only sadness and disappointment. Yet even that was starting to fade, along with the remainder of its eyesight.

Its vision went completely black and its last thought was of how it had disappointed the Queen. The Queen would be sad. It felt sadness too. Then it felt nothing.

JOIN THE ADVENTURE

Thank you for reading this book! If you enjoyed it, please consider leaving a review on Amazon or tagging me on social media.
Tag me @authorjohncresı on Twitter and @authorjohncressman on Facebook and Instagram!
Reviews help readers like you find this book. More readers means more sales, and more sales help independent authors like me to be able to write more books!
To learn more about the author and his other books and projects, visit the author's website at:
https://www.johnecressman.com
Or visit him on Facebook
https://www.facebook.com/authorjohncressman/

LITRPG

To learn more about LitRPG, talk to authors including myself, and just have an awesome time, please join the <u>LitRPG Group</u>.

MORE LITRPG

For more information on this book and other exciting LitRPG/GameLit books, please visit the following Facebook groups:
LitRPG Books
https://www.facebook.com/groups/LitRPG.books/

and

GameLit Society
https://www.facebook.com/groups/LitRPGsociety/

ACKNOWLEDGMENTS

I'd like to acknowledge all the members of the LitRPG Authors' Guild who helped me in so many ways! Without your help, I could never have gotten this far!

Also, a big thank you for everyone who had bought one of my books. Your support really means a lot to me.

ABOUT THE AUTHOR

John E. Cressman is an author, magician, mentalist, hypnotist, programmer, and longtime lover of roleplaying games and fantasy/sci-fi books.

As a teen, he wasted long hours creating D&D fantasy campaigns for his friends to play. He has tried several pen and paper roleplaying games from the original Dungeons and Dragons, Traveler and Star Frontiers to the new Pathfinder games.

He still enjoys computer RPGs and MMORPGs, with his current favorite being Elder Scrolls Online. He used to play Skyrim, but then he took an arrow to the knee.

John has published two books on hypnosis and is now trying his hand at the fantasy LitRPG genre with his new LitRPG trilogy, VEIL Online.